IRIS MARTIN COHEN

The Little Clan

PARK
ROW
BOOKS

PARK
ROW
BOOKS

Recycling programs
for this product may
not exist in your area.

ISBN-13: 978-0-7783-1282-6

The Little Clan

ParkRowBooks.com
BookClubbish.com

Printed in U.S.A.

For Matthew, for handing me the match.

The Little Clan

"The tradition of all dead generations weighs like a nightmare on the brains of the living."

—*Karl Marx*

"It would be a thousand pities if women wrote like men."

—*Virginia Woolf*

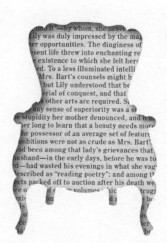

PART ONE

1

Ava waited, watching the stopped clock. Just before the hour, every hour, a faulty mechanism caused both hands to pause a moment too long, delaying their loud rhythmic clicking. The intrusion of this sudden silence into the room, no matter how regularly it occurred, always grabbed her attention. She remained trapped, stuck in pointless suspense until released by high, tremulous, inevitably disappointing chimes and then the ticking began again. The sphinx on the mantel who cradled the clock face between its breasts looked back at her, bored and imperious. Finally, the gold beast condescended to strike noon, and Ava returned to her writing.

She pushed down too hard on a rusty quill, and it sputtered and burped ink—Prussian blue. The noise of the clock receded back into the oblivion of her creative absorption; she was practicing her signature. Unable to find a satisfying way to connect the second letter of her name to all the flourishes she wanted for her first initial, she was coming around to the idea of a terse "A. Gallanter" which seemed to denote a masculine seriousness of purpose. She was writing a novel, or more accurately not writing, a grand panoramic, perhaps multiple-volume indictment of what she considered the callow ugliness of modern society. It hadn't been going so well.

Her models and inspiration were close at hand—Balzac, Zola, Trollope, Proust, Dickens, Dostoyevsky, all her favorite great men of the nineteenth century, lined the shelves of the Lazarus Club library, dusty and bound in morocco leather—the intellectual patrimony of the grand but faltering social club where she worked as a librarian.

Once in a while a club member came to finish a brandy or nap in one of the leather chairs scattered around, but for the most part Ava's duties were pretty nominal, and she was free to while away her days in the magnificent building that lined up so nicely with her aesthetic preferences and dream of authorial grandeur. Even if, for now, this ambition was spent covering pages in the overly elaborate twists and whorls of her signature.

But this club, where stained glass doors and creaky hallways opened onto ballrooms and parlors where old ladies roosted, as glassy-eyed and immobile as the stuffed peregrine falcons perched above the front door, seemed to comfort and abet her lack of industry. Once the Lazarus Club had been bustling, an opulent and exclusive playground for the upper echelons of New York Society to gather, to dine, to dance, and, according to its oft-quoted mission, discuss arts, letters and philosophy. One hundred and fifty years later, it persisted on a quiet uptown street, barely solvent, a last refuge for its affluent and elderly members to hide from an increasingly diverse and democratic world, eating Waldorf salads and snoring through the occasional social mixer.

Ava loved it. It was as if someone had conjured an Edith Wharton novel all around her, a magnificent setting in which she could be the star, the main character in all of her novelistic daydreaming. Here, beneath the chandeliers, surrounded by the dim glow of sumptuous, slightly frayed interiors, she never saw anyone her own age, and was more than content to chat with the old ladies about fountain pens and light operettas and third-rate Victorian detective stories, while managing to ignore their more egregiously antiquated opinions.

Ava took a quick sip from the bottle of cheap port in her top drawer and hiccuped, the goofy pop echoing loudly in the empty room. Drinking alone always made her maudlin, but today she had good reason to be sad. It was her twenty-fifth birthday, and this felt like a crisis. Having always thought of herself as an ingenue, the winsome, young Estella character in *Great Expectations*, she was now having to consider she might be curdling into Miss Havisham. At what age did being a virgin cease to be cute and start to become ridiculous? Twenty-five was too old, an invisible line had been crossed; she was past her prime, an expired commodity, and it made her feel a little desperate.

She had had that last chance two years ago, at the going-away party for her best and only friend, Stephanie. After college graduation, Stephanie had convinced Ava to move with her to New York, where "everything important was happening," only to abruptly decide to leave town—and Ava—a year later. Ava had tried to convince her that "The International Model Agency" offering her representation and based in Kiev was surely a scam, but such was Stephanie's fearless commitment to her path, the blazing, and often confusing trajectory that was going to lead her to an ill-defined stardom, that Ava hadn't been able to talk her out of it. She had never been very good at arguing with Stephanie.

Among the packed-up boxes of their shared apartment, Stephanie had pushed Ava and a very drunk bartender of her acquaintance into the tiny windowless closet that had been Ava's bedroom. "Here, he loves books, you guys talk about literature." Soon Stephanie wouldn't be around to engineer these kinds of situations, and, worried that this might be her last chance, Ava had tried to enjoy his sweaty hands under her shirt while he mumbled something about *The Catcher in the Rye*. But thinking of Stephanie's imminent departure, tears kept rolling down Ava's face and falling into the crest of this stranger's dark, greasy hair. Silent weeping would have probably even been fine, but no one can have sex with a girl who is crying the wet, snotty wail of true abandonment. And so that evening her virtue had remained intact. And had these past two lonely years.

The waxed hallway floor creaked, and Ava quickly hid her bottle as the honorable Lazarus Club president, Aloysius Wendell Wilder III, shuffled into the room. Pink-cheeked and boyish despite his seventy years, his hair fluttered around his head, a stark and unnatural shade of black that wandered onto his forehead and made him look like he had been carelessly dipped in ink. He lived in rooms at the back of the club and never seemed to leave the premises. Ava liked him because he had hired her without any qualifications. She had been standing on the sidewalk, gazing up at the awning and the cryptic insignia of its wrought iron doors, amazed that such places could still exist—it seemed to have just sprung from the pages of books she loved so much. Lurking in the foyer and sensing a kindred spirit, Aloysius had swept her in through the doors like a hawk retrieving its young and hired her to manage their books for an absurdly low salary. But because his offer included a tiny rent-free apartment in the back of the club, exactly the safe haven she had been looking for since being tossed roommateless into the storm of New York, she'd gratefully accepted. She'd moved in with her cat, Mycroft, determined to finally write her novel, and since then had hardly left the premises either, another source of kinship with the club president.

Aloysius fingered a small cherub on the mantelpiece, then slipped it into the pocket of his navy blazer. He liked to rearrange things. "You like dogs," he said in a sudden, accu-satory mid-Atlantic bray.

That morning in the hallway they been discussing Persian cats, but Ava nodded politely. "Yes."

He pulled a brochure from the inner pocket of his navy blazer and handed it to her. "Westminster. The pooches are glorious this year. Miss Wharton's pug once did his tinkles in the parlor fireplace. She was a member of this club, you know. A wonderful animal."

"I love dogs." He was her boss and her landlord, and having not formally signed a lease, she generally tried to be obliging. "And Edith Wharton too, I guess." Ava did, fer-vently, but pretended to prefer Henry James. He seemed more respected, and she didn't want people to think she wasn't serious.

He fondled the figurine in his pocket. "I've come for a book."

Surprised by the request—this was an hour usually spent trying not to wake the club members snoring off a lunch-time gin and tonic—she sat straighter with what she hoped was a professional alertness. "Yes?"

"I need *The Adventures of Sherlock Holmes.*"

"That's easy. You don't have it."

"Are you sure?"

She was. She would have known if one of her favorite books had been hiding among the transcendent randomness of the Lazarus collection: the nineteenth-century manuals on brain surgery, the firsthand accounts of racially suspect ex-plorations, lesser novels of lesser novelists. As a kid, her copy had become thick and crinkled, the pages coarse from hav-ing been dropped too many times in the bathtub, the only place she could be sure her mother wouldn't wobble by, sti-letto heels in a cloud of Cutty Sark, and scold her for being "odd and unsociable." As Ava grew, the fancier annotated edition that had replaced it had become almost black from enthusiastic underlining. If it had been on these shelves, she would have known.

"I have to say I'm very disappointed." He looked at Ava sternly. "Imagine guests coming from all over the world to discuss some very important irregularities in this work this afternoon, and we don't even have a copy to put up on display. It does not look good. Not at all. I just don't know what I am going to tell them." He started to wander away, scratching the back of his head, and muttering.

"Wait," said Ava. "Are you talking about the Baker Street Irregulars?"

"All very irregular. Couldn't agree more. Actions will have to be taken." With this not very clear clarification, he left.

Ava folded her wrists, lightly scarred with the marks of teenage sadness, over her desk, drumming her fingers, trying to stay calm. It had to be them; the Lazarus Club was always hosting odd groups and fellowships. The Baker Street Irregulars were the pinnacle of Sherlock Holmes fan clubs; she had always dreamed of joining. But by the time she fell in love with Holmes and Watson, too many years of bullying she had endured at school had left her terrified of any kind of group or social dynamic, her shyness calcified around her.

Ava couldn't say when it originated—her conviction that life was full of unspoken rules that she was sure to be on the wrong side of. In their big suburban house on the outskirts of New Orleans, icy with air-conditioning year-round, her mom, smelling sweetly of alcohol, had seemed vaguely disappointed in her for reasons Ava didn't understand for as long as she could remember. Her sense of transgression only worsened after she was plucked from a cozy synagogue preschool and sent to the elegant and prestigious Academy of the Bleeding Heart of Jesus, where she struggled mightily to understand the many obscure rituals and ways of the gentiles. Her early youth was just a blur of anxious fretting.

But one day, a sympathetic school librarian had given her *Little Women*. All at once, Ava discovered the world of books, warm, inviting, forgiving, and she fell into it and in love with Jo March in particular, deciding that she too would grow up to be a writer. Her identification was so passionate that after reading the chapter where Jo sells her hair, Ava also cut all of hers off with a pair of blunt scissors from art class. This hadn't gone well. Laughingly calling her a boy, her classmates had blocked her from the girls' bathroom until finally, in terrible humiliation, pee ran down the long white knee socks of her uniform. When her mother came to pick her up, she too had seemed inexplicably enraged at her daughter's short messy hair—a disgrace to the family, she had said, lighting another cigarette, and making Ava ride home, damp and ashamed, on the crinkly plastic of an old Saks shopping bag.

When Ava returned to *Little Women*, desperate for solace and finding it in the loving idea of the March family, after that, old books were all Ava would read. As though her only hope for love and acceptance was somehow tied up in petticoats and horse-drawn carriages. Thereafter no matter how many times she was pushed into garbage cans or excluded at lunch, or teased or mocked, she was sure it was just a symptom of being born in the wrong time, and the thought consoled her, and pushed her further into the open arms of classic literature.

But if Jo March was the light of her childhood, Sherlock Holmes was the lodestar of her adolescence. What joy she found, watching him slice through people's lies and deceptions—those motivations that held such fear and mystery to Ava—and see him triumph, his oddness and his introversion brandished proudly and unapologetically. His victories became Ava's. He was smart and moody, vain yet self-defeating, overly sensitive, rather lazy, resplendently his own prickly, complicated self, and still, somehow, he was loved; he had a friend. And so there was hope for her. She often skimmed past the actual cases, hunting instead for those moments of intimacy between Holmes and Watson, burrowing into the warmth of their companionship, their little nation of two. Such was the whispered promise of the Sherlock Holmes books, and Ava read the stories over and over, late at night, turning pages with an urgent, clammy, confused yearning.

But the Baker Street Irregulars would understand all of this. And they were coming to her domain because, like Ava, they also loved the nineteenth century's greatest detective, and this building was right out of his world. Persian rugs and rusty chandeliers and busts of forgotten notables, the Lazarus Club let dreams of empire linger, the twilight remnants of a dying tradition that for the shy, the strange and the bookish, was more real, more welcoming than the bright, jangling city passing just beyond the bay window. They were her people, and they were coming here.

The afternoon crept on with the gentle imperceptibility that time acquired inside the club, as Ava paced and fidgeted, retwisting the complicated mess of heavy braids she always wore as if just the right arrangement of hair might crystallize her resolve. The port dipped lower and lower in the bottle, and a violet stain was spreading unnoticed across her lips. A summer draft stole through an open window, barely stirring the room. Eventually sounds of movement and conversation drifted up from the bar. The event must have started. She unhooked a stocking from her garter and pulled it up to smooth out all of the creases and sags. Real silk stockings always pooled around her ankles, but she clung to arbitrary rituals—no panty hose, no typewritten letters, no ballpoint pens, the candlestick beside her bed, a boar bristle hairbrush—

that made her feel closer to the characters in the books that still dominated her emotional life and kept her company.

But again, this was the sort of thing the Baker Street Irregulars would sympathize with. The tremulous demarcation between fiction and reality was their raison d'être; their core tenet was that Sherlock Holmes really existed, and that Arthur Conan Doyle was the fictional construct. She would go down, she who was such a stickler for etiquette, despite not having an invitation; she belonged by right of common sympathy.

Down the long dark hallway that led from the library to the bar, portraits of former club presidents watched her sternly from behind walrus moustaches and glistening pince-nez. At the top of the stairs, an antique wicker pagoda of finches rattled and shook. She paused next to a gold nymph whose outstretched torch lit the foot of the banister. The foyer was still. It was only four in the afternoon, but heavy carpets and velvet drapes dampened the noises of life passing on the streets outside. Here, beneath a large painting of a seraglio—ladies sprawled in pillowy idleness—life was reassuringly immobile. No breeze ever stirred the crystals that hung from porcelain lamp shades or the enormous tasseled ropes that hung in the doorways. Someone laughed in the bar, and Ava felt the old ache of standing alone on thresholds where life seemed to be always taking place on the other side. But for once, she took courage and crossed the hall.

Under a dusty Tiffany skylight, the mirror of a carved oak bar caught the lights reflected in bottles in a twinkling line, and Rodney, the club bartender, arms crossed, was yawning. Tall and thin, with the pale, ascetic face of an Eastern Orthodox icon and the politics of the former Eastern Bloc, he greeted Ava happily. "A vision from the one place in this dump that doesn't smell like old people. I swear you bring the scent of vanilla cake and jelly beans with you wherever you go."

"I don't think that's me," Ava said. "What's going on?"

"Well, these guys are stealing the fruits of my labor through the historical accumulation of capital." Rodney had been trying to raise Ava's consciousness, unsuccessfully, for as long as she worked there, and she was never sure when he was joking with her or not. It made her nervous.

"I mean this afternoon."

"Well, it's a constant process." He smiled. "But if you're referring to these bozos, they are apparently a bunch of people that think Sherlock Holmes is a real person. Want one?" He held out a sugared orange slice wrapped in cellophane. Rodney was good at pilfering the candy bowls of various Lazarus employees' desks, or as he liked to refer to it, redistributing the spoils.

She took it. "And maybe a glass of scotch? Neat." Because she always dressed so nicely and lived on the premises, Aloysius allowed her to use the club facilities, a privilege not extended to the other employees. It was a strange in-between place to occupy in the establishment, but Ava liked it because it made her feel like a governess. Unfortunately, Aloysius was no Mr. Rochester.

She sucked her candy and tried to casually look around the room. There were only a few stragglers left, chatting in small groups. A slim older man approached the bar, and Ava nervously sipped her glass. He spoke to her with the friendly ease of conventioneers. "Whiskey is the thing to drink while we are in New York City, yes?" He had a Pepé Le Pew French accent. Ava picked a cocktail napkin from a stack nearby and wiped her nose though she didn't need to, nodding just enough to be ambiguous, in case he wasn't actually talking to her. "I see you have chosen the same. To America." He raised his glass.

Rodney flicked at a spot of dust on the bar with the towel that hung from his waistband. "She's drinking scotch," he muttered.

Ava obligingly clinked glasses. He had a slightly formal way of speaking, although the way he was looking at her left her trying to remember whether she was wearing nice underwear. "I don't believe I saw you at last year's gathering." His dark hair was sprinkled with silver, his eyes above heavy circles were cerulean, his tweed blazer fit ostentatiously well. "I'm sure I would have remembered."

"You didn't. I'm not supposed to be here. I'm not actually a member of the BSI." It seemed better to confess right away.

"I thought not. A member of the Lazarus Club then?"

He didn't appear offended or about to turn her out of the party, and this gave Ava courage. "Yes, well, no. I work here. I run the library upstairs. Or at least I keep a bunch of old books company."

"Lucky books." It was only the slightest lift of the eyebrows.

"I heard that the Baker Street Irregulars were downstairs, and I got so excited."

"Really?" The Frenchman looked genuinely surprised. "Well, what luck." He turned to Rodney. "Another round for fate. For strangers who pass in the night."

Rodney shook his head. "Maybe it's a librarian thing."

Ava downed her scotch. "I've read every story a million times. I have all the annotated works with the Sidney Paget illustrations, everything." She felt hot as she spoke, a prickling heat that made her eyes water for no clear reason. To speak out loud about something so close to her heart was harder than she anticipated, and she tried to talk quickly so as to be able to stop sooner.

When the Frenchman extended his hand, she felt very

relieved. "Allow me to introduce myself. Jules Delauncy, BSI, president of the Sherlock Holmes Society of France."

"Ava." The pause after her name seemed so empty of Holmesian credentials, she almost resolved to turn and run back to the library.

Jules Delauncy didn't seem to notice and, resting his elbows on the bar, spoke to the dim skylight with a drawling satisfaction. "Delighted. You know, Holmes had relations particular to France."

Ava glowed with the opportunity to prove herself. "His grandmother's brother, the painter, Vernet."

Despite the low illumination of the room, his eyes visibly lit up. "You must meet the others."

"But I'm not even supposed to be here."

He took her elbow. "As my guest, please, you're obviously one of the enlightened. And I have certain privileges as the president of the oldest and most influential Sherlock Holmes society in all of France. Please." He gently inclined her toward a group of men nearby, chatting with the satisfied air of long-tenured English professors. The circle rippled open at her approach with some surprised throat clearing and tie straightening. One gentleman's gesture of welcome was so enthusiastic, Amstel Light bubbled up and spilled all over his wrist.

A few hours later, perched on top of her desk, Ava floated in a cloud of bliss. The treasurer of the Welsh Deerstalkers and the president elect of the Maiwand Jezails were perusing the shelves, delighted to have found a complete set of *Hunting in Zambia*, vols. I–IX. The great-grandnephew once removed of Arthur Conan Doyle hovered behind them, tall and thin, peering at the titles with a nearsighted squint, while a member of the Cimbrian Friends of Baker Street snored quietly in a chair by the cold marble fireplace, a copy of *How to Be Your Own Barrister* splayed open on his chest. The Baker

Street Irregulars had been delighted to accept her invitation for tea in the library and had made themselves at home. She felt as though their appreciation of the surroundings reflected back on her, and while she wished more of them were actually talking to her, she didn't want to push herself forward.

A draft from the window ran across her neck. Against the late turning of a summer evening, the president of the Sherlock Holmes Society of France was sitting on the windowsill, letting the smoke from his calabash pipe float out into the streetlamp-spotted twilight. He gestured to her, and she sat next to him on the windowsill as if acknowledging a previous intimacy. There was something in the way he watched her, smiling, as she served tea to his colleagues, as though she was a discovery that he was showing off. She liked the feeling and had started leaning plantlike toward his warming approval. Finally after all those years of failure with the opposite sex, here was a man who understood her. He removed his pipe and indicated the room with it. "You are very fortunate to be able to work in such a Holmes-looking place. It makes you glow. I can imagine you there, trembling behind your veil, asking for his help, maybe to find a missing lover?"

She paused. She never really imagined herself as a client like this, those inconsequential strangers just passing through the intimate world of Holmes and Watson, but her gratitude to have someone to talk to about these things made her overlook the slight. "I still need to hang up a Persian slipper," she said finally. He chuckled and she flushed with pleasure.

He looked closely at her. "But don't you have somewhere you need to be on a Friday night, a beautiful young woman like yourself? No?" He began refilling his pipe. "How could you be unspoken for? What knowledge of the canon you have."

She waited, thinking this was perhaps the moment when

he would invite her to join the BSI, but he didn't. Maybe she was being presumptuous, and she coughed a little to cover her disappointment.

The noise roused the great-grandnephew once removed of Conan Doyle, and he wandered over. "Is our Frenchman bothering you, the dirty old reprobate?" He elbowed his colleague. "Not that I blame him." He lifted her hand, and his moustache tickled her knuckles. "You are a breath of delight in the musty halls of our middle-aged lives, like Miss Morstan in *The Sign of the Four.*"

Ava dipped her shoulders in what would have been a curtsey were she not sitting on the window ledge. She wasn't thrilled about the comparison with Watson's wife either, so forgettable, he often forgot he was married in the later stories.

"I hate to tear you away, Delauncy, but we've got to go check on the preparations for tonight. There's not a damn hotel in this town that stocks a good Madeira, and my tails aren't going to press themselves."

"Our annual banquet is tonight," Jules explained, "and as mentioned, I have certain responsibilities."

Ava was so close to asking for an invitation, but she assumed the desire must be written all over her face, and if these two gentlemen were ignoring it, they must have a good reason. "Please, don't let me keep you," she said, and to cover up a yearning that was raw and ugly and very familiar, she picked up an empty teacup and saucer.

Jules slid off of the ledge, tapping his pipe out of the window and slipping it into his jacket pocket. "Let me help you with those." He picked up a teacup from the desk and followed her as she hurriedly thanked the other Irregulars, feeling ashamed of her temerity, and carried other cups into the hall.

She ducked into a small alcove that had been fitted out with a sink and a hot plate, but Jules Delauncy stopped her.

"Surely you don't expect me to find her, the one, my very own Irene Adler here in this perfect building and let her escape from me so soon?" The sudden warmth in his tone surprised Ava; she was certainly no glamorous, mysterious Irene Adler, the only woman Sherlock Holmes could be said to have loved, but it was nice that he was still talking to her.

Jules was handing her his teacup, but then somehow it appeared on her other side, and when she turned around, she landed right against the ardent lips of the president of the oldest and most prestigious Sherlock Holmes society in France. Ava's first instinct was revulsion at this strange man's tongue in her mouth, then flattery that such a preeminent Holmesian desired her, then surprised fascination at the kiss itself. She had never kissed an older man before. A succession of literary Frenchmen flew through her mind—waxed moustaches and champagne and amatory dexterity—and she was, finally, for one glorious moment, every Victorian ingenue, helpless in the arms of a passionate seducer. He had a warm smell that she couldn't identify but that was all the same expected—leather, vetiver, bay rum, expensive shirts, masculine, slightly formal. With a dizzying sensation like trying to focus the two sides of an old-fashioned stereoscope, the outline of all her romantic fantasies came into line with the very real man pressing against her, and when he asked her to meet him later for a drink, she agreed. It was not exactly what she had imagined, but it was better than going home and drinking cough syrup and pretending it was laudanum.

Later that night, reeling slightly from the three absinthe frappes Rodney had made for her and leaning heavily on the arm of Jules Delauncy's dark tailcoat—she had never actually seen one in real life before and was thrilled to be allowed to press up against its severe elegance—she was crossing the marble foyer when Castor, the doorman, called to her.

"Came today, Miss. Mr. Savoy tried to take them for you,

but I wouldn't let him." He pointed at a bunch of daisies in a purple vase.

Ava opened the card. "Happy Birthday!!! Do you know how hard you are to find? Do you even have a phone? I'm back. Call me. Stephanie." There was a number on the bottom.

"I knew it." Jules Delauncy looked at the flowers suspiciously, pulling the cuffs down from his sleeves, and flashing links that read 221b. "An adventuress."

Cheered enormously that her friend was back and a bit pleased at the aspersion as well, Ava pulled him gently toward the elevator. Stephanie was going to love hearing about this.

2

A gentle whistling sounded somewhere in the distance. High, whining like the deflation of a tire, it rose, subsided and then summoned her again—insistent, exasperating. The press of a mattress, a strand of hair caught against her cheek—from the deep well where memory and sleep curl their fluid boundaries, Ava felt a gentle dissuasion urging her from waking up. A thick, queasy feeling whispered that she might be hungover, and from there she fell quickly into a vague, but seemingly significant awareness that she was naked. She opened her eyes and then shut them again immediately.

Unfortunately, this only allowed the memory of the night before to reconstitute itself that much more clearly in the darkened screen of her eyelids. Jules Delauncy on one knee, in sock garters and graying undershirt, proposing to her in a fake Sherlock Holmes vernacular—would she be Irene to his Holmes, etc. Jules Delauncy taking down her hair and clumsily ripping long strands between the bobby pins despite the gravity of his gestures and expressions. Jules Delauncy climbing on top of her, and her romantic imagination receding before the tactile reality of flesh in flesh and leaving her alone and stranded beneath an unknown male animal.

The college boys with whom she probably should have had this moment appeared to her mind with their fresh, American smell, deodorant and laundry detergent, innocent and eager, and in this moment as appealing as puppies. But a persistent romantic impulse had always kept her from this final gesture of surrendered intimacy; she had been saving herself. But when Delauncy entered her apartment and sat on her one chair, a green velvet chaise lounge, and looked around at her framed engravings, the candlesticks, the jumble of antiques lovingly collected over the years, and nodded with approval, her gratitude burst forth, a reckless courage propelling her past her reservations. Here was a man who cared as much as she did about the books that defined her life, who deserved her, who would understand her. At last she would be able to call her mother and tell her, "You see, Mom, I have a boyfriend. I'm not hopeless." This impression of essential sympathy, however, had ended immediately upon penetration. He smelled musty, musky, old, and worse, once he began rocking away in his wheezy rhythm, it was like she wasn't even there.

An unpleasantly smooth, pale arm reached over and caressed her shoulder. She felt obliged to open her eyes. Jules Delauncy, looking even more French and craggy in the cool morning light, smiled a yellow smile at her. *"Bonjour."* Her revulsion was visceral and she crawled out of bed avoiding the evidence of his continued interest poking at her sheet. "Irene, come back. Don't leave our bed of love."

She was mortified for both of them. "My name is Ava." Nearly tripping over Mycroft, who was rubbing against her ankles, she picked him up and brought him with her into the bathroom where she lay down on the floor, pressing her forehead against the not very clean tiles and aggressively rubbing the cat as if the repetitive motion could somehow soothe

the anxious state of her mind. She wondered how long it would take this inconvenient stranger to leave on his own.

A long time, apparently. Eventually, she opened the door and yelled through the crack that he needed to go. After a protracted negotiation and the proffering of very hurt feelings, he left swearing that he would return to win her heart and that, "as there was only one woman for Holmes, there could be only one woman for him, and that he would best her in this game of hearts." Ava noted with annoyance that he still didn't mention her joining the BSI.

Alone finally, and back in bed, a satin pillow monogrammed with someone else's initials sheltered Ava from the disappointed frown of a plaster Athena on her bookshelf. Little pads of pressure soon manifested against her forehead as Mycroft made himself comfortable on the pillow, the vibrations of his loud purring resonating through the down. No wonder ladies reacted so poorly to their deflowering in books. Throwing herself into a river seemed a perfectly reasonable response to this overpowering nausea, a deep physical disorder that started between her legs, radiating up through her body to her throbbing head. What did normal twenty-first-century girls do when they lost their virginity? Cry? Paint their nails? Clean their closets? Sleep? Maybe she would do all those things, but the last option seemed the nearest at hand, and she surrendered to its blessed oblivion. She dreamt of low, sweaty, overcast skies.

When she woke, she stared at the ceiling and thought about making coffee, which seemed like a lot of effort. Then she remembered Stephanie's card, and, happy to chase away the thoughts of the night before, she got out of bed to find out what exactly her tempest of a friend had been up to.

As the phone rang, Ava thought about the few emails she had received from Stephanie at long and random intervals, discursive and enthusiastic, and conveying almost no information, except that she was alive, and that the worst of Ava's imaginings hadn't come to pass. She had quickly abandoned "The International Model Agency," but the flurry of adventures narrated from internet cafés across eastern Europe had not cleared up what she had been doing to support herself instead. But somehow in her tales of midnight trysts on cobblestone streets and passionate discussions in basement cafés, Stephanie cast herself beyond the realm of these pedestrian questions. She was living *The Sun Also Rises*, she was Lady Brett Ashley, the glittering expatriate, at least by mail, and Ava was curious.

When the connection finally clicked through, Ava heard a familiar breathy hello. Stephanie always tried to speak in a register slightly lower and more sophisticated than her natural speaking voice, but often forgot, so her speech patterns had a constant rising and falling that always made her sound just a little drunk. Because it had been a while since Ava had heard this voice, it suddenly called to mind the first time she had seen Stephanie, the unlikely introduction to the woman who would become her devoted friend, an inseparable pair at the small liberal arts college they'd attended.

Sprawled in the grass of the main quad, her blond hair spread like swirling buttercream, Stephanie had been sunbathing in a hot-pink bikini and enjoying a package of red licorice whips with casual obscenity. Passing professors nervously averted their eyes. A group of students in torn black clothes scornfully pretended not to see her. Even the hippies playing Frisbee affected to not notice her remarkable display and the audacious misplaced confidence of it all, like a cheerleader who wandered into the chess club. And Ava couldn't help but notice the way that even just by making these different groups strain so hard to ignore her she had forcibly commanded everyone's attention. Everyone's gestures, especially those of the men, had taken on the unintentional awkwardness of people performing for an audience. Ava was

spellbound by the whole performance, but Stephanie somehow always demanded that kind of irresistible, complicated
attention. It had seemed impossible that when she had chosen a friend, she would have picked Ava, alone in the dining commons, reading Zola, and picking at the lint of her
cardigan. But indeed she had.

"Hello?" Stephanie said again with a quick, mounting
impatience.

"It's Ava."

"Ava! I found you. Jesus. Do you ever check your email? I
had to call your mom. You sound hungover, are you drinking alone again? Sylvia Plath with her head on the oven and
whatever?"

"I've never read *The Bell Jar*," Ava said, annoyed. Stephanie was always getting her inspirations just slightly off. That
book in particular was a bête noire; it had swept her high
school, and Ava had resented seeing so many of her former
tormentors now turned enthusiastically literary and writing poetry. It had felt important to distinguish herself, and
so she'd stopped reading books by silly women and prid-
ing herself on only reading big, important masterpieces like
Moby Dick and *War and Peace*, a distinctly, self-consciously
male pantheon.

"Glad to see you haven't changed. You know what I
mean."

"I was celebrating. It was my birthday. Thank you for the
flowers, by the way."

"You're welcome. I still have the company account from
that temp job, if you ever need to send flowers. It's amazing."

"It's been years. They haven't noticed?"

There was a pause. "I don't do it a lot. Now that I think
of it, I must have switched it over to my name at some point,
so anyway…happy birthday! I have a million things to tell

you. Stop moping around or canning tomatoes or whatever and come have brunch with me."

"That's really what you think I do when you're not here? I don't even know how to can tomatoes."

"I bet you do, but we won't argue about it. Come meet me. A Bloody Mary will fix whatever is making you sound like a dying squirrel. My treat."

A Bloody Mary, why hadn't Ava thought of that? That would fix so much. Also, she needed to get away from the stale air of Baker Street that seemed to linger in her apartment. Stephanie would have no theories about Moriarty's disappearance or Watson's regimental colors. Today this was a virtue. "No place too loud."

"I know, I know."

In the disorientation of the morning, the act of letting Stephanie persuade her to do something felt familiar, and because of that, deeply soothing. They made plans to meet in an hour or so.

Hanging up, Ava decided against making coffee and poured a slug of bourbon into a coffee mug. It felt appropriately hard-boiled, the action of a woman who has fallen from the path of virtue, but her stomach objected and she promptly threw it up. Noticing a trail of dried slime running down her thigh that she was pretty sure hadn't come from her, she ran to the shower, the exculpatory ritual of young women everywhere who have made unfortunate decisions.

Later, clean but not cleansed, Ava waited for the elevator. The back half of the Lazarus Club had been built as temporary residences for members, pieds-à-terre maybe, or artists' studios. Most of the thirty or so tenants had been there since anyone could remember, and the uncertainty as to who got apartments or why or when they might ever leave created a feeling of disembodied permanence that reminded Ava of

The Magic Mountain. Also, she heard a lot of coughing. Some of the apartments remained inexplicably vacant; some Ava suspected were occupied though their residents never ventured out. A reclusive woman, Mrs. Grierson, shared her floor and smiled at her ferociously whenever they accidentally met in the hall. Decorative cat statues had proliferated on their landing, very much in the way, but Ava didn't dare move any of them, suspecting tenants had had heart attacks over less.

The other five floors were equally cluttered with dead plants, stacks of newspapers, novelty doormats, ashtray stands and statuary, reaching an apogee at the floor of Aloysius who used his hallway as an impromptu closet, clothing racks and cardboard boxes rendering it nearly impassable and highly noncompliant with fire codes. A mildewed air of hoarding and missed doses of Thorazine hung over the whole building. Ava found it all very comforting.

The rattling elevator and long narrow corridor turning and twisting under the dining room and ballrooms and offices of the Lazarus Club let out eventually into the grand marble foyer of the main entrance. It created such a sense of psychic distance from the bustle of New York City that all of the questions that had seemed so urgent after college and in Stephanie's company—who she would become, what she would do, how she would satisfy her dark, restive ambition— seemed to drop away, curling like dust in the cracked wedding cake moldings. Walking into the bright June sunshine, it felt like she hadn't gone outside in a very long time.

As she came up out of the subway downtown, and the pedestrians around her became increasingly stylish, the sallow veil of Ava's hangover turned inward, and she noticed the crooked buttons of her dress. Leaving the house, she had hoped she resembled a Godard heroine, rumpled, debauched, a girl who couldn't care less. But this impression evaporated as soon as she was on the pavement moving among the busy streams of other people, and she remembered she was a girl who would always be a little off, and who cared too much about everything.

Clothes were so complicated. Her old-fashioned mannerisms, the feel of a long hem against her calves, stepping from a curb in stiff leather shoes, allowed her to embody for a fleeting instant the physical sensation of the ghosts of history that populated her daydreams. This made her feel happy and safe. In the snap of a garter against her thigh, she could be a bright young thing navigating the shiny chaos of the modern city. The brush of a fur collar against her cheek turned her into a courtesan off to an assignation, and she became mysterious, desirable, romantic, filled with the preoccupations of lives more exciting than her own. Slipping in and out of the various characters in her head, her body became a bridge between her imagination and the world she had to walk through. She felt alternately protected and invisible. But then every so often the illusion shifted, like a slide slipping from a projector, and she was left exposed in the world as it was, awkward, eccentric and acutely self-aware. Then the imagined glances of passersby felt like a judgment until just walking down the street became torture. Today her whole skin itched with self-consciousness, and this discomfort spread through her body and the clothes that hung on it, now seemingly very tight and bunchy and ill-chosen.

She checked the address. She should already be at the restaurant, but 65 Rivington Street was a boarded-up tailor shop. Next to that was a tattoo parlor, and next to that was a jewelry store. She walked the length of the block a few more times, then gave up and stood beneath a lamppost, trying to read a "historical landmarks" sign from under its palimpsest of graffiti.

A tall blonde in tight jeans brushed past on a cell phone.

Hair disheveled, fitted blazer, nipples just visible under a man's undershirt, with a large expensive purse and dirty sneakers, she evoked a bedraggled, downtown cool, Patti Smith by way of Brigitte Bardot. Or, Ava thought with some chagrin, a Godard heroine.

Normally Ava would have recognized this combination of carelessness and cultivation—the perfect eyeliner and glossy bounce of her hair somewhat belied the hipster ensemble—but because the last time Ava saw her, Stephanie had been trying to reinvent herself as a gallerist, running an eponymous art space and wearing only expensive natural linen and heavy leather belts, it took Ava a moment before her friend's familiar outlines materialized from this particular pretty, affected stranger. She tapped the passing shoulder and the stranger turned and smiled, radiant, and the feeling of being suddenly swept into an exclusive, privileged circle while somehow feeling worse about her outfit was instantly familiar: Stephanie.

"Darling." She casually hung up on whomever she had been speaking to. "You look amazing as always. I love the fucked-up thing you're doing with your hair."

Ava felt for her braids. "Thanks."

Stephanie bent toward her, and her hug was warm and she smelled like rose water. She had always been physically affectionate, and Ava remembered the pleasure of receiving this open, magnanimous embrace, even if the difference in their heights meant she was uncomfortably jammed against Stephanie's hard breastbone. "I can't believe it's been so long. Traveling the world is exhausting. Look—" She pointed at what Ava assumed were supposed to be wrinkles. "But that's the price of wisdom. You haven't aged a bit. Your Anne Frank tendencies are so good for your skin." Ava started to object, but Stephanie disarmed it with a grin and held her chin for further examination. "You look pale, though, but maybe you just need a hair of the dog. I see some things haven't changed." She put an arm around Ava's shoulders, guiding her toward a frosted glass door. "You still need someone to take care of you."

"Why doesn't anyone have signs anymore?" Ava asked as they entered the closed tailor shop, which led to an unexpectedly large open space.

Circular light fixtures reflected off of waxed, pale wood, slick and shiny as a skating rink or, Ava thought, maybe a Finnish airport. She waited, shifting her weight and bumping a couple nuzzling next to her in the vestibule, while Stephanie air-kissed the maître d' and the bartender, still talking to Ava over her shoulder. "New York, it's such a small town. You're away for one minute and it's like you're a celebrity." She waved at a group of middle-aged men in hooded sweatshirts whose skateboards were stacked on the banquette next to them, and they responded with an unconvincing show of casualness, one offering a lazy peace sign.

"Didn't you work here for a little while?" Ava asked. Stephanie's rapid succession of postcollege jobs had been hard to keep track of, bartending or hosting things, events at nightclubs or fancy clothing stores, all which had vaguely to do with art or fashion, and all seemed to be paid for by sneaker or alcohol or bottled water companies. The main thread was that it all occurred in the twenty or so blocks that bound the Lower East Side, and all seemed to be attended by the same people. Ava had gone once and been so embarrassed and ill at ease that she spilled her wine on an important someone's limited-edition white sneaker and got removed from the event. It had been very traumatizing.

There had been a strange feeling in the air when Stephanie convinced Ava to move to New York with her just two years after the events of September 11. Ava had been expecting to find a solemn city—but like the Rostovs returning to Moscow in *War and Peace*, they had found a city churning with money instead. Determined that Ava was going to be a famous writer, Stephanie had urged her into a job as a fact checker at a magazine, acquired with surprising ease, while Stephanie herself seemed to float on an endless stream of capital, paid for being young and beautiful and knowing the right people. Her gallery had only lasted a few months before she got into some kind of disagreement with her landlord. Her artists also had some issues about work maybe having been left in a damp storage closet by Stephanie's assistant or someone, a long convoluted story of betrayal that Ava had listened to sympathetically, without really grasping the particulars.

At their table, Stephanie ordered a warm water with lemon from someone who wasn't their waiter and leaned back rolling a large ring around her middle finger. "Tell me everything."

Ava was still just a little hurt that Stephanie could reappear so casually. Of course Ava had had no intention of moving home after graduation, to be back in her mother's orbit of luncheons and charity clubs and blind dates with eligible young men who would hate her, but moving to New York, and with Stephanie, for whom her mom had a stubborn and irrepressible aversion, had made her parents abruptly cut her off financially. It hadn't mattered, being poor with Stephanie had been strangely painless, an adventure almost, to siphon from the city all that it had to offer two young, pretty, hungry girls, but still, Ava felt she at least was owed some kind of apology for then being so abruptly abandoned. "I'm not the one who's been all over the place. Maybe you should begin."

"Oh my god, you just won't even believe the couple of years I've had."

Ava couldn't help interrupting, "I told you that place was

a scam. I still don't understand what made you think that was a good idea."

"Well, I was broke, if you remember," Stephanie started. "After I was cheated so terribly by that slimy landlord,"

"We were both broke, but I had a job. You could have just gotten a stupid job like everybody else and stayed here instead of handing yourself over to human traffickers."

"They weren't human traffickers." Stephanie dismissed the idea, annoyed. "They were way too disorganized for that. I was practically running the place before I decided it was a waste of my time. So I have ambition," she said, twisting her ring, "I think wanting more out of life is something to be proud of. Why are we having this fight again? It's like you're not even happy to see me. I thought about you all the time while I was gone."

"Why didn't you answer more of my letters then?" Ava reached for her water glass to try and distract from the inadvertently high pitch of her voice. She didn't quite want Stephanie to know the raw, miserable extent that she had missed her. She studied her menu. Everything was written in a sparse, serif-free, lowercase font that made her think the portions were going to be too small.

"I was busy. I was trying to make a career."

Ava couldn't help a small snort. "Leaving like that was totally insane."

"Okay, it was a little *unconventional*." Stephanie rubbed her forehead and pushed her hair back so that her bangs stood up for a moment, pale golden feathers that fell slowly in a gentle cascade. "It was so bad," she laughed. "You don't even want to know. Although, weirdly I almost made the inaugural cover of *Vogue Ukraine*. But then it folded. I did date this Russian guy for a second. He had his own plane. That was cool."

"What did you do all this time? What did you do for money?"

"This and that." Stephanie spoke vaguely, suddenly intent on her menu. "Some journalism and stuff. I started a newspaper in Lodz—expats are really into that kind of stuff—but it didn't really work out. A lot of bartending. For a while I was serving drinks in this crazy hundred-year-old spa—Czech people really like to get drunk in slippery marble rooms—but I got some kind of mineral poisoning and had to quit. I got paid for a while just to hang out in the lobby of this fancy hotel. I don't know, stuff." She put down her menu and insisted a busboy take their order despite his objections.

These sorts of things were always happening to Stephanie, and as Ava listened, she felt a returning wonder and a kind of admiration at the relentless flow of life that her friend got to sample. Nothing ever happened to Ava. Except, it seemed, during those times when she hooked herself to Stephanie's momentum and swung out behind her, pulled into the thrilling, confusing, sometimes disastrous stream of experience, something she seemed incapable of doing on her own, and for which she was grateful. "Why didn't you just come home? I was here."

The bread that she was not eating sent little showers of crumbs onto the shiny table, which Stephanie then pushed into neat little rows with the side of her pinky. "I guess I kept waiting for something awesome to happen, so I could have something to tell everyone when I got back, but then it just got kind of lonely and boring. And I got pneumonia. That sucked." She brushed the crumbs off the table. "My mom was so psyched to say her daughter was finally a model and in Europe, too. It was like all those years of spending our rent money on Weight Watchers and teeth bleaching had finally paid off. I just couldn't take that away from her." She shook her head, an unconscious bristling that often arose after mention of her mother, a trait she and Ava shared, and pointed dramatically at Ava. "Let's talk about you. Did you write your book? When I was in Budapest, I kept telling people I was writing a nineteenth-century epic because I missed you."

The abrupt transition from Stephanie's tale of adventure to the blank of her own life took Ava by surprise. "Stephanie." She shook her head against a wave of embarrassment. The lines of her vision became too sharp, and a surge of adrenaline reared up, but with nowhere to go it just rose up to her ears and hung there, insistent, ringing. "I've never told anyone but you about my book."

"Yeah, but that's your weird issue. Everyone I met was super impressed. I think this one poet guy only went out with me because he thought I was a novelist. You waste a lot of opportunities." Stephanie watched her closely. "Still not going well? Don't worry. You're a crazy genius, you'll do it." She patted Ava's arm.

"Can we talk about something else?" Ava blinked, waiting for the world to shrink back to its normal perspective and volume. Stephanie's ardent faith had been a mystery since the early days of their friendship. They had been in an English class together, but after it ended, to Ava's astonishment, Stephanie had sought her out, finding her in the halls or the cafeteria, dragging Ava around arm in arm, as if Ava's shadow somehow made her own radiance shine more brightly. Ava had been dazed, but grateful for the attention and even years later never really got over a fundamental confusion that the homecoming queen in all her blond glory, chose to curl up in Ava's narrow dorm room, eating cookie dough and trying to quench a seemingly endless curiosity about all things "fancy and intellectual."

"I've just been thinking a lot about literary stuff these days. You're really the only one I can talk to about that kind of thing, so few people seem to genuinely love books the way that you and I do. I should have never tried modeling. I can't live a life that is so unintellectual." Stephanie pushed the bread basket toward Ava. "I'm off carbs." She unfurled her napkin. "But more on that later. What about your job? The magazine?"

Ava buttered a roll emphatically. "Never again." After Stephanie left, she had only lasted a few more months at her prestigious publication. It was full of handsome, condescending young men who let her know that of all the innumerable books she had read, somehow none were really the right ones, not like Carver, or Franzen or Foster Wallace. Without Stephanie's reassurance and encouragement, she found she believed them. Also, one particular senior editor was always cornering her in the break room to regale her with vaguely ribald stories of the magazine's early days, standing so close she could smell the coffee on his breath, and suddenly everything had just reminded her too much of high school, so when she found the job at the Lazarus Club it had felt like salvation.

Stephanie nodded sagely. "I think you're right. I think working our way up the ladder isn't right for us anyway. It's kind of a sucker's game."

Ava took a long sip of the drink that had arrived and noticed the muscles of her shoulders relaxing a little. Whenever Stephanie spoke of them intertwined like this, which she often did, Ava felt a kind of safety in the association. She wasn't sure that their priorities aligned quite as closely as Stephanie liked to imply, but that assumption felt so validating, smoothing the edges of her quirks and weirdness into something much less shameful. The rigidity of being on guard against a hostile world broke a little at the affectionate tones in Stephanie's voice, and Ava felt acutely how much she had missed her friend. "So what are you going to do now?" Ava asked. "I'm not moving back in with you. I had to cover our last two months' rent when you left, and it almost killed me."

"No, no." Stephanie dismissed the past with a sweep of her bangs. "But I'm working for myself, that's for sure. I want to start something of my own, do something meaningful." Stephanie leaned forward, gold bangles clattering against her folded arms. "You know my love of books, maybe something to do with that."

Ava had learned that Stephanie often liked to talk about her love of books, but in an abstract sort of way, and that in particular she didn't like to be interrupted by Ava talking about any specific books. But climbing through the ranks of teen pageant circles of the depressed agricultural towns of the Midwest, she had memorized the whole first chapter of *A Tale of Two Cities* as her talent, something Ava could never picture without a rush of affection—beautiful Stephanie, teased and lacquered, quoting Dickens with steely intensity to a bunch of bored judges for scholarship money. Although, apparently, she won every title she ever competed for, something she liked to remind Ava of a little too often.

"Or I don't know, like a bar or something. You can make fierce money with the right kind of club in New York. I've worked enough of them to know."

"Aren't you broke? How do you open a bar without any money?" Ava fished a pickled green bean from her drink.

Stephanie waved a hand in the air, bored. "You just get investors. You're missing the point. You remember how 9/11 was the death of irony?" Her pause didn't really invite questioning, so Ava just waited. "There was a *New York* magazine article about it a little while ago. People want a place to go where they can be a part of a community, be a part of something classy. All that bottle service stuff is so over. I don't know, I'm still working on the concept. But I'm done fucking around." She sat back as a plate of salad was put in front of her. "Also, now that I'm back in the country, those student loan people call me like ten times a day. I would have to work a real job for like forty years before I could pay it off. No thank you. I plan to be debt-free by thirty."

"I think *Little Dorrit* takes place in a debtors' prison," Ava said as her plate was set down, as well. As she predicted, the dish was so spare that she considered ordering a second entrée, but, fearing Stephanie's horrified reaction, she ordered a side of bacon instead. Which still earned her a startled look.

Stephanie pointed with her fork. "But tell me about you. You're working in a private club, right? So you get what I'm talking about."

Ava laughed. "Everyone at my club is eighty years old, and my boss tried to pay me in expired Bergdorf gift cards the other day, so not really." A mimosa replaced her empty Bloody Mary glass, and she drank, finding the fizz of it mildly contagious. "You should come see it. You always liked all my old stuff—the Lazarus Club is like the 'House of Usher.'"

"I remember that story, it's Edgar Allen Poe," Stephanie said, a little pointedly. "And if you basically raised yourself in the Glamour Shots storefront of a suburban shopping mall, you would think it's cool, too." Ava knew not to interfere with the rage with which Stephanie spoke of her upbringing, the complicated indignities of being poor and almost disastrously pretty. "But I've been rambling, and you still haven't told me anything yet. Like who you were drinking with last night. You've probably read a hundred books since I last saw you. Having more fancy, fascinating 'only Ava' adventures. I want to know everything."

Somehow when Stephanie spoke of her like this, her life seemed to rearrange itself, shedding the dull sheen of reality and transforming into something worthy of Stephanie's attention. "Well, actually…" Ava felt a glow, she *was* having adventures, and she related the incidents of the night before with more enthusiasm than she had felt in the act.

"What? Finally!" Stephanie's bracelets rang out in a celebratory jostling. "After all this time. I always figured it would be like a Civil War reenactor or something."

"You weren't far off." As she went into detail, Ava realized how long it had been since she'd actually spoken at length to anyone. The sound of her voice pouring forth in unaccustomed loquaciousness, framing her experience into words and offering it to someone else, soothed the disorder of her feelings that had lingered all morning. She felt lighter, easier, happier than she had in a long time. "It wasn't such a big deal actually," Ava said finally as their plates were cleared with the indecorous promptness of New York restaurants. She didn't quite want to admit just how unpleasant the sensation had been, the sharp residue of disappointment it had left her with, the feeling that she had implicated herself in some terrible failure.

Stephanie yawned. "If men knew how not big of a deal their dicks were, the whole fucking world would collapse." She paid their check from a wallet that had been duct-taped shut and stood up, taking a large pair of sunglasses from her purse. "Come on. Let's go for a walk."

Ava waited patiently while Stephanie stopped and hugged two more acquaintances on the way to the door.

They left the restaurant and bought coffee, strolling the busy sidewalks arm in arm. The bilgy tide of Ava's hangover had receded, leaving the world distinctly less menacing. Stephanie's skinny arm was light on her own, and this casual pressure reminded Ava of a companionable ease she hadn't even noticed she had been missing. They instinctively fell into step. There was a simple physical pleasure in being doubled, the proximity of a warm, affectionate female body so close beside her, and it made her realize how alone she usually was. She stopped worrying about the accidental contact of passing strangers, an unwelcome comment or a judgmental gaze. With a friend, the painful alienation of being a body passing through the world was alleviated. She sipped her coffee, hoping that Stephanie wouldn't notice the intensity of her gratitude. From this new perspective as part of a pair, her previous self seemed so pathetic. "I'm glad you're back," she said finally.

"Me, too." Stephanie got very interested in the window display of a shop they were passing. "No more hiding away, Ava. We're going to do great things together."

Ava watched Stephanie's reflection shimmer, vanishing, then reappearing in the flapping shadow of an awning overhead. She thought of the night long ago, walking the empty corridors of her college dorm, book of poetry in hand on a Saturday night, when she heard the sounds of sobbing, and glancing into an open door, she had found Stephanie, that confident, bikini-clad vision from the main quad, howling with rage and ripping what was clearly a corrected essay into long thin shreds. She had looked up at Ava with such despair that Ava instinctively offered the only consolation she could think of. And so Ava had spent the evening reading Pushkin to the most beautiful girl she had ever seen until her sobs subsided, and she fell asleep, head on Ava's knee. When Ava had woken with a crick in her neck and got up to leave the next morning, Stephanie scowled. "You can't imagine what it feels like to have everyone think you're dumb," she'd said, then turned away, pulling the covers over her head and leaving Ava to show herself out. They had never spoken of that night since.

Stephanie was already pushing open the door of the shop, and not wanting to be alone on the sidewalk, Ava hurried after her. Clothes hung on a tangle of welded iron branches, and three bored salesgirls draped their willowy bodies against the racks. She waited while Stephanie flipped through the tiny dresses on display. A salesgirl frowned and demanded her coffee, which Ava immediately relinquished.

"I think you're the only person I've ever shopped with," Stephanie was saying. "It's way too intimate for anybody else. You should try this on. It was on sale a while ago."

"I thought you just got back. How long have you been in town?" Ava picked at a smudge on her collar that she couldn't help noticing in the lights of the store. "I don't wear short things."

Ignoring the salesgirl's efforts to relieve her of her coffee cup, Stephanie shoved a dress into Ava's arms and pushed her toward the dressing room. "You should, you've got great legs." She pulled the curtain closed. "I basically just got back. It's been a little hectic."

Ava looked at the dress in her hands and decided to try it. It was a comfort to hear Stephanie's voice out there, arguing with the salesgirl for a discount on a blouse she had found with a missing button. When she had the dress on, tight, black, barely falling to her knees, she opened the curtain. "You don't think this is too slatternly?" A stranger looked back from the mirror. "Like a Balkan trophy wife?"

Stephanie flung the blouse dismissively toward the cash register. "I don't know what slatternly means, but I've seen those wives and no. You should get it. You look hot, but smart, like a sexy young author on a book tour or something."

The strange weightless feeling she used to get around Stephanie was coming back to her, the sense of previously inconsiderable courses of action unfolding all around, the tight self-imposed boundaries of her life expanding in an infinite array, and she was left free of herself and fearless. Not alone. It felt wonderful.

By the time they left the store, Ava's world was shrinking back to her accustomed limits, and she was glad to be in her scuffed oxfords and dowdy skirt, but still, she didn't quite regret the dress that was wrapped in plastic and slung over her arm. Maybe she'd never wear it, but the rustling weight murmured with possibilities and tickled her arm as she waited to cross a street. What did she need those scruffy old men in the Baker Street Irregulars for anyway?

3

And so, as if she had never left, Stephanie poured back into Ava's life, filling up space that Ava only now recognized as empty. Having been so accustomed to being alone as a kid, it was only in the bright Technicolor warmth of companionship that her previous state of existence acquired the cool chill of loneliness. She began to look forward to the regular phone calls, the quick comparing of insignificant daily events. A funny anecdote about her neighbors or Aloysius's latest absurdity now sat awkwardly within her, waiting to be released, their rough edges smoothed by the easy laugh or commiserating disgust that Stephanie was always so ready with. The first time she came to visit Ava, she walked into the large marble foyer, her mouth a perfect O, and turned to Ava with shining eyes. "This is the most amazing place I've ever seen. I feel like Montgomery Burns." And after, she came over as often as she could.

On Sunday afternoons, she liked to lay around in Ava's striped silk pajamas spinning plans for her future, while the quiet mortar of friendship rehardened stealthily and silently, holding Ava in an easy grip she barely even noticed.

"How can you stand it?" Ava turned another page, fruitlessly attempting to read, while Stephanie banged around her kitchen corner.

While deciding on her next venture, Stephanie had gotten a temporary job cocktail waitressing. Each weekend, she took a bus to Long Island to work Friday nights, came home in the morning, slept for a few hours, showered, then did it all over again on Saturday. She made the commute with the other working girls, young and beautiful, waiting for the jitney as the sun rose over the manicured lawns of East Hampton.

Stephanie crawled into Ava's bed with a pint of mint ice cream, rubbing her eyes through the leftover accretion of last night's mascara. "I'm making a lot of good connections for my project. The guys there are loaded."

"Are those the kinds of people you want to be in business with? Isn't your whole concept substance and sincerity or something?"

"The place is crawling with artists and publishers and movie people. Seriously, you meet everyone. Bartenders are like the secret masters of the universe. Anyway, can't have art without commerce." The bed sank under her weight as Stephanie shifted closer, digging in to the ice cream and sighing with a guttural satisfaction as she closed her mouth around the spoon, shutting her eyes against the full measure of the pleasure. The fan by the bed spun, and strands of blond hair waved in the breeze and tickled Ava's shoulder. "Read to me." Stephanie's voice was thick with melting cream.

"It's *Vanity Fair*. I'm right in the middle," Ava cautioned.

"Don't care."

Ava had read it before anyway. Thinking Stephanie might profit from the moral example of a young woman a trifle too determined to make her way in the world at any cost, she flipped back to the first page and began to read out loud. But Stephanie was asleep in minutes, the ice-cream carton tilting dangerously from her limp hands. Ava removed it carefully, and Stephanie's hands curled around the empty space in a protective knot.

The next time Ava sat down to write, she felt unusually optimistic. Things felt like they were happening and Stephanie's conviction that success was easy, inevitable and theirs for the taking made Ava feel unusually intrepid. The library was silent, a cup of Earl Grey steamed on the desk, a single ray of sunshine painting its blushing porcelain almost translucent. Her quills were clean, composition book open, she was ready to start again. The pens and nibs she had to buy from an art supply store didn't last; after a few pages she always switched to whatever other pens were lying around. But it seemed an important ritual, a declaration of principles. A writing teacher in college had scolded her for her ornate style—"You can't write an eighteenth-century novel in the twentieth century." She had immediately dropped the class in tears, but now, determined to do just that, she started out each time scratching the sharp nib out of spite. When in the end it turned out that she could and had written a grand old-fashioned novel, full of beautiful words and long elegant sentences, she would send a copy to him with a sharp note.

It wasn't industry that she lacked. She had composition books already filled with sketches of her dashing hero, Agustin, and the run-down mansion where he lit candles and stared out of windows. She seemed to get stuck, however, when she needed him to do anything else. She had recently thought up a love interest, Anastasia, who was already displaying a similar dispiriting tendency to sit in chairs and look sadly at the floor. The situation was getting dire. Reading and writing were the only things that Ava had ever been any good at, and if she didn't figure out how to make things start to happen soon, she was going to have to come to some hard understandings about herself.

She wasn't trying to write historical fiction; rather she liked to think of it as timeless, a reflection of the veil of old books through which she saw the world, and which colored her impressions after their own image. But really, what else could she do? New books, she assumed, were about people that had friends and boyfriends, that went to parties or dated, a well of common experience that she always was skirting the edge of. But from the distance of another time, obscured by cravats and bustles, people seemed at once more familiar, because of the books she read, and also more abstract, and therefore easier to identify with. Or maybe it was just that Ava had sort of continued to associate the deepest, most private aspects of her emotional life with high button boots, and codes of honor and rattling cabriolets, and she struggled to articulate her feelings in the only language she knew.

With her weekdays free, Stephanie hung around the Lazarus Club nearly every day. At first, Ava had been worried that someone would object, but she soon learned just how porous and poorly enforced any sort of rules were around the place; no one seemed to really notice or care. And then somewhere along the line Stephanie had acquired a remarkable ability to look rich. She had always dressed well, but recently she had perfected many of the subtle cues, the kind of handbag, the right shoes, that when coupled with her brazen self-possession, no one even questioned her right to be there. Ava knew her purses came from the sidewalk vendors on Canal Street and her shoes from consignment shops, the glittering facade was just paint and moxie, but it didn't seem to matter. Even Aloysius had fallen for her when she told him his whole look was "very Cary Grant" and offered to put him in touch with some young designers who were doing great things with pocket squares. "It's so good for the club to have young people around," he had fluttered and asked Stephanie to sit closer to the windows so that all those journalists writing nasty articles about the encroaching end of the establishment could see that the Lazarus Club had plenty of young, new members and was doing just fine thank you very much.

Currently, this breath of fresh air was sitting in a leather club chair, long legs pressed against her chest, absorbed in a biography of Nadia Comaneci she had found on the shelves. High heels abandoned on the floor next to her, she absent-mindedly cupped her toes in her hand while she read.

"This girl was pretty intense. Imagine being better than everyone in the entire world at one thing, and having everyone know it. How fucking satisfying that must be." She threw the book aside. "You know, I wish you would just go into business with me."

Ava was rearranging the library for her own amusement: a turn-of-the-century manual on brain surgery migrated to a shelf she had labeled *Hobbies*, Jane Austen she put under *Finance*, and P.G. Wodehouse went next to the Communist Manifesto in *Socialism*. She laughed. "Me? I would be terrible at starting anything. In case you've forgotten, I'm cripplingly shy."

"Well, that's what you would have me for. I'm not scared of anyone."

Ava flipped through a book on Euclid and considered filing it under *Foreign Languages*. "True. Rather, I think people are often scared of you."

"And I just feel like I need someone I can trust. You're my only friend." She noticed Ava's skeptical look. "My only real friend. Everyone else is just people."

"I already have a job."

"Well, maybe we could do something that ties in some-how, like a library-slash-bar or something."

"What you're trying to describe is basically my fantasy. I mean, not the commercial business part you're talking about, but I've always dreamt of hosting a salon. Every nineteenth-century novel has a salon in it, famous artists and beautiful women, drinking tea and talking about books and art and falling in love. But I think you need to be married to a duke or something for that to work," Ava finished, sadly.

They were interrupted by the arrival of an older woman muffled in a large fur stole despite the season. "I was almost married to a duke, but he called it off because I once wore slacks to the Sherry Netherland," she said through the fur.

"Good Morning, Mrs. Van Doren," said Ava. A former Argentinean beauty queen who had married into one of New York's oldest families, Mrs. Van Doren was a source of glamorous fascination to Ava.

"Hello, Ava. I wanted to see if you wouldn't mind switch-ing our mahjong to Tuesday afternoons. Mrs. Bellamy has some complications with her driver on Mondays."

Ava shrugged. "Sure. I never have anything to do."

"You're very agreeable, but you shouldn't admit that, dear. Even to a pack of old ladies. Always allow yourself some mystery." Mrs. Van Doren stopped in the center of the room and waited, expectantly. Ava knew what she wanted but de-cided to let Stephanie handle it. "This young woman is in my chair," she said finally, with a look at Stephanie's bare feet.

Stephanie immediately slid out of the chair and into her shoes like oil pouring off water. "Of course, I'm so sorry. I was just so caught up in this book. Don't you just love a li-brary?"

Settling into the chair, Mrs. Van Doren rearranged her silk blouse with a proprietary air and shifted the glittering eyes of the mink biting its own tail, pulling it up higher around

her neck. "I remember her, she was quite the impressive little thing." She pointed at Stephanie's book and closed her
eyes. "I'm glad we saved her from those godless commies."

"Oh I know, *dasvidaniya*, but what would we do without caviar?"

A smile fluttered over Mrs. Van Doren's pale lips. "One
of my ex-husbands practically lived for the stuff. A trip
to Petrossian and a bottle of champagne and he'd pay any
amount on my Saks charge."

"Wasn't Nadia Comaneci Romanian?" Ava asked.

They ignored her, exchanging bromides about men, which
Ava felt just a little wounded not to be able join in, until
Mrs. Van Doren tucked her chin against the pointed snout
cradling her cheek and promptly fell asleep.

"I love this place so much," Stephanie said, and began
to wander around the room. She put her book back on the
wrong shelf and poked her finger into the mouth of a brass
lion roaring on a side table. The tassels of a velvet bellpull
hanging from the ceiling brushed her shoulder, and she idly
wrapped them around her wrist, tugging a little too hard
for Ava's taste.

"It doesn't work anymore," Ava said.

"What's behind here?" Stephanie stopped at a dusty set of
double doors and tried a bronze doorknob.

"A storage closet?" Ava turned back to her books. "Aloysius keeps everything locked up, so who knows? Mummi-
fied bodies? Confederate bonds?"

"Aren't you curious? If you had a knife or something, I
bet I could pick this lock."

"How about a hairpin?"

"That only works in movies, Ava."

Ava set a stack of books on a rung of the wooden ladder.
She rummaged around her desk. "I have a World War One
bayonet I was trying to use as a letter opener."

"Let me see." Stephanie glanced at the weapon. "No. I need a thinner edge."

Ava put it back. "Yeah, it was a terrible letter opener. Aloysius probably has the key, but he's so weird about this kind of thing. I tried to open those glass-fronted bookshelves downstairs once, and it distressed him to the point of tears."

"I'll get it. He loves me." Stephanie stomped out of the room.

Ava re-scaled the ladder. Balancing on the top step, she slid *Coup D'état: the Technique of Revolution* under *Sports*, right next to *Married Love and Health*. Eventually Stephanie reappeared with a large bronze key and a frazzled expression. Ava rested an elbow on *Tales for Males*. "It's amazing that you can charm even a delicate old bachelor like Aloysius."

"Well, I had to hear a bunch of technical details about Pomeranian breeding and then he said I reminded him of a young Doris Duke. I don't even know who that is."

Ava carefully descended the waxed rungs. "A dead socialite." Stephanie, at the locked door, smiled at this and continued pulling on the stiff key with both hands. "Let me." Ava knelt down and tried to hear the teeth catching. She had once read that safecrackers could do this kind of thing just by feeling the vibrations with their fingertips. After a few moments, the key slipped in the lock with a loud creaking sound. Ava turned the doorknob, and they stood, struck speechless by the room that opened up before them.

Weak sunlight filtered into a cavernous space that nearly mirrored the library next door, illuminating the sprawling pile of garbage that filled it: rolled up carpets, a dressmaker's dummy, huge wads of newspaper, curtain rods, garbage bags sagging against each other in dejected lumps, an egg crate mattress folded and bent under the weight of a tarnished samovar. Dirty windows stretched to the ceiling crossed with dark iron mullions. On the other side, a smaller, connected room was filled with old appliances.

Stephanie stepped forward and prodded a molting teddy bear. "What the hell is all this stuff?"

Ava followed cautiously, squatting to examine a mason jar filled with what looked like sharks' teeth. "I can't even imagine." An upended sofa lilted dramatically to one side, supporting a jumble of empty picture frames and a stack of yellowing *Penthouse* magazines.

"The people in this club are insane. Don't they know what New York real estate is worth? Was this somebody's apartment?"

"No idea. There are a dozen rubber nipples for baby bottles over here and a glue gun. I don't even want to know. Maybe it was an art studio? "

"Check it out, this wall has bookshelves. Somebody covered them over with carpet." Stephanie yanked at the filthy shag carpet that had been carefully nailed over the empty bookshelves.

As she crossed the room, plastic sheeting and garbage bags slid under Ava's feet. A deflated Mylar balloon coasted past on a spray of dust that swirled into the air. "Maybe it was originally part of the club library?" Ava pulled a corner to help. "But what it looks like now is the apartment of a schizophrenic. I thought the rooms were bad where I live. I hope we don't find the corpse of the crazy person who used to live here." With a final tug, the carpet fell to the ground, revealing carved wood bookshelves even more baroque than the ones next door. "Oh my god. Why aren't they using these?"

"Because they are insane." Stephanie was picking her way toward the deeper shadows at the back of the room. "I think this was a kitchen." She sneezed and turned the faucet on and off. "This space—it's fantastic. I wonder if they would let us use it. If we fixed it up."

"What do you mean?"

Stephanie was laughing. "It's so perfect. If we do it here, it would solve everything."

"I don't understand."

As she began to pace, Stephanie moved through the gauntlet of junk with surprising grace. "What if, and I'm just thinking things through here, what if we open our own club up here? The Lazarus Club would make us look fancy and established, I mean, come on, this place is amazing, but we could have our own membership and host people here, it's like a bar-slash-library already."

"Why would they let us do that?"

Stephanie stopped and looked at Ava in disbelief. "Are you kidding? This place is asphyxiating. Ten years from now, all their members will be dead. You know how desperate Aloysius is for good press. With all my connections, we would be the best thing that happened to this place in the last twenty years. Fifty," she corrected herself.

A paint can at Ava's feet seemed a good place to sit down. It was unsettling to think that she had been working away in the next room for so long, unaware of all this. A mannequin arm left a dusty handprint on her dark wool skirt. The chaos of objects bristling, immobile, incongruous, seemed to whisper a story she couldn't quite piece together, a diorama of a dead civilization casting a spell. "But you're talking about starting a business. Don't you need to know about accounting and stuff? I don't know anything about running a business."

Stephanie swung a broken picture frame around her wrist and then tossed it back onto a pile. "How hard can it be? I've been reading about it. You just get incorporated in Delaware for taxes or something."

This was not reassuring. Ava leaned forward and wiped the dust from the toes of her low T-strap heels. "Stephanie. You know I could never be in charge of anything. I'm so bad with people."

In her hurry to cross the room, Stephanie tripped on a stuffed pheasant and, practically crawling over the piles of junk, came to squat down in front of Ava. She pushed a lock of hair out of Ava's face and took both of her hands in hers. "I can handle the people. There are so many rich people in New York. Everybody wants in on the cool new thing. This is about you, for you. This whole place—that stuffed bird, and bearskins, and paintings of someone's dead grandmother, all this Victorian stuff, it's going to be the next big thing. I can just feel it, and that's all you. People are going to come here because of you. You can curate the whole thing, we can have books and readings, it could be just like the salon you were talking about. Don't you want to host a salon and have everyone come and find out what an amazing writer you are?"

Ava wanted to pull her hands away but just nodded instead, retreating from this dizzying prospect to the safety of the particulars. "But it's such a mess in here. Wouldn't that be expensive to fix up?"

Stephanie stood up so fast, the restive energy always so present and barely contained, now let loose, filled up the room between them, all the empty space at once surging with wild possibility. "Investors are going to be no problem. All those years I've spent at every art opening and night-club and fashion launch—do you think I was just wasting my time? I was waiting for this. My moment. This is when I take it all back."

There was a fierceness to Stephanie's tone that made Ava look away, her gaze traveling over the clutter to the soaring height of the ornate ceiling panels. Still attempting to resist Stephanie's grandiosity, there was something about the equally outrageous grandeur of the room they were in that made it oddly appropriate. Not just appropriate—inevitable even. If fate were going to grant them a room like this, abandoned right in the middle of Manhattan, it would be irresponsible not to make use of it. "Do you think a bank would give us a loan?" Ava asked.

"No, they'll want collateral. I looked into it once. It's so stupid. If I already had something worth money, why would I be trying to get a loan? Look, don't get hung up on the details. I promise I will be able to get us funding. Think about the idea, the genius of it. Private clubs are so big right now—like three new ones opened up downtown, but they don't have a concept. But a literary club, in a place like this— every writer in town is going to join."

Ava didn't want to ask why exactly Stephanie had been trying to borrow money. From her vantage point on the paint can, she was having trouble thinking clearly. Events had escalated so dramatically that practical considerations seemed somehow beside the point in the face of Stephanie's operatic optimism.

The idea was absurd of course, but as she turned it over in her mind, Ava couldn't help a quiet thrill at the sudden prospect of one of her most beloved novels coming to life around her. She decided to read *In Search of Lost Time* in college because to be the kind of person who had read it gratified her vanity, but once started, she had been overwhelmed. Marcel, the narrator, his nerves and shyness, oversensitive and second-guessing, always wrong about everyone else's intentions and motivations, had spoken to Ava with an electric spark of recognition. His desperate desire to be a writer and his equal inability to actually write anything felt like someone whispering the irresolvable conflict of her secret heart. And then later as he made his way through the glamorous salons of Paris, it had summed up an entire shorthand for Ava, a descriptor of the life she one day wanted, a writer, surrounded by an admiring and glittering society, and so the book remained with her, more than just a story, a kind of fantastical template for her to recognize and measure her desires and progress against. And here was Stephanie, inflamed and fearless as usual, offering to create that very world around her.

"I don't know," she said finally.

A slow grin spread over Stephanie's face. "Just you wait."

Later that night, Ava's phone rang, shattering the quiet of the small studio. The bell still echoing in her head did not prevent her from being startled when the ring burst into the room again. She knew the futility of resisting the only person who would call her at two in the morning and threw back the covers, groping her way to the phone. "Hello?"

"You really need to get a cell phone."

"It's the middle of the night." Ava cradled the receiver in her ear, picked up the heavy body of the phone with her other hand, and began to drag its long cord to the bed. "I'm here, aren't I?" She pushed Mycroft out of the warm hollow of the mattress that she had recently vacated. Annoyed, he slithered to her pillow and respooled himself. "What do you want?" Ava realized she was still hoping for the token apology that should have started this conversation.

"I need you to get in a cab and meet me on Eighty-Third and West End Avenue."

"No." Ava paused. "What for?"

"I found the most amazing couch."

"What?"

"When we take over that room, we're going to need more seating. I'm thinking ahead."

"Stephanie, they're not going to let us take over the room. Stop thinking they will."

"They will," she insisted. "And this couch is amazing, and free. It's dark leather and has those button things."

"You mean tufted?"

"Yes, and it's just here on Eighty-Third Street, and I need you to help me move it before somebody else takes it. Just get in a cab."

"No." Then as Stephanie waited, silently, confidently, Ava couldn't help but picture the couch. She had always wanted a chesterfield. It really was the kind of thing every library needed, and if you were, somehow, going to have a literary club, it was exactly what you would want everyone to be sitting on, with the lights turned down low, brandy glasses warming in cupped palms, a murmured conversation about Thomas Hardy. She had lots she had always wanted to say about Thomas Hardy. "Oh, all right. But only because it's tufted."

Ava threw an old cotton dress over her nightgown. The thought of adding more junk to that crazy room was ridiculous. This was Stephanie getting ahead of herself as usual. Still, it was kind of exciting to get into a taxi in the middle of the night. She felt untethered, vaguely disreputable; like Mata Hari. What if she told the driver to go to Grand Central, took the first train out and just vanished? She saw a European hotel room, a new life, her one dress hung over a chair until she rose in the morning and slipped it over her head, the silk of her nightgown still nestling against her skin like a slip.

A warm breeze swept through the open window as the cab sped up a deserted avenue. The lit windows of skyscrapers looked like so many squares of an advent calendar, each holding their radiant secrets behind drawn shades. Apartment buildings glittered, a web of discrete worlds all held together in the muted glow of the city night. The car took a sharp left, and she slid across the slippery seat, enjoying her bare legs,

awkward and glamorous, the kind of legs that flung around
the back seats of rushing taxis at midnight. A pharmacy sign
flew by, and the lit torches of subway poles guarded empty
corners. When she arrived, she gave the driver a twenty for
a ten-dollar fare and told him to keep the change. Her dress
fluttered around her knees, and she slammed the door with
brio; she was that kind of girl.

She didn't realize that she hadn't actually believed Stephanie until she saw her sitting in a proprietary crouch in the
center of a large brown leather sofa, waving excitedly. "How
did you find this?"

Stephanie crossed one leg of a shimmery black cocktail
suit over the other and draped her arm over the back. The
proximity of a fire hydrant made Ava feel like she was in
a Buñuel movie, polished and urbane and not making any
sense. "Wednesday is garbage day on the Upper West Side,
and that's where all the good stuff is. The East Side gets
picked over too fast. I think all the doormen must sideline
as furniture dealers or something."

"How do you know all this?"

Stephanie shrugged. "I had to furnish my apartment somehow. I was at a party and then I figured I better walk up and
see if there was anything good out."

"You walked up here to go through the garbage?"

Stephanie smiled. "From Chelsea. At least I walked off four
vodka sodas." Ava sat, and Stephanie slid down and rested
her head in her lap. Ava noticed she hadn't quite walked off
the vodka sodas. "It's obviously a sign that I found a perfect
sofa. It's fate. We're a great team." She stretched her arms
and stroked her wrists absently. "Even though you always
thought I was uneducated."

This took Ava by surprise. "No, I didn't." But as she
spoke, she tried to consider the possibility, an uneasy tangle
of resemblance and comparison, envy and disdain, had al-

ways dominated their relationship, how they inhabited each of these categories, and perhaps more important, how the world around them judged and sorted the two. Maybe she did like to think of herself as smarter. "Why would it even matter to you? The way you look, you can have anything in the world you want, why even bother?"

"You're such an asshole sometimes." Stephanie reached a hand up and pressed it over Ava's lips, but affectionately. "You sound like my stepdad who couldn't understand why I even wanted to go to college. Because really, I'd rather not end up old and ugly, married to a mortgage broker whom I have to fuck even though he's fat because I'm forty, and no one else will ever love me, okay? This is why it's important to go into business for yourself," she explained to Ava.

Ava felt like there was an argument to be made here, but there was a vehemence to Stephanie's feelings that she felt bound to respect. She kind of wanted to stroke the silky hair spread across her lap, but didn't. Stephanie smelled like expensive perfume, like roses laid over smoldering embers, and Ava hoped that if a man ever got close to her again, she would smell as inviting to him as Stephanie did to her right now. Although maybe it was just one of those things about really beautiful women, one imagined they smelled so nice because of the aura that hangs around them and turns even their smallest acts into rare and intriguing mysteries; you had already been seduced. Was she doing exactly what Stephanie had just been complaining about? Ava decided she wasn't. "You smell good," she finally said.

"Thanks, I get free samples at Sephora every week."

The warm summer darkness hung around them, and Ava remembered the constant effort of Stephanie's beauty, and it made her feel tired. She let Stephanie put her head on her shoulder and idly play with the fingers of one hand while they sat in the never quite silence of a New York night.

Suddenly Stephanie spoke again. "Do you know how many county fair stages I had to cross in a bathing suit to get here? And how many times I had to shake the hand of some small-town Kiwanis club asshole, sweating and simpering and looking at my ass. But it was okay because I knew I was on my way out, to fame and fortune and everything I deserve. 'Here lies one whose name was writ in water.' You know that's on Keats's tombstone?" She hiccuped. "Not fucking going to be on mine. Call a car service to come pick us up. I'm going to take a nap."

Ava took the phone, a little surprised that Stephanie knew Keats's epitaph and she didn't. "The thing about a tombstone is, it doesn't have to be true. You can just say whatever. And why a literary club? How come you don't just want to be a movie star or something?"

"Because I'm fucking smart and I read books," she said sharply. Then, her annoyance passing in the easy fluctuations of her drunkenness, Stephanie curled her hands in the hem of Ava's dress. "You can't fool me, Ava. You're ambitious, too. It's just that you're a coward, but it's okay. That's why I'm here. I don't know what you would do without me. Ask for a van, but don't tell them we have a couch. Once they're here, they'll have to help us."

Ava dialed. She leaned back against the couch and looked into the strip of night sky visible between the projecting cornices of the roofs above them. In the shine of streetlamps, the row of granite buildings flattened like a stage set—two girls making it in the big city. Ava had been so sure she would write big important novels about love and society and the human condition, and she would ascend to that pantheon of stern beards and noble brows of all the authors she admired. But now? Maybe Stephanie was right, and her whole life risked fluttering away like translucent powder blown from an open compact.

"This is why we have to look out for each other. No one gives a shit about two pretty girls." Stephanie returned to her train of thought, her eyes still closed. "We might as well be potted plants."

"I'm not pretty enough to be decorative."

"All this false modesty is so boring." Stephanie yawned. "Why did Aloysius hire you? Because you're so good with Dewey decimal and stuff?" Ava was silent. She knew she had been hired because she and the Lazarus Club were made for each other, useless relics of a vanished time, but there was something so seductive about being grouped together with Stephanie in this way. What a delicious reality that would be, if it were true, that she was as universally desired as her friend. "Fuck 'em," Stephanie added. "That's why we have to be in charge. No one thinks of Leona Helmsely as a potted plant."

This was impossible to argue with, so instead Ava slowly ran her fingers through Stephanie's hair, humming a waltz she had learned from an unmarked batch of Victrola records. Stephanie was snoring quietly when the van arrived. The driver was furious, but as Stephanie predicted, he helped them load their couch. He grumbled at them all the way back to the Lazarus Club in a guttural foreign language, but Stephanie, slumped against the armrest, didn't seem to notice. Ava allowed herself not to care, still enjoying their strange errand like a kid up past bedtime. Gasping and straining, they got the couch up the stairs and into the pile of junk where it looked very much at home.

4

When they finally got Aloysius to come see the room they had discovered, he looked around startled and then his gaze grew distant. "Oh yes, this was the personal studio of one of our most illustrious members, Cornelius Alderdonck." He picked up a moldy teddy bear and stroked an ear affectionately. "One of the original Alderdonks, the direct male line, *not* the distaff side," he said, looking sternly at Ava for some reason. "Such an artistic soul. Did you know his ancestors used to own the Bronx?"

Stephanie sniffed appreciatively. "I just love a pedigree. It makes everything feel so homey. My grandmother always said, if there wasn't Mayflower somewhere in your family, you just couldn't be trusted." Ava noticed Stephanie was wearing pearl earrings she had never seen before. "Tradition was really what we were thinking about, Ava and I, when we were talking about how wonderful it would be to fix this place up and maybe host some select, artistic events here. My good friend Tom was just saying how few really exclusive places there are left in New York City. He's an editor at *Vanity Fair*," she mentioned casually as an aside. "I'm sure he'd love to do a story on us."

Turning pink around the ears, Aloysius cleared his throat. "They do such charming portraits, that magazine. I've always found it strange they never asked me before."

Stephanie put a sympathetic hand on his arm. "Well, we have to fix that. I've got lots of other ideas, different celebrities that might want to get involved, that I'd love to discuss with you. Maybe we can talk over a drink."

As she led him toward the bar downstairs, he stopped to pick up the jar of shark teeth, a mannequin arm and two dirty corduroy shirts that he pressed to his chest. "You would have to clear it with the board, of course, and the club really doesn't have any room in the budget for improvement."

"Oh no, we would handle all that, of course." Stephanie couldn't resist looking over her shoulder and winking while Ava followed behind, somewhat dazed, as she often was, by the full deployment of Stephanie's charm, a sensation that only increased as they drank glass after glass of sherry, and she watched Stephanie and Aloysius howling together in gleeful drunken conspiring.

After, Ava and Stephanie sat on their new couch, recovering. "What the hell did he mean about wanting in particular to attract new membership among our dusky friends and neighbors?" Stephanie asked. "Dusky?!"

Ava groaned. "I think that's just how he talks. He always refers to Mrs. Bellamy as 'la belle Creole,' and I want to die of embarrassment. I mean, she's from Milwaukee." Ava hesitated. "I think he means, well, in like a Nancy Cunard kind of way."

"I don't know who that is." Stephanie scrunched her nose in distaste. "But, if he really wants to drag this club into the twenty-first century, I would be more than happy to help in that regard."

Ava smiled a little in spite of herself at the thought. "Is this all really going to happen?"

"Yep." Stephanie stood and pulled out two large black garbage bags. "Let's clean this place up."

Ava accepted a bag. "How did you even know he would say yes?" she began and then decided not to press the issue. "I still can't imagine this will work. I couldn't even get into the Baker Street Irregulars. How can I start my own club?"

"Those guys are a bunch of losers, and no one wants to be in their dumb club anyway."

Ava almost started to defend the eminent Holmes scholars, but it was true they hadn't asked her to join, so she didn't. She started sorting through a box full of chipped rococo vases.

Volleys of old girlie magazines went thudding into Stephanie's trash bag. "So we need a name for this thing. I've been thinking about it—something old-fashioned." She looked at Ava to make sure this registered. "Just like you want, but also sexy and fun, I was thinking something like 'The Scarlet Letters.'"

"That sounds like a cheerleading team." Ava set down a dusty jar decorated with little gilt monkeys and stared off into space, considering. "Also Hester Prynne is kind of a dismal role model, especially if your aim is sociability."

"Well, you come up with something."

Ava thought for what she hoped seemed like the right amount of time and then suggested, very casually, "How about 'The Little Clan?' It's the name of the salon in Proust. He's kind of brutal about how they're all just social climbers with pretensions to culture, but it's still a cool name."

"Not catchy enough."

"But it's like the most famous salon in literature. I'm sure some people would get it."

"No one but you knows what that is, Ava." Stephanie didn't even bother to turn around.

Hurt, Ava decided she had work to do in the library next door. "I thought that was why you wanted me to do this with you—because I know things about books that other people don't."

"Don't be so touchy." Stephanie, busily sorting garbage, called after her, "You need to trust me on this kind of stuff."

As Ava began reshelving a stack of books, her silly categories didn't seem so funny anymore, just embarrassing and kind of pretentious. She could hear Stephanie puttering in the next room, and eventually, Ava gave up on the books and slouched at her desk, morosely refilling some fountain pens. At least she had mahjong on Tuesday, and those ladies thought she was just lovely.

Having secured tentative approval for their project, next was finding the funding. The board meeting they were slated to attend to argue their case was quickly approaching, and Ava and Stephanie both sensed their chances would be greatly increased if they could prove themselves financially independent. In Ava's experience, the club members huddled around the free cheese and crackers had a thriftiness inseparable from their Bar Harbor estates and Yale tie clips. The fraying carpets and unchanged light bulbs around the club also spoke to the members' lack of philanthropic spirit. For someone who subsisted almost entirely on bar nuts and the free hors d'oeuvres of parties she attended, Stephanie seemed miraculously unconcerned about it.

Instead, excited by the challenge, like a hunting dog, snout raised for the scent of blood, she cast off after investors, a campaign of cocktail parties and late boozy lunches among her wide-ranging acquaintance. Hair spray and heels waited in the bottomless bag that was always slung on her shoulder for when she heard the siren call of gathering affluence. Then touching up her makeup, she explained to Ava that, as wearying as these functions could be, she thought she would do better on her own, and why didn't Ava stay and keep sorting through the trash?

This suited Ava. Stephanie, dotting foundation across her cheeks with a cool concentration or frowning as she smoothed her hair and unbuttoned another shirt button, was sleek, coiled, hypnotizing to watch, and a little frightening. When Stephanie returned, cursing the stinginess of rich people, her manner, supercilious and domineering, carried an unconscious imitation of those she had just left, and Ava was very glad not to have gone with her.

As Ava cleared more and more junk out of the room, it became apparent just how extensive the decrepitude was—the hardwood floors were a mess, half of it covered in sticky linoleum, the walls were stained with mold, light fixtures hung broken. If their plan, as it currently stood—of charging membership dues for people to hang out and drink and attend literary events and readings—had any hope of working, they would need to invest in substantial renovations before they could possibly open. Ava often thought wistfully of the luxury of her parents' house.

Her mother was always rearranging things. Whenever Ava started to get used to the terrible matching prints her mother adored—flowers and monkeys and vines clambering over each other in frantic stasis—her mother, complaining of "dinginess," would rip it all out and start again. Then Ava would be subjected to a different room of exploding pink flowers whose aggressive newness and femininity made her feel like a guest, a stain on the meticulously conceived design of the rooms she lived in.

But it would be so nice to be able to call her mother now and ask for help and advice. Initially she had hoped that her mother would be excited about her job at the Lazarus Club—she was, after all, free of Stephanie, always dismissively referred to as "that person," and it was fancy and full of rich people. But after one visit, her mother had cast a withering eye over the place and summed up Ava's failure. "You'll never meet any men here." The thought of what her mother would think of her one conquest, Jules Delauncy, almost made Ava laugh. But not quite.

Finally with just two weeks until the board meeting, Stephanie called one morning excited—she had a potential investor on the hook and wanted Ava to meet him, to "seal the deal." Ava couldn't imagine she would be of much use in whatever that entailed, but walking farther uptown the next day, it was kind of exciting to be on her way to a meeting; she so rarely needed to go anywhere. She assumed no one would miss her at the Lazarus Club; Aloysius had always had very lax, not to say, confusing expectations about when she was supposed to be at the library. She stopped and bought a *Wall Street Journal*, a paper she associated with her father as it had blocked Ava's view of him for almost every breakfast of her life. The technicalities of his business, running a chain of local grocery stores, were unclear to her, and therefore, she assumed, must be important. What a novel sensation to be on this side of the divide, that of things that mattered.

When she arrived, the entrance to the restaurant corroborated her new sense of self-importance. A converted bank, its former name was etched in crisp serifs across a limestone facade rising between giant art deco lanterns. The architecture spoke so strongly of the confidence and bluster of the American Twenties that Ava's heart fluttered that such places still existed and that she had reasons to enter them.

She clicked through the revolving brass door into a room whose height and proportions dwarfed the leather banquettes and white tablecloths that now filled it. Chandeliers hung from the vaulted ceiling, their brass fixtures casting a discreet glow, a whispered promise of the responsible stewardship of wealth. Doors that now led to wine cellars or kitchens still bore the bright varnish that must have delighted their original occupants, men, she imagined, whose vests stretched tight over bellies and who yelled through bulky intercoms at their unimpressed, gum-chewing stenographers. A hostess led Ava toward a table at the back, where she could see Stephanie already sitting with a slender man in his fifties. As she passed, she couldn't help but notice many of the other tables also seemed to be occupied by beautiful young women picking at their food while older men appraised each other approvingly from across their separate tables. Electronic music was playing too loudly over the sound system.

Ava tried to pull out the big leather chair with a graceful hello, but it was unexpectedly heavy, and she had to be rescued by a solicitous waiter who pushed her into the table like a child. Stephanie's companion, Steve Buckley, was a bony man whose hair arched back from a wide yet angular face like the crest of an iguana. He shook her hand, and as his fingers lingered over her wrist, she had a sudden feeling that she might be very bad at whatever it was Stephanie wanted her to do.

"Hello, darling, this is Steve Buckley, who I've been telling you about. VC extraordinaire, visionary, the sort of man who really appreciates the future."

Ava didn't know what any of this meant, so she just smiled and nodded and accepted an enormous menu from the waiter. A tiny shake of the head from Stephanie confused her until she tentatively handed it back.

"The tartar." Steve Buckley indicated all of them with his finger. "And a goddamned vodka soda."

"He's part owner," Stephanie whispered loud enough to provoke a satisfied grunt. "And this is Ava, the brains behind our project. She has read absolutely everything." Ava thought she detected Steve Buckley's pale face start to collapse into boredom. "Tell him," Stephanie commanded.

Doubtful but deferring to Stephanie's experience, she complied. "It's true, I probably spend more time with books than with people." Her self-deprecating laugh was not contagious. Alarmed that he seemed about to yawn in her face, she tried again. "Are you a big reader?"

"I read big ideas." He paused to check one of two phones on the table in front of him. The subject of books momentarily put to rest made him happier, and he expressed his satisfaction by squeezing Stephanie's shoulder. "Isn't she fucking amazing?" he asked Ava.

"She's a delightful person," Ava said defensively.

"He's just trying to flatter me. Did you know Steve has been collaborating with Hermès? His media company is getting artists to design scarves for them which they are then going to install in certain luxury hotel rooms, as part of a special…" She started to trail off, unsure. "Anyway, he really understands the importance of literature and art to building a premier, first-class experience."

"A hobby, you could say." He smiled into his vodka soda.

"Please, supporting the arts is just the sort of hobby that makes for a better world. It's not as if you're playing golf, or something."

This struck Ava as a daring gambit, as he seemed very much like someone who might play golf, and she waited anxiously.

But Steve laughed. "I love this woman." And he and Stephanie exchanged a look of mutual appreciation. As the conversation rolled forward, Ava admired what she started to realize was a concerted strategy—by the subtle disparagement of certain people and activities, Stephanie was carving a complimentary portrait of Steve Buckley, cultured, discerning, different, and he eagerly received this vision of himself, that mysterious way that Stephanie had of making someone feel special. By the time the food arrived, she had spun a web that held them all aligned, a milieu she implied that was at once young, cool, entrepreneurial and, most important, rich.

"We will want some society people, of course, but it's important that things not get too 'Park Avenue' stuffy," Stephanie was saying. "Anyway, that's Ava's department. She's the Southern deb."

For the first time, Ava seemed to register in Steve's eyes, and he turned to her with a new visible interest. "Old money, huh?"

This so summed up the driving frustration of her mother's life that Ava almost laughed as she chased a slimy wad of tuna tartare around her plate with a fancy potato chip. She wasn't. Her grandfather had made his money with a chain of grocery stores which he later left to his son, and realizing he would never be more than his neighbors' Jewish shopkeeper, he bought up acres of recently drained swamp and built the suburb where Ava grew up, whose wide treeless streets and big brick houses aped the mansions uptown that wouldn't grant him entrance. This was why Ava, his only granddaughter, had been sent to the city's most expensive Catholic school; he was bankrolling another attempt to break his family into the exclusive social world of the goyim. It hadn't worked.

Instead, she had been presented in the ballroom of the Petite Lac Country Club, just off the strip malls of Route 90, forty minutes outside of New Orleans and a universe away. There, squeezed into a bridal gown and forced to curtsey deep into shag carpet while a Casio keyboard mournfully chirped *Tales from the Vienna Woods*. It was just as good as the other balls, her mother insisted, hanging her debutante portrait over the dining room sideboard and Ava had to look into her own eyes, sparkling with blue shadow and blank as a taxidermy deer, every time they sat down to eat.

Stephanie's smile hardened, starting to show little wolf teeth, so Ava took a large gulp of the champagne that had appeared on the table. It was too early in the day and tasted like sour pineapples. "Something like that" was the best response she could manage.

Stephanie smoothed her hair with the back of her hand. "Really, Steve, who doesn't want to hang out with a pair of sexy librarians, and also be a founding member of what is going to be next year's hottest club?" Embarrassed, Ava tried to put down her glass and knocked it onto a plate of untouched flatbread. Stephanie calmly handed her a napkin. "But let's talk specifics. We're looking for supporters at the five-, ten- and fifteen-thousand-dollar beneficiary levels."

Startled by Stephanie's daring, Ava almost started to cough, but managed to suppress it, carefully mopping up her spilled champagne.

Steve looked bored again and checked his phones. Without looking up, he asked where Stephanie had been going out lately. All the old places were so dead.

"Exactly my point. Clubs are dead—but a home for cross-cultural collaborations, where successful men like yourself can really relax and know you'll be surrounded by people who are your intellectual peers, that's the real goal. Who hasn't been inspired by literature? We all know that smart is the new sexy." Stephanie continued to describe their project, pitching and persuading, cajoling and teasing, while Ava watched, just astounded by the audacity of the whole thing.

When it was over, they declined his offer of a ride home—his driver had been idling outside the whole time—and walked together into the congested bustle of Madison Avenue.

Traffic bellowed, and a bus shot a plume of exhaust at

them. Ava felt like they had been inside for hours, and this busy sidewalk was too noisy, too bright, but Stephanie was triumphant. "That was fantastic. He totally loved us. Guys like that just need a little cultivating. I have a good feeling about this."

A lamppost seemed a good spot to stop and rest while the world spun. "I can't believe you thought anyone would give us thousands of dollars. I thought you were going to ask him for a hundred or something."

"You can't start small, it just makes everyone suspicious." Looking into her mirrored sunglasses, Stephanie reapplied lipstick. "Trust me. Anyway, he said he would give us some books."

"It's him I don't trust. He looks like he could just chew you up and spit you out. You'll waste all your charm and beauty and hustle, and he'll move on and you'll end up alone in a garret, proud and thirty and dead. Didn't you read *The House of Mirth*? That's how these stories end."

"Oh my god, that's perfect. I love it." The cap of the lipstick clacked into place, a flash of sliver in the afternoon sun.

"What do you mean?"

"As a name. Beyoncé just started a fashion line called House of Deréon. But also like the House of Windsor, but also kind of sounds like Shakespeare. I love it."

"You're definitely not getting the point. That title is a quote from the Bible about fools."

Stephanie ignored her. "Mirth is such a classy word. And it shows that our club will be smart and fun and not stuffy."

Ava shook her head. "No. You need to just read the book, please. Edith Wharton."

"Of course I will. I thought you didn't read books by women."

"It was assigned in high school," Ava lied. "It's pretty good. I just usually like serious books."

"You're a woman who wants to write a serious book."

"Mine is going to be different. Not some book about pretty, rich young women going to parties and trying to get married. It's going to be about art and literature and stuff."

Stephanie had rather pointedly stopped listening to her. "So how excited are you to get an entire library?"

Ava couldn't help but smile. While not committing any cash, Steve Buckley had recently purchased a large estate that had come with a library, and they were welcome to take all the books off his hands. "I wonder what's in it?"

They walked slowly downtown, passing a water bottle between them and arguing about what their fantasy library would contain. Stephanie wanted first editions of all Thomas Pynchon's novels, Ava, all of Balzac's human comedy. Eventually they agreed that provided they didn't have to read each other's choices, they would have a spectacular collection.

This lunch seemed to launch them in some way; the invisible currents that flowed through the city seemed to pick them up, carrying them along like a ship under sail. For Ava, this crazy idea was slowly shedding the timbre of the delusional. The more they talked about it, the more it took shape, emerging from idle fantasy into something external, something real—something that now had a name. For someone so accustomed to living in her own head, this transformation had something magical about it, and she credited Stephanie for this unexpected, thrilling act of alchemy.

Now that someone actually pledged to donate something to their improbable scheme, a course had been started, and they couldn't turn back. This inexorability energized Stephanie, launching her through a cavalcade of cocktail parties and business dinners. Ava was surprised that she could have found quite so many rich friends, but as it was described to her, each acquaintance brought out four more possibilities, and Stephanie hunted each of them down, relentless in her acquisitions, until she had a new soul mate every week: the recent divorcée who wanted a friend to shop with, the tech millionaire who wanted to go to the cool new clubs, the attenuated playboy looking to relive his youth. All this activity hadn't actually provided any resources yet, but it suddenly seemed that dozens of people knew of their club and its imminent opening.

And while Ava sat through some of these meetings feeling like the conversations were happening in a language she wasn't familiar with, there had been bright moments: the nightclub impresario who loved Victor Hugo, the fashion photographer who had heard of Wilkie Collins. There had even been one wonderful lunch with the head of a major publishing company. It was unclear how he had been swept up in Stephanie's otherwise rather downtown net, but Ava had spent a glorious hour impressing this leonine gentleman, who inclined his large snowy head toward her and spoke to them indulgently of young people, and the life of the mind, and Gertrude Stein. After, noticing the cloud of self-regard Ava was floating in, Stephanie brought her down rather abruptly. "He just wants to fuck you," she said irritably, extending her arm for a cab they couldn't afford.

5

Despite their lack of funds, the germinating impression of participating in a real business was beginning to flower. Stephanie did not read *The House of Mirth* as promised, but threw around the name so constantly, it was starting to lose its original association and become theirs by right of repetition. "What are people going to think we're saying about ourselves?" Ava asked.

"No one but you has read it. Stop worrying" was Stephanie's blithe response. Ava disagreed; they were starting a literary club, after all, but it was a beautiful phrase to have occasion to say so often. The eloquent formality of the King James construction managed to feel both familiar and yet elevating, and, maybe there was a hint of rebellion, a kind of brazenness in so naming themselves that Ava was starting to enjoy.

Stephanie had been right about Delaware being the cheapest state in which to incorporate themselves: a hundred dollars and a mail-in form later, they received a manila envelope of very official documentation proclaiming The House of Mirth Literary Society to be a limited liability corporation with two officers, Stephanie Anne Sloane and Ava Rose Gallanter. Ava liked being an officer. There were some questions about what to do next regarding the IRS, but Ava had found a book at the Lazarus Club, *The Mercantile Profession: Its Modes, Customs and Manners*, and fully intended on reading it. It didn't feel pressing since they didn't have any money, and anyway, April 15 was a long way away. The board meeting, however, with its sense of great consequence, was almost upon them.

Ava took the opportunity the following Tuesday to ask Mrs. Van Doren, whom she knew was on the board, for advice.

"Just be your usual charming self, my dear," she said, stacking her mahjong tiles with a lazy clatter. "I think it would be grand for this place to have some more nice young people like you around. It's getting to be like a nursing home around here."

"Speak for yourself, Flora," Mrs. Bellamy said sharply, organizing her own tiles with a brisk efficiency. In the thirties she had eloped with the scion of a grand New York family, but before his parents could disinherit him, they had been killed in a train accident, as Mrs. Bellamy had once explained to Ava with still evident satisfaction. She remained strikingly beautiful, and it mystified Ava that she would spend her last years at the Lazarus Club. But then, at times Mrs. Bellamy seemed equally confused about Ava. "You won't be banging around too much, will you? This city is chaotic enough. This is my sanctuary." She put down a tile and took another from the table.

"Oh no," Ava said. "Nothing like that. It's going to be nerdy girls like myself, and other quiet people who want to talk about books and writing. Three of bamboo?" she said putting it on the table.

The other women shook their heads. "I would just tell

them you plan on fixing the place up a little," said Mrs. Van Doren. "We've been having no end of trouble with the city. First they landmark you, then they harass you nonstop for every little thing. It's fairly outrageous."

"But surely the members are wealthy enough to take care of things like that?" Ava asked.

Mrs. Bellamy and Mrs. Van Doren exchanged a glance. "Let's just say Aloysius isn't the best bookkeeper."

Mrs. Bellamy picked up another tile. "I would keep all of this to yourself, dear. Chow," she added with satisfaction, laying down three tiles.

Mrs. Lowry, the fourth member of their game, turned up her hearing aid and suddenly yelled, "Mahjong." The others, as was their custom, ignored her and continued playing.

A few days later, Ava was sitting on the floor of her apartment making the final corrections to their proposal for the board with a gum eraser when her doorbell rang. She stood up, taking an Oreo from the open pack on the floor, and surveyed her work. Trying to come up with persuasive ways to make their case, she and Stephanie decided the first step would be to show the terrible dereliction of the space they wanted and the great changes they would make. As Stephanie was still being squired around town by various men of means, Ava volunteered. She knew, because Stephanie had shown her, that she wanted one of those computer-generated architectural renderings, little people wandering around enjoying the beautifully renovated space. Instead, Ava took some Polaroids and then created an imaginative projection of what it could possibly look like with ink and watercolor. She had taken a couple of drawing classes in high school, and while the perspective was a little off, the final product struck her as convincing. She mounted both the before and after pictures on poster board, in beautiful vintage frames. The feeling of accomplishment was very validating.

She split the Oreo and checked the peephole. Stephanie, dressed for their meeting, huge pearls around her neck and her hair teased into an immobile puff, leaned hard on the bell. Ava steadied herself just one minute before she unlatched the door. Dropping her purse on Ava's kitchen counter and knocking over a cup of cold coffee, Stephanie looked at the cookie in her hand. "What are you doing? Do you know how bad for you these are? We need to look our best." The open package sailed into a nearby garbage can.

"That was my breakfast." Ava mopped up the spilled coffee with a paper towel.

"How can we expect anyone to take us seriously if we can't show a little discipline? Truly successful women never break their diets. Even Oprah's clearly pretending to like carbs just to seem relatable." Stephanie gave a wistful sigh. "She's in an entirely different league."

"I don't think that can be true."

"Trust me. If you want people to think you have money, which is imperative because rich people will only give you stuff if they think you don't need it, then you've got to be skinny. It's like hair. I wish you'd let me straighten yours."

That she had wild, abundantly, gloriously curly hair was one of the overriding shames of Stephanie's life. Ava had only seen it in its natural state once, when Stephanie slipped in the shallow end of a pool, where she had been cautiously preening in a designer bathing suit, emerging afterward with wet, wavy locks in a sputtering fury.

"No." Ava had idolized too many Victorian ladies in curling papers to ever consider a flat iron.

"So unprofessional," Stephanie sighed. "Where's the presentation?" She looked around the room. "I need to psyche myself up. I feel like I'm out of practice. These old ladies can't be any worse than the Junior Miss Nebraska Teen Regional, right?"

"I still can't really believe you were a pageant queen."

"Why? You were a debutante. It's like the exact same thing except you don't win any money. I used to puke every time before I went on. Maybe we should try that. It helps calm your nerves."

Not used to seeing this side of Stephanie, Ava felt a kind of panicky response to this revelation of her friend's vulnerability "Wait, why are we even doing this?" She began to back away as the feeling gathered force, a rapid blossoming of sticky heat. "I can't do this. I can't go in there and convince them to let us take over their club and make a mess of things. They're never going to agree. This whole idea is crazy." She bumped up against her chaise lounge and sat down heavily. "I can't possibly do it, Stephanie. You know that I can't."

Stephanie, who had been anxiously rummaging around her purse, found a packet of Tums and looked up at Ava quickly. "Oh no you don't, Ava. You don't get to wimp out on me now. There is no fucking way. You don't get to get all faint and fluttery and run for your quill pens and start braiding your hair or whatever it is you do when you're about to pussy out."

The Oreos were surging around in Ava's stomach, and she was getting worried expelling them might not be a choice. "I like my quill pens. I like my job. I don't want it to change. I like it here. You're the one who left, not me," she yelled, surprising herself.

Stephanie's eyes got hard and there was a sudden flash, and Ava sensed an unspoken threat, and it scared her and she wanted to reach for Stephanie, but an overpowering feeling of helplessness prevented her. Of course Stephanie could always leave again. She could leave at any time, and life would rush up to greet her and carry her away to new adventures, new people, new best friends. She would probably never even remember the woman she left behind, alone and forgotten, stuck in a dusty library for the rest of Ava's life. The terrible weight of her dependency pressed in on her, and she trembled, hoping that Stephanie might somehow not notice.

But Stephanie noticed everything, and she clamped her purse shut and came to sit next to Ava, wrapping an arm around her shoulder. "We're a team, Ava. We have been ever since that day I made you go to that first party in college and you didn't want to and I dressed you up and you got so wasted you danced all night."

"You went home with that soccer player, and I threw up all over the guy you tried to set me up with."

"Sure, whatever, but the point is, you had fun. Look, you're going to be a writer, a famous writer one day, but you have to live a little first. This is how you're going to get from point A to point B. You just have to trust me."

Ava was trying not to burrow into the warmth of Stephanie's armpit, as if she could absorb strength and consolation through the slight pressure of her friend's bony ribs. "What are we going to tell them? We don't have any money to renovate with."

"We'll think of something. If you smile hard enough, no one pays attention to what you're saying anyway."

This didn't sound likely, but Ava didn't want to break the moment by arguing. "I finished our proposal." She pointed to her paintings, a little sad when Stephanie hopped off the chaise to examine them.

She looked at them for a long time while Ava nervously ate another Oreo. Finally, Stephanie rubbed the bridge of her nose and sighed. "Ava, those look insane. We're trying to be professional."

"I am being professional. I thought we wanted things to look old-fashioned."

The buzz of a BlackBerry interrupted them. "Hold on, I have to take this." Stephanie held up a finger and faced the wall as if this afforded any privacy in Ava's tiny studio. "Yes, love, I know, but if we can't get on the guest list by five, it's just not worth it."

Ava fed Mycroft the cream of her cookie, finding comfort in his eagerness.

"I know, but she owes me everything. I introduced her to him. Call her again and then call me back." Stephanie hung up. "God, sometimes it feels like I just have to do everything."

The BlackBerry buzzed again, and she started tapping in response, jamming her thumbs against the buttons with an aggrieved quickness.

In the sudden withdrawal of attention, Ava felt a chill again. Where exactly had Stephanie picked up so many other friends?

"I'm already killing myself trying to get us some money," Stephanie mumbled as she typed. "You're no help with that. Are you sure you can't just ask your mom again? She did bail you out that one time."

Soon after moving to New York there had been an incident with a rented U-Haul, and what the cop had called "reckless driving" when Ava, Stephanie in the passenger seat, had somehow hit one hundred miles an hour on a deserted FDR Drive. Ava's mother had bailed her out of a holding cell that night and swore that she would never again support Ava's vulgar and immoral lifestyle with that "unspeakable girl."

"She won't do it."

"Fine." The BlackBerry landed in Stephanie's open purse with a thud. "So what are we going to do about these?" She returned to the drawings, picking each up, holding it out and tilting her head as if the view from a different angle might align it more closely with her desires. "Oh, well, I guess we don't have a choice. Come on, get dressed. We've got to go knock some old ladies dead. I probably shouldn't say that, just in case."

Still a little hurt, Ava put on a necklace and slipped a dress over her head. "Fine, but you're overdoing it. You look like Pat Nixon."

"Well, your hem is coming out," Stephanie replied, and Ava didn't have an answer because it was, and she had been meaning to fix it for a while. As they waited in the hallway among the welter of cats, she consoled herself that her pearls were real, unlike Stephanie's, but then felt guilty for the thought and so let Stephanie enter the elevator first.

The meeting was at the top of the club across from Aloysius's office. He met them in the hallway with a whisper. "Important club business being discussed. You girls wait out here. I'll come get you when it's time." Directed to two chairs in the hallway, they waited primly, trying to ignore the yelling coming through the wall. Stephanie squeezed her hand, and Ava was grateful. It felt so familiar, waiting just on the edge of something and wanting to sink through the floor, but held in place by Stephanie's narrow hand. More shouting rumbled through the closed door. They looked anxiously toward Aloysius's secretary, a plump redhead in bifocals who rolled her eyes from the open door of his office.

Finally, Aloysius stuck his head out and waved them in. With one last squeeze, Stephanie led the way into a room filled with frowning old ladies. They took seats at a large shiny table, and after a brief introduction from Aloysius, Stephanie stood up to make their case. With the room's attention directed elsewhere, Ava calmed her nerves enough to see that there were only eight old ladies present plus two old men, one of whom was asleep while the other leaned forward, alert and suspicious, his chin on his cane. Mrs.

Van Doren smiled at her encouragingly and then continued turning the pages of a fashion magazine. The table was littered with sweating glasses of iced tea and cans of generic caffeine-free cola.

As Stephanie started her pitch, which from repetition was getting pretty breezy, about private clubs being all the rage for the young and hip, the animosity in the room quietly began to build. This audience didn't want to be lectured about the novel charm of exclusive clubs; they already saw themselves as the gatekeepers of these very values, tasked with defending their territory against invaders like Stephanie. She paused, and the board members began to pepper her with questions—Who would be employed by their club? How would Castor, the doorman, identify members? Who would be enforcing the dress code? What did they mean by "literary events"?

Stephanie, feeling that they were missing the essential genius behind her plan, was beginning to get testy, so Ava jumped in. "When I found the Lazarus Club, not only was it the most beautiful place I had ever seen, but for the first time in my life, I felt like I truly belonged somewhere. This amazing place felt like home. I want to share that love."

"I recognize you." A lady with a pair of glasses on her nose and another on her head spoke. "You're that little girl that's been hostessing in the dining room."

This was not true, but Ava smiled at her and pressed forward. "I'm just afraid that not enough people my age appreciate the Lazarus Club. I think so many would find it an honor to be in such an important place, architecturally, culturally, historically."

"Membership rolls, Arthur," Aloysius said ominously toward one of the old men, who snorted disdainfully.

"I like young people," another woman chimed in. "My granddaughter always has such amusing hairstyles."

"Exactly. Don't you think she would want to be involved? And since our idea is a literary club, with readings and famous authors, we would really be carrying on the Lazarus tradition of arts and letters while making sure to promote the club."

Stephanie was catching on. "I think the kind of publicity this would bring, the right kind of publicity, of course, could only help expand the next generation of Lazarus Club members. We want everyone to love this club as we, here in this room, already do."

"Why is the waitress going to start a literary club?" asked the first woman in a loud whisper to her neighbor.

"I actually work in the library, which is why this is so perfect." Ava brought out her watercolors. "See all the improvements we plan to make?"

Another old woman seemed to jolt out of sleep. "The lien for improvements was settled ages ago. The city has no grounds for any lawsuits. They want to bankrupt us. A pox on the building inspectors."

A quick shushing went around the table, and Aloysius scowled at her before loudly complimenting Ava's drawings.

A tiny old lady who had been silent thus far picked up one of the pictures. "Oh, this is lovely. Did you girls do this?"

"Yes, ma'am." Ava smiled again with the immolating politeness she had learned at an early age.

The woman passed it to her neighbor. "Margery, look at how nicely she handles the wash in this section of the background."

Margery nodded. "Very nice work indeed. Some of our members run a watercolor group every fifth Tuesday," she explained to Ava, passing it to a third lady who also nodded gravely.

Stephanie and Ava exchanged a quick, confused look,

but the tenor of the room seemed to have changed. A few strained smiles lit up around the table.

"Ava makes quite a good cup of Darjeeling," Mrs. Van Doren said to the woman next to her.

"Well, I'm willing to let them try it on a provisional basis," a fourth woman observed, drumming peach-polished fingernails on a can of cola. "Running the literature committee has been exhausting. We had a reading here three years ago. It was quite successful," she added defensively to no one in particular.

"There's nothing in the budget for this." The old man who was awake sternly introduced himself as a Mr. Dearborn, the club treasurer. The smiles vanished, as the whole room waited for Ava and Stephanie's response with such suspicion. Ava couldn't help but think of the gray-haired citizenesses knitting at the foot of the guillotine.

"Oh no, we would love to take all that work off your hands. This is really a passion for us. We just want to help the club."

"You won't get a penny from us," he repeated warningly.

"We plan to be totally self-sustaining. By cultivating a select group of patrons, and maybe charging a nominal fee for some of our more popular events, our plan is to help support the club, especially by undertaking some of the desperately needed historical preservation in the rooms we're talking about."

"Oh, that cursed landmarks commission," a lady sighed. "In my day, what went on in your own home was your own business. That inspector almost tricked me the other day, saying he was from Zabar's, but I figured it out and slammed the door in his face."

"Good girl." Aloysius patted her bony hand.

Mr. Dearborn folded his hands over his chest, the cuffs of his jacket extending over his knuckles. Ava thought his whole suit looked too big, as if he had been quietly shrinking inside his clothes and hadn't noticed it yet. "They look like a pair of strumpets to me," he said to himself, loudly.

Everyone ignored this comment, and Stephanie clapped her hands. "Fantastic. Provided we will fix the space up and operate independently, I think this will be a beautiful partnership. The Lazarus Club and the House of Mirth."

"I always liked that book." Mrs. Van Doren opened a flap in her magazine and the room filled with the overpowering scent of perfume. "Edie Wharton was such a firecracker in her own way."

There was some murmured agreement and a few burps.

"The subject is put to rest," Aloysius announced. "Conditional on certain repairs being made, these two are allowed use of the rooms adjoining the library. Approval may be rescinded at any moment. Also, could you girls please do something about that bathroom up there? It's just dreadful." And rather abruptly, he shepherded the girls into the hallway.

"Doesn't there need to be a vote or something?" Ava asked timidly.

"You have a call, Mr. Wilder," his receptionist called from the office. "The Department of Labor." She paused ominously. "Again."

"Later," he yelled. "You two have my full support," he said, pushing them each by a shoulder. "I've always liked the look of subway tiles in a bathroom." Then he disappeared behind the boardroom door, and they could hear the muffled skirmish start up again.

"I need a drink," Stephanie said as they walked slowly down the dark hallway.

"What just happened? I'm so confused."

"It's good enough for now." Stephanie shrugged. "They didn't say no. At least those old crones can recognize an opportunity when it falls into their laps."

When they arrived downstairs at the library, still arguing about whether or not they would actually be able to do the needed renovations in the space, they were surprised to find ten or so confused college-age students milling around the rubble. "Oh crap, I totally forgot, I told Castor about this." Stephanie hung her purse on a broken coatrack and ran her hands over her high bouffant. "I put an ad on Craigslist for an employee. I figured we're going to need another set of hands when this thing takes off."

"I thought this was just going to be us," Ava whispered. "We can't have an employee. We don't have any money."

Stephanie laughed. "Oh my god, you don't have to pay college kids. You just say it's an internship. We're going to be a cultural institution—such valuable experience for a young person. You've got to think big if you want to be big, Ava."

"That doesn't sound very fair."

Stephanie rolled her eyes and turned to address the students. "Good afternoon. Thank you all for coming. We will be interviewing you one at a time in the next room." She pointed at a candidate sitting on the edge of the egg crate mattress. "You first."

Ava's doubts about the necessity or ethics of the situation were soon absorbed in the novel sensation of being a boss. Each applicant, slightly sweaty in his or her button-down shirt, bore the unease of wearing clothes more formal than they were used to. Fidgeting, blinking like calves, they tried to explain with convincing enthusiasm why they wanted a career in literary event planning or hospitality. Ava had long known, without really believing, that no one in life was as confident and put together as they appeared, but she rarely got to see it this clearly from the other side. These kids squirming beneath her gaze would never know the extent of her shyness, and so for as long as they sat before her, it ceased to exist. It was liberating. Her empathy for their discomfort meant that she could have been friendlier, tried to mitigate the intimidating force of Stephanie's beauty and condescension, but it felt glorious to be among the victors, and she didn't. "You realize this will be a very exclusive club," Stephanie was telling a young woman in a misbuttoned cardigan. "I don't know if you're accustomed to dealing with celebrities."

"Not really," the girl sighed with the resignation of the already forsaken.

After two hours, they had a stack of résumés and were finally leaving for their long-desired drink when a young man burst into the room. "Is this where the donnybrook happens?" he asked, running a hand through his hair and looking around from under the raised tangle he had created. "That doorman downstairs—quite the gauntlet. I just barely squeaked past."

"Are you here for the interviews? You're late," Stephanie said coldly.

Taking a crumpled handkerchief from his pocket, he dabbed at the sweat running down his hairline. "Unforeseen circumstances of absolutely unavoidable import," he said, transferring the handkerchief to his left hand and extending his right. "George Harazi: scholar, poet, scrivener, bon vivant, jolie laide, intern extraordinaire. Bit of a history buff too, I've been dying to get a look inside this place." The cuffs of his shirt flapped around his forearms, and his striped tie had what looked like ketchup on it. He hurriedly put on the blazer he had been carrying under his arm. "It's rumored one of Ziegfeld's mistresses died on the premises, but I can't imagine they would have let a member of the tribe roam freely through these halls like that. Do they let Jews in here now?" He looked around nervously.

"You're Jewish?" Ava asked and then felt maybe it was indiscreet.

"Don't let my dark good looks fool you, it's the Yemenite heritage, although I won't lie, it's been a doubtful advantage these last few years. However, I'm sure the TSA guys are just doing their job. And the subway cops. And the crossing guards. And the guys that hang around outside the bodega on my corner." He sighed. "But anyway, I digress..."

"I'm sorry, I didn't mean," Ava started to apologize.

He waved her off. His sleeves were a few inches too short. As he smoothed his hair down into a part and shoved his handkerchief into the breast pocket of his coat, a debonair charm fell over him like a rumpled sheet. He rocked back and forth on the heels of his sneakers and looked around. "This place is fantastic. Astounding. Alistair Cooke, black magic after tea and crumpets sort of place. Crazy baronets in the familial keep. You've got to admire the unhinged ebullience of these upper classes." He smiled at them and bowed. "Ladies, my references." He handed over a piece of paper, carefully folded, from his back pocket.

Stephanie was still trying to look stern and commanding, but Ava was pretty amused. A junior at Hunter College, enrolled in honors classes, literary magazine, school paper, student government, he was probably more qualified to run this business than either Ava or Stephanie. They added the résumé to their pile, nodding to each other. There was a certain indefinable inevitability about George Harazi that bore acknowledging.

"Come on. We were on our way to get a drink. You can tell us more about yourself and why you want to work at the House of Mirth," Stephanie said.

He stood aside politely to let them go first. "That name," he said approvingly. "It's a bold choice, if I may say. You ladies aren't pulling any punches."

"Thanks," Ava said with a sigh as she pulled the door shut behind them.

★ ★ ★

At a nearby bar, George nursed a can of Schlitz and re-galed them with an exegesis of the Beach Boys' late oeuvre, the Aristotelian ethos of late-night television, and how an elbow injury ended his love affair with the accordion. By the time he started in on Tolstoy's sexual perversions, they hired him. Since they weren't going to be paying a salary, instead Stephanie offered her undivided attention. Lean-ing forward, chin in hand, she laughed appreciatively, her big blue eyes wide with interest and admiration. George, flushed and blooming under the indulgence of a beautiful, older woman, talked as if he might never get the chance again. He kept looking around the bar with dramatic in-tent, as if hoping for an unruly patron to subdue, a wind-mill to storm, an opportunity to prove his fealty. Eventually they also learned that he grew up in Queens, that his par-ents were dental technicians, and that to drive them crazy he dressed like Oscar Wilde all through high school. He got beat up a lot. His classmates at Hunter didn't care for him much, so he spent most of his free time in the main branch of the New York Public Library, reading yellowing Hearst newspapers and pretending to be John Jacob Astor. He was visibly, vocally glad to have found what he called "a pair of kindred spirits."

After three gin and tonics, Ava started to tune out the rambling monologue and watched him with pride. They had an employee. They had incorporation papers. They had a venue. Was it possible this unlikely thing was really going to happen? She felt transported, like those shots she had seen in movies where the background zooms in from out of focus, suggesting the passage of enormous distance without the main character moving at all, and she now occupied an entirely different sphere of life than she did just a few short weeks ago. It was dizzying and exhilarating, and she giggled into her drink.

"What?" Stephanie was sucking on the slice of lemon from her glass.

A worry about money rose in her, a tiny bubble which quickly burst amid her general effervescence. "Nothing." Ava finished her drink and licked at a drop of condensation that spilled from the lip of her glass and down her hand.

6

Stephanie set a date in the first week of September for their grand opening, an act of aspirational folly that Ava argued against in vain. As each day passed, the disorder of the rooms began to give her a stomachache, and she had to keep the doors closed and pretend it wasn't all she could think about. Aloysius, who popped in every so often to see how the renovations were progressing, was not happy that they had not even begun and muttered as much under his breath. Ava tried to work on her book, but each time she was distracted by thoughts of Stephanie, and now that this sparkling life had been dangled before her, it felt that she would never be able to be happy here again, alone, fruitlessly trying to make Agustin and Anastasia fall in love. Instead she sat sketching out various possible book groups and lecture topics, and writing out her introductions to them.

In order to ensure that their event would be well attended by "everyone who's everyone," Stephanie had doubled down on her promoting. Ava barely saw her, and so was secretly rather relieved one muggy Thursday night when she insisted that Ava accompany her to a party given by a famous literary magazine. They expected it to be filled with just the sort of people that needed to know about an exciting new literary salon and library. When he overheard them discussing it, George had asked to join them with an eagerness whose underlying desperation Ava thought she recognized, and they agreed. She knew what that felt like. She liked George, his oddness, his enthusiasm, his strangely affected accent—notes of Walter Winchell, Jimmy Stewart, William F. Buckley and just a hint of Bugs Bunny. His frame of reference and bemused delight with the Lazarus Club aligned him with Ava, while an obvious, unrequited and unspoken crush on Stephanie kept him sympathetic even to her most callous impulses. So he slid between them, oil on their occasionally choppy waters, a perfect, if sometimes extraneous, employee.

Stephanie led their way, head high, chin lifted, already projecting the invulnerability she wore to these kinds of events like an expensive accessory, while Ava tried to keep up and George ambled contentedly a step or two behind. Prince Street loomed, dark and silent around them except for a booming that reverberated every time Stephanie stomped across a set of iron basement doors sunk into the sidewalk.

Their reflections skimmed across the lit windows of a closed store. "This neighborhood creeps me out." Ava looked up at a window display. "Who decided that mannequins shouldn't have heads anymore—seems like kind of an essential organ even for a well-dressed lady."

Stephanie, losing the thread of an imaginary conversation she had been preparing, shrank from queenly impresario to annoyed teenager. "Ava, some of us are trying to concentrate."

"How do you do that?" Ava asked.

"What?" Stephanie rifled through the bag on her shoulder for a business card, then used it to remove something from her gums.

"That thing you do." Ava tried to imitate her friend's imperious bearing.

Stephanie threw the card on the pavement. "You've got to sell it. Confidence is everything."

"Joan of Arc had confidence."

"And she was pretty fucking awesome." This seemed like an elemental difference of perspective, so Ava kept silent. It was a little exciting to be going somewhere on a summer night when the air hung on them, close with possibility, and the breath of a subway grate exhaled the proximity of a million other people's evenings and hopes for the evening. Ava couldn't remember the last time she had gone to a party. And every time she started to shrink at the prospect, she remembered the salon, and it buoyed her. This time she had something cool to talk about.

Other groups of twos and threes coalesced, lightly shining with sweat in the summer twilight. "Are we all going to the same place?" Ava asked.

"The bigger the crowd, the better we can promote."

"Speaking of promotions." George handed them each a stack of papers from his bag. "I worked out a flyer like you asked."

"They look beautiful." Ava stroked the cover. "The font is perfect. It looks like Abigail Adams scribbled a condolence card."

"It's called 'Von Stackelberg Fancy,'" George informed her. "I thought you might like it."

Stephanie shoved the cards back toward his bag. "We can't bring those. We aren't promoting a comedy club on a street corner. It looks totally wrong."

"You specifically asked me to make them for tonight." George sadly closed his cotton satchel.

"I'm sure I probably didn't. How are my teeth?" Stephanie flashed her gleaming mouth at Ava. "I'm going for the editor-in-chief. His book on the atom bomb was awesome."

George was looking at his feet, and Ava gave him a pat on the arm, aware that consolation from her was only second best. "Why don't we skip this party and put on pajamas, and you can explain to me how hadron colliders work?" she asked Stephanie. "You used to do that kind of stuff. Sometimes."

"We can nerd out after we're famous. Right now we've got work to do." Stephanie pushed Ava through a set of heavy doors and into a small elevator. Girls in winged eyeliner and glasses carried tote bags, some of which prominently displayed the logo of the magazine, and pressed up against them.

George looked around delightedly. "This is what I've been looking for my whole life. I bet every girl on this elevator reads *The Times Literary Supplement*. Ladies," he said, smoothing down his hair, as one smiled back, encouragingly.

"I bet they don't." Ava looked around, comparing herself to all the pretty girls in cardigans, their thin arms and cold eyes, and this feeling of being surrounded by potential versions of herself—young women who liked books and maybe even wanted to be writers, and the impression, even more acute from being pressed up in a small elevator, that there wasn't enough room for them all, and that the subtle gradations of who would succeed must be sniffed out.

The customary silence of unacquainted New Yorkers felt particularly hostile. Women so often evoked this feeling in Ava, a yearning to be liked and approved of and the certainty that she would mess it up somehow. Women just seemed to be the only things that mattered, and each seemed to offer the possibility that if they would just accept her, grant her entrance to the unique sphere of their life and confidence, that the aching loneliness always looming around her would vanish forever. In some ways she felt she would always be eight years old, watching the laughter and the intimate whispers of her classmates, arms wrapped around each other, skinned knees swinging entangled, trying desperately to draw closer. But like keen-scented little foxes they always seemed to sniff out some essential difference and shut their ranks against her just as these young women probably would, if given the opportunity.

Ava wanted to run back to her apartment and renounce this complicated tangle of longing and fear, forever associated with the tight braids and blue polyester jumpers of school uniforms, but the elevator stopped with a jolt. A current of heat spun between the opening doors, and Ava pressed back and found Stephanie's shoulder. Then she remembered her friend, her beautiful, confident partner, and found refuge in the pressure of this resolute elbow. "I can't go in there," she said. More bodies spilled from an open metal door. A young woman blocked their path, commiserating over someone's success with an equally sweaty young man.

"Just go." Stephanie shoved Ava forward and slid under the outstretched arm of a man who was holding a full plastic cup in each hand and another in his mouth. "Thanks."

Ava had no choice but to follow, bumping up against warm damp bodies. "So sorry, excuse me." The more she apologized, the more annoyed people seemed, so she gave up, abandoning herself to the whorls and eddies of the crowd. When she finally landed inside the room, she looked around for help, but even George had melted away, and she was alone.

For a while, just staying out of people's way kept her busy with an advance and retreat of politely apologetic murmuring, but that brought her to another corner where, free of jostling elbows, she had nothing to do but stand. She noticed a doe-eyed girl a couple steps away who seemed to be all alone, just staring into a cup of wine. Ava spent a few min-

utes admiring the slope of her back, a narrow branch bending beneath the weight of its own boredom, and the way
the tilt of the wrist holding her cup managed to express such
contempt for this party. At last the misery of standing unac-
companied overpowering her fear of bridging the existential
gap between human beings, Ava resolved to say hello. But
just as she started to move closer, the sylph hooked an arm
around the elbow patch of the man next to her, and they
glided to another corner of the room.

Feeling inappropriately rejected, Ava directed herself to
the bar. After securing a cup of warm, sour white wine, the
obscure dynamics of the crowded bar area deposited her behind the white cloth-covered table where she found herself
facing a row of handsome boys. She smiled. They ignored
her and drank. Hedged in by the bar, stuck at the approxi-
mate distance of people having a conversation, the continued
avoidance of one was becoming excruciatingly uncomfortable. "Hi," she said finally.

Three dispassionate sets of eyes scrutinized her. She sipped
her wine. At last, a blond with a sharp Truman Capote part
sighed. "Do you work at Schuster?"

"No." Ava spoke from behind the clear plastic lip of her
cup.

"Oh, sorry. I thought you were someone else. Publishing?"

It took her a minute too long to realize he was still asking about her job. "No."

"Then you must be a writer."

From the way he said this, Ava felt a great pity for all the
poor girls who might actually answer yes to this question.
"Oh no."

"Then why are you at this party?"

She marveled that he could be so assured, inhabiting this
space with such a casual presumption of ownership while
she was called to defend her existence. "I'm starting a lit-

erary club, a place for writers, where people can go to talk about books." An undeniable feeling welled up as she said this—pride, excitement, she wasn't quite sure but something made her sip her wine with a slightly higher tilt of her head, a feeling that in the joust of conversation, for once, finally, she was armed.

"Why would I have to go someplace special for that?"

"So you could meet other people who like to talk about books." This seemed so obvious, Ava couldn't help the note of condescension that crept in to her voice.

"I already know lots of people like that. Watch." He turned to the man next to him, a pencil moustache tremulously bisecting a juvenile face. "Dan Blachovsky's latest?"

"Genius."

"Elizabeth What's-Her-Name."

"Domestic, middlebrow."

"Joshua Goldfarb."

"Hilarious." They looked expectantly at Ava.

"Um, I don't know those authors."

"Sounds like a great club."

They were right, of course. She wasn't doing a very good job, and tried a different sally. "It's going to be like the salon in Proust."

They all rolled their eyes at her, maybe one of them groaned, "Oh, please."

This wasn't her intention. What was she doing wrong? Ava tried again. "Or other classics, I guess, you know, get people together to discuss great works of literature."

"Sounds pretty dull, don't you think, Josh? I'd rather talk about bad books like yours."

Pencil Moustache shrugged. "No, no, I'm not great literature, after all. I'm sure her club will be awesome and not at all pretentious." He stopped and looked closer at her and then a light of recognition flashing in his eyes, his smile warmed just a hair. "Wait a second, I know you. Didn't you used to work at the *New Yorker*? I used to see you in the elevator with a weird umbrella."

It had been a parasol. "No, that must have been somebody else."

"I'm pretty sure it was you. I kept trying to ask you about it, but you were always staring at the floor."

Mentally erasing the moustache, she recognized him too, an editorial assistant, vegan, who asserted his prestige over mere fact checkers by "accidentally" removing her turkey sandwiches from the break room refrigerator. "Yeah, that was me."

He chuckled. "This all makes a lot of sense now. I always wondered what your deal was. Do you want another wine? I'm going to get one."

As he spoke, a faint glimmer of remembrance stirred— had he invited her to a party once? He had. She had been so flustered by the invitation, she had agreed to go and then, overcome with shyness, hadn't shown up. How mortifying. Did he remember? He must, and he must be thinking how despicably rude she was. "No, thank you." Now terribly embarrassed, she had to get away and sort of waved awkwardly. "It was nice to see you again." And ran for the protection of the long and winding bathroom line before he could respond.

Recovering, Ava wandered around some more. She didn't want to risk going back to the bar, and so found herself next to a table on which copies of the magazine were displayed. She picked one up and began flipping through it. On the other side of the table, two dark-skinned men in bright bow ties were doing the same. One had a small repetitive cough that Ava decided was an indicator of social unease, and she wanted to introduce herself in solidarity, but just as she had resolved to do it, they were joined by a larger group with much laughter and backslapping, and Ava had to assume she had been mistaken. Everyone had friends here except her. Now alone at the issue display, she felt even more conspicuous, and put her copy down and left. For a while, she followed random blond heads through the crowd, hoping that each might be Stephanie, but none of them were, and she was a little surprised that there could be so many unusually tall blondes circulating through this party. A bank of windows offered a temporary respite. She perched on the ledge, scanning the crowd every few minutes as though she were waiting for someone, but the ledge was at capacity, and the couple next to her were fighting loudly about Oxford commas. As they descended into personal slurs, Ava decided to pee again.

As she got in the bathroom line once more, Stephanie popped up at her elbow. "Hey, how's it going? After you go, come with me, I want you to meet some people."

"I'm ready now. I've been in this line three times already. Don't ask."

"Have you talked to anyone?"

"I met a few young novelists."

"See, I said you could do it." Ava accepted the congratulations with some shame. "I've found the really important editors, come on." There was a glow in Stephanie's eyes.

At the rear of the room, a group of men a decade or two older than the rest of the guests clustered together. It was less crowded here, airier. Success encircled and isolated them from the rest of the party like a cool breeze, an invisible moat across which sweaty aspirants cast longing glances. Stephanie sailed into the breach, pulling Ava along, and introduced herself to a man just going gray, in a wilted blazer. An annoyed ripple at Stephanie's audacity started behind them and made the back of Ava's neck feel even hotter.

Stephanie, with a disregard for preliminaries that Ava was starting to understand was widely accepted, started in brag-

ging about their club. Accustomed to letting Stephanie take
the lead in these situations, Ava looked down at the floor,
admiring the distinguished editor's shoes. Burnished leather
oozed over the soles as if any original stiffness had long been
worn away, Ava presumed, along the halls of Harvard. They
were the kind of shoes that could stand behind a lectern or
rest, crossed, on the guardrails of a jetty as the sun set over
Nantucket with the same composure that was now pointed
at Stephanie.

"And we will have only the best authors involved. Your
magazine is just the sort of partnership we need. Literature doesn't just live on the page. It needs to be nurtured
by art and conversation," she was saying. "We can provide
a space for that." Ava looked at Stephanie's toes, squished
into pointed white heels, and felt sad. She wanted her friend
to be able to stand equally at ease, bones splayed with entitled comfort. Maybe in their own establishment, she and
Stephanie could preside, just taking up space without all the
jostling and measuring and second-guessing that seemed to
be their lot as young women. For all her disdain for entre-
preneurship, some small slice of the value of ownership revealed itself to Ava. If, by force of will, they were able to
bend some small part of the Lazarus Club into something
that made enough space for them—maybe if you owned the
club, you wore comfortable shoes. This project wasn't just for
her. Stephanie had been squeezing into high heels to wrest
from the world what it owed her since she was thirteen years
old. She deserved this.

As she talked, a flush had crept over Stephanie's face and
down her low-cut blouse, a wash of dewy excitement at her
own eloquence. Ambition made her even more lovely, and
Ava wanted her to succeed, to reach a place where she would
no longer have to be out here prying status from the fleshy
grip of men like this, trading her beauty as currency. "Every

great literary moment had its salon. Intellectual life is inseparable from social exchange," Ava jumped in, wanting to help, to express a support Stephanie probably wouldn't even notice. She was getting so used to saying things like this that she was forgetting how much she disliked social exchange in reality. "For a movement to emerge from this disconnected modern world—"

"The internet age," Stephanie interrupted.

"—people need a physical space, like all the great libraries of history." She raised her eyes from the knotted tie she had been talking to. The eminent editor was still watching Stephanie hungrily.

The recipient of the prurient gaze was careful not to notice. "My partner, Ava Gallanter, has quite the historical perspective," she said proudly, patting Ava's back.

Ava held Stephanie's wrist to forestall any additional jiggling under this politely rapacious gaze. "Maybe we should go," she said.

A hand caressed Stephanie's free arm. "You should stay. I could introduce you to a few authors who might be very interested in your project."

The eager, flattered expression on Stephanie's face made Ava all the more desperate to rescue her. "We have to finish organizing the books."

"Just a few more minutes." She slid from Ava's grasp, led by a meaty hand.

As the bar in this part of the room was much less crowded, Ava was able to get a cold glass of white wine, handed to her by what she guessed from the earnestness of his smile was an intern. A man standing near the bar expressed his interest in her by engaging in conversation in a strenuously uninterested tone, and she answered his questions as best she could while keeping an eye on Stephanie across the room. In a thin silk blouse and linen slacks creased despite the heat, her body language was calculatingly seductive. One hand pushed a hip forward in provocative *contrapposto*, the other hand was engaged in a delicate choreography: touching her collarbones, coming to rest on a gentleman's arm during a confidential pause in the conversation, or pressing finger-tips lightly against her lower lips, an unsuccessful attempt to cover up a laugh, that made a shared joke infinitely more intimate. Held in the rapt attention of four or five older men, she looked small to Ava's eyes, a sparrow encircled by pigeons, who, if a little too paunchy to appear a threat to Stephanie's quicksilver being, still conveyed a suppressed hostility in their excessive fawning. Each jockeyed for the prize position at her side where her elbow was grasped by successive, avuncular hands. Finally after a flurry of busi-ness cards, Stephanie found her way back to Ava slightly sweaty and giggling. "They love our project." She took a sip from Ava's wine. "People are so responsive to a concept with substance."

"Can we get out of here, please?"

Stephanie nodded. "I've got what I came for."

Those that had been watching Stephanie's progress looked even less friendly as the two women pushed their way out of the circle of prestige. "Should we find George?" Ava asked.

"The last time I saw him he was chatting up two bru-nettes. He'll be fine." They fell out into the hall, and Steph-anie pushed the button for the elevator. "I'm just so excited that those famous writers and editors were so into our idea. The dream is happening." Sweat had caused Stephanie's mas-cara to run a little at the corner of her eyes, a faint smear that edged away from the broad curl of her lashes. Ava found she was overheated and longing to get out of her sweaty under-wear. She thought of cool water; she and Stephanie swim-ming somewhere in dark, cold waters, naiads—callous and free, far from the corrupting gaze of men. The thought embarrassed her. The elevator was too stuffy, and she wiped the dampness from her cheeks, checking for the smudges of her own mascara.

Outside, a hot wind was swirling down the empty street; a wooden sign banged against its metal pole, the heavy imminence of a summer storm approaching. Party sounds drifted from open windows. A strip of low-hanging clouds, visible between the rows of high-reaching cornices, sped across the night sky. "We're living the dream, Ava. We're going to do it. You're going to have a salon. I'm going to be a star."

Stephanie's elation made Ava suddenly very lonely. "But that wasn't very fun," she said sadly. "Those people made me feel like I'm wearing the wrong shoes and reading the wrong books, and that the two are equivalent. Although I don't know, maybe they are. Are they? Maybe this is a bad idea."

Stephanie frowned at her. "Do you know I dated one of those guys up there? He's an editor now, but then he was just some stupid DJ. He dumped me with a text message. Couldn't even be bothered to call me on the phone after almost six months. 'Not feeling it,' it said, 'We cool?'"

Ava stepped over a pile of newspapers that blew up against their ankles in the hot breeze. "That's awful. Why do you date guys like that?"

Stephanie brushed aside the comforting hand Ava put on her arm with some irritation. "But, you know what? Three months from now, he's going to be begging to be a part of my club. They're all going to read articles about me in the *New York* Fucking *Times*, and every last one of them who thought I was just some dumb blonde is going to show up spitting apologies."

"Why do you care about them?" Ava asked, reaching for her hand, and fumbling, finding her strangely difficult to grab on to. "They don't even know you."

"They're going to. Everyone's going to know me. And

everyone's going to know that the whole time I was smiling next to some stinking prizewinning sow, I was a million times smarter than everybody judging me." She paused for just a moment, lost in enraged retrospection. Ava almost asked if she meant the pigs and decided not to. "I know I can do it. I can make this whole thing work. I can get the publicity, I can get the members, if we could just get the stupid renovations money, I could blow this town wide-open." Stephanie slammed her fist against the iron grill of a closed store, and Ava was startled by the bang.

Ava was thinking that through her force of will, Stephanie probably could eventually wrest whatever exactly it was that she wanted from New York, but then hearing a quiet sniffling, she had the terrifying thought that maybe Stephanie was crying. Ava hadn't seen Stephanie cry since that first night when she had read *Eugene Onegin* until she was hoarse to stem the tears of a woman who wasn't even her friend yet. But now she was purposefully not looking at Ava in a way that made Ava again desperate to comfort her.

"We'll find it somewhere. There must be someplace else to borrow money. What about credit cards? I've never had one. I'm sure we're not established enough to get one. How does that work?"

The sniffling stopped, and Stephanie turned to her in disbelief. "Are you serious? You've never had a credit card?"

"I told you, I read *Little Dorrit* and it's all about being in jail for debt and it freaked me out."

"You've had a job since college, you totally have credit."

Nervous now, Ava picked at her fingernail. "It's just that's how so many novels go wrong. Someone gets into debt and then it's just one straight downward slide until you're dying of consumption."

"Jesus Christ, Ava." Stephanie looked mad, then laughed, and shook her head. "It just never occurred to me anyone could actually have credit. I don't even have a bank account because those student loan assholes keep me totally cleaned out."

"Well, I don't know if I would want—" Ava began but she stopped because Stephanie had wrapped her into a hug that lifted her off her feet.

"You're totally nuts. I don't know how you've survived in this world as long as you have, but I love you so much. I can't even believe you let me worry this long. You're too much, Ava. There's a million people I need to talk to now that this is settled." She set Ava down and reached for her BlackBerry and began typing. "I've got to go make some calls."

"I'm just not sure I want to do that," Ava said, but Stephanie wasn't listening. "The idea really scares me."

"I'll see you at the library tomorrow." An air-kiss was tossed in her general direction.

Ava wanted to ask her to stay, to keep her company in the midst of the terrible sinking dread, knowing Stephanie would be able to dispel it just with her presence, but she was already walking away. It felt silly to ask. "Um, okay, bye." Her voice was lost in the empty street, and she watched Stephanie until she was just a narrow strip of white fading into the darkness.

7

A dollop of mortar landed behind the toilet with a splat, and Ava, on her hands and knees, smeared it around with a wooden spoon. She was starting to get the hang of it and soon could justifiably add "tiling" to the list of unexpected skills recently acquired. She had applied for a credit card, and one had arrived with an alacrity that made Ava just a little nervous. It came with pages and pages of fine print, which she intended to read at some point, but Stephanie's joy was contagious. They had had so much fun that night sharing a bottle of five-dollar sparkling wine, giggling and building castles in the air until they both passed out on the library chesterfield, waking up with hangovers and the indentations of tufted buttons in their soft flesh.

To chase away the panic of sliding gently into the river of debt, Ava threw herself into their renovations, which proved distracting and surprisingly fun. Small hexagonal black-and-white tiles crept across the bathroom floor, filth was scrubbed away, vinyl flooring ripped up and disposed of. She marveled at her new proficiency. Her facility with reading and writing predisposed her to undervalue the life of the mind—surely anything she was that good at must not be very hard—and now that she did things with hammers and wrenches, she was convinced; true achievement lay in the daily application of manual work. Also she loved wearing the painter's coveralls she had bought that made her feel like a soviet agitator. Her associations for this kind of thing were mostly Russian novelists, and while she wasn't quite tilling the soil, she still felt vaguely noble and enlightened by it all. She knew renovating part of an exclusive club in order to create another exclusive club was not quite the greater social good, but whenever she started to feel like Marie Antoinette milking the cows, she rolled up her sleeves and worked harder, losing her reservations in sweat and effort.

She reached for another section of tile, but the mesh square that held the small tiles in their prearranged pattern didn't fit the narrow space behind the sink's pedestal. She sat back on her heels. "Use the wire clippers," suggested George from the empty claw-foot tub where he was smoking and studying for an English exam.

Ava pushed her hair back; cement dust left gray streaks in her bangs. "Thanks." She knelt and began slicing little hexagons free.

There had been some questions about the legality of doing all this work themselves, about the landmarks commission, and licensed contractors and things. When they asked Aloysius, he said of course all the work had to be aboveboard and not to worry too much and then winked and said he just loved flocked wallpaper. Mr. Dearborn told them that the rules were different for interiors and suggested they refinish the floors while they were at it. So they pressed ahead in good faith, but committed the most drastic improvements at night. As they snuck out the rubble in used paint cans and wastepaper baskets, Castor, the doorman, just shook his head and pretended not to notice each time they tottered past to dump their detritus in their neighbors' elegant wrought iron trash cans.

"Why did I sign up for midcentury American novels?" George flipped through his notes. "All this male malaise is starting to wear."

Ava started mixing a new batch of mortar. "I can't help you, too recent for me."

"And yet you plan to cater to and support the contemporary literati of New York?"

"No, I'm hosting a nineteenth-century salon."

"I think the madam may have a slightly different plan." He threw the cigarette he should not have been smoking into the toilet and lit another before handing her more tiles. "Though I have nothing but respect for her authority. Where is her ladyship anyway?"

"How come I never get any honorifics, George? I'm your boss here, too."

"There is honor in comradely affection," he replied. "Also you are much less scary than she is."

"Stephanie is out finding members and investors." Ava placed the hexagon gently on the floor, enjoying the mortar squishing through the tiles. "So many rich men in cool T-shirts and expensive sneakers. Somehow not what I expected for our salon."

"You prefer industrialists?" George's teeth clenched around an imaginary cigar.

"I wish. I'd love to see this place full of top hats and monocles."

"So your ideal investor would be a Scrooge McDuck." He nodded sagely. "Although I agree, I would never trust a financier in plimsolls." He knocked his sneakers one against the other.

Ava laughed. "I hate to ask, George, but do you have any

friends at school? What do the other kids at Hunter make of you?"

"I've always blazed my own trail. And anyway, I once sat next to a girl in the cafeteria." George returned to his notebook, whistling. Ava began to twitter along tunelessly as she laid another row of tiles. She didn't realize he was leading her in "The International" until a third whistle joined them enthusiastically from the hall before fading down the stairs toward the bar. Rodney had become even friendlier now that she was often coated in plaster dust.

They were aspirating a rousing and out-of-tune finale when Ava stopped. "I believe that will be her now." Stephanie had paid no attention to Ava's suggestion that a lady should learn to glide silently across a floor.

"How are my darlings?" Stephanie, in heels, stomped into the room.

"Wet mortar." Ava pointed at the ground. "Be careful. How did it go?"

She picked her way along one wall and climbed into the empty tub with George, plucked his cigarette from his mouth and began smoking it. "Amazing. Everyone loves our idea. The owner of Squeeze said he would be a member."

"I don't know what that is."

Stephanie sighed. "It's the most exclusive nightclub in New York City. You really need to read my emails. Hand me my bag." She rummaged around in the torn lining for a second. "Voilà."

Ava reached for the check. "Five thousand dollars?"

"I decided that was how much our top-tier patron level membership should cost."

"What's the matter with people? This club doesn't even exist yet. Are they just trying to throw their money away?"

"This club is happening and it's going to be amazing and no one wants to risk missing out." Stephanie waved her off.

"I said we would mail a membership card. George can rig something up."

George gave her a thumbs-up and tried unsuccessfully to take his cigarette back.

Ava pressed back against the wall, closing her eyes against the implications of this check. The illusion, already tenuous, that they were acting with the innocent enthusiasm of the Little Rascals opening a lemonade stand was crumbling before the cold reality of fiduciary obligations. Would this possibly count as fraud? If they didn't manage to pull off this ridiculous project, could they be sent to jail?

But how could they stop now, and what would become of her if they did? Against this shuddering possibility, Ava retreated into uncertainty. The risks felt enormous, but she thought of all these new skills she was gaining, this new sense of her own power and capability. Surely when she had time to get back to her book, once this salon was really going, she would have shed some of that everlasting timidity that plagued her. She was becoming a girl that did things, and if she could tile a floor, how hard could it be to write a novel? In a way she was securing the very future she was worrying about. And anyway, weren't these the sorts of things great novels were about when it really came down to it, the pursuit of love or money? Maybe she was done writing endless pages of people sitting sadly in ornate, velvet-upholstered chairs, beautiful though they were. She took a deep breath and passed over a book of paint swatches. "For the wall behind the bar."

Stephanie began turning the pages of colors with great studiousness.

George glanced over. "Those are all white."

Stephanie didn't answer, folding the page she was looking at to better compare two almost identical shades. Ava found this solicitousness endearing. It wasn't exactly perfectionism, this attention Stephanie paid to details, because it didn't quite feel like there was some larger moral framework behind it, but more just a great capacity for taking things seriously. It was something they shared, and for Ava, often equally picky, but embarrassed about it, Stephanie's willingness to take pains was oddly pleasurable.

Finally she tossed the thin booklet toward the lid of the toilet. "I think soft dove."

Ava caught it as it slid toward the wet floor. "Yeah, I thought so, too. I'm exhausted. What time is it?"

Stephanie, examining her hair for split ends, looked up. "We can't go to bed. We aren't finished."

George stood and brushed tile dust off of his jacket. "I have a test tomorrow. I have to head back home."

"Fine." Stephanie waved. "You can go. But Ava—" not getting enough authority sitting in a bathtub, she stood, hands on her hips "—I need to see some commitment from you. If you aren't willing to do the work, then I don't know how we're going to make this happen."

She spoke in the easy, casual knowledge that Ava wouldn't defend herself, but there was something about her rough coveralls, the cement splotches, the hard labor successfully accomplished that gave Ava courage, and she dropped her trowel into a bucket with a clank. "I've been here working all day. I'd say I've been very committed. It's you who's always out at parties."

"Let's not forget who's really making this thing happen," Stephanie said coldly.

Ava frowned silently at the paint swatches. Stephanie twirled up her hair and secured it with a pencil. "Come on, love, let's do some painting. We open in three weeks." When he saw Ava's shocked expression, George murmured his goodbyes and fled the approaching storm.

"What are you talking about? This place is a mess. It will never be ready in three weeks." Ava didn't mean to yell.

"Buzz, darling. I can't keep the excitement up forever. People will get bored and move on. We have to open, ready or not." Stephanie pulled her dress over her head, walking away naked in high heels. "Oh, by the way, we're going to be a nonprofit. It went over so much better."

"You can't just say that."

Stephanie turned, raising her head imperiously, her nakedness a silent roar of animal dominance. Ava didn't know where to look and blushed, feeling awkward and chubby and embarrassed. She plucked at the handle of the trowel.

Satisfied, Stephanie went into the next room. "I'm not just saying it. We should be nonprofit. And while we apply for status, we can tell everybody our paperwork is pending," she called.

"I think that's illegal," Ava sighed.

"It's not, because we are going to file. I already looked it up on the internet. We're creating a social good. We can add some literacy programs or something, too. We will do it tomorrow. Will you stop worrying?" Reappearing barefoot in an old Van Halen T-shirt, Stephanie had shrunk back to less intimidating parameters, but the residual effects lingered and Ava didn't meet her eyes. "There's a room that needs to be painted." Plastic sheeting billowed around her. "By the way," she said casually, "Steve Buckley came through with some money too, which is great because I really need to start drawing a salary for all this."

"Really? How much? I thought he was just giving us books. Do we really want to take money from people like that? He seemed so sketchy."

"I knew you would get all worked up. We're really not in any position to turn down investments. Don't worry. It's only another five thousand."

Against the rush of fear these numbers aroused, Ava rested her face in her hands. Her fingers were cool against her hot cheeks. She wanted to make Stephanie understand the implicit peril of their situation, but the feeling of traveling in a foreign country and not knowing the language and customs made her doubt her instincts and hesitate. She wanted to leave, but she thought of the silent darkness of her room, just a cat, an old review of books, a cup of Sleepytime tea, and the renunciation felt too great.

She took the paint can that Stephanie held out to her and crossed to a blank, dirty wall. Her roller swung in wide reassuring arcs. Her worries slowly seeped away as they worked through the night, singing Broadway show tunes to stay awake. The smudged traces of past lives disappeared beneath the growing field of white. When they finished, Stephanie hooked her arm through Ava's as they admired the pristine expanse. "This is really going to happen," she whispered, her breath hot against Ava's ear.

Ava found she couldn't speak, but she nodded, and her heart burst into a thousand tiny shards of crystalline possibility.

True to his word, and somewhat to their surprise, Steve Buckley also sent over the books he had promised, and the boxes crowded the room. Ava, excited by the prospect of so many new books, had scoured the empty bookshelves, climbing and clinging precariously to each ledge to clean and polish their many rows until they shone, ready to receive their burden. Unpacking and sorting through the shipment, she worked her way through yet another box of seventies romance novels and celebrity memoirs, and a certain equanimity took hold; these were not the books she had been hoping for, but it was still nice to sit on the floor surrounded by volumes exhaling their musty breath. The piles beside

her grew, and Ava relaxed amid the calming presence of so
many pages.

The next box was full of murder mysteries, but lying
alone at the bottom with a misleadingly lurid cover was a
copy of *Ethan Frome*. Unwilling to resist the temptation of a
good novel, Ava opened to the first page, and had the pleasant feeling of slipping into a familiar country. When a quiet
knocking at the open door roused her, she was more than a
quarter through, had a crick in her neck and no idea where
she was. She looked at the attractive young man standing
in the door and for a quick moment completely forgot what
century it was, and what were the usual forms of address.
"Oh, you" was the salutation that escaped her, but she realized that wasn't right and looked down again, putting the
novel back into the box before remembering she was supposed to be unpacking and taking it out again.

"I am," he agreed.

This was an encouragingly awkward response, but Ava
was so preoccupied by her embarrassment, she barely heard
him. "Help," she said softly without meaning to.

She had most certainly been addressing some higher faculty than this stranger, but he took it as an invitation and
entered, casting a friendly eye over the boxes. "A lot of unpacking to do?"

Being caught in the intimate act of reading made her feel
hot and funny, so she rose, and not knowing what else to
do, put the book in her hand on the nearest shelf where it
stood, alone, the sole occupant of the many empty shelves.
Because it looked so silly there all by itself, she picked it up
again, but then standing with this book in her hand like a
sudden burden she couldn't figure out how to dispose of, she
sat back down and put it on top of a very dog-eared copy of
Valley of the Dolls. "Yes. I guess."

He unhitched a messenger bag from his shoulder and

squatted among the cardboard, the curve of his body strung like a bow among all the squares and corners. "Seems like kind of a fun job." He pulled out a stack of books and looked at the spines. "I didn't know Zsa Zsa Gabor wrote an autobiography. Actually I don't know who that is, but I guess she likes fur." Ostensibly looking at the cover he held up, Ava was able to examine this apparition more closely; young men didn't just wander around the Lazarus Club.

And he looked very young. He had long eyelashes and a delicate pallor to his face, a veil behind which the possibility of a flush seemed to be constantly advancing and retreating. He was wearing work clothes that bore a fine layer of dust and a splotch of paint across his knee. The contrast between the gentle symmetry of his features and the assertive roughness of his clothes almost made him look like a girl who, wanting to pass as a boy, had picked an outfit that was overdone, laughably too masculine. Maybe he was a new maintenance worker? She didn't recognize him from the regular crew of the Lazarus Club, but then there was a lot that Ava didn't always notice. She wanted to say something, and so spoke quickly. "Are you on a job?"

"Just finished one." He piled a stack of books carefully with a quick dexterity. Ava noticed they were perfectly lined up. "But there's always something else."

Had Aloysius sent him? He had been so monumentally unhelpful up to this point, it seemed hard to believe, but this person was forty years too young to be a club member. "So you're very busy, that must be tiring," Ava said.

"I guess, better busy than not. My shithole apartment isn't going to pay its own rent."

Ava thought this was a little forthright, but she could sympathize with the sentiment. "I'm sorry for your troubles."

He broke down a box with the same fluid economy of

gesture that Ava couldn't help but admire. He was very efficient. "Thanks, I guess?"

It was getting harder to ignore the very striking fact of his appearance. It wasn't just the way his bad haircut, standing up just a little in the back, made him look like a civil war recruit posing for an awkward portrait; there was something more compelling and yet familiar as if she had known him from somewhere. He gathered the boxes into a neat stack and stepped gracefully over, looking past her into the next room.

"I just wanted to check out the space. See the dimensions." As she followed the direction of those light eyes—gray, blue, she couldn't tell—looking into the distance, Ava suddenly placed him. The boyish face, the poorly cropped tawny hair, the gaze fixed on the infinite like that, he looked like Arthur Rimbaud, more precisely, the exact photograph that had hung over her bed ever since high school.

For someone already defining herself as somewhat reactionary, it was funny that Ava would have fallen so hard for Rimbaud's wild, revolutionary poetry, and in point of fact, her feelings for the poems themselves were somewhat ambivalent. It was his portrait that she found flipping through an anthology one day, so pretty, so delicate, so young, and the romance of his story that entranced her—to have fled his provincial home and found love, fame, his genius recognized all by the tender age of seventeen. To a lonely sixteen-year-old with her own secret dreams of grandeur, his beautiful face seemed to hold the promise that all was possible, and she used to lay in bed staring at the poster yearning for both his talent and his slim, dirty teenage body. That he was famously homosexual struck her as beside the point. If only he had known Ava, things would have been different. That same poster still hung in her room, but now it served as a rebuke; she was so old, so much time wasted, and so little accomplished.

And now, incredibly, he seemed to be standing right in

front of her, surveying the room with his hands in his pockets and one shoelace that had come untied. "It's definitely a cool place," he said.

She bent over a pile of books using her hair like a screen for the erotic past she was sure was writ in her cheeks. "Thanks," she mumbled.

"I would normally stay and help. I find these kinds of activities weirdly relaxing." He indicated the boxes. "But I've got to get back. I'm just on a lunch break, really."

"Oh, okay, well, try to let me know your schedule if you plan to come by and do some work."

He gave her a curious look while he picked up his bag. "Sure. I guess I'm down to help." He smiled at her in a way that she couldn't quite decipher, but she also didn't try very hard because by this point she was kind of hoping he would just leave her to the uncomplicated ease of sitting alone.

That night, she called Stephanie to tell her about the morning's unusual apparition.

Stephanie groaned. "Oh god, you're both idiots. That was Ben. He's a brilliant artist. I'd almost talked him into building a bar for us, if you haven't ruined everything. Why didn't you just introduce yourself?"

"I don't know. I thought he was the new janitor or something."

Stephanie sighed. "All right, I guess I'm going to go call him and try to fix this."

"Okay, I'm sorry." And then because she felt there was some slight injustice, she added, "He could have let me know why he was there."

"Oh my god, he's like an art star. You're impossible, I've got to go."

Ava hung up still vaguely indignant that he hadn't introduced himself, but also a little gratified that her strange premonition had been correct. He was an artist, a genius even maybe. She wasn't exactly sure what an art star was, but it sounded impressive, and it was exciting to think she was in charge of a project that drew such people around her. Their plan was working just as she had hoped. She lay back against her pillows and looked up at Rimbaud and smiled at his pretty eyes, that crooked necktie. Why didn't all men wear tight soft-shouldered coats and white collars, their gaze intent on the infinite and beyond? She reached up and straightened the frame on its nail and then fell back, feet propped against the wall, ankles crossed, and gave herself over to pleasant contemplation.

8

As their grand opening raced toward them, Ava, thoroughly caught up in preparations, decided that this premature announcement maybe hadn't been such a bad idea of Stephanie's. Money was sliding through their fingers. Stephanie's salary, now that she had issued herself one, absorbed most of their funds while building supplies and furnishings scavenged from Craigslist took care of the rest with no hope of more until they were up and running and could accept members. While the list of things to be done, fixed and worried about seemed to grow exponentially, the pace and urgency prevented her from thinking too much about technicalities, like the mounting interest on her credit card. Stephanie was spending all of her time fund-raising, if unsuccessfully, but this was another reason Ava didn't feel she could object now that Stephanie had become their greatest expense; she had long since quit cocktail waitressing. Ava was still receiving her pittance from the Lazarus Club, so they decided she could temporarily forgo her salary as codirector of the House of Mirth with the expectation that someday in the future, she would also be compensated.

The next time Ben came by, they sheepishly introduced

themselves. "I just figured Stephanie would show up at some point and take over. I didn't ask because I guess she makes me kind of nervous." He unfurled a technical drawing across Ava's desk. "Did you ever notice that she kind of prowls back and forth while she's talking to you?"

"No, but she probably acts a little differently with me." She remarked the ambivalent raise of his eyebrows. "No? Anyway, I was the real idiot. I thought maybe you were here to fix the mold spots on our wall."

"I still could."

"Stephanie said you were an art star." The euphonious phrase slid from her lips with some envy, how wonderful to already have merited such a designation.

"Glorified craftsman." His laugh faded before it really started, and he chewed his lower lip. "For an art star, I sure have to make a lot of custom furniture to pay the bills."

Poverty seemed perfectly in line with her ideas of nineteenth-century bohemian poets, but she admired this humility. "I'm sorry to take up more of your time," she said.

"Oh, this?" He pointed at the drawings. "No, this is fun."

It looked like a very complicated endeavor to be merely fun. "I thought you might have been a Lazarus member," Ava lied.

"Do I look rich?" he asked, incredulous, but Ava thought, maybe just a little pleased. She shook her head thinking how Stephanie had recently mentioned that it would be absurd for Ben to expect to be paid, they clearly couldn't afford it and how it was fine because his work would get a lot of exposure among very influential people and it would probably bring him lots of new jobs. In fact, he would probably end up so well compensated for the whole thing, he should really be paying them for the opportunity.

"You're really going to make this for us?" she asked, looking at the elevations laid out before her, amazed that all these lines and numbers would somehow leap from two dimensions to three.

He laid a measuring tape on a corner of the drawing that kept trying to curl up. "I shouldn't. I've got like six other jobs I should be working on, eight if I don't want to live on salami sandwiches all month, but I don't know, the idea of contributing to a good cause makes me feel like a human again, the illusion of free will."

Ava played with the curled edge, flicking the corner between her fingertips. "Hopefully this project will make us all feel human."

He removed the paper from her fingers. "You look human to me." He erased something with the back of a shiny metal pencil that looked very official, possibly German.

This seemed very complimentary, and Ava savored it. "So how do you know Stephanie?"

"I don't. She cornered me at a friend's opening. We didn't discuss it, but my guess is she thinks I'm an idiot that will work for free. I get the impression she gets a lot of free stuff from dudes."

Ava came down to earth rather quickly and coughed. Ben glanced up while she pulled at the edges of her sleeves and then decided to go make them a cup of tea.

Two weeks later, sunlight eased through the broad, open windows of what they now called "the great room" and brought with it the summer sounds of children playing. In the distance, a jackhammer rattled like a swarm of bees, a buzzing undercurrent to a lovely afternoon, unexpectedly temperate for the end of August. The room bore no relation to the chaos of a few months ago. Bookshelves, freshly varnished, held their new collection: the least embarrassing of Mr. Buckley's bequest, a few volumes pulled from the original library next door, and every book Ava or Stephanie owned, all strategically arranged to show off the more decorative covers and disguise any sparseness in numbers. Other walls gleamed in new paint. In the unforgiving light of day, the gouges they had created refinishing the floors streaked across the room like gently rippling waves, but at night those floors shone like old money.

Ava sat vigorously rubbing wood stain onto the front of an L-shaped bar in the process of being built into a corner. Ben, in what he admitted was part of a greater self-defeating tendency, had spent way too many days making them a huge, unnecessarily beautiful object. Each time a shortcut presented itself, a means of making the process quicker and therefore more cost efficient, Ava watched him struggle and then make the more aesthetically satisfying choice. By now he had put in so many hours, the original quick favor he had been doing them had acquired its own trajectory, and Ava respectfully tried to stay out of its way.

She wasn't disappointed that this punctiliousness kept him around more. He liked talking about art and movies and never teased her even when she admitted her favorite movies were silent or that she liked equestrian statues best. His tastes were kind of elevated too, she realized happily, as he went on at length about foreign and art house films that she had never heard of. He spent an entire afternoon telling her the plot of *Fitzcarraldo*, his favorite, the story of the man so determined to bring Italian opera into the jungle that he pushes a boat over a mountain. When she went home and watched it, she understood at once why he liked it, and why it was taking him so long to finish their bar, and she decided she liked his company a lot.

Today, he was distressed that Ava insisted on staining before he had finished construction. He cantilevered himself over the counter yet again. "I swear, I'm going to be totally done by the end of the day tomorrow. Can't you wait?"

Ava wiped away a trail of mahogany stain that was running down her wrist and tried to ignore his displeasure. "We
don't have an extra day, if we still need to varnish this thing.
We open in a week."

"But you're going to get sawdust mixed in. The finish is
going to look terrible."

Ava turned to block his view of the area she was working
on which was, in fact, covered in a fine grit, now stained a
lovely chocolate brown. "Don't worry. No one is going to be
down here inspecting the finish. It's going to be beautiful."

He picked up his drill with a stricken expression and silently resumed affixing the cheap ornamental moldings that
were transforming the plain plywood box. She sympathized,
but Stephanie's brand of impetuousness had spread through
the House of Mirth and swept everyone along with it.

In the next room, Ava could hear Stephanie on her phone
wheedling mailing lists from people. So far she had amassed
a staggering four hundred names. George, at his laptop, was
grappling with a graphic design program and cursing. Ava
was enjoying her labor, the dirtiness and fatigue. Industrious,
surrounded by the tools of his trade, Ben had a simplicity
of bearing that made him look a bit like a Shaker. Also he
was wearing suspenders, and this made her very happy. She
would probably wear them too if she had a lovely flat chest
for them to rest against.

"I can't stand it," he said finally and put down his drill to
take the can of stain from her. "You just have to wait at least
until I'm not drilling. It's too dusty. I just can't."

"Okay, okay." Ava sat back on her heels.

"Thank you," Ben said, taking the stain to the other side
of the bar with him, which Ava found amusingly distrustful.

This philosophy of haste had gotten her and Stephanie
into some trouble. Ava had tried to install one of the antique
wall sconces they found in a junk store without finding and

turning off the breakers first. She hadn't actually known what breakers were until a shower of sparks sent them running to the internet. It was terrifying, but strangely exhilarating. And when they had wallpapered the bathroom, a task that seemed so simple in the enclosed sheet of instructions, the process had devolved into a Laurel and Hardy two-reel. Luckily they found a red Sharpie that almost matched the scarlet paper, so they could go back and color in the long uneven strips of white that kept appearing between vertical rolls. Some of Stephanie's hair had caught in the glue and now nestled behind the paper, a little telltale heart.

"Hell's bells," George mumbled in the other room. A minute later he slouched in, plucking at the collar of his Barthes is for Lovers T-shirt. "If you want these invitations in time, you guys are going to have to decide who's doing this reading, so I know what name to put on here."

"Phillip Goldman. I already told you."

"Who's that?" asked Ben from behind the bar.

"He's in charge of the classic books lectures at the New York Public Library. I used to go all the time and he's brilliant and he wrote a biography of Edith Wharton, so it just seems really obvious that he should read that at our inaugural event. He's perfect."

"So Ava thinks she gets to decide who should do our reading even though she's too shy to ask him, and wants me to do it." Leaning against the door frame, Stephanie held out her hand, examining her rings. "Which is pretty absurd, considering he hasn't published a book in almost ten years."

"You already did ask him and he said yes, so why are we even still arguing about this?" Ava asked.

"Because no one is going to come to that. There's no hook. Sam Bates is so hot right now. Not only is everyone writing about his book everywhere, but he just started a literary magazine in Brooklyn, it's like food and writing or writing about food or like readings at dinner parties or something, I'm not sure, but he's on fire. Also, and this is kind of beside the point, but he's black, so if Aloysius was sincere about wanting to expand their membership, this will make us look really good."

"It's odd, he keeps asking me where I'm from," George mentioned, looking at the ceiling. "And he seems very unsatisfied when I tell him Queens."

"I just don't know," Ava said nervously and then, realizing that the other three were looking visibly disappointed in her, sighed. "Fine. What is his book about?"

"Game shows, I think? Or like some show where the contestants eat each other? It's about appetites or something. I don't know, but it's very confusing and everyone loves it."

"I read it. It's pretty good," George said with a conciliatory shrug.

"Yeah, I've heard the name," Ben agreed.

Stephanie's smile was a little nasty. Ava put her paintbrush gently down on the lid of a can of stain and pulled her into the next room away from Ben and George. "I thought you wanted me to curate our events."

"I do. You will. You're the most important part of all of our programming."

"But what you're describing doesn't even sound like something I would go to."

"You're as bad as Aloysius says the board is." Stephanie rolled her eyes.

"No, I'm not," Ava said indignantly. "That's not why. But I've been telling you for weeks that we should do something about *The House of Mirth* for our opening."

"And I heard you," Stephanie said with some exasperation, "and we can and we will. I just need to make sure I can get people in the door. Don't worry, once we're established, you can be as fusty and boring as you want. But other people are interested in more than just dead Europeans."

Ava flinched a little. "I thought you thought this stuff wasn't boring." She wasn't sure if it was the desire to not be overheard in the next room that was causing the volume to winnow from her voice like a deflating balloon. "I thought you were on my side."

"I am. Of course, I don't think you're boring." Stephanie picked at a trace of wood stain on Ava's cheek. "It's just everyone else I'm worried about. Once we get them here, I promise this whole place, the project, us, it's going to seduce everyone, and we will be able to do whatever we want. But I need to get reporters here and they need a hook, and it needs to be contemporary. After that, whatever you want."

"I've tried to be contemporary," Ava whispered. "I just don't get it. It's not me."

Stephanie had already walked back into the other room. "It's decided," she announced to George. "Phillip Goldman is going to read—" she gave Ava a wink "—and Sam Bates is, too."

"All right, back to Kinko's." He unfolded himself and, grabbing his old postal satchel from a corner, loped out of the room.

Ben paused and straightened, wiping his forehead with his sleeve. "You guys are pretty good together," he said. "You've been friends for a long time?"

Ava was silent.

"I've even heard of that Bates guy, and I'm not much of a reader."

Ava sighed and then, realizing Ben was talking, turned her attention to him. "Really? You look like you would be into Walt Whitman."

"That's weird." He laughed. "I do like Whitman. What

makes someone look like they read one thing instead of something else?"

"I don't know, can't you just tell? What do you think I like to read?"

"I would ask you."

"Amateur." Ava smiled and then felt just a little shy, so she looked down toward his shins. The blue cotton looked very worn.

"I would never try to guess people's minds. Especially a woman's."

"Sherlock Holmes has a thing about that—you can't tell if a woman is sitting in the shadows because she's guilty or if she forgot to powder her nose."

"Well, now I know what you like to read. See how conversation works? Although, I don't know, that sounds a little sexist. I just meant because it seems like kind of a dumb thing to do."

"You just don't understand him."

"Are we still talking about Sherlock Holmes? Isn't he gay? Maybe that's why he's not into women."

"He's not gay," Ava said heatedly and corrected herself. "They're just friends. I always felt like those aspersions would really hurt Watson's feelings."

"This is a funny conversation," Ben said, then as Ava started to apologize, he stopped her. "No, I'm into it. Someday I'll talk to you about the different varieties of pine."

"Isn't all pine the same?"

"So you would think—" he pointed with his drill "—but, oh my, no, indeed."

Ava wasn't sure if he was kidding, so she kept talking. "Are you going to come and see your bar in action?" She lowered her voice. "It's not really the event I would have planned, but Stephanie's good at figuring out what people want."

"I've noticed." Ben raised his head toward the breeze

wafting in through the window. "I have to say, it's kind of inspiring what you two have managed to do in here. Not from a professional contracting standpoint so much, but you two sure are determined."

"Thanks." Coming from someone who was able to make monumental furniture appear out of nothing but inspiration and plywood, this felt significant, and she allowed herself a moment of pleasure at the acknowledgment.

Just then, a sound like the crack of a rifle rang out, and they all jumped. "Hello?" They heard Stephanie in the next room ask, "Can I help you?" Ava and Ben went to investigate.

Mr. Dearborn stood in the hall and whacked his cane against the doorjamb. "Who's in charge here?" he asked.

"Is there something we can help you with?" Stephanie asked with a smile.

He looked at her coldly, carefully remaining on the far side of the threshold.

Just like a vampire, Ava thought to herself.

"The board of directors of this club has reconsidered your proposal," he announced. Stephanie shot Ava a look. "As treasurer, it has fallen to me to inform you that while we will continue to allow your activities within the grounds of the club, you will henceforth be required to pay a sum of one thousand dollars for the use of these spaces, payable monthly."

"You're going to charge us rent?" Ava noticed and then tried to ignore that his fly was open.

"I'm Stephanie Sloane," she reminded him, extending her hand. "Let's discuss this further. Please come in and sit down. Have you noticed the floors?" she asked.

He looked at her hand. "I've been a member of this club since V-day. I don't need you to invite me in anywhere."

Stephanie put her hands on her hips. "This is not the agreement we discussed with Aloysius."

"Aloysius does not own this establishment, whatever he may think. The board has the final say in all club matters." He spoke with a fury that hinted at previous battles with their errant president.

Ava hurried forward before Stephanie could say any more. "Of course." For extra politeness, she let her Southern accent seep through. "We are so honored to be able to participate in such a prestigious institution." His eyebrows curled, thick and heavy like a Muppet. "Have you noticed all of the improvements we have made? Would you like to see the rest of the work we have done to preserve this valuable architectural history? And also—" she bent down and ran a hand along the shining parterre "—look at how beautifully it came out."

"Not bad," he sniffed.

"Maybe we could see if there is some way to mutually benefit each other. We are all members of the Lazarus Club here, and we all only want what's best for the club, of course," she continued in high, affected Dixie.

"I demand another meeting with the board. This is outrageous. I have a Pulitzer Prize winner coming next week," Stephanie interrupted.

"Only board members are allowed to call meetings. There is nothing to discuss." He turned to leave.

"Does Aloysius know about this?" Stephanie called after him. "Aloysius is very pleased that we're here. He loves us."

The only response was the angry stabbing of a cane on the hallway floor, as he inched away toward the main staircase.

Ben discreetly slipped back into the other room, and they heard the high whine of the drill. "Those no-good, sneaking geezers." Stephanie paced, stomping her heels against their sparkling floors. She grabbed a book from a shelf and threw it, but it landed in the plush of an armchair with an anticlimactic silence. "You realize what happened, don't you?

They waited until we had invested all this work and money to spring this on us."

Ava picked up the book and sat in the chair, worriedly flipping its pages. "You think?"

"Definitely. Just because they're old doesn't mean they aren't a devious bunch of scheming schemers."

"But I thought we were all supposed to be part of a big cultural family. Didn't Aloysius say we were the future of the club?"

Stephanie snorted. "More like Social Security."

"What are we going to do?"

"We'll just ignore them." Stephanie allowed herself to be distracted by the buzzing of her cell phone. "It's not like we've signed a lease or anything. What can they do?"

"They could kick us out and congratulate themselves on finding the world's cheapest contractors." Ava folded her legs and pressed the tops of her sneakers despondently.

Stephanie looked up from her texting. "Look, if worse comes to worst, we'll just have to hustle more. I can raise the cost of the patron membership."

"Oh, is that all it takes?" Ava tensed to the tapping of buttons.

"Okay, I've got to run. I have a meeting. When George finishes that invitation, email it to me, and I can send it out from home." She threw her phone in her purse.

"So you're really not worried about this?" Ava asked.

"We're obviously not going to stop now when we've come this far. They don't have a leg to stand on." Stephanie fluffed up her hair in the mirror over the mantelpiece. "Don't sweat it. Ciao, love."

Ava didn't answer. She sat, squeaking a rubber-soled toe against the floor. The renovations were done, their bank account, now that they had one, was at zero, Ava's credit card balance enormous. Stephanie seemed to think that once they made it to their grand opening, money in the form of membership dues would start to rain down on them. Ava was far from sure, but what else could she do at this point? She went back into the bar. A smell of varnish rose from the wood, toxic, bracing. Ben was making notes with that mechanical pencil Ava liked so much. She leaned over to look; it was the same drawing of the now built bar. Sharp lines laid out the form quietly and assertively, and there was something entrancing about this proof of conjecture now made real. How nice, she thought again, to be able to turn thoughts into objects that then became filled with their own ineluctable presence. "I still can't believe you made this," she said.

"You're easily impressed." He smiled and snapped open a measuring tape, checking it against the edge of the bar in one quick motion. "We all have our talents."

"Do we?" She picked up her can of stain again. "I'm not so sure."

"You definitely have a talent." He didn't elaborate, and Ava felt it would be unbecoming to press him. It occurred to her that all of the things he must consider her talents, the wrangling of boards, the convincing people to join, finding writers to participate, the whole bustle of activity that had led to this point which had excited his admiration, were all just manifestations of Stephanie's powerful id. "So Stephanie said you're a writer."

Ava looked up in surprise. "She did? Why?"

"I asked. I was curious about you, why you're doing this."

For one moment, Ava thought of confessing everything. Of all people, maybe Ben would understand the desire to create something out of the undifferentiated mass of impressions that flowed through her mind. But this shiny bar looming before them seemed to make the difference in their status so clear that a shyness overtook her. "Nope," she said.

"Really?" Ben asked, confused. "Why would she…"

Ava didn't allow him to finish. "We don't have a lot of time before we open."

"Okay." He drilled a few more screws. "That's cool. I'm sorry." The drill screeched again. "So I couldn't help over-hearing before, but do you guys really not have any kind of lease here? You're either really big optimists or you're nuts."

Ava didn't want to look at him. "Yeah, one of the two."

"A thousand dollars is insanely cheap for this space. You guys should really sign a lease. Like, tomorrow."

"When you're broke, everything is equally expensive." Ava laughed, but started to chew on a thumbnail, spitting it back out when she realized it was bitter with mahogany stain. "I don't have a lease on my apartment either." Ben didn't say anything, but something about the way he opened a new packet of screws felt very expressive. Ava couldn't de-cide if she was indignant at the implied slight on their busi-ness acumen, or flattered that it betrayed an interest in her well-being.

9

The morning of their big event dawned hot and muggy, and Ava and Stephanie spent most of it haggling at the flower market, where Stephanie convinced an annoyed florist to sell them eighty alabaster Easter lilies for thirty dollars. Ava was impressed as usual by Stephanie's acquaintance with the vast network of thrift that pulsed just beneath the unaffordable surface of New York, while Ava felt more and more adrift in a world whose rules she didn't understand. Her knowledge of books had so far proved almost completely inessential to opening a literary club. Somehow they didn't end up getting in touch with writing programs to find young writers, and they didn't try and partner with any of the public libraries; no book clubs had been planned or talks with rare books dealers. But they had a liquor sponsorship and a lot of people coming that night, which Ava supposed was maybe more important, and they had been very busy. Once they opened, as Stephanie was always saying, Ava had hope they would get around to it.

Back at the Lazarus Club, Stephanie, her arms full of flowers, pushed open the heavy front door with her back. "Cab drivers make so much money. They're all, like, millionaires. I never tip more than a dollar."

Ava frowned, knowing her silence would be read as consent, but the brown paper wrapping around the bouquets in her arms crackled sharply as she entered the dim foyer.

Castor rose from behind the front desk. He was a small man, almost as small as she was, and he carried himself with the quick, careful confidence of a sailor. When he was still, he sat behind his desk, his elbows propped and fingers tented, a pose of stern deliberation that also kept the cuffs of his predecessor's uniform from dangling over his wrists. He liked Werther's Original candies, and so did Ava, so she sometimes bought him a pack or he offered her one, and they shared a smile of understanding of the most blistering insignificance.

"Thanks, Castor." Stephanie tossed her hair over one shoulder as he took the heavy door.

"Mr. Wilder is looking for you two." His many years at the Lazarus Club had smoothed his manner of speaking to a perfectly uniform blandness. Sometimes, Ava felt like she could almost hear the deeper veils of meaning shimmering behind his politeness, but she'd never yet been able to catch him voicing an opinion.

They paused on the shallow marble steps of the club's parlor floor and exchanged a nervous glance. Since the specter of rent had passed their transom, Aloysius had been avoiding them while leaving cryptic messages with the Lazarus staff that he "wanted to see them urgently," a baroque game of hide-and-seek that was making the girls thoroughly paranoid. "Did he say why?"

Castor shrugged in a way that made Ava want to commiserate about the irrationality of their boss, but just as she was about to say something, he seemed to be very intent on the top corner of the door frame, and she lost her nerve.

"By the way," Stephanie spoke from behind a scrim of

flowers, "we're going to have a lot of guests at our event, and they might not all be Lazarus Club types."

"Less than a hundred years old," Ava tried to joke.

His smile was civil—cold, and fleeting.

Stephanie did not like being interrupted. "Among other things. This is important. Some of them might not be wearing sport coats. You know, the Lazarus dress code doesn't really apply for our events."

"Oh no." Spending so much time surrounded by the three-piece suits and panty hose of the elderly bourgeoisie, Ava had forgotten that most normal people wore jeans and sneakers. "What are we going to do about that?"

"Nothing. I'm not going to get the downtown elite to come to an event and then say they have to change into a disgusting, borrowed club blazer, for god's sake."

"Yeah, but those are the rules."

"Well, they'll just have to get over it, Ava."

"Mr. Wilder won't notice," Castor said, and Ava almost thought she caught him acknowledging the distracted mania that was Aloysius, but when she searched his face, he looked at her blankly.

Stephanie was already striding up the stairs. "Thanks, love," she called over her shoulder without turning around.

"We really appreciate your help." Ava gave him a lily from her bouquet, which he accepted, graciously noncommittal, and turned his attention back to the small notebook he was often writing in, and which filled Ava with curiosity.

In the library, Stephanie threw her bouquet onto their sofa to answer the frantic summons of her cell phone yet again.

"Flowers don't get put in water all by themselves, you know." Ava picked up the bundle, muttering, and brought both to the sink behind the bar. She had installed it herself, and it only drained if she pressed a hip against it to compensate for the slant of the floor, but it was big and silver and looked very professional. She stuffed the flowers into a couple of dented aluminum garden urns that almost looked like grand silver vases and then paused, her palms pressed against the cold metal. She had read somewhere that people who did yoga could change their emotional state by just adjusting the rhythm of their breath. After a few arduously calm inhalations, she gave up. "What if nobody comes tonight?" she said.

"On the phone."

"Or what if Aloysius doesn't let anyone in because they aren't dressed right and then we have to explain to Phillip Goldman that he has to read to an empty room?"

"Still on the phone."

She almost put the urns of flowers on top of the bar and then stopped, gingerly pressing on the shiny surface with her fingertips. The varnish was still tacky, and she saw a vision of the event to come: plastic wineglasses all stuck to the bar like a carnival game. The vases clanged back against the bottom of the sink. At least the mural was finished. Thanks to the confluence of Ava's new enthusiasm for the decorative arts section of the public library and the discovery that Craigslist was filled with talent willing to work on spec, they now had a mural of a giant art deco peacock flashing its tail in black and silver behind the bar.

Ava walked back into the great room. "The varnish on the bar isn't dry." Stephanie, her phone cradled against her ear, was plucking her eyebrows in the mantelpiece mirror. She didn't respond. "What time are the authors coming?" A stack of paint cans had been forgotten in a corner, and Ava hurried to put them away. "Are we ready? We aren't ready, are we?" As she tried to stuff the cans into a tiny closet, already filled with drop cloths and a ladder and a cardboard file box that held two months' worth of mail, loose rolls of wallpaper tumbled around her. She kicked back a roll of duct tape and shut the door. "I hope no one tries to put away their coats. It's September third. No one will be wearing a coat, right? Did we get enough cups? What about the alcohol, when is that getting delivered? And the ice? We don't have an ice chest. Will people think we are unhygienic if it's just in the sink? Could you please get off your phone for one second?"

"Hold on." Stephanie pressed her phone against her chest. "George is coming with some volunteers he picked up at school in, like, two hours, and he can use my blow-dryer on the bar before everyone gets here. He can get the ice. Stop worrying. I'm kind of doing something here." She picked up her phone again. "Oh I know, but he never goes out with her in public."

"What about hand soap? Is there enough in the bathroom? Maybe I should refill it." When she opened the closet door again to get the soap, the paint cans crashed free, banging her ankle and rolling with a lopsided heft until they rested against the wall.

"Ava."

"It's okay, they didn't spill."

"Go home. You are driving me crazy."

A wall sconce beside the closet hung dispiritedly on its side, and Ava straightened it. "Yeah, maybe. Okay."

"Don't forget your record player. We don't have any other music."

"Won't the Lazarus Club be mad if we're playing music in the library? Do we even need it? I don't know what I'm wearing. Do you know what you're wearing?"

"Goodbye, Ava."

"Okay, bye."

She started down the twisting corridor that led back to her apartment but saw the back of a head that could have been Aloysius, so she fled in the opposite direction that led her to the main doors. Outside of the club, she immediately felt better. Midmorning sunlight fell through the trees, a dappled spray that trembled on the sidewalks, and she crossed the street grateful for each step that took her away from the Lazarus Club. She ought to remember to leave more often, but those thick limestone walls exerted a strange pressure, a gentle suasion bidding her to stay deep inside the building, a force she didn't notice until, stepping onto the sidewalk, it vanished and the sensation of the sky above her, even the dense, muggy sky of New York City, made her feel as light as helium. Hands in her pockets, she stepped gingerly on her toes, taking care to avoid the burst ginkgo berries that dotted the sidewalk, pink and pearlescent and smelling like vomit.

This evening was advancing toward her inexorably and with it the strangers who had paid membership dues to be part of a club that didn't even exist yet. What if it didn't work? What if Stephanie was wrong, and everyone came and scented out whatever it was that made Ava such a failure and a weirdo? She was the wrong kind of person, and when she tried to write, she wrote the wrong kind of books, and she liked the wrong kind of clothes, and she knew all of this and tried to stay out of people's way, and now Stephanie had tricked her into putting herself forward, and it was all going to be a disaster.

She tried the breathing trick again, trailing her hand against the black railings in front of a brownstone as she walked, in the hope that the childish act would comfort her. It didn't. After a few steps, she noticed that her fingers were gray with filth. A tree trembled just beyond the iron bars. She thought of the blocks surrounding this neighborhood that had become her life, stretching out and out in geometric precision, limitless. A multitude of people and lives pressed in on her as if she could physically feel the weight of so much accumulated aspiration and desire. And now here she was in the middle of it, as filled with wanting and the possibility of failure as any of them. In a rush, New York was too much with her.

And then, out of her panic, a familiar sensation came to her rescue, an inner retreat, and she sank into the distance it offered, looking at the streetlamps and letting her eyes glaze over, as she imagined a different city, the stench of the gingko trees and the heat of the afternoon evoking the thick, organic decay of a jungle climate, French Indochina perhaps. Marguerite Duras floated through her mind; she wasn't a fan, overwrought and overwritten, she thought, but in this moment, that was the ambience of her inner life that spilled over, recasting the ordinary street in vivid colors. What if she were the kind of woman, sensual, impetuous, who slunk into adventures without a moment's introspection? The hum of traffic and taxis on adjoining streets took on the rounded shine of cars in black-and-white movies. Soon she would enter a bar and drink scotch out of small, bright glasses, and someone across a round marble table would light a cigarette and yearn for her. She bloomed under this look of imaginary desire, glancing flirtatiously at a line of parking meters as she rounded a corner, a creature of seduction. Once this perspective had rearranged around her body to a comfortable weight, she felt she could again move through the world.

This mask of colonial eroticism and its borrowed courage carried her right up to the green awning of the Lazarus Club, but deflated at the sight of Aloysius, pink and sweaty, and screaming at Castor. She guiltily pressed the back of her hand against the perspiration gathering on her neck, and ascended the stairs, her ankles wobbling in the thick plush of the carpeted runner. Maybe she should think more carefully about some of these old books she loved. But the bonds of affection that held her to the books of the past pushed her to elide some of history's more unpleasant truths, the way one might, without too much effort, overlook the brutality of a caddish boyfriend who happens to be very nice to you personally. Maybe Stephanie was right, and it was good that Sam Bates was coming to read that night, but Ava was still a little nervous about it. It wasn't her habit to make waves.

When she got back to her apartment, she sat down for a minute at her desk. The composition book lay in front of her, and she opened to a new page, rows and rows of faint blue lines of possibility. She took up a quill, smooth and light in her hand and, dipping it gently in a pot of ink, paused for a moment, thinking and then wrote, "So it begins," in her florid, precise script. She wasn't sure what to say next, so she stopped again, resting her chin in her hand. To her left, plane trees tossed their wide fluttering leaves beyond the open window. A bird on a nearby branch gave her an alert, worried look. She smiled and sat, unwilling to move lest she dislodge this novel feeling, as bright and weightless as a soap bubble that transfigured the familiar scenery of her apartment, layering the dark, cluttered space with a fresh, shimmering translucence.

10

That evening as Ava crossed the landing of the main staircase, Rodney, catching sight of her, waved from the bar. "Big night tonight," he yelled, earning a frown from an old lady sipping a sherry. Ava's portable Victrola, squat in its leather suitcase, creaked against the rings of its handle, and she hefted the weight, as she wondered once again if her outfit was too dowdy. She had spent the whole afternoon fretting in her apartment, trying and rejecting clothes, until finally, the time for the event almost upon her, she had landed, impractically, on a favorite blazer. It was definitely too hot for velvet, but the deep blue lapel resting against her blouse made her feel like Oscar Wilde or Baudelaire, and somehow this seemed appropriate.

The gaudy wallpaper, gold fleurs-de-lis on a field of scarlet that they had found on remainder in the back of the paint store, shone darkly in the dim light of recently installed fifteen-watt bulbs. The many imperfections of its application were swallowed by shadows that grew deeper at the far end of the hallway that led toward their rooms. Locked doors on either side emerged as Ava passed, marking the space between low pools of light and drawing her along toward the hushed darkness, playing with her sense of perspective. Her shoes clapped on the wooden floor. At the end of the passage, a head popped out.

"Ava, uh, I think we may have some issues here." George spoke with a contained urgency that dispelled the tranquility of the dark hallway and prompted her to hurry toward him.

"Take this." She handed him the Victrola.

Surprised by the weight of the unassuming little suitcase, it slipped from his fingers and landed on the floor with a bang, followed by a hard rattle. "Oh, geez, sorry."

Ava knelt and unlatched the case, propping open the lid to examine the turntable beneath. She plugged in a brass side arm and began to crank. The black disc slowly started to revolve. "It looks okay."

"Oh, wow, the very latest in Edison technology." George knelt beside her and tapped the metal interior of the lid. "This amplifies the sound?"

"Yeah, it's for picnics and things, yachting. Wherever you need a fox-trot on the go. There's a place here for records." She opened a metal case in the lid and drew out a pile of heavy shards. "Oh." They looked silently at the black mosaic she spread out on the floor. "Well, it looks like a couple survived intact—'Down Among the Sheltering Palms,' the 'Merry Widow Waltz' and the overture to *Tristan and Isolde.* That's something, I guess."

"I feel just terrible."

"Don't worry about it. We'll play what we have." Ava gathered up the broken records, holding on to them for just a moment of memoriam before handing them to him to dispose of. Many hours of solitude had been spent listening to these same twelve recordings. "You look nice. I like your suit."

He held out a lapel, examining it as if he had never noticed before. "Thanks, it was my great uncle's, a somewhat unsavory character. There's this little burn on one sleeve that I suspect is gunpowder. He didn't get along with those Murder Incorporated fellows, Ashkenazim, you know," he added conspiratorially.

"Yes, George." She patted his arm. "So what are these issues you were talking about?"

Instead of answering, George guided her toward the bar. The art deco bird strutted at the moldings, and molted silver feathers gently coasted across the wall. Four undergraduates in thrift-store suits and ties struggled to look at ease. "These are the volunteers I found. They're all in the poetry department." George leaned in to whisper, "Probably not the most efficient bunch, but poets seem to be the rare students at Hunter without multiple other jobs, and therefore time on their hands. Also it was the only department I remembered to flyer."

A phalanx of poets at her disposal tickled Ava. "Thanks for helping out. You can have all the booze you can drink."

"Yeah, that's one of the issues." George spoke to the floor. "That liquor sponsor that Stephanie was supposed to have lined up?"

"The documentary filmmaker or whatever?"

"Yeah, well, the rest of the time 'he reps for his dad's booze business' was her construction, I believe."

"And?"

"It was never delivered, and he's not answering the number that Stephanie gave me."

"Are you serious?" Ava began circling the room as if she might find the previously overlooked cases of liquor, a pointless activity she couldn't seem to stop.

"Yeah, it's not here. I've been waiting all day."

"Give me your cell phone."

George reached into his breast pocket. "Also the party rental place only brought fifty chairs."

She took the phone. "We were supposed to get a hundred."

"Those guys were way sketchy." George frowned. "I tried to argue and got quite the dressing-down. Armenian, I think the language was? Jeremy was here." He pointed to a small young man in a not quite matching gray suit who nodded vigorously.

Ava, waiting for someone to pick up the other end of the ringing line, tried to look mature and composed, while the young man shifted his weight, catching the rough tread of one sneaker against the laces of the opposite foot, and wobbled precariously. "This place is really awesome," he said, regaining his balance.

Ava smiled at him and then spoke into the phone in a panicked whisper, "Stephanie, where is the liquor?" To preserve her dignity, she walked back into the hallway. "It's not here."

"That's totally absurd," Stephanie informed her. "It has to be there."

"What are we going to do? People are going to be here soon."

"Let me work on it." The line went dead.

Ava ran back into the bar. "Why don't you guys start setting up the chairs we have? Let's put the reader in the big room in front of the bookcases." She handed the phone back to George. "Have you set up the microphone?"

George straightened his collar. "You should come look at it. The Lazarus microphone is really ancient and made a lot of noise when I tried to plug it in to the speakers, so I had to reroute an extra cord through my laptop." Ava had no idea what he was talking about, but at least someone else was worrying about it. Behind her, boys began unfolding and setting up chairs with a lot of clanking and shuffling. "And we had the wrong kind of extension cord, so I just left this part of the plug sticking out, but I covered it with electrical tape, so it should be okay, but it might be a good idea for one of us to stand near it, just in case it catches on fire."

"Um, okay."

"Then I was going to print out the guest list, but our printer, which is really crappy, by the way, ran out of ink, so I went to the copy place." He pulled a sheaf of paper from his back pocket. "I think the girl who works there and I are really starting to come to an understanding."

Ava flipped through the list. "Why is it so long? We can't fit this many people in here."

"I guess Stephanie got more emails? I figured me and the guys could work the doors."

"I guess that's a good idea." She turned around. The chairs stretched in two long lines, one behind the other. "Okay, guys, why don't we make more rows here? Sort of bunch everyone up closer to the reader. I'm going to see what else I can find for people to sit on."

"Oh, by the way," George called after her, "I think I got the bar dry enough as long as we don't use cocktail napkins. Skin is okay, but paper still sticks to the varnish. So there's that."

"Thanks, George. There is that."

As Ava tapped back down the hallway, she held out her arms, trying to dry the damp spots starting to seep from her armpits. She thought of taking off her ridiculous blazer, but by now the white silk underneath was probably visibly damp. She passed the bathroom, considered trying to throw up to relieve her growing nausea, but decided it would take too long. At the main staircase, she peered cautiously over the banister for signs of Aloysius before slinking up to the third floor. Here, there was another large parlor that no one ever used.

At the top of the stairs, she checked to make sure that Aloysius's secretary was gone for the day. It was hard to tell;

every surface was piled with paperwork, and manila folders teetered in arbitrary and precarious stacks. Except for a blue parakeet that immediately started shrieking, the office appeared empty. She proceeded to the parlor, where to her dismay there were no chairs, only couches and divans, all of which looked too heavy to haul downstairs. She didn't feel right asking her poets to risk their backs. There was, however, a large Persian carpet.

Once she had cleared all the mismatched settees, Ava knelt on the hard floor and began rolling up the carpet, kicking it when necessary, sliding around in her stocking feet. When she finished, she realized whatever movie image she had in her head of someone jauntily carrying a rolled-up rug on one shoulder was totally inaccurate. The carpet weighed a ton. Only by wrapping her arms around the tight circumference of one end and exerting all her might, could she just drag it along the slippery floor. It smelled of wet goats. "Hey, boys," she called breathlessly. Two poets wandered in with an irritating lack of alacrity. "Will you set this up in front of the microphone and line the chairs up behind it?"

"Ava," George called.

"Give me a second." Ava scurried back up to the third floor, sliding a little on the hardwood and reminded of being a kid and barefoot in stockings at her grandmother's elegant parties. She reappeared, her arms full of sofa cushions, which she dumped on the carpet, kicking them into piles. "People can sit on these. It's kind of bohemian. Will you guys go see if you can find any more?"

George squatted and ran his hand through the nap of the carpet. A plume of dust sprang up. "This rug is really dirty."

Ava set an old brass vase on one corner and grouped pillows around it. "Hopefully everyone won't notice until they stand up to leave. Have you heard from Stephanie?"

George stood up. "Uh, yeah, the liquor isn't coming."

Ava stopped scattering lily petals around the rug. "What do you mean?"

He assumed the kind of distant air that he had developed lately as a coping mechanism. "She said we should go to a liquor store."

"Phone." Ava held out her hand.

"She said her phone was about to run out of battery but that she would be here as soon as she could."

Ava sat down heavily on a metal folding chair. "People are going to be here in fifteen minutes." None of this was fun anymore. She wanted to be alone in her apartment with the door locked, so alone that she could be dead for ages before anyone noticed, until Mycroft began to eat her. After three days, a household pet will start on your mouth and eyes. Where had she learned that? It didn't sound so bad.

"She says we could have it delivered."

Ava looked up. George was reading from his phone. "I thought her phone was dead."

"The text says 'fone almost dead. have liq store deliver. charge it.'"

"'Charge it,' says Eloise." Ava put her head down, allowing one more brief moment of despair. "Okay. The closest liquor store is on the corner. Buy three cases of their absolutely cheapest wine. My purse is over there. There's a card in it. At least with wine you can't tell how cheap it is from the bottle. Buy bottles, by the way, no boxes."

"Or I could buy some bottles and a funnel and we could just refill them from boxes."

"George, in our darkest hour, you shine ever brightly."

"I endeavor to be of service, milady." He bowed deeply, his orange socks visible under his safety-pinned cuffs.

The poets came in with more cushions, and Ava kicked them into place. "What took you guys so long?"

One of them answered, "We ran into this crazy guy that thought we were stealing and started screaming at us."

A different one corroborated, "He was wearing a yellow bathrobe over a tuxedo. He called us Bolsheviks."

The first one interrupted, "He called you a Bolshevik. He called me a Sandinista. I don't even speak Spanish, and anyway, I'm Puerto Rican." He frowned.

"I'm sorry. That was Aloysius, the club president. He's just like that." Ava started biting her cuticles. "Did you tell him you were bringing them here?"

"He said he was going to come talk to you about that."

"Okay, fine. You guys see if George needs any help."

Calmly, Ava left and walked to the bathroom. She closed the door and crawled into the empty tub. She pressed her foot against the faucet and felt the metal behind her toes. Then, she leaned her head against the side of the tub and counted the tiles on the floor until eventually, there was a knock at the door.

"Ava? Are you in there?"

It seemed pointless to lie, especially as she now remembered she had forgotten yet another thing on their list of absolutely essential tasks to take care of before the opening—installing a lock on the bathroom door. "Yes."

Stephanie opened the door in an avant-garde confection of a dress, a sort of cardigan from which revealing sections had been cut away, the end result both grandmotherly and strangely indecorous. She kept one hand on the neckline that kept sliding off her shoulders. "What are you doing in here?"

"What are you wearing?"

Stephanie looked down and laughed. "I know, funny, isn't it? A designer friend lent it to me. I thought it was kind of librarian-y." She put the lid of the toilet down with a bang and sat, a large glass decanter cradled in her lap. "Why are you hiding in the bathroom? Aren't you hot in that?"

"Yes," admitted Ava. "I was hiding from Aloysius."

"You're such a wimp," Stephanie groaned. "We have just as much a right to be in this club and using the facilities as anyone. Anyway, I just ran into him and told him someone from *Vanity Fair* was coming tonight. He practically kissed me. He's coming later."

"He's not mad about the cushions?"

"You're so silly sometimes. Look, I brought this for the wine." She held out the decanter.

"I thought your phone was dead." Ava started to get mad again. "What happened to this guy who was supposed to be giving us all that free booze?"

Stephanie shrugged. "I don't know. He's a flake. If we use pitchers like this, no one will see how cheap it is." She hitched up the falling shoulder of her dress again.

Ava slid farther down against the smooth back of the tub. "I don't want to. I hate parties. Why are we doing this?"

Stephanie glanced into the mirror above the sink, running her finger along the corner of her lips to remove excess lipstick. "Because otherwise you would be in that tiny room making pickles."

"Why do you always accuse me of preserving?"

"Well, something equally boring. This party is going to be filled with writers and people who like books, and you know more about books than anybody I know. Everyone's going to love you. That's what this is about, right?" She put the decanter under her arm, pressing its slender neck against her ribs, and grabbed Ava's hands. "This is it. This is the moment you become a fabulous salonista. When I think of you rambling on about Proust and writers and salons, in that tiny dorm room all wrapped up in those silly flannel nightshirts you used to wear—who would believe that we would actually make it happen? But we did. We made it happen. Come on, get up."

Ava allowed herself to be pulled and stepped over the side of the tub. "I know I'm going to say something wrong. I don't know how it happens, but it always happens, and it's going to hurt so much after all this work when no one wants to talk to me."

Stephanie wasn't listening. "Where are your shoes?"

"I left them upstairs. I'm wearing the black T-straps and they were kind of slippery."

"I don't think you should wear the black shoes with that outfit."

"I'm being serious, Stephanie."

"So am I. Everyone's eyes will be on us. We need to look right." Stephanie's smile was implacable. "Go grab another pair. Hurry, so we won't be late."

"I really don't think it matters right now."

"Just go. I'll wait for you." She pushed Ava out of the bathroom and toward the hall. "Wait until you see. I bought tea lights. Hurry."

Rather than argue any more at this critical moment, Ava followed Stephanie's instructions. Maybe she was right, she did seem to have an unshakable faith in her priorities, while Ava was constantly wavering in her own. A kind of power emanated from conviction, and Ava bowed to its force. She didn't want to spoil everything.

When she returned, Stephanie nodded her approval and rubbed Ava's shoulders. "Wait until you see."

They stopped at the threshold of the library. Small candles flickered on the mantelpiece, measuring out the marble expanse in dots of flame, their reflections repeating in the mirror above. In the spacious twilight of the grand room, the silhouettes of interns passed back and forth, placing dozens of white tea lights on the bookshelves, now nearly hidden in shadow. Seduced by the delicate glow of so many lights, Ava still thought of, but decided not to mention, the fire hazard. In the flattering light, the dirty Persian carpet and pillows looked like the artist's studio of Ava's intentions, and she fleetingly wished she could plop herself down next to the urn and the lilies, naked, and be painted in oils. This was the nineteenth-century novel she had dreamed of—candles and wine and the importance of art and men of genius and literary ideals. Out of the longing of her solitary and romantic imagination, the space had sprung into being like Athena from the head of Zeus, and now it lay there, realized and tangible. Any minute now, other human beings would float through the most secret and unironic regions of her heart; she would preside over this magnificent salon—charming, admired, envied, like the beautiful Duchesse de Guermantes. She wondered why, in the reflected glow of the scenery she had worked so hard to create, she felt a small internal deflation, a sigh, a hesitation; it didn't quite feel as satisfying as she had expected. Also the red heels she had changed into always pinched her feet.

11

The trickle of people that started the evening had quickly become a river flowing toward the bar, and Ava let it swirl around her.

A quartet of tall, thin blondes were clustered nearby. One, hitching a tiny bag farther onto her shoulder, asked, "Is this the way to the booze?"

Ava nodded and heard George calling from the next room. "May I offer you ladies a libation?"

Alarmed by the size of the crowd, Ava hurried into the bar. "Do you need help?" she asked George.

He answered with a harried look, so she grabbed a bottle of wine and began handing cups to outstretched hands. The blessed repetition of required motions: opening another bottle, turning, extending, smiling, gave her something to do, and each drink had a set exchange, friendly and impersonal, that passed before Ava had to worry about what to say beyond hello and you're welcome.

Eventually, she began to enjoy the sensation; she was performing, and the impression of having an audience spurred her to enact the part of someone serving drinks with an extra concentration and vivaciousness, a slight fillip at the end of each pour, smiling brighter at faces whose features she didn't even see. She perched forward, imitating the queenly posture of a barmaid she vaguely remembered from some impressionist painting. The bustle of the bar lapped around her like so much froth from which she, the owner and founder of a literary salon, rose like Venus from the sea, delighted to hide for a minute in this flattering image. A tall young man in a sport coat with an upturned collar asked her, "You guys serve whiskey?"

"No." Ava indicated the field of red wine being raised toward mouths.

"A pretty thing like you should serve something stronger than wine," he said with a smile.

This statement seemed such a thrilling confirmation of her metamorphosis into a new and dazzling creature that, unconcerned whether he wanted it or not, Ava handed him a cup of wine, which he frowned at and left behind on the counter.

Phillip Goldman had arrived, and Stephanie had backed him into a corner of the bar where he kept laughing loudly and yelling, "Oh, you girls," in a plummy accent that carried over the rest of the noise. Ava noted with grudging admiration that his tie was a double Windsor, although she didn't like how often his hand seemed to slip down the small of Stephanie's back.

At some point, Stephanie grabbed her arm. "Stop flirting, we have to talk."

"I'm the one who's flirting?" Ava objected, as Stephanie pulled her from behind the bar and into a corner.

"He doesn't want to read his Wharton biography," she whispered. "That was his last book. He's got a new one that he wants to read from."

"What do you mean?" Ava tried to loosen the desperate grip on her wrist.

"He's working on a novel, and he wants to read from that. He didn't even bring the other one, and I don't have a copy. Do you?"

"Did we really not even buy the book that we based this whole big event around?" They looked at each other. Ava finally pried Stephanie's fingers loose, but not to be dissuaded from whatever support she was gleaning, Stephanie grabbed Ava's other arm. Ava thought about how drowning people occasionally down their rescuers with the insistence of their grip. "I guess we have to let him read what he wants. What's it about?"

"A married professor who has an affair with an intern or something."

"Oh, gross, no. I hate books like that."

"I don't think we have a choice."

A young woman in a pair of sea-blue eyeglasses bumped into them, and they both smiled forcefully at her. "So this will be our first event," Ava said in what she hoped was a cutting voice. "I hope you're happy."

"What do we say? I had a whole intro prepared, and now it won't make any sense. I can't just blab about how our name comes out of this great tradition if he's not even going to talk about our name."

"I guess you have to tie it in to a different book. Talk about *Lolita* or something."

"Can't you be more specific?" Stephanie asked, annoyed, and Ava guessed that she hadn't read it. Then, in a surge of excitement, Ava knew she would be able to use her particular set of skills at last. "I could do it, if you want. I think I could do a good job. I have a lot of feelings about that book."

"Oh no, I know how shy you get. We don't want to bore everyone." She stopped, thinking. "And where is Sam Bates?"

They looked around and spotted him immediately, standing by the windows and reading the spines on the shelves nearest to him with a self-conscious concentration. At the same moment, the same thought occurred to both of them. "Oh god, there aren't any other black people here," Ava said with a feeling of acute shame on behalf of herself, Stephanie, the Lazarus Club, the world at large. "What happened with your mailing list?" she asked.

"I tried. I swear. But my friend Sasha was busy."

"You only have one black friend among all these people?"

"It's not like you're any help," Stephanie hissed back.

"Yeah, but that's because I don't have any friends at all," Ava said, feeling it sounded a little thin. "And I spend so much time at the Lazarus Club..."

"Well, we don't have time to worry about it now." Stephanie dragged Ava over to where Sam Bates was standing. "Sam," she exclaimed, embracing him with two loud air-kisses, "you made it. Ava, this is Sam Bates, Brooklyn's hottest young author."

Ava waved shyly and thought she managed to say "hi" but wasn't sure, and maybe just kind of bleated. Since she was looking down, she noticed Sam Bates was wearing beautiful chestnut wingtips with light blue socks.

"This is a cool space." He paused and his tone was ambiguous. "Different, I mean."

Stephanie laughed. "Oh, I know, it's not your scene." She leaned in to whisper, "This crowd is totally not our usual crowd either, but it's so great to be able to use a place like this to promote real talent like yourself. There's going to be a lot a press here tonight, so the publicity should be stellar. *Vanity Fair*'s here," she added, while Ava wondered if Stephanie had ever felt ashamed about anything in her whole life.

Sam Bates looked around, interested. "Photographers?" he asked.

"Of course. Come on, let's get you a drink. I want to

hear all about this project of yours, this magazine. It sounds amazing."

As Stephanie, still chattering, led him away, Ava saw him adjust the strap of his shoulder bag across his chest defensively, then find the knot of his tie with a quick resigned touch.

Someone bumped into Ava, distracting her, and she remembered she had an introduction to write. These social affairs were Stephanie's concern; Ava's job was thinking and writing and talking about books. She looked around for a pen to jot down some notes. What should she say about Nabokov? His weariness, his elegant nostalgia, his contempt for everything obvious and vulgar and stupid, that he sent forth in perfect, hilarious, uncompromising sallies of wit and satire, but satire etched with a razor blade, not a thing out of place, not an unnecessary word. Oh, this was going to be so much fun, she realized. Faces rustled by, crowding, jostling, laughing, their physical proximity adding to Ava's happiness, the impression of collective purpose. This was why they were all here, and she would finally give voice to her rush of deeply held feelings about literature and authors and style and books. For one glorious moment, she would fulfill the frustrated dictates of her deepest self and connect with a room filled with other people about the things she cared most about.

She sat by the record player, scribbling notes, while the room around her quickly filled. Tipsy models and publicists leaned against each other, cooing in mutual appreciation. Gallery owners and book agents chatted with the strident cheer of salesmen. Well-dressed women tolerated their dates with an air of leisurely distraction, checking their phones for other, more essential parties. Somehow Stephanie managed to corral the mob toward the lectern and got them to be quiet as the overture from *Tristan and Isolde* began lugubriously booming yet again. After some urgent waving, Ava silenced it, and as she started to push her way to the front, she heard Stephanie take the microphone.

"Good evening. I would like to thank you all for coming to the inaugural night of the House of Mirth Literary Society and Library." The microphone sputtered quietly. "I know that you are all here because you share a common passion for literature. But literature doesn't exist in a vacuum. It must be cultivated and nurtured. At our soon to be not-for-profit literary salon and writers' club, we have created an environment where literature is paramount. Not only will we be presenting more impeccably curated cultural events like this evening, in addition we provide this beautiful space for writers to work in during the day, complete with wireless internet and printing free of charge." There was some appreciative looking around. "Not to mention our bar, where our celebrity-curated wine list and rare whiskey selections from around the world will provide just the right amount of inspiration." A faint "Whoo!" escaped one of the tipsier models. "We are an exclusive membership society with several tiers of VIP, patron and platinum levels. If you are interested in applying, please see our membership director."

The broad backs of two pin-striped suits blocked Ava's path, and she waved to let Stephanie see that she was coming. Stephanie turned away from her and addressed the audience. "But literature would be nothing without its men of genius. Tonight, I am thrilled to introduce one of today's master wordsmiths, Phillip Goldman." Despite mounting evidence, Ava still thought Stephanie might be about to call her out of the crowd and hand over the microphone. Her notes wilted in her damp hand. "Tonight he will be honoring us with selections from his new novel, a forbidden romance between a brilliant man and his young student." She paused and Ava waited with one last, fading hope. "Controversial, yes, but that is why we look to our writers to be truly brave, to have the courage to tell the stories that make people uncomfortable, to speak the great truths, to challenge all of us. A sexy book for a sexy space—who says that literature has to be boring? We think it can be sexy as hell." There was a mild cheer. "Please join me to give a warm literary welcome to Mr. Phillip Goldman."

Ava slid to the back of the room, hoping no one would notice the crestfallen expression that she wasn't able to hide. There was a sprinkling of clapping that got more assured as the eminent reader stood and ascended toward the front of the room. Accepting the microphone, he clasped Stephanie's hand, kissed it and brought it to his chest while Stephanie smiled and tried to gracefully disengage. In a corner by the coat closet, Ava faced the wall and tried to compose herself. It was such a small thing, no big deal, why did it even matter; she tried to contain hot tears, embarrassed. "Our charming hostess. You can't have her," Phillip Goldman reprimanded the audience. "She's mine. I was here first." Stephanie laughed uncomfortably and clapped before retreating to a seat in the front row.

Ava found George in the bar and stood next to him, finding comfort in the familiar slump of his posture. He frowned. "I didn't realize this guy would be such a pompous ass. Although, thinking on it now, it seems rather obvious that he would be."

Ava just sighed.

Mr. Goldman pulled a pair of silver-rimmed glasses from his breast pocket and, placing them on the far end of his nose, shuffled a few pages. He began. "*To lose everything to a goddess is no shame. A goddess who walks into your office in a damp sundress who carries with her the breath of spring, and strawberries just going to rot in sun-warmed furrows, and who says hello with the same sweet exhalation of a woman cuming softly against your face; there's no shame at all. It's a fucking mitzvah and you grab it and thank the gods you're still alive and that your cock still works, at least for this week. Lacrimae rerum."*

Ava decided to rest, her forehead pressing into the musty fabric of George's shoulder, for just a minute longer.

A side door next to the bar opened with a loud creak, and Ava turned to scold whomever it was, only to meet eyes with Ben. Scanning the room with a bewildered expression, he looked like an envoy from a different planet. Incredibly glad to see him, Ava turned just as George tugged at her sleeve. "We're out of wine, by the way. And there's supposed to be a reception after."

"Okay, okay. I'll figure it out." She slipped from his grasp and crossed to Ben. He was wearing a tie and the narrow rear tail dangled several inches below the front.

"How's it going so far?" he whispered, leaning in close to her. "You look nice."

"Thanks." She had become so accustomed to seeing him in his dirty work clothes that this new cleaned-up person in front of her felt like a stranger, and it made her feel shy. Scrubbed of some of his comfortable familiarity, the fact of his maleness suddenly felt more noticeable, pushing itself between them, reminding her of his essential otherness. This new perception of distance and the slight fear that accompanied it made it hard for her to look him in the eye. "The bar looks good," she said, pointing, wanting to reassert the common interest that had fostered their previous safe friendliness.

He looked and shook his head against some internal reservation. "It's not perfect," he said sadly, turning away from whatever invisible mistake was chafing him, and messing with the buttons on his cuffs. There was a silence. Ava wondered if maybe the sudden shyness she was experiencing was actually a response to his discomfort. Maybe without the support of having something to build or sand or fiddle with, he was the one manifesting a social distress that she was merely echoing. For some reason it seemed a small but important point—to determine who was more uncomfortable.

He indicated the other room. "The place looks packed." George held a finger to his lips, shushing them, which Ava thought a little uncalled for. She and Ben turned toward the lectern. With her eyes facing forward, her other senses strained toward him, an acuity totally focused his nearness. Each time he shifted his weight, each measured exhale, the simple fact of standing next to this person absorbed her full attention. At one point he cleared his throat, and her whole body tensed in the expectation he was about to whisper something to her, so intent, she didn't even notice that Stephanie took the microphone again to introduce Sam Bates.

It was only in spite of herself that, when Sam accepted the stage, he called Ava's attention away from Ben. He thanked Stephanie and the audience for gathering to hear him read "his little efforts," and his resonant voice held a touch of laughter in it, a private amusement, one that he wasn't going to share, and this small note of withholding seemed to draw the audience into a new measure of curiosity, a desire to ferret out the source of the small smile not quite passing his lips. "But I hate it when authors talk too much." He again touched the knot before smoothing the plane of his perfectly uncreased tie. "No one has time for that." He paused as though expecting a contradiction, or rather pretended for a minute that he did before resuming with a new swell of rising elocution. *"To consume, to be consumed, an action that can exist in both the active and the passive construction. A duality tied to its very notion, a two-way street of ravening hunger. I consume my lunch. I consume my lover's body. I consume art and movies and television and advertising and medication and all the fruits of the world, desperately trying to sate this hunger, the Hunger that only grows, while this obsession consumes me. Let us examine, for*

*a moment, my lunch, a cheeseburger, this pullulated mass which al-
ready contains within the many levels of my own desiring but also
the desiring that came before my arrival: the deliberate chewing of
verdant grass, the calf suckling the milk that would then rot into
gruyere, the layers and layers of consumption and consuming that
bursting into my mouth will satisfy only one of my hungers leaving
the rest that much more noticeable. I am starving. I grab her wrist
and it yields beneath my mouth."*

As he read, Ava and the rest of the audience remained
slightly shocked, riveted, until he was done, after which he
plugged his next reading, his book tour, his magazine and
some collaborative design/idea/writing lab in Williamsburg
that Ava didn't quite understand but applauded mightily
along with everyone else. In the roar of acclaim, she pushed
Ben gently into the dim hallway and closed the door behind
them. "It's so crowded, we ran out of wine. Would you be
willing to come with me to get some more?"

"Sure." He ran a hand through that rumpled daguerreo-
type hair and seemed relieved at the suggestion. "That was
pretty awesome."

"Yeah, I guess it was." A couple making out blocked their
way downstairs. "Hi, would you mind heading back to the
event? Our guests aren't really supposed to be in this part of
the club." The couple untangled, annoyed. Ava shook her
head and glanced at Ben, hoping for an acknowledgement
of the couple's rudeness, a passing moment of intimacy, of
experiencing themselves as a pair in opposition to the rest
of the world, but he was rolling up the bottom of his tie,
and the awkwardness between them remained. "Sorry about
that," Ava apologized.

He looked up, letting the tie drop. "What? Oh, sorry I
got a little distracted. I guess I didn't expect you to have so
many people. I think I was picturing something different
from the way you talked about everything."

"Yeah, I think I was, too," Ava agreed, glad to have some-one else articulating her vague unease of the party for her.

They left the club in silence. Ben seemed to be so much on the verge of talking that Ava kept looking at him ex-pectantly, only to be disappointed and then confused. She was starting to wonder if now that their shared task of con-struction was over, maybe they just didn't have much to say to each other. She touched her earrings, reassured by the smooth hardness of rhinestones.

When they arrived at the store, Ben stopped, his hand on the brass handle of the plate glass. "You know this place is really expensive. There's a cheaper one over on Lexington. I don't know if that kind of stuff matters to you." He smiled at her nervously, then looked away.

Hoping this might be a pretext to draw out their walk, Ava nodded, glad to rest from the tumult of the party in his company. "Of course it matters. If we had a penny to spare, it would go to you first."

"Yeah, I spent way too many hours on that stuff for you guys. I'm kind of screwed." They waited for a light to change. "You want to do something nice for someone and then you have to act like an asshole because you can't pay your elec-tric bill." He kicked at an empty cigarette pack. "You guys are going to pay me for it, right?"

"Of course. As soon as we start accepting members."

"It looked like a pretty fancy crowd," he acknowledged. "I was doing some construction in a gallery today, and the girl there had heard of you. She was planning on coming tonight. I wonder if you would have even noticed if I hadn't shown up." He checked her reaction.

"I would have definitely noticed," she said, distracted by the information that a random gallerist knew of her and her plans. No one had ever recognized Ava for anything before. The idea that her name had a life outside of herself, that it had acquired a set of associations and interests that extended beyond her physical presence, felt like a violation, scary and strangely exciting. "What else did she say?"

"Who?"

"This girl you were working with." Ava wondered that Ben could seem so uninterested in the amazing fact of her celebrity.

"Nothing much. I guess Stephanie really does know a lot of people in this town. This girl was not a fan and had some pretty choice things to say about a gallery she used to run or something, but I don't know the details." His voice trailed off a little. "You just might want to be careful, I guess."

At each person she passed, she wondered just for a moment if they were on their way to her event, and if they knew that she was right here walking among them. She, who had built an idea, a salon, a real, tangible thing so alluring that strangers in art galleries wanted to visit it. Outside of a deli, a stack of newspapers rustled like applause. For the first time, she felt herself moving through the streets solid, consequential, not like the ghost she so often felt like, floating outside the web of interconnected lives and noise and motion. An empty soda bottle skidded out of her way. "Stephanie's got her problems, but it's amazing what she can pull off sometimes. She's the most driven person I've ever met."

"Yeah, driven to do what, though?" he asked and Ava couldn't quite put it into words. Men always wanted such clear definitions of things. She felt she understood Stephanie's blind need to make her mark on the world, in whatever capacity that took, to find in success, any success, the respect, the approval, in essence the safety otherwise denied her. "I just got the impression that maybe she's burnt a couple of bridges at some point," he said. "But maybe that's not correct."

He was walking too fast, and Ava wanted to put a hand

on his arm to slow him down, but she didn't. She felt the need to keep defending Stephanie even though something about the conversation felt distracting, as though they were actually supposed to be talking about something else, but Ava couldn't figure out what it was and didn't want to risk another lapse into silence. "Being as pretty as she is can really mess with your head."

"You're pretty, and you don't seem messed up." He looked back at her and, noticing he was ahead, slowed, suddenly causing Ava to bump into his shoulder.

She snorted. "I'm not pretty like that. I'm the awkward best friend with her nose in a book, who no one ever notices."

"Yeah, that's not quite how I would describe you," he interrupted. A taxi brayed and accelerated past them with a lurch.

Again, he got that look, a certain impression of immanence, like he was about to say something else, but he didn't, so Ava just kept filling the space between them with words. "Well, I could never have done this without her. And it's pretty amazing, like I might finally find someone who wants to talk about the Franco-Prussian War and Flaubert or something. That's why I'm doing this."

"I could be into the Franco-Prussian War." Ben smiled.

"Really?" Ava asked, excitedly. "Did you know the front lines came right up to Rimbaud's home, and he kept running away right into the middle of it? What a fearless little troublemaker he was. It's so attractive." She cast a sidelong glance in Ben's direction, flirtatiously.

"I'm sorry. I don't know anything about either that war or who that person is. Would the Boer War count?"

Ava tried to hide her disappointment. "The Boer War is okay."

"Man, Ava, a guy can't make jokes around you. I don't

know anything about the Boer War either. How much homework would I have to do just to ask you out on a date?"

This was exactly the sort of thing Ava had been made fun of for her whole life, and the nerve, when touched, sent little waves of shock and dismay through her that Ben would stoop to such a thing. The quick fierceness of her reaction made her realize just how much she'd come to expect his friendship, proud that someone so smart and talented would bestow his acceptance on her, and the abrupt removal of that feeling of security made her whole body stiffen. "I don't mean to be the kind of person you would have to do research for. It's not my intention to be so nerdy."

Ben, who had been watching her intently, shook his head as if confirming something and sighed. The silence between them resumed.

Even in his silence, Ava was drawn to him. He had that faraway look, an impression of distance she associated with the portraiture of another age that made him so easy to transpose into another century, and this made her want to hold on to him, to find some way to reassert their friendship, force him to keep talking. She couldn't think of anything.

"So do you know what I do for fun?" he asked suddenly.

"What?" she asked, glad for his initiative.

"Bird-watching. See," he said when she laughed incredulously. "Now who's the nerd?"

The admission felt like a gift, and for the first time that night, she felt a tremulous connection, a coil of human warmth binding her to another person. She liked the thought of Ben leaning against a tree in rapt contemplation of the birds, alone and lost in his imagination. "Is that where you think about art stuff?" she asked.

He shook his head. "Not really, it's just a hobby. Actually, I do so much other work these days, I guess making art is my hobby now. That's pretty demoralizing." He spoke to the steps of a brownstone. "I'm sorry. I haven't really tried to be charming in a while. I've become such a downer. New York City is spoiling my game." He sighed. "Not that I ever had much of one. In college, I thought the way to a girl's heart was making her big heavy things in the wood shop. I'm just going to shut up now."

Ava had stopped paying attention, caught on the implications of the word "game" he seemed to have just used in relation to her. However, true to his word, he did stop talking, and when she finally noticed the quiet, she realized she should say something. "Did the girls like the things you made?"

He laughed as they entered the bedlam of Saturday night at the liquor store. "Only the weird ones."

Ava watched two drunken women count out the price of a bottle of Prosecco in quarters. "I think it sounds like an amazing thing to be able to do for someone."

Ben's smile was so fraught with meaning that Ava actually turned around to see if anything unusual was happening behind her. "Let's get your wine," he said, happily striding down one of the narrow, crowded lanes of the store.

When they got back to the Lazarus Club, Castor opened the door. "It seems like a very successful party," he said to the top of Ben's head, and Ava got a creeping feeling along the back of her neck.

"Oh god, come on." She gave Ben a gentle shove. His back was ever so slightly damp, and she felt the hard ridge of his spine bristle at the touch of her fingertip.

12

By the time they arrived upstairs, the crowd, no longer contained within the library, spilled into the hallway, rolling like lava. The noise had increased exponentially, and Ava, as she pushed between sweaty backs and laughing faces, was taken aback by the enthusiastic din. A man, a peony wilting in his lapel, tapped her on the arm. "Isn't it just too Gatsby in here for words?" A woman in a party dress shrieked with delight. Ava smiled politely, glancing back to make sure Ben was following. He looked besieged and wielded the case of wine in his arms as if to ward off the clamor. Seeing that she was watching, he managed a weak smile. Everyone was smoking, and a thick anachronistic haze floated above the party. The windows were open, but the warm summer night disdained to enter, and the heat was intolerable. From across the room she heard George's quavering baritone singing "Pack Up Your Troubles in Your Old Kit Bag." She looked around for Stephanie, noticing empty and half-full cups on every surface.

As she followed the singing, she passed Aloysius gesticulating plaintively at Sam Bates. "I mean, the way people talk about the club, it's like they don't even know that W.E.B.

Dubois once gave a talk here and even had lunch in the club dining room—well, maybe not in the dining room exactly, but pretty near it, I believe," he said earnestly. Mrs. Bellamy hovered nearby watching Aloysius suspiciously. Sam Bates looked stupefied. Ava was pretty sure he wasn't ever coming back.

They found George, and Ben deposited the case of wine at his feet with a rattle. "George, what is going on in here? It's crazy," Ava asked, horrified.

"We're a long way from Sunnyside," he agreed gleefully. George had lost his jacket, and his tie hung loose around his neck. He held out a bottle for her inspection. "The liquor guy showed up right after you left."

"Marshmallow-flavored vodka? Are you serious?" A ring of crystals lined the neck of the bottle. "That looks vile."

"They've already been through nine bottles of it." He swung an arm at the room. "You may think it looks like something for Russian oligarchs, but this gang can't get enough." He drained the last of a clear liquid from his cup and grimaced. "It's not that bad." He took the bottle back to refill his glass and those of two giggling young women who appeared at his elbow. "Ladies."

"Who's behind the bar? And where's Stephanie?"

"I haven't seen her. Rodney's bartending. Apparently my mores were not up to his professional standards, which is funny because it's not like we even have anything to mix with this swill." He took another swig and rolled it around his mouth. "It's like the taste of a Tampa debutante."

"How would you know?"

"Every Jew can dream, can't he?"

Someone yelled compliments at someone else farther across the room. "Have people been complaining about all this noise?" Ava asked. "Club members?"

"Nonstop." George nodded, pointing at Mrs. Bellamy

who was in fact now yelling something angrily at Aloysius. George continued, "But Aloysius was being interviewed by somebody and kept chasing everyone away for trying to 'dim his limelight.' That guy really wants to be in the newspapers."

Ben tapped her on the shoulder. "I need a drink." She felt she should make excuses, but she wasn't sure how to explain all of this, and he slipped away before she could start.

She picked up the case of wine, and almost tripped over a pair of models who lay entwined on the Persian carpet. A tall man fanned them with the galley copies of a fashion magazine. "You look so good in front of all of these books," one was saying to the other admiringly.

When she got to the bar, Ben was nowhere to be seen, but Rodney, a bottle of vodka in each hand, was holding forth. "It's called dialectical materialism, but the really fantastic part is that you don't really have to do anything. You've just got to wait." He grinned, topping the glasses of two men in cravats who listened attentively. "Maybe hurry it along if the occasion presents itself. Vodka?" he asked Ava.

"No, thanks." She dropped the box and joined him behind the bar, grateful for the relative safety behind two feet of polished wood. "I'm a little overwhelmed."

Rodney poured himself two fingers of liquor. "I haven't seen a crowd like this in here—" he threw back his shot "—well, ever. Some of these guys are a real kick."

"Aren't you supposed to be downstairs?"

"Nah, the barback is covering for me. How'd you get so many hot girls to come to a book thing?"

Ava opened a bottle and smelled it. "That's a good question. I have no idea." She screwed the cap back on. Rodney leaned his free hand on the bar, his willowy torso bent taut, and looked down at her from his superior height. "What?" she asked.

"You, gals." He shook his head. "You gals are a piece of work." He said this with great affection and a curt, approving nod. "I thought I was doing my part just getting them drunk downstairs, but this is some next level infiltration."

"I don't think I can take credit for any revolutionary intent," she began and then, suddenly worried he was about to lurch forward and kiss her, Ava took a step backward, nearly upsetting the drink of a redhead in turquoise jewelry who was discussing her colonic. The woman scowled and ashed her cigarette on the sleeve of someone else's pink linen suit.

An effete boy in a school blazer ran into the bar. "Someone's taking a bath," he announced. "This gorgeous thing just took off her clothes and got in the bathtub." There was a quick exodus as everyone hurried toward the bathroom.

"Aren't you curious?" Rodney was around the bar in two long strides.

"I don't think so, although maybe tell George."

Rodney ran toward the hall, and Ava assumed George would have to find out on his own.

In the nearly empty bar, Ava took a minute to smooth down her hair. That guy was right; it was getting pretty Gatsby in here. And while before she would have thought such a statement would thrill her, now that she was surrounded by beautiful drunken people behaving stupidly, it was not as fun as she expected. But then, she hadn't read it in a while. Wasn't that the point really, that no one was actually having fun? She again made a mental note to revisit some of the classics she had loved, maybe a little indiscriminately.

She pulled a bottle of wine from the case and opened it to chase away the discomfort she was feeling. She recognized one of her poets, sitting alone on a window ledge, his smudged glasses reflecting the nearby candles. He raised his eyebrows hopefully, and she poured him a cup, as well. "This is the most amazing reading I have ever been to," he said, taking a big gulp. "Please let us come back and help at your other events." He staggered into the other room.

Ava drank half of her wine in one long slow sip. She could hear yells and laughter; they would pour back in at any minute, and her moment of self-interrogation yielded before the crazed energy of this party. Even if it was not quite what she had expected, the undeniable success of it all broke around her, and she felt giddy, unsettled, as if on a carnival ride that has just changed directions, and she was plummeting one way while the rest of her floated a moment behind, unmoored by centrifugal force.

Ben came in and put his glass down on the bar, shaking his head as she moved to refill it. "Did you know your whole party is watching some girl get naked?"

"Pretty decadent." Ava refilled her own instead.

"For some reason I thought you might be upset."

She was adrift in a current, unexpected and glamorous, and it felt as if Ben was trying to pull her back, to set her once again on the dismal shore of her life where nothing ever happened and all she ever did was read. "You have to admit, it's very Gatsby," she said and wondered if that man's peony had shed all of its petals yet.

Tenderly, Ben ran a hand over the bar, brushing away ash and wiping a puddle of wine. "You shouldn't let spills sit on here. This finish isn't that strong."

"Don't be such a worrier." She laughed in a higher register than usual. "Have another drink."

He looked at her in a funny way that she couldn't decipher. "I think I might just to go home."

She was tempted to ask if she could come, if only so they could stop before they reached the subway, and sit for a while on the steps of a brownstone, under the watchful beam of a streetlamp, and talk. About anything, it didn't matter, just the pleasure of hearing his voice echo her own, locked in the soothing advance and retreat of conversation. She wanted to bounce her innermost thoughts against him and let him take each one and turn it around, molding it to the as yet unknown cast of his mind, and offer it back to her, changed and fascinating. But she was here, in her private club, supporting this wild tumult like Atlas on her shoulders. And maybe she liked it. "Okay," she said.

"Okay." He waited for another minute, and Ava almost thought he had changed his mind, but then he left, his hands in his pockets. "Bye."

A returning flood of thirsty guests soon shook her from her thoughts, and she and Rodney were kept busy serving drinks. Phillip Goldman took up a permanent position at the bar where he presided over the admiring attentions of young women, filling glasses from a bottle and loudly extemporizing lines of poetry. In the other room, someone had discovered *Hunting in Zambia*, vol. III, and was reading excerpts to hysterical laughter. Ava, distractedly spilling vodka over someone's Kaballah bracelet, was tempted to rescue the maligned volume. Another pile of books fell somewhere with a clatter. Ava dabbed perspiration from her forehead with the edge of her sleeve, and swallowed a glass of wine. Rodney patted her on the butt in a comradely manner, and they resumed filling the ceaseless procession of empty glasses.

Two hours later, the crowd suddenly left, obeying an instinctive swarm that this party was over and that other more exciting things must be happening somewhere in the torrid night. Ava sat on the bar, playing with one of the foil labels that littered its slick wooden surface, surrounded by empty cups, many of which had been used as ashtrays. "It's going to smell terrible in here tomorrow."

George, his arms splayed over the sides of a club chair someone had dragged into the bar, propped his feet on a radiator. "Like an off-track betting parlor." In answer to her quizzical look, he added, "I've spent an afternoon or two playing the ponies."

"You aren't old enough to bet on horses."

"True, but I had a drunk uncle who used to take me along when I was little."

"You kind of look like someone's drunk uncle right now."

He brushed his wrinkled shirtfront. "That's not what the ladies thought. I got two phone numbers this evening." From his pocket, he pulled a bunch of crumpled papers. "The proof is somewhere here. The rest are people that want to become members." He fanned out a handful of business cards. "Seriously." He passed them to Ava. "I believe the House of Mirth may be the end of my age of innocence."

She tossed a wadded-up napkin at him and flipped through the cards, names of strangers, each somehow substantiating their crazy project. "I can't believe this worked. I can't believe how many people showed up."

"Yeah, I don't know what I was expecting, but it wasn't this. Everyone was so—" he searched for a moment "—expensive-looking. Here it is." He held out a torn Post-it. "Digits. I really owe you two. I haven't been this universally admired since my bar mitzvah."

Stephanie poked her head in. "Here you guys are. Don't you want to come in the other room? I'm chatting with an internet billionaire about Ayn Rand."

"No," she and George said together.

"Okay, but his grandfather was like an Indian prince or something, so it's pretty cool." Stephanie leaned drunkenly against the doorjamb. "He's got a shark tank in his living room." Then, tilting her head back against the wall, she smiled with postcoital satisfaction. "Wasn't tonight amazing? Can you believe how many people came?"

"No." Ava held out the business cards. "Who were all these people?"

"Amazing, right?"

"I don't even know. It was kind of rambunctious and well-dressed for a book reading."

"Isn't she a snob?" Stephanie asked George. "I serve up your wildest dreams on a silver plate, and you're finding things to grumble about, silly girl." She hiccuped.

Ava wanted to ask her about the introduction she never got to give, but she had lost the thread of urgency; it felt like a petty thing to be upset about.

"Anyway, that guy with the lazy eye won the National Book Award last year."

"Who?"

"You never pay attention to anything important." She took hold of Ava's hands. "We should be really proud of what we accomplished here."

"Are you? Is this what you wanted?" Ava asked.

Her drunken gaze cleared slightly. "Yes, it was everything and more. I want what's best for us. You just need to trust me."

She wrapped her arms around Ava's waist and leaned against her, bending down so that they could be forehead to forehead. In the soft inebriation of Stephanie's embrace, Ava tried to frame the discontent that had been lurking around her all evening into words, but it kept dissolving in the tender pressure of small arms around her back. She closed her eyes and felt the cool breath of her friend against her cheek, sweet and slightly sharp, the smell of strawberry gum and grain alcohol. "Your reader was better," Ava said finally.

"I know." Stephanie didn't move but she smiled.

A voice called from the other room impatiently, "Where is our librarian? The driver's downstairs. I'm starving."

"Just coming." Stephanie raised her head and gave Ava

a kiss on the cheek that missed and struck air. "Duty calls. Give me a ring when you wake up."

"I feel like I could sleep forever."

"You should. We deserve it." She turned away. "I know the most divine little tapas place where we can really talk." Her voice receded as she left.

"Well, George, shall we pack up?" Ava tapped his shoulder to rouse him. "I say we leave the cleaning for tomorrow. I'm exhausted." She strolled into the other room, trying to remember where she had put her keys. The beginning of the event felt like a million years ago. She blew out the remaining candles.

He followed, bleary-eyed, rubbing his head. "Indeed, I think I may avail myself of our lovely accommodations for the evening." He flopped down full-length on the Persian carpet. "Too many ardent spirits."

"Gross. That thing is so dirty. I saw like three people spill drinks on it."

"S'okay." His voice was muffled by the pile of the rug.

"Come on." Ava grabbed a limp arm. "You can sleep on my floor. It's better than this." He allowed himself to be pulled to his feet.

"Casualties of success," he muttered, draping an arm over her shoulder for balance. "You're a nice boss."

"Thanks, George." Steadying him with a hand on his bony waist, she turned off the lights as they passed.

Downstairs, Castor glanced at George. "I see he enjoyed your party."

"Yeah." It was all an undeniable triumph, and yet now, standing unsteadily before Castor's sober gaze, all Ava could summon about the whole thing was a sneaking feeling of embarrassment.

"Someone left this for you." He handed her a small cardboard box.

"Thanks." She examined it with one hand, supporting George with the other, and they moved slowly down the long corridor in a wide, swaying pattern like a roll of ribbon gently unraveling. "Are you humming Wagner?" she asked as they waited for the elevator.

"Bugs Bunny." He waved his finger in time to the music. "That Tristan overture is too damned hard to whistle." Her ear was pressed against him, and the vibrations in his chest rattled—not quite in tune, but soothing. When she got him into her room and onto her chair, she took off his shoes and, after a worried glance, unpinned the safety pins holding up his pants hems. By the time she put a large glass of water on the floor next to him, he was already asleep, clutching a velvet throw pillow, his steady breath rustling its tassels.

Ava changed into pajamas and turned on her fan. The roar of its metal blades filled the room, and she climbed into bed with a large bottle of seltzer and her mystery box. Mycroft leapt to her side to investigate, dragging his tail across the sweating plastic bottle and leaving a trail of hair on its label. He chewed tentatively on a corner of the box, purring and rubbing its sharp point against his gums. When she opened it, he pressed his face between the rough edges of the open flaps, rearing back and blinking against the pressure, then reapplying himself until his whiskers bent far back. She gave him a shove and out of the cardboard box removed another box, smaller, wooden and perfectly square. A tiny brass latch held each side to the lid and when she opened them all, and lifted the lid, the side fell open to reveal another wooden square, almost the same size, made up of smaller wooden cubes stacked on top of each other. They started to slide precariously without the support of the walls and Ava carefully set the whole thing down on the floor. Each cube was made of a different kind of wood and together they formed a sepia-hued mosaic, like a Rubik's Cube made a hundred years ago.

She picked up a cube and held it in her hand, amazed at how smooth and slick and satisfyingly tactile each was, then she carefully placed it back in its proper corner. She closed up the box again for the pleasure of working the tiny, intricate golden latches and then let the sides once more splay open revealing this incomprehensible object, orderly, but nonsensical, burnished yet mathematical, hidden but totally exposed.

Ben.

She should call him. She should thank him. Somehow this silent object spoke to her so eloquently, its message of kindred sympathy was so clear, yet so peripheral to the broad gestures of language that it seemed that anything she could try to put into words would confuse or discolor this perfect confession. It was strange, but she had never had a male friend before. After so many years of Catholic school, men seemed to her like phantoms, alien creatures dimly visible from the female planet on which all of her emotions were centered. She felt proud and grateful to be the recipient of such a remarkable thing and a little jealous that he could make something like this exist. She wished she could answer in kind.

She took a small ivory card from her desk and, with the one fountain pen that currently had black ink, wrote in the middle of the page in excessive, ornate script, "Thank you." Looking at the two small words, she felt overwhelmed by their paucity. The frustrations of the entire night seemed to well up around the blank space of the small page, a silence that pressed in on her, dense and impenetrable. She tossed the card aside.

George snored quietly from the chaise, and Ava struggled with a dissatisfaction that she couldn't articulate but that seemed to reverberate in the creaking of the old walls and floors, groaning around her small body in the rich darkness of the summer night.

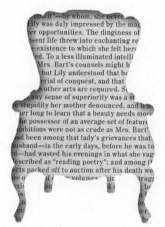

PART TWO

13

After the indisputable success of their grand opening, the next few months passed by in a swirl of parties and events, and Ava was amazed at how quickly what had seemed like a total reversal of her previous life could become routine, and even begin to slide into monotony. Every day she was at her desk in the library as before, but a new churning pattern of tasks kept her busy—arranging mailing lists, writing up invitations to events, ordering chair rentals and plastic cup deliveries, a daily race to keep the parties happening. Or else she was navigating the stream of unhappy Lazarus Club members who poured in to complain about whatever the previous week's festivities had been. Ava's neighbor, Mrs. Grierson, no longer smiled at her on the landing, and worse, her mahjong group had quietly relocated to the parlor downstairs, and Ava had pointedly not been notified of the shift.

But it had quickly become clear that the clientele of the House of Mirth was interested in parties, and since a few had actually paid membership dues and so many others promised they were going to "officially join" any day, Ava and Stephanie felt obliged to keep giving them what they wanted. So Ava stood in front of querulous old ladies, eyes downcast, apologetically murmuring promises she knew she had no intention of keeping—about keeping the noise and the crowds and the general uproar down.

Their situation with the Lazarus Club was tentative already. At the next board meeting, after they had done their best to answer to a barrage of outrage over their first event—how could they bring that kind of element into the club, what were they thinking, the smoke, the noise, the chaos, it was an absolute betrayal—Ava and Stephanie had been able to hand over a check for three thousand dollars, and the tenor in the room changed fairly dramatically.

"Very good, very good." Mr. Dearborn had examined the check with a relish that Ava was starting to get confused by—weren't these people all rich?—and then told them that since their rent had been prorated from the beginning of the summer, they were actually still two months behind, and this would need to be paid as soon as possible in the interest of everyone maintaining civil relations. Luckily they had recently been the subject of a full-page article in the Sunday Styles section of the paper that included a large flattering picture of Aloysius. So again he assured them that he would look out for their interests and not to worry. The further they entered into the workings of the Lazarus Club, the odder and more byzantine it all became. Fortunately, Ava was too busy now to think much about it; there was always a new event to plan, a bathroom to clean, lipstick and heels to put on for the next event on their calendar.

Today, she was looking at the evidence of their latest destruction. Things were definitely getting out of hand. At the reading of the night before, a guest, beautiful, young and very drunk, had decided to try and climb onto the mantel to reach a book on a nearby shelf. When she fell, she landed safely in the arms of the hedge fund trader who had been admiring her from below, but she broke off a chunk of the antique frame of the mirror over the mantel.

The huge mirror now leaned precipitously away from the remaining corner of its frame, showing Ava a grossly elongated view of the bottom of her legs. She had already tried stacking books against it, but they didn't seem to be offering any real support, and it was pretty clear when the mirror came down it would just do so, unimpeded by a shower of books. An air of suspended catastrophe permeated the room. While the snow blew high against the windows, and the cold radiators stood silently below, Ava waited for Stephanie to arrive so she could yell at her about the mirror. The incident seemed somehow so representative of the distasteful direction that their literary club had taken.

It was almost dismaying how right Stephanie had been: people who spend all of their evenings at fancy parties desperately wanted to think of themselves as people who read. The House of Mirth Literary Society brilliantly accorded them that illusion. But book parties, it turned out, were still parties, and "readings followed by a cocktail reception" felt more and more like cocktail receptions saddled with preliminaries, and Ava was starting to get despondent. People came in ever-increasing numbers. Businessmen in smooth silk ties pushed their midlife bellies against the bar—magnanimous patrons of the arts. Willowy girls who had majored in literature but now worked in PR found the bohemian parties they had moved to New York dreaming of, and chased the rich men, their ambition lit by the glow of artificial bronzer. Young artists complained of being broke in the international accents of Swiss boarding schools, Riviera vacations, and trips home to South American rubber plantations. Stephanie presided over them all. Fellow strivers gratefully hitched themselves to her upward trajectory, while those on top found her continually charming—always so well dressed, so amusing, so clever. It was left to Ava to pour drinks and mop up spills, watching the world she had helped to create from the other side of a growing despair.

She started to go numb from the chill and stomped her feet to warm up until she noticed the mirror trembling and contented herself with briskly rubbing the arms of her coat, shedding vintage rabbit fur as she did. Something was wrong with the heat. She drained the last of the cold tea in her cup and unwound a length of black tulle from her bag. Her plan was to hide the damage as well as she could before any of today's old ladies saw it. She was engaged in this effort, hanging from the side of the library ladder that didn't quite reach, when Stephanie finally arrived swaddled to her ears in white cashmere. "What on earth are you doing?"

"It's the best I can think of," Ava answered curtly.

"How bad is it? Does it look as bad today as it did last night?" Stephanie moved a swath of fabric aside and groaned. "I can't ask her to pay for it. Her dad owns most of Times Square. If they hear we're broke, we're done for."

"I don't understand why we put up with these rich idiots if they aren't ever going to give us any money."

"They will. It just takes time. Spare me the lecture, Trotsky. We need to figure this out."

"That's a rather ominous comparison." Ava twisted the dark fabric into a concealing valance. "Why not Lenin, if that's what you're accusing me of?"

"Because unlike some of us, you have no stomach for the necessities of running an empire." Stephanie picked at invisible lint from the sweater that encased her like swan's down. "I had one of those posters on my wall in college, if you remember."

There had in fact been a brief moment when Stephanie had been the toast of the student workers collective and had taken to wearing a jaunty cap with a red star that made her look like a French movie star flirting with communism until she did end up dating the very tall, charismatic president of the whole thing, at which point he began to bore her and she moved on to men who didn't have philosophical objections to buying her expensive dinners. Ava thought wistfully of this uncanny ability Stephanie had to evoke desire in even the most unlikely places. Someone always wanted her, and this state of affairs gave Ava a funny ache, small but raw, and she tried to chase it away by pointlessly stacking more books against the leaning glass.

Stephanie watched her trying to drape fabric over the broken frame. "You know what we have to do," she said finally.

"Stop inviting the daughters of oligarchs to our parties."

"There you go again. But seriously, Ben would know how to fix this."

Ava had one fleeting moment of thinking that Stephanie was joking and then, as so often seemed to happen these days, realized she was perfectly serious. "We didn't pay him, remember? He hates us."

"He just had a fit. Artists are temperamental people. I'm sure you could get him to do it."

It seemed impossible that Stephanie could be so unaware of the sacrifice that the whole incident had exacted on Ava. It wasn't that long after their opening night that Ben had asked her point-blank to pay him for making the bar. They hadn't spoken of his gift, but in a shy smile, a quick exchange of understanding glances, they seemed to have agreed that they could leave their declarations of sympathy unspoken, taking their time in the exciting silence of immanent possibility. "Acting like idiots," had been Stephanie's annoyed way of putting it.

He brought up the money at the end of another wild evening, while Ava was drunkenly consolidating the dregs of multiple wine bottles to recork and be served again. "I know it's my fault. I spent too much time on it. I wanted to make it really special." Ava looked up, noticed him blush, and spilled a little wine. "But I'm kind of down to the wire, and I can't afford to put it off anymore." He watched the dark liquid slosh in quick circles around her plastic funnel. "It's really humiliating to have to ask."

"More humiliating than what I'm doing right now?" Ava pushed in a cork and started a new bottle with a tipsy attempt at levity. But he didn't smile. He looked at the floor with a discomfort that made Ava sorry for joking. "It's so beautiful," she said. "We love it so much. It's just that we're so broke."

Just then, Stephanie wandered in looking for a corkscrew. "One of the owners of the Knicks just proposed to me." She giggled. "I told him he better buy a platinum patron top tier membership. Which I just made up." She waited, hand upraised for Ava to strike in celebration, then shrugged and did a little dance.

"I know you guys are, but I paid for all the materials out of pocket." Ben pressed forward, reluctantly.

"Oh my god, are you guys talking about the bar? Please." Stephanie picked up the corkscrew and waved it dangerously close to his face with a wobbly assertiveness. "You've gotten so much exposure. Everybody loves our bar. You should be paying us." Then to Ava's dismay, Stephanie wrapped an arm around her shoulders, pulling her close, in a mistaken display of consensus.

Ben looked at Ava, and his disgust seemed to confirm an esteem that she had just forfeited. His expression hardened. "I should have known." Then, despite his anger, unable to resist first wiping up a puddle of spilled wine on the surface of the bar, he threw the soiled paper in the trash and left. Ava hadn't heard from him since. Sometimes she looked at the little wooden box on her mantel, and its presence there offered some consolation like the stinger of a bee left behind, some piece of Ben embedded in her life, a link to the things she still associated with him—art, poetry, genius, all manner of higher things that Ava wanted in her life but that seemed to be drifting ever farther away in his absence.

"Now, Ava, I know you liked him. This is a perfect way to get you two back together."

"Stephanie, I'm not like you. Guys don't just fall all over themselves to do stuff for me. That was like my one chance." She felt all choked up for a minute and, embarrassed, stopped.

"One chance for what? For a boyfriend? Please."

"I even told my mom about him and then I had to call her back and say he disappeared, and she made the most dis-appointed sound I've ever heard, and I've made her make a lot of disappointed sounds in my life. She told me I was ut-terly hopeless. And she's obviously right." Ava didn't mean to sound quite so hurt, but it didn't seem to matter because it didn't appear to faze Stephanie in the least. The cavalier way she had become accustomed to brushing off Ava's concerns—that this whole project wasn't like a salon, that it wasn't even about books at all—had become rather second nature.

"All the more reason to patch it up. It will be good for you to have a project. I handle too much of everything these days. It's bad for you. You're getting shy again. Come down, I have something to show you. Our article is out."

Ava secured the tulle with one last tack, bruising her thumb as she did so, and descended the ladder slowly to ex-press her disapproval. Reluctantly, she took the magazine Stephanie was holding toward her. "House of Flirts!" read the headline. Ava had gotten so used to this kind of press she was able to grudgingly admire the pun. She and Stephanie had proved irresistible; reporters could pretend to be writ-ing about culture, then file a shiny pictorial of New York nightlife, and the requests for interviews kept coming. In this latest photo, Ava sat on a pile of books in a borrowed evening gown, champagne glass upraised, propped on one hand like a tipsy odalisque. Stephanie crouched behind her, staring down the camera, chewing on the arm of a pair of glasses without lenses. "Oh dear," she said.

"You look fabulous," Stephanie countered angrily.

Ava decided against trying to explain the uncomfortable amalgam of pride and embarrassment the picture evoked in her. While it was a little dismaying to be so stripped of her usual identity, that she could be this beautiful stranger, even if only frozen on the glossy pages of a magazine, fed a hunger that she didn't really want to acknowledge. In the silence of two dimensions, she and Stephanie looked almost evenly matched, equivalent. She turned away to avoid the dark, self-immolating thrill of it, handing the magazine back.

Stephanie read, a slight furrow of concentration between her brows. She sighed, running her fingers gently over the page, and when she finally looked up, a smile lay over her features, elated, serene. When she failed to find this ecstatic reaction mirrored in her friend, her face closed, the shimmering pleasure retreated, and her voice was brisk. "They called us a nightclub again. Why do people keep doing that?"

"Because stuff like this doesn't happen in a goddamned library," Ava said, pointing at the mirror and getting mad again. "And why is it only socialites? How come we still don't have any young writers, or MFA students or artists or anyone who might actually want to talk to me instead of just people that want to get their pictures taken with you?"

But Stephanie was lost again to the hypnotic thrall of the pages. "I have to send this to my mom. She's so proud of me."

All at once, Ava deflated. Stephanie's mom had come to visit three years ago, right after Stephanie's gallery had been shut down, and she hadn't even stayed twenty-four hours, complaining that Stephanie's apartment was dingy and her friends weren't going anywhere and if she wanted to hang around a bunch of losers, she might as well have stayed in Cedar Rapids. Ava had shared the quiche Stephanie baked for the occasion and then picked Stephanie up off the bathroom floor when she passed out that night, hair damp with vomit and vodka. "Do you want a cup of tea?" she asked.

Stephanie nodded as Ava placed a kettle on the coils of an old hot plate. "So we've got another gala to go to next week. There'll be some people there that I think might be able to help us with the board if they become members."

"No, I'm not going." Whenever the rich friends, so generally evasive about membership dues, found themselves with empty seats at charity events, they often called Stephanie to bring her entourage of somewhat famous writers and beautiful young women. At first, Ava had gone too, seduced by the chance to spend an evening in the grand cultural spaces of New York—libraries and museums and historic mansions—but invariably it involved a series of older men with sweaty hands taking unseemly pleasure in Stephanie's company. Also, galas were boring and it took like four hours to be served any food and then it was three sprigs of asparagus and a chicken breast, small recompense for the creepy transactional feeling of the whole evening.

"It's outrageous of them to want money from us. Before this, when was the last time the Lazarus Club was mentioned in a magazine? We're such an asset. They just need to hear it from other fancy old people. All we need is one big philanthropist to back us, and the board will drop the whole thing. I'm sure of it."

"We should pay rent. We signed a lease. It's not their fault all our money goes toward paying you a living wage. What kind of tea do you want?"

"I swear you are being obtuse on purpose. Roar of Thunder."

"These are charging bison on the package—why do you want tea to turn you into a buffalo?"

"I'm a raging bull. It's us against the world. I need my strength."

"I'm pretty sure this is not the world. This is a very specific and absurd predicament of our own creating."

"This from the girl who had spent two years here alone, darning socks. Is that what you want?" Ava looked away. "I'll take care of the board, and you get our stupid mirror fixed before we get evicted and can't make any money to pay off your dumb credit card."

At the mention of her debt, Ava felt a familiar rise in her throat, but she was learning from experience that she wouldn't actually throw up. It was just the bilious manifestation of the state of indenture. She swallowed it down and dropped a tea bag of Lady Grey into a delicate lilac cup. The cups steamed, and Ava realized she had forgotten to warm them first. She had been clinging to such traditions lately, as if by enacting the rituals of the great estates, she could inhabit for a moment the security of the ruling class. It didn't work. She cradled a cup in her hand, grateful for its heat. "We have to pay off that debt. We have to," she said finally.

"So let's not get kicked out." Stephanie drummed her fingernails against the bar.

"He looked so disappointed in me."

"Here's a thing about men—the worse he thinks you are, the more awesome he will feel about himself when he forgives you. It actually works out better this way." Stephanie had been checking her eyebrows in the reflective dome of the kettle but noticed Ava's expression. "What?"

"Nothing."

They carried their tea to the desk and sat opposite each other. Stephanie, her legs crossed on the desk, computer perched on her lap, chewed a clump of hair as she typed. Ava, whose chair had wheels, had been imperceptibly slipping farther and farther away from her typewriter as she wrote letter after letter begging donors for contributions until her chin was practically level with the desk. It made it convenient to rest her forehead against her keyboard after writing some particularly egregious untruth. The radiators boomed every now and then, causing both girls to look toward them hopefully, but no heat was forthcoming.

After a while, Ava noticed the absence of keystrokes from Stephanie's side of the desk. She was picking at her nails. "I really do wish you were coming with me. I always feel so much better when you're there. That financial journalist always tries to kiss me. And it's awkward. He smells like VapoRub."

Ava shivered. "You should punch him in the face."

"No, he might be useful to us at some point." Stephanie looked up. "Oh, you're joking."

Ava felt bad. "I wasn't really. Take George as a chaperone."

"Rich guys never take him seriously. Not like you. It's weird, it's like they get embarrassed or something. It's that look you get. It makes them way more respectful." She closed her laptop and began opening their mail.

Ava plucked at the fur of her coat. Fluff escaped from her fingers, borne away on a passing draft. "There must be some other way to make all this work."

"When you figure it out, let me know."

"It's just so gross," Ava said, but fear of what she would do without Stephanie, now that she had somehow allowed herself to be sunk into thousands of dollars of debt, silenced her objections.

When things had been going well with Ben, and her mother seemed suddenly disposed to ring her up for bright, chatty conversations about clothes and what hairstyles might suit her better than her helmet of braids, Ava had tried mentioning her debt. Her mother had so much money, after all. And her mother's voice had immediately taken on that chill, the feeling for Ava of the sun suddenly going behind the clouds, and had asked, "It's for the project with that girl, isn't it? When will you ever learn?" and the subject had somehow permanently been put to rest.

Stephanie made a sudden sound of strangled rage, and Ava looked up. "What?" Stephanie folded the letter she had been reading and jammed it into its envelope; Ava could see the twinning letters of the Lazarus insignia in one corner, and asked again, more urgently, "What do they want now?"

Stephanie stared straight ahead, a panicked, unfocused expression that looked right through Ava, as if she were about to cry and then, just as Ava, unnerved, asked one more time what was the matter, the color returned to her face like a slide clicking into place, and she blinked, as if Ava had just come into focus from a long way away. "Nothing. Don't worry about it."

"What? What was that? What just happened?"

"I have to go. I'm meeting a fashion editor for drinks. She might do a shoot here, and I'm going to charge her a ton of money to do it. Have you seen that pair of heels I left here last week?" Stephanie crossed to the filing cabinet, rummaging around the collection of high heels that had for some reason accumulated in the bottom drawer, taking the letter with her.

"You're leaving already? What's going on? What about our nonprofit application?" Ava asked, a catechism to which they paid daily, desultory obeisance.

Stephanie kicked the drawer shut. "That one is your responsibility." She gave Ava a funny look that Ava couldn't quite decipher, but suddenly Stephanie seemed very far away. Ava wanted to call her back, to feel her fingertips on her friend's warm forearm and draw the inevitable, wordless comfort that Stephanie's skin always seemed to offer. "Do it today," Stephanie added with a strange emphasis, at once an echo of some great unspoken feeling and a deflection of further inquiry. "And don't forget you said you would go with Steve Buckley to that party for me tomorrow."

Ava had totally forgotten. "No. I don't want to. I hate that guy."

"Someone has to. He saw one of our articles and now wants to get more involved. There's more money there. If we're ever going to pay this rent, we can't not try." Stephanie paused as she tied the ends of her scarf in the slice of mirror still visible under all the tulle. "I can't do everything, Ava."

Again, a strange shift in tone occurred; an unaccustomed solemnity that coursed in the low tremble to her voice made Ava want to reach out and pull Stephanie to her, and offer comfort. And she felt guilty about not going to Stephanie's gala. She always felt guilty about something these days. "No. I don't know. Maybe."

Stephanie looked at her through the mirror for one long, pregnant moment, her face like a duckling lost in the swelling of her scarf. "Thanks." Then she hurried away, the letter still clenched in her fist.

To silence the queasy, confusing feeling Stephanie left behind her, Ava looked around for a task—something tangible and productive to do, a defiant push against the sinking paralysis that she sometimes felt in her friend's company. She started looking up the different grants available to literary organizations, but she had done this many times before, and as always, everything she found required them to have 501(c)(3) status. She had promised she would do it, so from under a pile of accumulated junk mail, she found their copy of form 1023, "Application for Recognition of Exemption Under Section 501(c)(3) of the Internal Revenue Code." She flipped through the thick stack of instructions for form 1023 that she had printed out. Once again, she tried with steadfast heart to answer the questions that seemed so straightforward, but which immediately unfolded into an infinite number of possibilities like a philosophical proof whose foundational principles she hadn't grasped. She had actually tried to read Spinoza once because he was quoted in a Wodehouse story, and she had felt similarly defeated. At the fourth question, she started drawing little top hats on all of the letter *o*'s. Then a bunch of ostrich plumes in the margin and then a horse underneath them that was soon pulling a great catafalque across the whole of question six. She sighed and put down her pen. Instead she printed out a bunch of new letters asking for membership dues from Stephanie's rich friends and then to hide from the twinge of self-reflection, she opened a book of Edwardian detective stories. But other worries and concerns soon pressed upon her mind, and she closed the book without noticing and stayed at her desk, lost in anxious thought.

14

Because she didn't have the courage to refuse when Stephanie showed up the next day with a dress in a dry cleaning bag and lots of helpful suggestions as to the best ways to ask for money, Ava agreed to go to Steve Buckley's party. Since so little of their project had involved discussing books, Ava had few occasions to feel that she contributed anything useful, and more and more she felt prey to the worry that Stephanie might one day wake up to how unequal their relationship had become and cast her aside. This whole thing wasn't quite what she had envisioned, but any of her alternatives seemed terrifying. Her house, her job, her best friend, all were now inextricably tied to the fate of the House of Mirth. Also, there were some moments when the two of them were dressed up, shining with youth and sparkly eye shadow, standing arm in arm in front of a crowd of glamorous, fashionable people, that Ava felt a breathless wonder that this all somehow belonged to her.

So that night, Ava ended up at the rooftop bar of a fancy hotel in the meatpacking district, trying to make small talk while waiters circulated around a pool lit in a rotating kaleidoscope of neon colors, and stars shone in the clear night above. Because Stephanie had lent her clothes, the feeling that she was an impostor, an inevitable disappointment of extra pounds and dark hair, weighed even more so on her already stilted conversation. Luckily, Mr. Buckley proved so talkative, little was required of her. Words poured from him as if he were afraid the lingering notes of each previous sentence might somehow occlude the passage of the next, his intonation building in enthusiasm and urgency until the conversational crescendo subsided without any obvious cause, only to immediately start swelling up again. Ava found this unpredictable torrent of verbiage a little exhausting. He also seemed to require a lot of reassurance, and finally, sick of smiling and nodding after every thought, Ava looked away, vainly pulling up the front of her dress as it dipped and fluttered past her sternum.

Because of the season, they were enclosed in a glass box. An icy wind blew off the river, banging the awnings of the buildings below, while here, thirty floors above, people lounged on low chairs around a gently lapping pool lit by glimmering lanterns. The women were barely dressed; to be so nearly naked on a rooftop in January seemed just one more manifestation of the magical invulnerability of wealth. The men surveyed the women with self-congratulatory approval. Ava watched a waiter's fleeting expression of disgust as he mopped the spilled drink of a woman laughing loudly into a cell phone. A man in a sport coat and jeans lit a cigar, and the young woman next to him smiled through the smoke. A hungry-looking teenager in a sparkling dress sang along to a pop song as she squirmed on someone's lap, tapping an expensive shoe, her feet puppy large at the end of her spindly calves.

After a while, Steve Buckley stopped jiggling one crossed leg over the other and stood, professing a desire to mingle. Ava shrank from him, sure that this would be the moment when everyone's displeasure that she was not Stephanie would become too obvious to ignore, but he took her firmly by the elbow. A little shocked at this untoward self-assurance, Ava followed. To each new group of people, he introduced her as "my private librarian," and she was confronted with a shadowy, sexy fiction that fell over her like a painted flat obscuring the dusty, cluttered backstage of her ungainly self. She found she didn't actually mind it so much; it seemed to have such an immediate effect on people, everyone lighting up with a flirtatious eager welcome. There was something oddly relieving at being so labeled and therefore not responsible for explaining who she was in any real capacity. Sailing beneath the protection of Mr. Buckley's money and influence, she was complimented, cooed over, asked about her literary club, her answers hung on. His wealth commanded such a sphere of deference that for the first time she really understood why this mode of life appealed to Stephanie. She felt charming, commanding, safe. Disgracefully expensive bottles of champagne were ordered, and Ava drank immoderately, realizing that all those counts and barons she liked to read about must have felt like this their whole lives. A woman with slanted green eyes and a tragic Romanian lilt to her voice twirled one of Ava's curls between her fingers. "So beautiful," she murmured in her ear. "Thick like a horse's tail."

Beyond the diminishing reflections of their translucent enclosure, New York City glistened like a present offered just for her. How smart of them to drink in the sky like this, she thought, as her glass was replenished again unasked, like gods on Olympus. A few bottles later, a girl, six feet in heels with the soft, ripe face of a child model, brought Ava to the bathroom, giggling and whispering racist jokes of the former Soviet republics that Ava didn't understand. But this girl was beautiful, and to be the recipient of this passing affection almost seemed to raise Ava up, to include her in the sisterhood of striking beauty, and Ava responded eagerly, hungrily. Her arms grasped at the tiny waist and the friendship of a passing hour. The bathroom had plum-colored walls and a black glass chandelier, and the beautiful nymph offered her cocaine. Ava almost refused, but as the girl, whose name Ava hadn't caught, bent toward her, rummaging in a small silver bag propped against her thigh, the temptation to slide into this identity, one for which she was already dressed, proved overpowering. She didn't want to break the gossamer intimacy that bound the two of them, just two extravagantly beautiful women living the life that attends beauty. She had done cocaine once in college to feel closer to Sherlock Holmes but, as she inhaled, she realized that whatever she had done before was so inferior to what she was now consuming, it barely merited the same name.

The evening became more impressionistic after that, scenes of glimmering lucidity alternating with stretches of patchy darkness. She ended up in the pool at some point, in her cocktail dress, cavorting with other scantily clad young women like Rhine maidens keening for gold. One of them nibbled her ear while another, laughing, swam a lazy backstroke around them. Ava was overtaken by a blissful immediacy, and she floated in a succession of quickly passing moments where nothing had any consequences. Her past fell away, her boring previous life immaterial to this sparkling now, while the future consisted only of finding the glass of champagne she kept misplacing. She accepted offered cigarettes, delighting in the smoke, a substance as ephemeral as she felt, as if she had smoked her whole life. Everything was glorious.

At some point, she found herself in an animated conversation with Steve Buckley, urgently agreeing with everything he said, while his hands played against the silk dress that clung to her body like a wet tissue. The dark corner they had found almost demanded confidences, and she was absorbed in his recitation of a tragic childhood when he surprised her by wrapping his arms around her neck and leaning close over her ear, asking for a blow job.

At first, she wasn't sure she had even heard him correctly, but then, looking into his slightly unfocused but intent eyes, she realized that she had, and for some reason she felt flattered. An evening's worth of fawning and blandishments had worn down her critical faculties; if his wealth and status could be as admired as they seemed to be at this party, surely that must make him admirable himself, she figured. The champagne, the cocaine, the effervescent buoyancy of her evening all seemed a gift from this man, an act of generosity in bringing her with him into these giddy heights where pools floated thirty stories in the air and the winter wind couldn't touch you. It even struck her as affecting that among all the models and starlets, he had chosen her, and this seemed the final validation of the person she had started to become in the bathroom so many hours ago. She was glamorous, beautiful, triumphant; she owed it all to him. A blow job seemed the least she could do. Her knees hit the slick marble harder than she would have liked, and the thought that she would have bruises tomorrow was the first glimmer of her capacity to think about the future returning, but it was quickly swallowed by the darkness around her. She undid his pants and noticed with a disdainful twinge that he was wearing silk boxers, her disapproval of his fashion choices another indication of her critical faculties trying to surface. He wasn't erect, but as he was still looking down at her expectantly, she took him into her mouth. Then, as the cocaine in her system fought a valiant stand against a quickly approaching sobriety, she wondered what on earth she was supposed to do with this flaccid penis. She started to giggle. Giggling and the subsequent bouncing of unresponsive flesh against her tongue made the situation even more ridiculous, and she could feel that she was careening down a slope of amusement from which she wouldn't be able to recover. Steve Buckley didn't give her very long to try and removed himself with disgust. "Fuck the both of you," he said, walking away from her increasingly uncontrollable laughter.

It wasn't until she was shivering in the back seat of a cab, wet and mortified, that the thought cracked through the lingering haze of drugs and alcohol, that probably Steve Buckley would not be offering any further support to the House of Mirth, and that she had messed everything up once again.

When she told the whole sordid story the next day, looking for sympathy, while they waited in line for coffee, Stephanie was horrified. "Ava, that's one of our members, for fuck's sake. How unprofessional can you possibly be?"

Ava snapped the lid back on a bottle of ibuprofen, and put it back in her purse. "What, are you saying you haven't slept with him?" she said around the two pills on her tongue.

Stephanie offered her iced coffee with a disappointed shake of her head. "Of course not. What do you take me for? This is business."

"Can we just not talk about it anymore?" Ava drank most of the coffee in one long sip trying to ignore the brutal sweetness of Splenda that was setting her teeth on edge and then realized she needed to go home, immediately, and stay there for at least a day.

A day spent in her darkened bedroom did nothing to relieve the vertiginous feelings of regret and dismay that surged up and over Ava in successive waves. How could she have come to this? She tried writing, but every time she sat down to the quiet of her own head, it immediately filled with recrimination about the night before. She tried reading Thomas Hardy, but his heroine Bathsheba Everdene was so noble and virtuous and independent that Ava couldn't bear the comparison. She moped from bed to chaise and back again, trying to avoid the condemning eyes of all the portraits around her apartment—the plaster Athena, the portrait of Balzac looking all rumpled and sweaty, as if taken aback at her transgressions, and worst of all, Arthur Rimbaud with his beautiful eyes and his noble brow, and that other young man that he still called so strongly to her mind. Even Mycroft seemed to be avoiding her and spent the day napping behind the toilet.

Every time she accidentally remembered the feel of Steve Buckley against her tongue, the sharp acrid smell of him resurfaced and filled her with nausea. Why did women agree to do such things? How perfectly revolting. Eventually her stomach was protesting so much, she started to wonder if maybe she was just hungry; she had already gone through the last of the saltines, the one crumpled sleeve was all she had to eat in her apartment. She waited anxiously for four o'clock, the hour that the Lazarus Club laid out the cheap Brie and pâté for its members at cocktail hour. Now that she was so desperately poor, she often made do with this for her dinner.

She brushed her teeth and ran her fingers through her hair and, slipping into the reassuring dowdiness of a cardigan, ventured out into the world. As soon as she entered the ballroom, she was glad to see George. In a black overcoat whose previous owner had been about six inches shorter and fifty pounds heavier, George was hovering over a table laid with a white cloth with a cracker in his mouth and one in each hand. The strap of a messenger bag across his chest seemed the only thing preventing him from falling headfirst into the hors d'oeuvres.

"Hi, George, just arrive?" she asked.

He nodded. "Had to tie on the feed bag straight away. My dining hall credits ran out last week." A dab of spinach pâté fell out of his mouth and onto the strap of his bag.

"You're going to come down with gout if you keep eating all of your meals here." She delicately spread a tuft of goat cheese on a cracker. "I guess we both are, although once in a while I go home and eat some greens."

"Vegetables." Indicating a green mound of dubious vegetarian pâté with his elbow, George made little sandwiches out of cheese and Melba toast, wrapping them in napkins for later. "I have a hard time picturing you returning to the quiet homestead and butchering a head of kale."

She took a sprig of grapes and bit one off. "True, those were richer times, but still. This stuff is pretty bad."

"I'm supposed to go to a party with Stephanie later, some launch for a fitness magazine or something, so maybe their offerings will be a tad healthier."

"I feel like you've been out with her every night this week." Ava tried not to watch as he spread a layer of pâté on a layer of Brie and laid a slice of cheddar on top.

He popped the whole edifice into his mouth before he answered, so Ava was privy to each stage in its mastication. He smiled. "I know. They keep putting me on the guest lists, and not just as a plus one. To my astonishment, George Harazi has become quite the social commodity. I'm considered an excellent raconteur, and not a few women have complimented my style. This acclaim is so unaccustomed, I have a theory I was actually in some terrible accident the morning I got this job, and all that has followed has been the fantastical imagining of my dying breath, à la Ambrose Bierce." He began filling his pockets with napkin-wrapped bundles of cheese. "I mean, surely you agree that all this can't possibly be real."

"I wish none of it were real. I'm never going to one of

Stephanie's parties again." A squeal floated across the room from Aloysius. "So Stephanie and I, we're only figments of your imagination?" Ava asked.

George looked down at her with a funny gentleness. "You two are the least believable part of the whole thing."

They crossed into the parlor, with its distinctive odor of floor wax and mildew, a smell George referred to as "pine-scented funeral home." An old man snored on a damask settee, his chin resting on his crested blazer. A woman clawing a *Reader's Digest* looked up as they passed and frowned, muttering to herself about trollops and Saracens. Ava looked at George, but he seemed unconcerned, carefully putting away several napkin-wrapped bundles of crackers into his shoulder bag.

"Just be careful, George," Ava said, rubbing her temples that had started to throb again. "I would hate to see you lose yourself in all this. High society can be very corrupting, you know."

They sank into chairs on either side of a large bay window. It had started to snow. "I know, I know, I've read all the novels too, how easy it is to stray from the path of virtue, et cetera, but when such opportunities present themselves, some of us, and I'm not necessarily including you in this denomination—" He cleared his throat. "Some of us need to seize the day lest we end up old and alone, in shit-stained pajamas, living on cat food and the lost promises of our golden youth. You're a pretty girl, so such an end is far more unlikely, and in truth, for me as well, now that I'm so damn popular, but really, why take chances?"

"Jesus, George. That's pretty dark." They sat for a moment and watched the snow, and Ava was taken by a longing so strong to return to the path of virtue, she could actually feel it rising up her chest and constricting her ribs. But at this point, she couldn't even imagine what that would look like.

George cleared his throat. "So speaking of Stephanie…"

"Were we?"

"Aren't we always, really?" When he recrossed his legs, Ava noticed a small dab of Boursin embedded in the corduroy of his knee. "She mentioned you might be taking steps to get our mirror fixed? Aloysius stopped by today, and I managed to distract him with some well-timed questions about Portuguese water spaniels, but I'm not sure how long I can keep up the subterfuge. My knowledge of dog breeds is sadly limited."

"She put you up to this, too?"

George considered. "It seems our best option, and also, I kind of miss having Ben around the place. He had a kind of uprightness that really elevated the tone. Also he was teaching me how to rewire our lamp, and I'd like to finish the job." He handed over his phone. "His number's in there from coordinating lumber deliveries. *Per aspera ad astra*, as my high school yearbook urged repeatedly."

As she held the phone, Ava felt just how much she desperately wanted to see Ben, a longing that made her insides ache—his bright, clear expression, his soft work clothes, his dedication and his blameless poverty—fuck it, she decided, and pressed his number.

When the phone clicked through, she thrilled to hear the familiar voice.

"Hello?" He sounded a little different than she remembered, higher, softer. Absent the righteous anger that had only grown in her memory, he sounded like such a nice, forgiving guy.

"Hi, it's Ava. Don't hang up."

The pause was only a breath, but it was enough to let Ava know his indulgence was precarious. "That would be a pretty rude thing to do," he said. "I'm not a total jerk."

She felt the aspersion. "How are you doing?" she asked.

"I'm fine. How are you?"

An expectation that she would explain her call seemed to weigh on each word, an awkward lag to the normal rhythm of conversation, while she frantically tried to think of an excuse besides the favor she needed and which felt totally inappropriate. She happened to glance at George who gave her an enthusiastic thumbs-up, and it struck Ava that he would never offer such condescending encouragement to Stephanie and then thinking of her partner, a solution popped into her mind and she lunged for it. "I just called to let you know I've got some money for you. I wanted to pay you some of what we owe." She turned her back on George's surprised expression.

"Oh. Really?" The hopeful rise in his voice must have betrayed some conflict on Ben's part because there was a pause, and when he spoke again, his voice had resumed its normal register. "Thanks." When he continued, he sounded embarrassed. "That would really help me out right now."

"Maybe we could get together sometime. I could give it to you in person."

The promise of payment made him amiable. "Sure, we could get a drink or something. You can fill me in. I saw you guys in the *Times*. It sounds like you're doing pretty well."

A flush of embarrassment at the thought he might have seen her latest article was joined by an equal flush of pleasure that he had. "It was just the style section, so..." She laughed a little too brightly. "But yeah, it's been pretty crazy. Sorry it took me so long to call."

"Yeah."

This seemed dangerously ambiguous, so Ava wound up the call before he could elaborate. They made their plans to meet the next week, and she gave George back his phone with the funny vertigo of finding she had quite easily accomplished something she had been determined to refuse.

"You're in charge," George said with a shrug.

This confirmation of authority was gratifying, and seemed to reassert her place in everything. She was safe. He offered her another cracker, but Ava shook her head, distracted by the large window through which she could see the early winter darkness pressing against the snow. Ava found the shame of her lie dissipating rather quickly in the benevolent glow of the fast-descending hibernal twilight and the promise of seeing Ben again so soon. And Stephanie would be so pleased.

15

In the distance, his narrow figure stood dark against the snowy street. He was facing away from her, and she recognized the hunch of his shoulders; from behind he almost looked as if he were cradling something against his belly, like a knot whose tensile strength rests deep in its center. Ava thought of ships and rigging, twisted hemp straining against the elements. As she got closer, she saw these impressions of sailors and the sea were maybe just due to the fact that he was wearing a peacoat.

He turned as she approached, and she instinctively walked slower, wanting to pull away, suddenly shy, but he had seen her, so she continued her advance, experiencing the pleasure of being so obliged. She thought she remembered what he looked like, but in trying to piece his features together in her memory, she saw now she had forgotten the bones. The way the smooth planes of his cheekbones and prominent brow ridge formed a topography so hard and unyielding, her own face, pretty as it could be on occasion, was like a pile of uncooked dough next to his, her features floating in softness. This quick reminder of his essential difference registered as a threat, but it was such a quicksilver impression, it had fled before she covered the few feet left between them, only to return with an electric shock when he smiled at her.

"Hey, nice to see you." She looked into his face for a reprimand, but saw only a raw glow that made her think he just had shaved. "I thought you might be into this place." Hands in his pockets, he extended an elbow toward the door of a bar. "It's an old speakeasy, but I guess it's closed."

Ava cupped her hands against the window. "It looks nice. Thanks for meeting me."

A gust of wind keened down the short street—two blocks lost among the convoluted geometry of the West Village. Ben rested a boot against an iron rail that was guarding the roots of a wide, bare tree. He kicked once, and a little shower of snow shimmered onto the sidewalk. "Sure."

Now that he was relatively close to her and speaking with his familiar intonations, the pleasure of his company made her momentarily forget her anxiety at how she was actually going to proceed with him. Being so far from Stephanie's company made it harder to assume her gestures and her cast of mind; a lie that had slipped so easily into being on the phone seemed almost impossible to imagine face-to-face like this. Maybe he wouldn't ask for a while, and she could enjoy just being here with him. She shed the snow that had been accumulating on her head and shoulders with a canine shake.

"Let's just walk," he suggested. "I'm sure there's a million bars around here." She agreed and held down the wool pleats of her dress as wind cut up her black stockings and brought its icy breath to the bare strip of thigh above her homemade garters. The thick elastic she sewed into satin ribbons to hold up each separate leg, while very Victorian in spirit, was impractical without a couple of layers of long flannel petticoats. And, as Stephanie often mentioned, made her thighs look bulky. "I'm usually better prepared. I could source you any kind of building material in the tristate area, but this kind of thing is hard. I wanted to impress you."

He said this casually, tossing the compliment at her feet as if such things were of little consequence, and to maintain that pretense, Ava had to try and pretend he hadn't said it in order to hide the embarrassing flood of happiness it gave her. They started walking, leaving deep footprints behind them in the snow. In a crosswalk, a Boston terrier sat in protest against the sinister substance pilling around his argyle sweater. Ben smiled. "My dog, Betty, doesn't like the snow either. I tried cutting holes in an old wool sock to make a balaclava for her, but she wasn't into it." The light changed, and they left the dog in a mounting furrow, paws extended against the leash's persuasion.

"I didn't know you had a dog." This sudden insight into his domestic life acted like a flare, and in its sudden illumination, she saw just how vast the expanse of his life was that was obscure to her.

"A dachshund, and you did know because you told me they were called 'liberty pups' during World War One."

"Oh." Ava conceded that this sounded like her. "I make stuff for my cat, Mycroft, too. I tried to make him a ruff out of paper doilies once. It looked very regal, but he wasn't having it."

"It's a funny thing to have in common."

It was, and as Ava tried to layer this new paternal dimension across the scaffolding of her idea of him, it occurred to her that none of the heroes of her novels seemed to have pets. It then struck her that few of the books she read had animals in them of any kind, and it seemed a strange omission. She would put a dog, maybe even two, into her book if she ever got back to it. She so rarely thought of her book these days that just the fact of it crossing her mind seemed like an excellent sign, an indication that Ben's company had, as she hoped, an inspiring, not to say ennobling, effect.

They passed a wine bar, dark and cozy, its name scrawled in gold across a wide front window, just made for watching a snowfall. Ben didn't seem to notice, so Ava kept silent. She would have happily paid for the privilege of getting out of the snow, which was coming down heavier all the time, but maybe the lovely wine bar would be too expensive, and she didn't want to embarrass him. Or bring up the subject of money.

A little farther on, he stopped in front of a different bar. "I don't care what it's like. It's bound to be warmer and drier than out here."

"Agreed." Ava passed through the door he held open.

They shuffled between rickety tables and chairs crowded with jackets to the only available booth, a sticky table glowing in the light of a Genesee Cream Ale lamp. As they passed, a young woman in a pink hooded sweatshirt raised an arm and squealed at them with impersonal friendliness, "Whooo, snow day!"

Ben shook himself free from the stern navy coat and rubbed his hat between his hands. "Can I get you something to drink?" he asked, rather gallantly, Ava thought, for someone who was owed a couple of thousand dollars.

She flexed her pale, cold knuckles. "Whiskey? Or whatever you're having." He seemed like a whiskey drinker. He probably distilled it himself. She then realized that this sounded an awful lot like the kinds of things Stephanie always said about her, then tried to dismiss the thought. As he went to the bar for their drinks, she slid out of her pelts and tried to check her hair in a mirror on the wall, but the angle was wrong, and all she could see was the red, laughing face of someone she felt sure wasn't old enough to drink. Patsy Cline was playing on the jukebox, and she hummed along, mistaking the lyrics. In the warmth of the bar, everything felt easier, less weighted with consequence.

Ben returned. "I hope bourbon's okay." She smiled to let him know that it was and clinked her short heavy glass against his. The whiskey was sharp and oily, blistering and perfect. "So here we are," he said. "It took a while." When she glanced up, she knew that he was not referring to having found a warm, dry place to drink, and she couldn't stop from smiling in a kind of hopeful way. "I've never been very good at seizing the day," he continued by way of apology. "I take too long to do everything, as you know."

"You are very conscientious," Ava agreed. "But so am I. Usually," she amended.

"And I'm sorry I was such a jerk about the money." Ava's stomach seized up, but he was looking at his thumbs. "It's just that I wanted to be able to make it for you for free. And I couldn't. That's why I got so mad. Not at you so much. At New York for being so expensive. At myself for being poor."

"No, you were totally right. You're so nice and generous. I'm so sorry. I should have stood up for you. Stephanie is just so fierce sometimes, and I lose heart. She can be very persuasive."

"I get that, but still, it's funny that she has such sway over you. I mean, she does have a kind of force, like a hurricane or a bird of prey. I feel like I've seen hawks with a similar look in their eye, but she's just a type. New York is filled with girls like that."

Ava was torn between the urge to defend her friend and a kind of relief at hearing someone voice the suspicions shared in her darker moments. "I always thought it might be nice to be a type. If people have a way to place you, I think you draw less ire, less attention, less bullying. Or at least you'd know why it happened. I feel like I'm always a mystery."

"You're a type," he said confidently. "You're those girls

that like *Anne of Green Gables* and then get into swing danc-
ing or something." Ava wasn't at all sure she liked this, and
Ben noticed something in her expression because he clarified. "I'm a type, too," he offered. "The last of the gentleman artist scholar naturalists, a great tradition. Science and
art and the study of nature used to all be complementary
activities, now not so much, unfortunately."

"Nabokov chased butterflies," Ava said.

"I know." He smiled.

"Well, if you're the last, aren't you lonely?"

"Sometimes you find other weirdos."

A large gulp of whiskey hit Ava's chest, blooming warmth.
"Wouldn't that be wonderful? That's why I started all this.
But somehow I keep not getting it quite right. Maybe it's
just too fancy. I thought I would find the oddballs and out-
siders and thinkers and writers, but they don't really hang
out with the rich and successful crowd that Stephanie does."
She stopped. "It seems so obvious when I say it out loud.
The person that I actually want to meet is sitting in a room
somewhere, shy and lonely, filled with weird, unmanage-
able feelings, reading and writing books for the pleasure of
watching thoughts become words. Not at a dumb party." Ava
stared at the table. Was it possible she hadn't really thought
this through before now? But another feeling quickly sprang
up—the shape of Stephanie, and with it, a piercing need to
hold her close against the threat of separation rustling at the
logical end of her train of thought.

"So you are a writer."

It took Ava a moment to refocus her attention on the man
in front of her, surprised to find him across the table, extending a cheerful inquiry into her innermost thoughts. She
hesitated. "Ridiculous three syllable words and subordinate
clauses used to just pour out of me," she admitted. "I used to

want to describe the whole world in a million overwrought, old-fashioned, unnecessary words."

"That doesn't sound so bad. What happened?"

"I realized how tiresome it was for everyone else." She started a quick succession of small sips that drained her glass. "And it's really hard. I keep trying, but I can't get everything to click. So I just keep writing around stuff and nothing ever happens." It felt nice to be able to confide in someone.

"Maybe you're not being honest." Ava started to get indignant, so he quickly added, "Or maybe that's just me. When I get stuck, it's usually because I'm hiding from something or getting caught up in my own bullshit. But what do I know about writing books? So what's up next for the House of Mirth?" he said, politely switching topics.

Ava twirled her empty glass in slow circles on the table for a minute, unsure whether to defend herself further. She decided not to. "More parties? I wanted to have lectures and talks and things, but the dumb truth is that I'm just really bad at setting stuff up. You have to call people on the phone, and that gives me stomachaches. So I don't do it and then the parties Stephanie wants to have just seem to happen all on their own."

"I could help if you want." He leaned forward too eagerly and then, catching himself, leaned back again and looked at his drink. "I used to run a lecture series at school. I've always wanted to start up again. That kind of thing can really get you noticed. And your place is so amazing."

His eagerness touched a sympathetic chord in her. "Are you sure you want to? Our events always seem to get a little—" she paused, looking for the word "—dissolute."

"I suspect I'm a little less fastidious than you are." This hadn't been Ava's impression at all, but she chose not to argue. "I would love to start the House of Mirth inaugural lecture series on Art and the Natural World, whoever decides to come, however dissolute." She clinked the glass he held out to her. Finally someone was going to organize something substantive in her club. The prospect of another shared project also reassured her; she would get to see more of him, and maybe this time she wouldn't mess it all up again. Also, there was a chance that he wouldn't want to host a lecture under a mirror that was about to fall and kill someone. "I've been thinking a lot about old navigational charts lately. Maybe we can do something about that." He stood, extending a hand.

"I would drink to that." Ava relinquished her glass. He was being really, unnecessarily generous.

While he was at the bar, Ava again felt that funny feeling she noticed in his company, admiration, and its long dark shadow, envy. What would it feel like, she wondered, to have such confidence in your interests? To walk through the world, broad shouldered and self-content, bringing forth the fruits of your imagination as if they deserved to exist? Even now, she envied him across the room ordering their drinks with the casual entitlement of vertical parity; how nice to ask a bartender for what you wanted without the supplication inherent in being a foot shorter. His easy occupation in the world seemed to imply strength, and out of strength, courage, and his appeal melted into a moment of covetous longing.

"Did you know you can still navigate boats using sixteenth-century charts?" he said, when he got back. "It's kind of amazing."

"I like that you like old things." Ava spoke softly, twirling the crumbled red plastic straw from her previous drink. "What with your suspenders and hobnailed boots."

"Belt buckles get in the way if you use a table saw."

This felt a little like a repudiation of her, and Ava looked at him skeptically. "I don't think you look like a Civil War soldier home on leave without trying to."

He laughed. "I think from you that's a compliment, but I don't like stuff just because it's old. Old things are well made."

"That's important to me, too. I'm obviously a kindred spirit. Look—" she brought her knee up to the table, lifting her skirt as modestly as she could "—I'm wearing garters. Sometimes, also called suspenders." It occurred to her that she was getting a little drunk.

He looked at his glass. Then his eyes slid over to her thigh, and she put her leg down. "To be honest, you're the first person I've ever met to have such a distinctive aesthetic that wasn't an artist. I don't mean just your clothes or anything. But your way of looking at the world is unique and strangely coherent. It made a lot of sense when I found out you were a writer." He toyed with his glass for a minute, and Ava tried to stay calm against the desperate surging of her heart; he was describing just the person she had always dreamed of being and felt so far from at present. She focused hard on the uneven rolls of blue oxford shirt bunched tightly on his forearms. Pushed up like that, they seemed so redolent of a task only just abandoned, something industrious, a drafting table, a carpenter's level. He finished his drink in one swallow. "I'm bad at articulating these kinds of things."

Ava noticed a callus on the soft hollow between his forefinger and thumb and wanted to touch it and see if it was as rough as it looked. She wanted him to keep talking forever, so that she could gaze at herself in the flattering image he was creating. "I wish you were right. My project is a mess. My life is a mess. I'm so compromised."

"Ugh, me, too." He laughed. "It's hard not to be. Maybe we need more drinks."

In the rest of the bar, the festive atmosphere had escalated. Sweaty girls in thin tank tops danced in the center of the room, a chair was knocked over, a young man let forth a booming laugh. Ava and Ben's desultory attempts to·settle on a new topic of conversation faded softly as the noise in the room increased. Everything they brought up felt too pedestrian, but they both sensed that a further incursion into the sticky recesses of their deeper selves would be too much. "Maybe we should just get out of here. It's getting kind of loud." Ben looked past the bare arms and swinging hips of the dance floor to the plate glass windows. On the other side, snow was gusting sideways in grand, sweeping arcs that alternated with a slow, dreamy falling. "Although I don't know where we could go. It's crazy out there."

Ava leaned out of the booth to see for herself; New York had become a violently shaken snow globe caught in the four corners of the dirty window. "I don't have anywhere to be," she said.

"We could just walk. It's kind of beautiful," he suggested timidly.

Suddenly Ava, who had spent so much of her youth inside watching the world from over the rim of a book, wanted very much to be outside with him in the wild, fraught, cold of the storm. She agreed. He held her coat for her, tucking it around her shoulders with careful attention, and they passed through the young sweaty bodies and left the bar.

Outside, the snow was knee-high. Patrons of different bars poured into the street, chasing and grappling with school yard enthusiasm in the thick, white evening. A gust of wind sent a shower of snow from the top of the streetlamps. Someone yelled, "Blizzard Party!" and a snowball flew overhead. Stepping carefully around a pair of Ugg boots making a snow angel, Ava and Ben turned into the first street they came to, and a perfect stillness caught them. Here, shielded from the wind, snow fell constantly and gently onto the steps and eaves of facing brownstones. The demarcation between side-walk and street had disappeared under the unbroken drifts, and they pushed forward with large slow steps. It was as if no one had ever walked down this street before. The smell of wood smoke crept from affluent homes. "Listen." Ava's whisper carried surprisingly well in the hush of the snow-dampened night.

Ben closed his eyes. "I never thought silence could be so loud."

She kept talking, unwilling to relinquish this luxury of whispering on a New York street. "I'm glad we came out."

"Me, too."

Ava wanted to glance at him but didn't, and her ears got hot. She laughed, but it was a fake laugh, and it came out too loud, and the quiet of the street only made it more grating. "This cold is making my nose run," she said wiping a glove under her nose, which wasn't, in fact, running.

"Yeah." Ben sniffed violently, proving that his was. They moved forward unsteadily through the deepening snow. "Are we walking too fast? Is my stride too long? I'm sorry." Cour-teously he slowed down, even though she had been setting their pace.

"No, it's me. I'm really not dressed for this weather."

He looked disturbed by her wet skirt and stockings. "I feel like I should carry you." Then, as if embarrassed at having made the offer, he starting going through his pockets. "That was a dumb thing to say, but seeing girls look cold always gets me. I feel like half the women in New York don't wear socks in the winter, and I'm always worried about their feet." Ava tried to think of how to articulate the many contrary pressures that lead women to such seemingly impractical choices, but she suspected he wouldn't understand. He held out a small silver flask. "I had the bartender fill it up before we left." He faced her, his back making a bulwark against the flurries. "At least you won't notice your wet feet as much."

"It's not so bad, really." She took the flask and sipped from it, feeling just a little silly as she pursed her lips around the delicate spout.

He took back the flask and drank with just a hint of urgency; then, replacing it in his pocket, he didn't turn and resume his place beside her. He didn't move at all, looking at her instead with the directness of a person unaware that the steadfastness of his expression loudly signals his intent. "I'm glad you called," he said. "I felt really bad about how things ended."

"Sorry." She was about to confess everything when, glancing up, she realized he was coming toward her, and a flash of confusion stopped her words, followed immediately by concern. The distress of seeing someone so vulnerable, a fear for his sake of being rejected, or rather, an empathetic terror of imagining the fear of rejection that he must be experiencing overwhelmed her, and to save him the unpleasantness of it, she quickly threw her arms around his neck and kissed him first.

When they made contact, Ava slammed into the possibility that his reality didn't follow the lines of her imagination so closely. He didn't kiss like a man relieved of a terrible anxiety. He wrapped his arms around her furry back and pulled her toward him with leisurely intent. His mouth pressed against hers, and she realized that Ben did not need any of her help. His habit of diffidence seemed to recede along with the necessity of words, and she giggled from nerves and surprise.

He pulled back only about as far as her nose to look at her questioningly. The upturned collar of his coat cut a sharp angle against his flushed cheeks. She was trying to process this new development, whether this additional interest meant that at some point she might be entitled to breach that air of self-sufficiency he exuded. A possible future presented itself in which she was allowed to trespass on his person, to unbutton the double-breasted armor of this coat and press against him, burrowing into the imagined warmth of his chest. She thought of the wealth of things he could potentially make for her if, in fact, he liked her like that. He was everything she had ever wanted.

She tried to say something but, instead, breathlessly shook her head because she had no idea what she should say, and let her arms around his neck bear more of her weight as he kissed her again. The snow that hit their faces melted into little streams of cold water that made everything slipperier and sloppier, and Ava kept accidentally bumping up against the hard lines of his jaw. She realized she must be a terrible kisser, she'd had so little practice, and the more she tried not to focus on this fact, the harder it was to forget. He pressed forward undeterred, and a new sensation leapt up from deep inside, filling her with heat and delight. He was so smart and talented and full of admirable virtues, and he was choosing her. "Why don't we go somewhere warm?" she asked.

But Ben was already walking toward the subway, pulling her along with a flattering hurry.

The snow had stopped when they got off the train, arm in arm, smiling awkwardly in unspoken acknowledgment of what was to come. It was dark, and the lights of Chinese take-out counters and dollar stores lit up the street under the elevated subway tracks. Families hurried past, kids bundled in strollers. Different Spanish radio stations banged up against each other from adjacent bodegas. A guy hanging out on a corner puckered his lips at Ava until, noticing Ben, he murmured an apology. The train clattered overhead, and they turned onto a desolate industrial block.

Ava thought they must be near the river because the wind

howled down the wide expanse of low warehouses, rustling
cardboard boxes tied for recycling and flapping the shred-
ded plastic bags caught in the razor wire of empty lots. She
could see the appeal of coming home to a street like this; it
made her feel lonely, in a bleak, romantic way, a street that
made you hunch into your jacket and feel alone and think
about art. If she lived on a street like this she would probably write bad poetry about windblown plastic and the moon
and the promises of a spring that never seemed to arrive. She
considered saying something about it, but a wave of shyness
hit her, and she kicked an empty cigarette pack, lying for-
lorn in the snow.

When Ben opened the graffiti-covered metal door, they
walked into a large open space where two unshaven young
men were bent over a soldering iron. They looked at her
without curiosity. "Roommates," Ben muttered as they
walked past into another large dark room where various
machines bristled with blades and parts. An easel leaned in
the corner. Two drafting tables stood side by side, next to
a dusty record player, a pile of scrap metal and a large dead
plant. A dachshund ran toward them in abbreviated bounds,
only to stop a foot away, snout raised in suspicious inquiry.
"Oh, is this Betty?" Ava knelt, glad for something to do, and
held out her hand. At the gesture, Betty sprung backward
and looked at Ben, vindicated.

"Don't let it bother you. She's shy." He opened a narrow
door. "We use this as a studio. I keep meaning to clean it
up one of these days." The skittering of claws on concrete
followed them. "After you."

The room was tiny, only as wide as the length of the
double bed, which sat on top of a platform built of drawers, each with a single brass handle in the middle. A desk, a
bookshelf, everything was handmade, white and compact,

orderly as a ship's cabin. "Where's all your stuff?" Ava asked
before she could help it.

"Around." He pointed to a few drawers ingeniously hidden in corners of the room. "I don't have that much."

"I couldn't imagine living without all my things."

"I'm sure." Ava didn't know how to take this, so she
looked around again. A book lay open next to the pillow,
and she picked it up. "Contemporary art; not your thing,"
he said with a note of apology.

"I'm interested," she objected, but he didn't pursue the
matter. She could understand why, and yet there was something in this idea of her, as accurate as it probably was, a de-
lineation that felt constricting. A single lamp lit the room;
its muted glow bouncing off all the white walls evoked a
kind of serenity that alienated Ava even as she couldn't help
but admire it. "What about those?" She pointed at a stack
of books on his desk. "Tell me about those." She curled her
legs under her skirt.

He didn't and instead moved to sit next to her, very close,
on the edge of the bed. "You're very beautiful," he said.

If he was going to go that far, Ava felt obliged to let herself be pulled by the warm current of breath coasting across
her collarbones and turned her head. He kissed her again.
And again, an inconvenient focus on the awkward and kind
of absurd mechanics of his tongue in her mouth kept pulling her out of the moment. She closed her eyes and concentrated, trying to remember exactly how kissing was supposed
to work. How was she supposed to breathe? The line of his
teeth felt very hard and kept bumping up against her with
an untoward aggression. She tried to ignore the stubble just
above his mouth that was hurting her lip. But his head against
her cheek smelled of fresh soap, and the hair at his nape bristled under her fingers, and she didn't want to discourage him
when he looked searchingly into her face. "I'm sorry. I'm

not very good at this," she apologized. "I've only ever been with one guy before." She started to tell him about Jules Delauncy, but he was now kissing her ear and didn't seem to be listening. His mouth felt cold and wet behind her earlobe, and she had to suppress the impulse to ask him stop.

"Oh, Ava," he said with an indulgent chuckle, when she finished her story. "You're too much."

This was clearly intended as a compliment, so Ava felt her objections to the unpleasant feel of his kisses on her neck were ridiculous, and she attempted the kind of sigh that seemed appropriate under the circumstances.

Soon she was naked, as was he, and the knowledge that things were going to proceed in a fairly predictable order without much being required from her was a relief. He would be busy and not notice if she wasn't doing all of this correctly.

At some point, Betty woke up and, curious about the rustling, nosed her damp snout against Ava's ear. Ava was glad for the interruption, thinking this might be a moment where she could reconnect with him from across the aching plain of his desire; maybe they could start talking about books or art or something and she would feel that thrill from earlier in the evening, but Ben removed the dog with a perfunctory shove. He looked into Ava's eyes, but something made her want to avoid his eager, flushed expression. She turned her head against his shoulder, trying not to notice the cool, embarrassed awareness of the parameters of her body and the places it was being invaded. When it was over, he rubbed her arm in what almost felt like a consolatory way, and this made her pretty sure that she hadn't done a very good job, but he fell asleep before she could question him further.

The next morning, she watched him get dressed, hoping that to see him standing on one leg getting into his pants or baring the bony ridge of his spine would reassure her of an intimacy that she was already doubting, but he was as self-contained in a pair of silly white briefs as he was fully clothed. Men inhabited their bodies with such dumb ease that looking at a man naked was as unrevealing as looking at him clothed. He caught her eye and smiled, and she saw with a hint of jealousy that his shoulders were relaxed, his smile nonchalant. Her observation didn't bother him at all, and this bothered her very much.

16

When she got home, Ava was surprised to see Stephanie was there, slouched against her door, picking at the beading embroidered along the neckline of her low-cut gown. "What are you doing here?" Ava fumbled with her keys.

"Where did you sleep last night?" Stephanie asked, rubbing under her eyes, her fingers coming up black with mascara. "Is he going to fix our mirror?"

"Maybe? I don't know. We have to pay him. Seriously. We have to," Ava said, opening the door. "I can't live like this."

"Sure," Stephanie sighed, not looking at her. Her shoulders slumped forward, bare under the thin straps of her gown. "Whatever. I just don't want you to be mad at me anymore."

This sudden change of course was much more disconcerting than the argument Ava had been expecting. "Wait, what?"

"I just want us to be on the same team again. I feel like we're always arguing." A wrongly pulled thread sent a stream of beads from Stephanie's dress onto the floor with a rattle. "Fuck, this is borrowed." She crouched on the floor, hunting for her lost beads.

Still confused by this sudden capitulation, Ava stood aside

to let Stephanie pass through the door. "Where did *you* sleep last night?"

"Don't ask. I just don't want to be alone right now. Can I stay here?"

Ava followed. "Of course." Then she remembered why Stephanie was in evening wear. "How was the gala?"

Stephanie stopped fumbling with the clasp of her shoes and looked up, excited. "Guess what? I think I got us a new patron—Howard Steward."

Ava's stockings were still damp from the snow, and she hung them over the radiator. "I don't know who that is."

"He's a super famous investor guy. He has like a million companies. I met him tonight. He's a big philanthropist, and he's like Caribbean or Spanish or something. I told him we were going to do a bunch of youth literacy programs in Harlem."

"But we aren't."

"We will. As soon as we have more money, I think we should definitely do things like that. At least I'm trying to make us sound good, Ava. What else was I supposed to tell him?" Stephanie said, irritably. She shed her dress and was already crawling into Ava's bed. "I didn't make the world we live in. Howard Steward is rich."

Ava didn't quite follow, but she decided to let the matter drop. She crawled into bed beside Stephanie and curled up against her back, and a tension she had been carrying all through the previous night melted, sliding through their tangled limbs, and it felt like the most natural thing in the world to trust herself to Stephanie's care. The soft sound of Stephanie's breathing fell between them, and Ava welcomed it, her bones dissolving in ease and quiet. "Hey," she whispered. "I think I might finally have a boyfriend."

"Congratulations." Stephanie yawned, not bothering to turn around, settling deeper into the warmth of Ava's bed.

Maybe they would talk more about it tomorrow, Ava decided, and together they drifted into a hungover sleep, reeking of alcohol and men's embraces, overlaid with the barest hint of rose.

Over the next few days, it became impossible to ignore a certain chill around the Lazarus Club. The board's displeasure drifted like a pall down from the upper floors. In the hallways, Ava's polite greetings had been getting even icier responses. A creeping impermanence hovered around them, like living at court under a sovereign's displeasure. Ava tried not to take it too hard that her cozy nest had become so prickly and unwelcoming, and concentrated her attentions on the House of Mirth instead.

On a cold Sunday a few weeks later, corduroy blazers and coarse wool sweaters filled the library with the muted color of autumn leaves, over which a reader's voice billowed, a mellifluous rumble of sharp constants and orotund vowels. Ava and George, in a small rebellion against Stephanie's overwhelming influence, had allowed the volunteer poets who helped out at events to organize a series of poetry readings. They had gone about it with impressive enthusiasm, convincing all sorts of established poets to participate, and Ava was pleased. This was just what she had imagined her salon would be—young poets, elder statesmen, eager readers, gathered under the glow of her hospitality and a shared love of literature.

In the bar, George was piling scones too high on a chipped blue-and-white platter, while Ava dried teacups. She handed him another plate, and he accepted it reluctantly. "You have no sense of architectural adventure."

"Not with my homemade pastries. I watched five hours of *Daniel Deronda* on PBS to make that many scones. Did you know that book was about beautiful Jews? Somehow I had no idea."

"Our sex appeal is generally underrepresented in Victorian novels," he agreed. "I was writing a paper on Thucydides."

She refilled a marmalade pot. "I keep forgetting that you have a bunch of other obligations. How many classes are you taking this semester?"

"Six."

"Six? George, how? You're here all the time."

He smoothed out the wrinkled stripes of his tie. "It's a lot more fun than 'Intro to Calculus.' Also at school, unlike here, the girls are impervious to my charms." Clapping began in the other room and with it, the rustle of movement, listeners slowly shifting out of absorbed immobility. "Here they come."

Ava turned on the kettle. People began filtering into the bar, scanning the food with a show of indifference, while Ava smiled at them with the most open expression she could conjure, pouring hot water into porcelain cups. Sometimes, it looked as though one of them were about to start a conversation, and she felt a surge of anticipation, but then nothing seemed to happen. A young man in a flat cap stared at the shimmering peacock painted on the wall and met her searching eyes by accident. "Did you enjoy the reading?" She handed him a cup of tea.

"What is this place?" he asked.

Eagerly, Ava launched into an explanation that somehow got kind of jumbled by the end. "So it's just perfect for people who like poetry. We plan on having many more of these readings."

"It looks expensive," he apologized and slid backward into the crowd before she could argue with him.

An older woman in a sweater vest rifled through a basket of tea bags, and Ava wanted to talk to her, but the professorial bearing that drew Ava to her also made her feel shy. She checked the clock. Stephanie had been calling all day with instructions—where to pick up the cake, when to come over, wanting to know whether twenty-six was the beginning of middle age. Each year, Ava got excessively withdrawn on her birthday, insisting that no one make a big deal and then hid, brokenhearted, all day because no one cared, and this was making her more irritable with Stephanie today than she meant to be.

She poured herself a cup of tea and ventured from behind the bar. The tweedy crowd looked exactly right. Overhearing a woman with Ana May Wong bangs and horn-rimmed glasses admiring the chandelier, Ava braved herself to butt in. "Thanks, I helped mount it up there myself. It's crazy how heavy a twenty-foot chandelier is." The woman blinked, and Ava tried to volunteer further friendly information. "It was surprisingly cheap. I guess not a lot of New Yorkers want Versailles-sized lighting fixtures."

"Not a lot of New Yorkers have the room." The woman turned back to her companions, leaving Ava embarrassed, aware that she had transgressed but with no idea how to fix it.

She sat on the arm of a sofa for a while trying to look approachable while poetry fans stepped carefully around her, retreating into clumps of previous acquaintances. Maybe she shouldn't have worn red lipstick. The bright smears on her cup seemed proof of her lack of seriousness. She wanted to go home and eat pea soup for dinner, savoring the sensation of creamy ham-flavored satiety on a dark, lonely Sunday evening. Maybe wash her hair. Maybe wash her cat. Why after all these months was she still so bad at this?

A young man with a dusting of freckles and a paperback rolled in the patch pocket of his coat bumped into Ava. "I'm sorry." She nodded to accept his apology, but he didn't keep

walking. "I love hearing Patterson read. It's like a bear gar-
gling with marbles."

Ava laughed and then, as she realized he was going to
continue the conversation, stood up so eagerly tea sloshed
all over the saucer under her cup. "That glass he had on the
lectern was full of vodka by his request, so maybe that has
something to do with it."

"You helped put this on? It's pretty great. What an amazing place to hear poetry. Are you a poet then? Pound or
Carson?"

Trying to decipher this gnomic question, Ava made a
guess. "Carson?"

It was clearly the wrong answer, and rocking back on his
heels with a marked relish, this young man seemed about to
explain her mistake, when Ava felt something in her crumple.
These were the conversations she was looking for, and yet
in the face of his cheerful assurance and her mistake, a fear
welled up within her, overpowering and irrepressible. She
was not in high school anymore, she reminded herself. This
smiling young man was not going to superglue her back-
pack shut or throw her gym clothes in the cafeteria dump-
ster because she said the wrong thing or failed some kind
of mysterious test. Real life didn't work like that. This was
her event. She belonged here. It was only conversation, not
some resolution on her worth as a human being. Yet, she
just couldn't tamp down the fear. It kept rising up until the
ringing in her ears drowned out whatever he was saying, and
she watched his lips moving, cursing the fact that Stephanie
wasn't here to save her. Why had she decided to throw an
event by herself? This was madness, foolhardiness; she ex-
cused herself, moving quickly away from his confused expression, and back to the safety of the bar. "Wait, I'm sorry,
what's your name?" she heard him call behind her.

"I'm so bad at this," she said to George, refilling the kettle at the leaking sink to quiet her racing heart. "How does Stephanie do it? How do you do it? Surely you had a hard time in high school."

"I am possessed of a burly older brother, so nothing too disastrous. And anyway, none of that matters now." Ava felt there was a slight in this, and she watched silently while George cleared a few cups, tossing the used tea bags in a soppy arc into the sink. She had assumed anyone she got along with must have been tortured in elementary school. Wasn't that the glue that bound all worthwhile people? "Speaking of disasters, has Stephanie mentioned anything to you lately, of, I don't know, maybe catastrophic import?"

The dense squares hit the steel sides with a splat and slid slowly toward the drain. "No, what do you mean?"

"Nothing," he answered, suddenly evasive, and when his phone rang, he answered it quickly. He held it toward her. "Speaking of."

"Again?" Ava took it tentatively, hoping Stephanie was not going to scold her anymore. "Yes?"

"I just wanted to remind you that Le Sucre closes at six, and it's all the way over on the West Side. The event's almost over. Leave George in charge. Please? I'm making salmon. It's good for your skin. I miss you. Come over." Ava gave George back his phone with a sigh. She wasn't able to refuse.

When she finally left, dirty teacups were piled as high as the deep walls of the sink. George was leaning on the bar, drawing shapes through little puddles of spilled tea, while a man in a loosened tie offered him a job as a personal assistant.

It was a cold night, and Ava walked south enjoying the hard black midwinter sky. Wind gusted down the desolate stretch of avenue, and she ducked into the small shelter of a bus stop. Snow lined the street in drifts, a rough terrain over which the wheels of cruising taxis crackled and snapped.

An old man joined her at the bus stop, his face sunk into

his scarf, and the shared interiority of strangers insulating against the sharp air made her feel even more blissfully alone. When the bus finally came, Ava took a seat by the window, watching the shadowy outline of her fluorescent-lit reflection, occasionally pressing a cold hand against her cold cheek, happy on the hard blue seat. She wished the bakery were even farther away.

She arrived just as it was closing, but after knocking on the glass and some quick pleading, she continued her pilgrimage downtown, feeling slightly more cheerful to be carrying a large white box tied with ribbons. Stephanie lived on a small side street in the financial district, a narrow alley of Chinese restaurants and delis that served the grand old banks and investment houses of the surrounding area's daylight hours. On a Sunday evening, it was deserted. The flickering yellow sign of a boarded-up dry cleaner shone on a row of overflowing dumpsters awaiting the end-of-the-week pickup. The metal gate of an Asian massage parlor rattled suddenly, and nimble shadows darted from underneath, careening down the street like dark, earthbound birds. Ava hurriedly pressed the graffiti-covered buzzer at Stephanie's address.

"Come up," a familiar voice crackled, and Ava pushed through the creaky iron door, starting the long climb to the sixth floor. Stephanie was waiting for her in a triangle of light that cut sharply into the dim stairwell. "How did the event go? Did we get a lot of people?" She stepped aside to let Ava in.

Breathless from the stairs, Ava nodded and threw herself down on the large leather sectional that Stephanie had scavenged a few months ago with that strange knack she had for finding sofas. "Here. Happy Birthday." Stephanie beamed and took the white box from Ava's hands. She was wearing her glasses, thick Coke-bottle lenses that gave her the earnest, inquisitive look of an adolescent at a science fair, and her hair almost had a wave to it, a natural buoyancy straining against yesterday's flat-ironing. "What's all over your face?"

"Zit cream."

"I just saw you yesterday. You didn't have any zits."

"Sunday is my maintenance day." Stephanie gingerly touched a few of the thick white spots dotting her face. "Hold on, I have to check the fish. I made a salad, too." She shuffled into the kitchen in thick wool socks.

Ava kicked off her shoes and pulled a torn cashmere throw around her legs, enjoying the smell of olive oil and dill that infused the apartment with a pleasurable domesticity. An unfolded pile of laundry filled an armchair, and a library book lay spine up next to three tabloids. The room had a cluttered comfortableness, the soft, intimate charm of a discarded bra still warm from another woman's body; and Ava felt very cozy as the cold of the street seeped from her muscles. "What time are people getting here?"

"George is coming after he cleans up."

"It's just us? I thought you were having a whole party. What about all your celebrity friends?"

"Oh god, in this dump?" Stephanie answered from the kitchen. "No, I always go to their apartments. This is just family."

Ava contemplated this new, preferable prospect for the evening, staring at a large discolored spot on the ceiling. "Doesn't that make you feel weird, like a call girl or something?"

Stephanie came back and handed her an asparagus spear. "No. I mean, I'll have people over when I have a nicer place." The slender stalk waved between them, a drop of water cresting from its prickly head onto Ava's lap. "I have you guys. Come to the kitchen. Let's make a drink. I bought umbrellas to make tiki martinis. I call them 'Tiki-tinis.'" Ava allowed Stephanie to pull her to her feet. "I was going to go get stuff to make fancy rum drinks, but then my mom called, and I forgot. All I have is vermouth, so they're just martinis with pink umbrellas. But if you call them 'Tiki-tinis,' it's more festive." Stephanie kicked a pair of dirty underwear under the couch as they passed.

"How bad was your mom this year?" Ava bent down and picked up the underwear, folding it on the arm of the couch. "You're going to forget those."

Stephanie shrugged. "Not that bad. One of her friends gave her a ton of diet food, so she's sending me like a month's worth of nutrition bars. Which is pretty cool, actually. Those are expensive." Ava groaned. "Well, last year she gave me all those sessions at a tanning salon. I mean, yes, it was super convenient, but still, thanks, Mom, for the cancer." Stephanie pushed her hair out of her face with her elbow, picking at an invisible spot on her chin. "Gin or vodka?"

"Gin." Stephanie's glasses flashed as she shook a silver cocktail shaker. Ava considered trying to explain to her friend how desperately adorable she looked right now. That if she ever let a man see her like this, her romantic problems would be over and whoever was so honored couldn't possibly help but love her, but Ava knew Stephanie would never believe it. She accepted a drink and tried to drink it in one swallow, but the pink umbrella poked her nose.

Stephanie watched her, amused. "Slow down, tiger." She fished out a cocktail onion and dropped it in Ava's glass. "It's all I have, although now I suppose it's a Tiki-Gibson, which is much less catchy. Sit. I'm going to make a hollandaise."

"Seriously?" Ava sat on the counter, her feet resting on the opposite cabinets of the tiny kitchen.

"It's not that hard." Stephanie, an egg carton in her arms, swung the refrigerator closed with her hip. "It's very Atkins. Move. I need to get to the stove."

Ava complied. Stephanie carefully separated the whites of

her eggs, nestling each yolk in the cup of a broken shell before sliding them into a pan. "So it's silly, but I kind of had this worry that you might not come tonight."

Ava watched the hypnotic calm of the process as each yellow puddle oozed past. "Why?"

"I don't know. Now that you have a boyfriend and stuff. You seem pretty distracted and all. And now is really when we need to be making plans for our future. You know we might not be at the Lazarus Club forever, and I want to make sure we're looking out for our members and their interests." Her glasses kept slipping down, and she pushed them up, with a quick glance at Ava. She squeezed a lemon into the pot and handed Ava a whisk. "Don't let these burn."

In her whole life, Ava had never heard anyone refer to "her boyfriend," and an overpowering satisfaction filled her heart. She hesitated. She had been wanting to ask Stephanie about relationships, about the awkward silences that sprang up between her and Ben whenever they weren't talking about books or art or movies, or why every time she had slept over at his house she had left with a funny creeping feeling across her skin, a strange knot in her stomach that kept her from ever really being able to lose herself in the moment with him. She wanted reassurance that this was what it was like for everyone, and Stephanie had lots of experience of men, and yet Ava waited. If she gave voice to all the reservations that kept sneaking up on her when he left his sweaty hand in hers too long, or chewed on her nipple sending sharp alerts of discomfort down her shoulders, maybe this lovely dream would shatter. What if Stephanie thought it sounded crazy, or told her that everything was supposed to feel different? What if she lost this hard-won, long-awaited pleasure of feeling that she was just like everybody else? Little bubbles sprang around the edge of the pan, and she swished them away with each turn of the whisk. "Where did you learn to cook anyway?" she asked to change the subject.

Stephanie leaned deep into the refrigerator. "I don't remember. I've always liked being self-sufficient. But I guess you know all about that now, now that you're so busy with your own life and all."

Millions of little yellow bubbles now rose in the pan, some bursting with a slow yawning gasp, others climbing into a cresting foam. "I've barely spent that much time with him," Ava said. "You don't have to worry. You would never have to worry about me," she added softly.

Stephanie dropped the butter she was cutting and grabbed the pan, removing it from the stove. "Too hot." She examined the curdled eggs for a minute, swirling the pan through the air before dumping them into the sink. "Okay, let's try this again. I'll stir, you cut up that stick of butter."

"Sorry, I wasn't paying attention."

A fresh egg cracked against the side of the pan, and Stephanie, pacified, began the process again, pausing to finish the last of her cocktail. "Well, I never loved you for your practical skills. But don't forget, we're partners. Until the end."

"But I seem to be bad at everything we do—all these parties and collaborations with *Vogue* or whatever. At least Ben likes to hear me talk about Zola and the Hapsburgs and stuff. At least, I think he does. It's hard to tell sometimes."

"I was first." Stephanie sniffed indignantly as she set the pot aside. "I've been interested in all your boring stories from the beginning. It was always me." She spoke sternly to the oven door. "You can't leave, just because of some guy. I need you."

Ava reached out and touched her shoulder, amazed as always at the heat on Stephanie's skin and the way it transferred instantly to the pads of her fingertips. "I'm not leaving you."

Stephanie shook her off. "That's right, remember, I would

fucking destroy you." She laughed uneasily. "Set the table while I wash this stuff off my face. I left some flowers in the sink."

As she arranged the stiff deli roses in a vase, Ava slipped on the thorns. She sucked the thin trickle of blood from her palm, the taste of iron and salt, and then laid out plates and silverware.

Eventually, George arrived with an overnight bag and a small package, wrapped in the brightly colored ads for escorts from the back of a free weekly, that he put next to Stephanie's plate. "It was all I could find on the way here." He looked at it for a minute. "I didn't notice just how buxom some of those ladies were."

Ava realized she had forgotten to get Stephanie a present. "What's with the bag?"

Stephanie reappeared. "Georgie." She gave him a hug, sloshing a little bit of the drink she was carrying onto his shirt. "Here, have a cocktail. He sleeps over when he has class in the morning," she said to Ava, before sitting down at her plate and picking up her present.

"My parent's house is really far away," he explained.

"You parents don't mind?" Ava asked.

"They think I have an internship at Bear Stearns." He smiled. "That buys me a lot of freedom."

Stephanie ran her fingers along each fold of wrapping. "We wear jammies and watch game shows on cable. George is weirdly good at *Wheel of Fortune*."

"Really?"

"I played a lot of Hangman with my brother. Family road trips."

Ava fiddled with a fork next to her plate. "No, I'm just surprised that you stay over. I never knew you two were so secretive."

Stephanie sniffed her present. "Mmm, dusty. You could

come over too, but you never want to hang out. You're always so ready to go home."

Ava pressed the tines of the fork into the tablecloth, producing a scattering of little dents. She realized that she had always assumed that George liked her better than Stephanie. This revelation of an intimacy to which she was so peripheral made her suddenly insecure, and very jealous. "I just thought you were always going to parties."

"Sometimes we go to parties. Everybody loves George." Stephanie picked at a piece of Scotch tape with the edge of her nail.

"It's really not worth being so careful with that wrapping paper. The hookers won't mind," George said, watching her progress.

"I don't want to rush." When the wrapping was finally off and neatly refolded and tucked under her plate, Stephanie held up an elegant used volume. "Amazing. *The Sun Also Rises*, only my favorite book of all time."

"It is?" Ava felt strangely petulant. Stephanie was always pretending to read books, and somehow the reminder that she actually had books that she had read and loved felt like a betrayal. She already had so much else—did she have to take this from Ava, too? And George knew and was complicit, and this hurt, as well. Did either of them need her? "Where did you find this?" Ava resentfully turned the thin, gold-edged pages.

"Bookstore." George sniffed hopefully in the direction of the kitchen.

"George, you're amazing. I love you both. Best birthday ever. Let's eat," Stephanie commanded.

They feasted on fish, then cake. The hours passed, and Ava tried to stop looking enviously at the book next to Stephanie's plate. She felt unmoored, disoriented, adrift in a world that felt too inconstant. With a start, she realized she hadn't read a book in weeks. This fact that had somehow skimmed past her notice in the long busy days of their project now seemed enormous, casting its shadow over everything else. If Ava wasn't someone who read, who was she? And what was she doing? She drank another cocktail to quell the feeling of panic.

Stephanie was holding forth. "Being as broke as we are is just the universe inviting us to try harder, to prove that we're better than everyone else. I've always loved Nietzsche." Stephanie pushed the sagging crown Ava had fashioned for her out of tin foil back up on her forehead, a gesture she had repeated so often static electricity had caused a halo of hair to poke out of the top.

Ava spit a cocktail onion back into her glass. They were giving her a stomachache. "I thought that was just because you were kind of a Nazi in college."

"She's joking," Stephanie informed George.

"He knows," Ava said, putting her drink down on Stephanie's book by accident.

"Knows you're joking or knows I was a Nazi? Because I wasn't," Stephanie clarified a little testily, moving the glass.

"*Vergangenheitsbewältigung,*" George said to the remains of the salmon.

"Anyway, we can't afford not to succeed. If this all falls apart, I'll end up living in my mom's basement, getting my boobs done every year, just waiting to die." She plucked the petals off of a rose, scattering them dramatically over the ruins of German chocolate cake. "Let's play Scrabble," she said suddenly. "Ava always gets grumpy because I beat her, but it's my birthday, so I get to choose."

"It's only that I have no competitive spirit. I just don't get it. I know so many more words than you," Ava protested.

"You lack strategy, my dear." Stephanie tapped her forehead. "Strategic thinking."

"All right, fine."

"I'll get the board." George stood and stretched, brushing a few crumbs from his tie. "I know where it is."

"I'll bet you do," Ava called after him, finishing her third, or perhaps fourth, martini.

When he returned, they settled into the game and a silence of strenuous concentration. The evening wore on to the small clacking of square tiles on Stephanie's Deluxe Special Folio Edition board. George beat both of them handily. Ava came in last, as usual, but found that this evening, for some reason, she was more upset about it. She left soon after and walked all of the long way back to her apartment, weaving slightly, glad for the chill, and the wind and the comfort of the deserted street.

17

The next morning, Ava lay looking at the stack of books next to her bed. Her nightstand was piled with new releases, books by authors Stephanie wanted to court for events, and Ava realized this was a great part of what lay behind her recent ambivalence—reading to facilitate Stephanie's ambition was as disheartening as wearing someone else's clothes. In the past, her habits had been directed by an almost unconscious process that had led her from book to book, an intuitive train of interest from one author or time period to the next, and a great part of the pleasure she took in reading was this sensation of building the scaffolding of her intellectual sense of the world in so many literary increments. But the process seemed to have stalled. Thinking of it now, she remembered she had occasionally, somewhat guiltily, abandoned Stephanie's list of suggestions, and had tried to go back to the books she liked—a couple of minor Balzacs she had been meaning to read for a while—but still she ended up putting them down, as though she had lost some essential connection to the process. Her beloved novels and, by extension, her whole worldview had begun to seem irrelevant, pointless, something that she kept talking to Ben about in the way that one might refer too often to someone who has died in order to affirm their continued importance.

Ben called to cancel again. He had been promising to repair their mirror, and each time he was swept away into a paying job, and Ava felt the delicacy of her situation, how unreasonable it would be for her to complain. She still hadn't given him any money, and inexplicably, he hadn't brought it up again after that first date, but it hung between all their interactions, a reproachful presence that haunted Ava like the ghost of Jacob Marley.

Ava, somewhat reluctantly, accepted his invitation to a movie later that week. He kept taking her to see films, gritty, arty things that she mostly hated. "Isn't Cassavetes great?" he had asked excitedly as they left the theater the last time. "I really wanted you to see that one with me, the dialogue is incredible."

"I couldn't really hear anyone. The seventies were so ugly. Why even make movies if you're not going to have nice costumes?" She'd offered him what was left of her popcorn, but he shook his head and kept noticeably quiet for most of the walk back to her place. She'd walked beside him, chomping her popcorn, and thought of what an oddly mercurial person he so often seemed to be.

She hung up the phone and then in a burst of resoluteness, decided she didn't want to wait on Ben anymore. The sight of that mirror bound in its doleful tulle was making her too sad. That library, that one little corner of the club, had been her comfort and her refuge, and she was not going to sit around any longer while it buckled under their callous attentions. Also, she was glad for the excuse to turn away from her bookshelf.

At the hardware store, the clerk seemed willfully confused by her explanation of what she was trying to accomplish, and kept trying to sell her a variety of ornamental mirrors instead. Eventually she was able to buy a few metal brackets and, later that afternoon, managed with varying success to drill them into the wall, somewhat securing the mirror. The black metal arm looked awful cutting across the glass, and the mirror was not flush against the wall and wobbled a little, but it no longer strained forward at such a terrifying angle. The frame was still missing a corner of gilt cherubs and garlands, but at least there was no longer any danger. Ava kind of even liked the change; it now looked like a mirror that had seen some hard times, and she could identify with the impression of having lost a bit of shine over the last few months.

When Stephanie arrived visibly hungover, she was not pleased. "That looks horrible. Why hasn't Ben fixed it?"

Ava, pressing hard on a screw, hadn't heard her come in, and almost grabbed the mirror for balance before catching herself and holding on to a nearby shelf. "I didn't feel right about it. We still owe him so much."

"What's the point of dating a man without any money if he won't even fix things for you?"

"I thought you would be proud of me. What about self-sufficiency and being a team?"

"It looks awful."

There was a silence. Ava noticed she and Stephanie were wearing very similar shirts, and she wanted to tell her friend not to copy her style, but then this seemed ridiculous. No one had ever imitated Ava's odd way of dressing, so she had to wonder, had Stephanie always worn Peter Pan collars and Ava had just never noticed? It seemed essential to draw a distinction by right of previous habit as to who was dressing like whom. She was just about to say something about it when Stephanie yawned. "See if he'll fix the latch on the bathroom door, too. It keeps slipping. I brought some more books for you to look through, and some mail you should really look at." She put down a stack of new hardbacks bristling with envelopes.

Ava decided she would do neither of those things today, although she did not say this as she climbed down from the mantel and went to change into a sweater.

A few evenings later at an event—unemployed starlets reading excerpts of Shakespeare—Ava was trying to wake an unnervingly thin PR girl who had passed out on the main Lazarus stairs, while Mr. Dearborn watched, offering his objections from the step below.

"I know, I'm sorry, I'm trying to get her out of the way." Ava again shook a frail, limp arm.

"Absolute degeneracy. What's wrong with her anyway? I've never seen such goings-on in all my life. This isn't a bawdy house, for crying out loud."

Finally the young woman's eyes fluttered open. She smiled at Ava and then vomited all over Mr. Dearborn's feet.

He turned purple and left before Ava could apologize again. She hoisted the hiccuping young woman up and dragged her back towards the library where she deposited her into Stephanie's arms with suppressed fury. "Oh, gross." Stephanie immediately dropped her; the young woman happily curled up and went to sleep again.

"These people are going to ruin everything."

Stephanie looked at her coldly. "This is hardly my fault." She pointed at the woman on the floor. "And if you're not happy with our club, why don't you just invite all of your friends to our events instead?" She turned back to a previous conversation.

Ava was still smarting later when a tall older man trying to make conversation confessed, "Oh, you know I've always meant to read *The House of Mirth*," in that funny way that people often seemed to be asking for absolution from her, and she decided she had had enough. She would start a book club. They would read *The House of Mirth*. Goddamn it.

The resolution cheered her through the rest of the interminable party. It seemed an obvious choice, a "hook" even Stephanie would not be able to argue with, and through it, Ava hoped to return to that familiar country of big elegant books, a way back to herself through all the confusion of the last seven months. Not to mention she would finally get to sit in this library in her literary club and lead a discussion about a book she cared about. At last.

When she announced the project to their huge email list, nearly six hundred of Stephanie's acquaintances, eighty of which were actual paying members, she got a lot of responses from people she had never met saying things like "Fabulous!"

"Too exciting!"

"I've always wanted to read it." But following up, not a single person actually wanted to join. Even Stephanie backed out, citing her schedule. Determined, Ava insisted George read it with her. Rodney was also persuaded, and Ava knew she could count on Ben. This was the sort of thing he would be great at. When she asked, he said yes, and they settled on a date for his art lecture, which Ava was a little surprised to realize he had already fully organized.

One last piece of dim sum, "Golden Shrimp Treasure," sat squat in the round metal canister, empty variations of which covered the slick lacquered table. Ava poked it with a chopstick. It quivered, and its cold, larval shell split, a blob of filling, the shrimp treasure, she supposed, rolling free.

"I'm pretty sure that must be breaking some rule of Chinese etiquette," Ben said, flushed from eating too many dumplings.

She put down her chopsticks. "You're probably right. It feels rude."

He had arrived at noon to set up for his event. Once the bottles of wine were laid out, the AV set up to his approval and the empty chairs arranged in rows awaiting a speaker, there were still hours before the event, so they decided to go get dinner. Watching Ben's meticulous, thorough preparations and the neat list he'd checked off throughout the day had been relaxing, and also made her wonder why exactly she and Stephanie seemed to have such trouble in this regard. But even as she admired his calm efficiency, she found she almost resented his stepping so easily into the space they had laboriously wrung out of chaos.

Still, it was nice to sit here with him, with his soft, scuffed wool jacket that made him look like a young Romantic, and she wondered if anyone else in the restaurant had noticed them, the curious, envious gaze that she used to turn on others who had somehow become part of that mysterious dyad—the couple. "I'm thinking after *The House of Mirth*, we should probably read some Henry James, right? I can't decide if it would be more fun to have the reading group be Victorian Americans or maybe just novels obsessed with money and status, like throw some Trollope in next or something," Ava said, returning to their previous conversation.

"Don't you ever get excited about living people?"

"No." She seemed confused. "Do you?"

"Sure. I mean if you make art, it seems like maybe you might want to be in conversation with other people. You want to be a writer—don't you want to know what other writers are thinking about and working through these days?"

This seemed so beside the point that all at once the effort of trying to communicate with another human being consolidated into one intense knot of pressure behind her left eyebrow. She gave up for a minute and felt the hard lacquer slats of her chair dig into her back, watching a plastic cat next to the cash register wave its paw in delirious repetition. "No," she said. "I want to give voice to all the million shades of experience that I live through every single moment and never get to communicate with anyone. The important stuff, the real thoughts and feelings that no one ever says out loud." As she spoke, life seemed to well up around her proving her point—the keening murmur of a woman on the radio singing in Chinese, the breeze fluttering the dusty curtain that divided the kitchen from the rest of the room, the tap of someone's fork against a plate, the current of minutes inexorably passing.

"Yeah, but no one experiences life alone. We're communal creatures."

"I do."

"You don't." Ben sounded a little aggrieved. "I'm sitting right next to you."

"Is this just because you don't want to read my books with me?"

"I don't think you're hearing me. Sometimes I don't think you listen to me at all."

"That's ridiculous, the other day I listened to you talk about what's-his-name for like an hour."

"Lucian Freud. And it's because I think you would like him, if you would just trust me a little."

"Didn't sound like it." Ava wrinkled her nose.

Ben sighed. A waiter picked up the hard plastic bill tray for the second time in five minutes and put it down again, loudly. "Sorry, maybe I'm nervous about tonight. I'm sure you know that feeling. I've got a couple of big-name gallery people coming."

"You sound like Stephanie," she teased.

Ben did not like the joke and frowned, reaching for his wallet.

"Oh, she's not that bad," Ava felt compelled to add in the face of his palpable disapproval. The Gordian knot of disdain and admiration that bound her and Stephanie together seemed impossible to explain to one so clearly used to living in the clean strata of masculine categorizations.

They left the restaurant. Outside, the night was warm, an early, unseasonable balminess that offered a fake promise of spring and made Ava homesick for the South. A row of ducks in a butcher-shop window hung from twisted necks, glistening in their oily, roasted skin. "We've got time, want to walk for a while?" he asked.

The gutters of Chinatown ran shimmering, iridescent patches of oily water foaming with suds and the smell of bleach. Fish piled on shelves of ice grimaced through tiny jaws or swam despondently in white plastic buckets, and Ava watched them with a detached sympathy. It was fun walking almost in step with a tall handsome man. They were going to her salon where very important art people were gathering to talk about important things. This, from the outside, was pretty much exactly want she had wanted. As they moved through the crowd, she hung back just behind his shoulder, coasting under his forward momentum like a remora on a shark. "What sort of books would you want to read?" Ava asked.

"What?"

"In my book group. If you were going to be in conversation with the zeitgeist or whatever?"

"You really want to know?" he asked, surprised. Then his arm slid around her shoulder, and he gave her a squeeze, rambling enthusiastically about that winter's big important novel he had been wanting to read. "I always wanted to date a writer," he finished. "A cute girl with pens in her hair and a bigger vocabulary than me."

She felt a funny twinge, but it felt so safe here, enveloped in his glow, a kind of radiant confidence that included her in its generous invulnerability. Against the oncoming stream of people, she pressed a little closer to his side, as they walked north hand in hand. After a while, their palms got sweaty, and Ava suspected they were both waiting to see who would let go first. Ben rather sneakily accomplished the break by stopping to pick up a free newspaper, and Ava felt glad for the rush of cool air across her palm. But then, a few blocks later, to her surprise, he reached for her hand again and held it in his loose, relaxed grip as he walked with her all the way to the Lazarus Club.

At the event, Ava's feeling of security soon fled. The crowd, maybe a hundred people, was a little less shiny than Stephanie's; there were quite a few pairs of sneakers and paint-splattered windbreakers, but more studied, as if every aspect of their appearance had a well-considered theoretical position. Statement necklaces and asymmetrical hems predominated. A lot of the women's clothes didn't have any discernable fastenings, no zippers or buttons, but rather what Ava decided might be called "architectural" draping. In comparison, she felt ten pounds too heavy, as she did at most events, but more specifically, something about her neat skirt and heels also now seemed kind of obvious and pedestrian; everyone here was very forward-looking. She kept seeking out Ben, hovering awkwardly at his elbow, but he was busy greeting people, and finally feeling foolish, she retreated to her usual hideout behind the bar.

A gruff, handsome man in a thick turtleneck sweater, who reminded Ava of Captain Haddock, gave a PowerPoint presentation entitled "Intersections of Forest and Manhood," images of his elegant log cabin and handsome Weimaraner. A short Dutch woman with a heavy accent spoke for an hour about the destabilizing construct of the ocean as means of self-invention. A slender young man, cherubic in a backward baseball cap, talked about grass. Ava poured wine, mystified. The audience nodded appreciatively.

Their conversation, rippling with theory and unfamiliar portmanteaux, was impenetrable, but they all seemed very smart, and as the evening went on, very enthusiastic, especially about Ben. Wherever he moved, admirers circled around him, little eddies that gathered and broke according to his progress through the room. He blushed a lot, and seemed a little sweaty, often looking at the floor with the happily embarrassed mien of someone receiving compliments. His ears were pink, and he listened with earnest attention to each person, before apologetically moving on to the next firm handshake, the next congratulatory pat on the shoulder. Ava didn't doubt that he could have genuine relationships with so many people, but from a distance, especially if she squinted, his movement through the party didn't look all that different than Stephanie's. Ava wondered how the same set of basic gestures when hung on Stephanie's slender frame could look so frivolous, and so sincere and substantial when enacted by Ben.

Eventually he ended up at the bar beneath the arm of a beaming man whose bright pink forelock only accentuated the tight, hard lines around his eyes. "Isn't he just the most?" The man pinched one of Ben's cheeks hard. "The speakers were perfect, but this space. Too decadent, too gloriously bougie. I love it."

"This is Ava, it's her salon actually." Ben made introductions.

His attention shifted to her reluctantly. "Can I have a glass of that, dear?" he pointed at the wine in her hand.

"I thought you were going to talk about nautical charts or something," she said to Ben, pouring a glass. "Gentleman scholars and naturalists."

Pink forelock accepted the wine. "Whatever is Babycheeks Gertrude Stein here going on about?"

"Well, I want to have a career." Ben spoke into his swirling wine. "You always make me feel so defensive," he apologized.

"No, I don't," Ava countered, rather stupidly she realized.

But he was already being pulled back toward the other room. "Come, Ben," his friend said. "We have other important people you must be introduced to."

Ben looked at her regretfully over his shoulder as they merged back into the crowd. She heard excited greetings and a high giggle. All of a sudden Ava remembered Stephanie's words of so long ago. Was Ben an "art star," and what would that mean exactly? She had become so used to thinking of him as a paragon of artistic rectitude that it was hard to now see him engaged in what was very clearly self-promotion. If this was the sort of thing he was interested in, why was he dating her? More somberly, the thought struck her, was this perhaps the reason why he was dating her? Luckily, a row of empty cups and impatient expressions pulled her back to the present and away from her confused thoughts. She opened another bottle of wine, feeling the strain in her wrist as she yanked the cork free.

Later as Ava waited, still hoping Ben would come back at some point and talk to her, an older woman walked into the bar with a distracted air. She was petite and thin, perched on very high heels from which she surveyed the room, balanced delicately like a bird on a twig. Dark hair fell to her shoulders lit by two streaks of silver, and the bow of an enormous aquiline nose sailed forth from her face. She looked like a raven or a vampire, Ava thought approvingly. She seemed to part the crowd around her like a knife slicing through cake.

Noticing Ava's attention, she waved a voluminous cashmere sleeve, a gesture that both sought to end Ava's examination and yet excuse it, as if she were accustomed to the admiration her appearance evoked but disinclined to prolong it, and she wobbled over.

A little awed by this new guest, Ava offered her wine, wishing it wasn't in a plastic cup, the paltriness of the offering even more embarrassing after it was declined.

"No, thank you. I was having a drink with a friend downstairs, and we heard the ruckus. The bartender told me there was a writers' club up here, so I decided I had to see for myself. Although this building usually gives me quite the heebie-jeebies. Don't you feel like you're about to wander into 'The Cask of Amontillado' or something?"

"I always thought of the 'House of Usher.'" Ava had to smile.

The smile was returned. "It does seem like it's about to come crashing down. Wouldn't be the worst thing. You know that nutty president has gotten them into one lawsuit after another. From what I've heard, they've been bankrupt for years."

While this revelation had more than a glimmer of the truth about it, Ava wasn't ready to relinquish the aura of staid grandeur she had always associated with the club. "It's a beautiful building, though."

"It is. Those robber barons did well for themselves. So what exactly is it you're doing up here? Apparently it's giving all the old ladies, of which my friend is one, the fits. And you, my dear, seem about forty years too young for this place, if you don't mind my saying so."

Ava explained their concept as well as she could. At this point she barely knew what they were doing anymore. She may have said something or other about Proust.

"And you're in charge of this whole thing?" The stranger looked impressed. "I'm a writer myself. It's been a while since anyone has done something eccentric like this in New York. The city's been dead since everyone got rich."

"I am in charge," Ava said proudly. For what might have been the first time, she realized.

Introductions were made. Constance Berger was a writer, an essayist mostly, who, in her own words, now wrote for all the fancy publications she used to make fun of when she was a young troublemaker. "So I get it, loving all the fantastic old institutions like this but wanting to rough them up a little from the inside. You're a woman after my own heart, I suspect," she added with a smile.

"I'm not that exciting," Ava demurred. Constance Berger was hard to look away from. To Ava, who had spent so many years bemoaning her own prominent features, there was something magnificent about the unapologetically Semitic cast of her face.

Ava kept expecting her to leave at any moment, and was trying to prepare herself for the disappointment of it, but Constance Berger seemed disinclined to end the conversation, and lingered. As Ava rather more intently pressed hospitality upon her, she accepted the wine. "You picked a great name for a thing like this," she said. "That's such an underrated book."

"Thank you." Ava nodded emphatically. "I was just arguing that point with someone earlier tonight."

Constance turned and extended her arm. "Well, come on, show me around." The invitation felt like an honor, and Ava stepped out from behind the bar with an eagerness that made her stop short of taking the arm that was offered to her, just in case she was mistaken.

But Constance wrapped her arm around Ava's wrist anyway and pointed with the wineglass in her other hand. "Now, did you really do all this wallpaper?" It occurred to Ava she might be a little drunk.

As Ava led her through the large crowded room, she looked around the familiar space with new eyes, anxiously trying to preempt and excuse anything Constance might possibly disapprove of. She wasn't sure why she wanted to impress this woman whom she had only just met, but this was the first time that anyone at an event had paid her so much attention, and Ava responded with all the gleeful intemperance of a puppy who has been neglected for an afternoon. They stopped beneath the mirror, and Constance looked up appreciatively. "I have a strange affection for poorly made repairs, when you can see the seams. Something broken can never be made whole again, after all."

"I really did a bad job with this one."

Constance took a big, messy sip of wine and then daintily wiped away a drip from her chin. "It keeps this whole place from feeling too precious, you know. A palazzo where the roof leaks is infinitely more glamorous somehow."

Ava giggled. She noticed Ben watching her from a loud group of people. She turned her back on him, and continued her perambulations with Constance.

At the end of the evening, Ava was surprised to find he was remarkably petulant about her neglect. "You barely even acknowledged me," he said.

"That's not true. You were the one who was so busy all night."

He looked unconvinced, and Ava, who had never had occasion to be accused of ignoring anyone, wanted urgently to relieve him of a suffering she was only too familiar with. So she offered to switch books for their reading group to the one he wanted to read. She got a funny pain in her chest, but maybe it didn't matter so much to her in the end, and when he smiled and wrapped her in hug that pressed her uncomfortably against his hard collarbone, she consoled herself that at least she had a boyfriend and she would always be able to read *The House of Mirth* again some other time.

18

When Ava finally dragged herself to the bookstore to pick up the novel she had agreed to read, she was dismayed to find that it was a nine-hundred-page tour de force about an internet start-up. The back cover called it a "blistering indictment of contemporary America, a call to arms for the cubicle age, courageous, monumental, a work of genius."

"It's great." A bookstore employee passed by and grabbed a copy to give to someone else. "Really, really funny."

It was hard to imagine the author, a young man deathly serious behind thick glasses, ever having smiled, but, resigned, Ava put the book into the crook of her arm where its enormous weight dug into the skin of her forearm. Then, wandering the warmly lit, soothing aisles on her way to the Penguin classics, Ava stopped and asked someone to look up an author for her, and she spelled out Constance Berger's name with a funny shyness. Soon, she found herself in an unfamiliar corner, the essays and criticism section, and when she came upon the name on a spine, it was with a little shock as if she had uncovered something secret, private. She almost felt like she should have asked Constance's permission first; to pull this slender volume from the shelf seemed too intrusive, as though she had suddenly invaded the intimate terrain of someone else's thoughts. She flipped through a few pages. There were essays on art she hadn't seen, new books she hadn't read, a lot of queer theory that she didn't understand and then, with a quick flurry of surprise, Ava saw a mention of Proust. Constance liked Proust. Ava had mentioned Proust to her without this previous knowledge, and this filled Ava with an inexplicable elation. She hurriedly bought her books, not wanting to read any more in the exposed jostling of such a public place.

Ava dutifully read the entire grand, ambitious chronicle of Silicon Valley while drinking tepid prosecco from a coffee mug, and sighing a lot. George and Rodney had sounded suspiciously relieved when she called and told them about the change.

On the evening of the book club meeting, an icy rain was beating against the windows, and Ava was filled with conflicting emotions. It was exhilarating to have brought one element of their project in line with her aspirations, and to know that a whole evening stretched before her with the happy prospect of talking about books. However, she was not looking forward to talking about this one.

"Who wants to start us off?" she asked. George, his computer resting on his knees, was trying to organize their financial records with a program called Taxloop. He looked up apologetically. "No, you keep working on those," she said. Though she had come to accept that she was never going to get around to filing for nonprofit status, it had become an important aspiration to cling to, like Chekhov's sisters planning their never-to-be-made trip to Moscow. Stephanie in particular had become increasingly insistent that they at least enact the legal outlines, the empty gestures, of their grand altruistic project.

Rodney scratched his chin with the edge of the monstrous paperback. "I thought it was pretty funny. Especially all the stuff about TV."

"These guys do seem to talk a lot about TV," Ava agreed. "TV shows and masturbation."

"Yeah, that scene where he jerks off to *The Golden Girls* and feels so bad about it. I love that part, so honest. Also hilarious."

"Really?" Ava asked, and Rodney shrugged.

"Sure," Ben interjected. "He's making fun of himself."

"Okay, but still, like forty pages about his testicles seems kind of self-aggrandizing." Ava played with the corner of a page, unsure. "It all reminded me of when people laugh at their own jokes. No one actually talks like that, do they?"

"This from a woman who warned me the other day that 'the way ahead was fraught with discord.'" George didn't look up from his typing as he spoke. "I do it too, I'm just saying, we should be tolerant of each other's lapses into grandiosity."

"Fine," said Ava. "Point taken." A squall of rain lashed the dark windows, and it felt very cozy to be inside. Even being outnumbered couldn't totally destroy the pleasure of talking about a book. Mrs. Van Doren, whose loyalty to Ava had somehow outlasted the enmity of the rest of her circle, had agreed to join their book club. She thought they were still reading *The House of Mirth*, and a beautiful leather-bound copy sat on the arm of her chair, while she snored gently. "Can we at least talk about how there are no women in this except that one who does pornographic webcam stuff?"

"But the main character's in love with her—she's a huge part of the book," Ben argued.

"Yeah, but she's always in his computer. You can't think that's love."

"I think the author's making a point that love and desire aren't so easy to separate, especially for men sometimes."

"All the books I ever read are by men, and they aren't like this."

"Do you really think those stories are so different?" Ben asked, testily.

This premise momentarily shocked Ava into silence. "I think that's a very mean thing to say."

"How is that mean?"

"To compare classic books that elevate and tell real truths about the human condition with this." She waved her copy accusingly. "I think you're turning this into a personal attack."

Ben was starting to get exasperated. "I think you're making it personal. I'm just trying to have a discussion. I swear, you don't actually listen to anything I say."

"Why should I listen to you disparage all the things I love? To say that they are equivalent to this pointless waste of pages? I can barely even call it a novel."

"I liked this book," Ben objected angrily. "It's a good story and has some neat ideas. To expect real life to look like Victorian novels is crazy and a very limiting perspective."

"Are we still talking about the book?" George asked.

Before Ava could answer, Stephanie's laughter interrupted them. A cluster of well-dressed people, flushed and drunk, burst through the threshold, shaking the rain from expensive umbrellas. Waving a bare, unseasonably tan arm, Stephanie spoke loudly. "And this is our reading group, where we are paying tribute to one of the great women of literature, our namesake, if you will, Edith Wharton." An elderly man with a deep tan and a pocket square peered through a folded pair of reading glasses and wrapped a hand around Stephanie's waist to hear her better.

A girl in heels laughed from behind a curtain of blond hair. "I would just die of boredom," she said in an unexpectedly Borstal accent. "Could you ever?" she asked a sallow young man in a skinny suit who was holding her up, though just barely.

"Ghastly," he agreed.

Stephanie leaned toward them, whispering. "I know. You couldn't pay me to be in it."

As they moved toward the bar, Ava noticed a dark, quiet man in a very well-cut suit walking beside the most beautiful woman Ava had ever seen. Stoop-shouldered and small, he seemed content in his humble role, the terrestrial support of the goddess wrapped in hot-pink silk who towered above him, resting a lazy arm on his shoulder, diamonds flashing on her finger. Stephanie made a very emphatic face at Ava as they passed.

"Holy shit," said Rodney in a loud whisper, "that's Howard Steward. He's like a billionaire ten times over. I've seen his picture on newsletters—the Wobblies hate that guy."

"What?" Ben craned toward the bar. "How do you guys find these people?"

"Our boss works in mysterious ways, her wonders to perform," said George.

"Maybe I should go surveil them," Rodney said, rubbing his chin. "Also I think that drunk blonde lady is a famous supermodel."

"No. We're here to talk about books." Ava felt unreasonably antagonistic.

Laughter and the sound of popping corks came from the bar. "A glass of wine would be nice at least." Ben spoke petulantly to a stuffed peacock on the mantel behind Ava's head, borrowed from one of the downstairs parlors.

Ava frowned at him as she got up. "Can you guys keep talking about the book? Please."

Behind the bar, Stephanie was leaning forward on her elbows, conveying the playfulness of wealthy people serving themselves for a lark. "Bartender," the pocket-squared gentleman said with a flirtatious tilt of his head, "I'll have another. The same."

Stephanie winked. "Coming right up. Specialty of the house—red or red?" Then seriously, she added, "You know, when you're just a humble soon-to-be nonprofit, you have to do things on a penny. When we have our own town house, I'm going to put in a whiskey and cigar bar. For writers who need a place to relax." She pivoted to Howard Steward, who was checking his phone, his beautiful wife looking silently and scornfully at Stephanie. "Part of our expansion will include our literacy outreach to underserved areas. We believe the children are our future." She laughed a little at herself, but not nearly enough, in Ava's opinion. "And your youth philanthropy is famous all over the city."

"I try to give back." He looked sleepy. His wife handed him a handkerchief from her bag unasked. He blew his nose and declined the wine Stephanie was offering.

"Ava," Stephanie introduced them, "Mr. Steward gave us a ride here. In his Maybach," she whispered excitedly, though maybe a little too loudly.

Ava felt embarrassed for all of them. "Very nice to meet you." She took a bottle of wine and glasses from behind the bar. "Excuse me. I have to get back to the reading group."

She felt a pull on her sweater, and Stephanie again whispered, "Can't you stay and hang out? He likes a crowd. This could be very big for us."

"I have only ever loved brilliant women," Mr. Pocket Square was telling the room.

The presumed supermodel leaned against the bar, smoking with her eyes shut. She slightly opened one eye. "I was top form in my A levels," she said, then ashed into her designer purse and burped.

Her date placed a hand on her ass. "She's fucking brilliant."

"I can't," Ava whispered to Stephanie. "I just can't."

"Jesus, you're so totally useless," Stephanie hissed back.

"I'm not being useless," Ava objected. "I'm doing what we set out to do. That book club in there—" the wineglasses she was holding by their stems rattled as she pointed "—is the only time we have ever done anything remotely like our original mission. Although to be honest, at this point, it's getting hard to remember what we started all this for."

"Librarians can get so worked up when discussing literature." Stephanie laughed toward Mr. Steward before yanking hard on Ava's elbow and pulling her a few feet farther into a corner. "This is serious money and you are fucking it up right now. Nobody cares about your stupid book club. Stop acting like it matters and do what I tell you before this whole project tanks."

"What do you mean nobody cares?" Ava wrenched her elbow from Stephanie's grasp. "It matters to me."

"You're being so childish right now. I don't know how I've gotten as far as I have with you as a partner. You're just dead fucking weight sometimes, Ava." Stephanie turned away from her. "You know we're going to be reading Baldwin next," she said to Mr. Steward. "You should really consider joining our book club. We would really love to hear your unique perspective on things."

The prospect of reading James Baldwin with Stephanie must have left Mr. Steward unmoved because he yawned and checked his watch.

The wineglasses in Ava's hand gave a high warning chime as she struggled to control her angry trembling. How dare Stephanie think of her like that when this whole project had come to be because of Ava's job at the Lazarus Club, a job she already felt she was on the verge of losing because of all of this nonsense. How could Stephanie say she, her best friend, didn't matter next to that gruesome bunch she had collected? It didn't seem possible. It didn't make sense.

She returned to the library feeling a little like she had just had the wind knocked out of her.

"I think I just remembered," Rodney was saying. "That big fashion show where the models wear bras made of diamonds? I think she's one of those."

"Really?" George glanced over his shoulder with a heroic effort at casualness. "Maybe I should go see."

"I promise you guys don't want to go in there." Ava poured herself a very full glass of wine, while the three men around her seemed somewhat unconvinced. She sat, stewing in hurt feelings.

"I think we were getting to something interesting," Ben said, leaning forward and tapping the book in his hands. "About the ways that some of the themes people used to write about get rearranged for a different age, like what does a romance look like now? Would Anna Karenina be online dating for example?"

It took Ava a minute to realize he was still talking about the book, and when she did she got mad all over again. "Not Anna! How could you compare the two?" In her already emotional state, Ava felt a passionate defensiveness for Anna Karenina and, by extension, Tolstoy. "Why are you being such an asshole?"

Surprise made his ears stick out, and Ava decided he didn't look at all like Arthur Rimbaud. "Ava, what are you talking about?"

"You don't like any of the things I care about. You think the books I like are old and stodgy and weird, just like me. That I'm just dead weight."

Ben's confusion was quickly turning to anger. "I have no idea what you mean, dead weight, but what I do think is that it can be very difficult to talk to you when you aren't interested in hearing what the other person has to say."

"You didn't want to read *The House of Mirth*," Ava countered.

"So what?" Ben almost yelled. "That's not some referendum on you as a person. It just means I like to read other stuff, too. And see other movies besides costume dramas. And I want to be able to talk about it all with you and discuss the things that interest me, but you just stop listening and it can be very frustrating." He paused, thinking. "No. It's not just frustrating. It's hurtful. Rude."

Ava had never ever been so accused, and as she had stacks of old etiquette books that she followed to the letter, this felt like an outrageous slur. "I'm not rude."

"You are. You ignore me in the rudest ways all the time. Every time I try to tell you about something that didn't happen in the nineteenth century. But for just one more example, I consider it very rude to tell someone you're going to pay them for the work they do and then lie about it."

A wave of embarrassment made Ava's ears prickle, and before she could stop and think about it, she quickly answered him, "Well, I think it's rude that you don't seem to care that whenever we fool around, I never have an orgasm."

There was a deafening silence in the room, which George broke by humming quietly at the ceiling.

Rodney cleared his throat. "More wine?" he asked George, and filled his glass to the top.

"I think I'm just going to go see what's on and about in the other room." George put his computer aside, and left, sloshing a few drops of wine behind him as he went. Rodney, however, sat back in his chair, crossing his legs with the barest hint of a smile.

"Yeah, okay, Ava." Ben stood. "I'm going to go now. I think you're an interesting person, but you're not nice. And you don't seem to have any idea how relationships work."

"I know I don't," Ava said softly, looking at her lap.

"Well, that's the first self-aware thing I think I've ever heard you say. Good luck with all this. I still think it was a cool idea." He slung his bag over his head and onto one shoulder and waited.

Ava looked away.

"Okay. Fine. Bye, Rodney," she heard him say, while she stared hard at the book in her lap until the title wavered in the edges of her vision. She hated Comic Sans so much. She heard the door close.

"Cheer up, comrade," Rodney said, a little too brightly, she thought. "Romantic love is a bourgeois construct anyway."

She gulped some wine. She had messed it up again. She was going to end up a spinster. How could she be so bad at this? Stephanie's laugh floated from the other room. Mrs. Van Doren snored, a gentle cooing whistle. Rain fell. A quiet helplessness welled up within her, and she yielded to it, glumly staring at the last few glittering feathers of the peacock's tail beside her.

Eventually something banged, startling her out of her reverie. When she looked up, Mr. Dearborn was standing by the door, leaning both hands on his cane with a more sprightly air than usual. Ava almost thought he was smiling. And then, even though he had her attention, he banged his cane on the floor again and seemed pleased at the sound of it. "Yes?" Ava asked.

But Mr. Dearborn just waited. He was definitely smiling at her, she decided, and it was very unpleasant. She considered asking him to just please go away as she had already had a very difficult night and didn't need him grinning at her like the specter of death when she had just this minute been broken up with, but before she could figure out a reasonable way to phrase such a request, Aloysius entered the room with a bundle of Kleenex and a *World Book Encyclo-*

pedia. His preternaturally black hair stood on end, and Ava noticed a short halo of white roots at his scalp that made it almost look like his hair wasn't attached to his head but rather floated above him like an angry cloud.

With a nervous glance at Mr. Dearborn, he spoke loudly to Ava. "I've just come to tell you that things are not going to continue as they have been around here, no, sir. Don't think for a moment that they will."

Ava allowed herself a short moment of rubbing her eyes. Finally, she opened them and looked at the blurry figures in front of her to face what was coming. "What's the trouble, Aloysius?"

"It's just beyond all reckoning." He shook his hands violently for a minute and tucked the book under his arm to press the bridge of his nose. "We have never had such problems in the club. The very idea of our members being assaulted, *assaulted*, by bodily fluids on the very steps of this institution, by plague-ridden harlots. Who knows what Mr. Dearborn could have caught? That you would bring such an element into my club, putting not only our reputation but our very health at risk, it's just unsupportable. And that—" his voice rose to a shriek pointing at Ava's poorly repaired mirror, which he appeared to be noticing for the first time "—you're tearing this place apart!"

Mrs. Van Doren, roused by the baying of the Lazarus Club president, opened her eyes, shifting into wakefulness with a reptilian stillness. "Oh, hello, Aloysius. How have you been? I missed you at Westminster last month. The Lhasa Apsos were tremendous."

Aloysius glided toward her and melted over the back of her chair. "Oh, Mrs. Van Doren, I didn't see you there. You know what I've been going through." The high ridge of her wingback chair seemed to prevent him from nuzzling the silk scarf around her neck, and he sighed so hard it almost ruffled her stiff curls. "Trying to keep this place together, trying to make everyone happy. I work my fingers to the bone—" Aloysius extended his chubby pink fingers for Mrs. Van Doren's inspection "—just like a slave."

"Oh, hello, Arthur," she sniffed in the direction of Mr. Dearborn.

"Flora." He nodded coldly.

"I know what the board said, Aloysius dear, and they're a bit high-spirited, but it's so lively having young people about." Mrs. Van Doren patted him on the arm. "I just know I would miss them."

"Miss us?" Ava asked.

Aloysius unwrapped himself from Mrs. Van Doren and handed Ava an envelope. "I suppose you'll have to go, too. I've given that other one two of these already." He leaned in to whisper to Ava, "I would be careful about her. I suspect she's somewhat fast. Rodney, go back downstairs," he commanded as he left. Mr. Dearborn gave Ava one more of his death's head smiles before turning and clomping slowly after Aloysius.

"Are you on the clock?" Ava asked.

Rodney ambled past her in no particular hurry. "All wages are theft."

Inside the envelope, folded into an unfamiliar and official-seeming four folds, a properly formatted letter of business was, as it declared, a third and final notice of eviction. The lessor (The Lazarus Club) desired to inform the lessee (The House of Mirth Literary Society, LLC) that due to repeated failure to pay the stipulated monthly rent of $1,000.00, under due process of the state of New York, the lessee was hereby required to pay the full amount owed, $7,000.00, or vacate the premises before the end of the current calendar month or immediate court proceedings would be instituted. Sincerely, Andrew Henlow Tilley IV, Esquire, Attorney at Law.

Three notices? They had received three notices already, and Ava hadn't seen one of them?

Stephanie. Of course.

Ava should have known, should have expected. Stephanie always thought she knew better, that she didn't have to concern herself with pedestrian matters like debt and eviction or just the simple human decency she might owe a friend who has put her life and job and house on the line for her. And why would she, if she considered Ava useless? She glanced toward the bar, but a loud peal of laughter stopped her. She couldn't possibly confront her friend, her best friend, her only real friend, with all those people around; betrayal had stripped the skin away, and she couldn't subject the raw wound of her feelings to the casual scrutiny of strangers.

She noticed that Mrs. Van Doren, clawed hands resting on her armrests, was watching her expectantly. "You knew about this?" Ava asked.

Mrs. Van Doren waved a hand sort of apologetically, then cracked her knuckles, flashing a gold leopard biting a diamond chain that took up most of her index finger. "You mustn't put too much faith in Aloysius, dear," she said. "I've known him since he was a child, but according to the board, he's a bit of a snake. I believe they are planning on getting rid of you two and renting this space out to someone else for much more money now that it's so nice here. I agree it's a shame after you've worked so hard, but as a woman who's put more than a few husbands into the ground, may I offer some advice?"

Ava nodded.

"Don't waste your time around here. Marry rich while you still can. And read books. Lots of books like this one." She tapped a coral nail on the Wharton next to her. "A girl's got to find her way in this sorry world." She reached a bony arm toward the shelf closest to her. "This one, too. I almost dropped out of Vassar because of this one." She tossed it to Ava, chuckling at the memory and twirling the leopard around her knuckle. One of the estate books Ava hadn't noticed before, *Three Guineas* by Virginia Woolf. She was so sick of everyone always telling her to read Virginia Woolf.

"Um, thanks for the suggestion." Ava took the book. "Please excuse me one moment."

Down the familiar hallway, she fled with the impression that the building swayed above her head, just waiting to crash around her ears. Everyone had betrayed her. Ava knew better than to be caught like this, a lesson hard learned in all those terrible years of grade school, but she had forgotten, her longing had made her weak and lazy, and she had let herself be baited out of her solitude just to be deceived and humiliated. She ran down the stairs to the main entrance, but paused with the uncomfortable realization that there was nowhere she wanted to go. New York was full of strangers and elbows, and she couldn't face the bruising that navigating that human stream would entail. The Lazarus Club was all she had, and now it wanted to chew her up and spit her out.

Through the iron grill where the curling initials of the club were held captive by a profusion of iron vines, Ava noticed something big and shiny and black. Howard Steward's Maybach glistened in glorious, anachronistic repose, as though the Duke of Windsor had just pulled up, and Ava admired it even as frenzied thoughts ran through her head. *Three weeks. What would they tell their members? They had events scheduled that would have to be canceled. Deposits had been paid, swallowed up by the ceaseless accumulation of daily costs. How could they possibly pay back everyone who had paid membership dues? And where would she live? How was she going to pay off her credit card? What was she going to do?*

"Nice car."

"What?" Ava started in the cold marble lobby.

"It's a nice car," Castor repeated. "Mr. Steward is quite a successful man," he said with what Ava almost thought was a note of friendliness, the first she had ever heard from him. "He's a good person to have on your side."

"I guess." Ava watched rain bounce on the polished roof outside. "I don't know if he'll be much help."

"Are they kicking you out?" he asked.

Ava nodded. "How have you managed to stand this place, Castor?"

"Not my name."

"What?"

"It's not my name," he said a little more curtly. "It's just what they call the doormen here. Weird ass name it is, too."

"I'm sorry." Ava wasn't sure if she should say more and waited, hoping he might introduce himself properly.

But he licked the tip of his pencil, and looked down to let her know their conversation was over. "Burn this place down someday," he mumbled to himself, writing in his small black notebook.

Ava desperately wanted to ask what his real name was and what he was writing, but it seemed intrusive, and she decided it was time to go home.

Back in her apartment, she pulled off her clothes, turned on the taps, and sat down in the cold tub. Not quite warm water swirled around her, and she shivered, closing the drain with a clank. She didn't get up to turn on the lights. With her chin on her knees, she held her toes in her hands, watching as goose bumps made the hairs on her shins stand up. *Eviction. Evicted.* All that work, all that debt, all those seven months. He couldn't mean it. He couldn't cast her out. There had to be a way. Aloysius liked her, he always had. She would figure out how to reenlist him in their cause.

Mycroft leapt onto the lid of the toilet where he sat, cleaning his lips with large, rhythmic passes of his tongue. Ava held out a finger, and he licked a drop of water from it. Purring bounced against the dark of the small, tiled room. As water crept up the side of her ribs, Ava had to acknowledge that despite the looming catastrophe, she was relieved to be here, alone, in the bath.

Eventually, she heard a loud banging on her door, which she ignored. After a few minutes of knocking and yelling her name, Stephanie gave up. "I know you're in there, Ava. We have to talk. I gave you copies of this ages ago. It's not my fault you don't read your mail." Ava draped a wet washcloth over her eyes; funny that the collapse of her entire world could feel so warmly relaxing.

19

The next morning, Ava woke up to a note under her doorstep.

I knew you would freak out. Stop worrying. It takes months to evict someone. Everything is fine. We'll fix it. Call me. We've got work to do. (Sorry we got into a tiff, you know I love you heart heart kiss kiss, but seriously you were being a little unreasonable. Smiley face)

Ava didn't call. She also didn't answer the phone later when it rang. Unable to face Stephanie or the Lazarus Club, Ava decided to have the stomach flu. And every time Stephanie called thereafter, Ava told her she was puking and promptly hung up, despite Stephanie's outraged sputtering. Ava spent the next few days in her apartment crying over her losses—her boyfriend, her apartment and her salon—and rearranging her bookshelves, separating the doomed love stories from the happy. In the end, the cheerful marriage plots outnumbered the death and despair shelves by so much that she demoralized herself all over again. Everyone could pair off successfully except her, apparently. The poster of Arthur Rimbaud lost its place of privilege above her bed, and Ava spent many long hours studying the blank space left behind. He had been there fluttering her heart for ten years, and now his pretty face was consigned to the darkness of the closet. Her heart had not quite yet closed around the loss, and she didn't have the energy to shift all her other pictures around to disguise the visible reminder of what was now forsaken. She couldn't even bear to think about the rest of it.

She considered calling her mom, but she was pretty sure nothing her mom was going to say would make her feel better. She even dug up *A Room of One's Own*, thinking maybe she would find some vicarious maternal consolation in it, but at the last minute the gauzy picture on the cover of a lady looking sadly out of a window into a swirling pink cloud was just too unappealing; she was not that limpid creature.

The one bright spot that kept Ava from total despondency was that Constance Berger called and, since Ava was still mostly not answering the phone, left a message inviting her to tea. And then as if she knew, as if she could see right into the heart of Ava's timid equivocations, told her not to bother calling back, she would just expect her the following Wednesday at three. What a gift that brisk directive was, and Ava listened to the message over and over just to hear her say that wonderful, absolving phrase again.

By the time that day arrived, Ava was sick of canned soup, tired of hiding from Stephanie and very glad to get out of her house. She washed and set her hair. She found a nice tweedy dress that didn't make her look too lumpy. She wound her pocket watch. The front door of the Lazarus Club banged behind her as she left.

When she came out of the subway, the Upper West Side was filled with sunshine. Ava was drinking a cup of peppermint tea, trying to calm her nervous stomach, but it was scalding hot, and each time she tilted the cup, a little burst of liquid welled up through the small plastic hole in the lid and burned her lips. She winced, wiped her mouth, and minutes later, when in anxious anticipation of where she was going, she forgot and nervously took another sip, the unhelpful lid did the same thing again. She gingerly touched her tender lip and threw the full cup of tea into a garbage can where it landed with a wet thud. A dog walker passed, a stern charioteer behind a web of leashes, the dogs all wearing coats. She looked up at the numbers, searching for Constance Berger's building.

In all her time in New York, she had never really been called to the wide avenues near Riverside Drive before, and she was surprised at how grand and vaguely French it all seemed. She had never been to France, but in so many of her favorite novels, these were just the sorts of buildings she imagined adulterous lovers and governesses and courtesans hurrying in and out of. The decorative stonework erupting over the doors and around the parapets of the heavy square blocks of apartments called to her mind just the mix of frivolity and bourgeois virtue that she associated with Second Empire Parisians. When she finally found it, the building impressed Ava with its stateliness, and she lurked outside for a minute trying to remember the name of the main character of *Sentimental Education*. He had been another of her nineteenth-century heroes, and from what she remembered he had walked down a lot of unfamiliar streets like these; she was surprised that she couldn't think of his name; it was unlike her.

It seemed that, like reading, she had also lost the habit of daydreaming, staring at her bookshelves, invoking the phantoms of the past and her imagination. Life had rushed in, her books had receded. Now trying to summon the characters and situations she would have previously used for guidance, she found them distant and immaterial. It was a little terrifying to be out in the world and feel so unequipped. Life felt strangely indistinct. But at least here she was far away from the Lazarus Club and the terrible troubles looming there.

The doorman of the building watched her indifferently but steadily enough to make her feel guilty, and it was the desire to prove that she had legitimate business in his dominion that finally pushed her into the lobby. It would have been nice if the elevator had been older. She imagined in a building like this that she would have the satisfaction of slamming a metal cage before being whisked upward, but it was sadly modern and nondescript. Ava wiped her sweaty palms against her skirt and then tried to remove the little strands of gray wool that came off on her fingers. Eventually, released into a mint-green corridor, she hesitated by the call buttons, admiring an old brass mail shoot. An eagle struggled to free itself from a profusion of ribbons on the cover that she lifted and let fall with a clang. With a slow rattle, the elevator cast off on its next trip.

Ava pressed the bell and hoped she had misunderstood the invitation and would have to leave after just a few minutes of polite apologies with promises to return some other time. Instead the door opened, and Ms. Berger stood in front of her as wild and strange-looking as before. Ava felt she could almost see herself reflected in the black, glassy, slightly convex eyes. Just as her gaze was giving Ava the terrifying impression that she could see into the depths of her soul, she smiled and turned, waving at Ava to follow. "So glad you came," she said. "Call me Constance."

Hunched and frail, she swayed on the points of another pair of very high heels, an unsteady gait that made walking seem like an impromptu imitation of the common activity, one she was trying out for a lark. Ava felt an impulse to put a supportive hand under one of her elbows, but refrained.

They entered a living room lined with bookshelves and filled with stacks of books on every surface. The disorder gave the impression that these were objects of utility to their owner, as if a system of organization would betray a purely decorative or superficial cast of mind that Constance Berger had no time for. Instead these books stood waiting to impart their knowledge as practical as a sandwich or pencil, casually functional. It made her own newly ordered shelves feel very superficial in comparison.

Despite the clutter, the room was peaceful. There were no sounds of traffic. Faint squares of March sunlight traced the high windows on a faded carpet. Ava accepted a seat on a blue velvet sofa and sank much lower into the cushions than she expected to. She felt a strange urge to lie back among these overstuffed cushions and take a nap. She imagined she would wake up with that same calm that comes at the end of an illness, when a fever has finally broken and the world feels cool, filled with ease like a glass of cold water.

They sat in silence for a moment while Constance smiled a friendly, slightly unfocused smile. "Were you able to find the place okay?" she asked.

Ava nodded. "I've never been to this neighborhood much."

"I like it, reminds me of Europe."

"That's what I was thinking," Ava said, excited, and then wanted to talk about Flaubert and Zola and government building projects of the Second Empire and the triumph of the haute bourgeoisie and whether demimondaines were as tragic as they seemed. But she didn't. "Although I've never actually been," she clarified for fear of sounding presumptuous.

"You should, a girl of your temperament. The whole continent is practically the Lazarus Club, antiquated, fusty, totally delightful. May I get you a cookie?" Constance crossed one leg over the other. "My neighbors have been on an entrepreneurial frenzy, and I figure Girl Scout cookies are the tithe I pay for being childless on the Upper West Side." She smiled again, self-effacing and apologetic, but then looked at Ava with a glance so quick, but so piercing, Ava had the impression she was enacting these dowdy mannerisms like a shield, a defensive scrim behind which Constance was a much sharper woman. The perception gave Ava a tiny thrill that she didn't quite understand, and disarmed by her own observation, she nodded. Constance rose slowly as though climbing tentatively into her own center of gravity. Seeing her standing, poised and delicate on the tiny points of her heels, it struck Ava again that this awkward fragility was some sort of a deliberate affectation; Constance wasn't actually very old, and she was very self-possessed. Ava was fascinated. "I'll fetch us some. The Samoas are particularly good."

While she was gone, Ava scanned the bookshelves, pleased to recognize many of the spines. There was something thrilling about this alignment of tastes; it seemed to imply a possible intimacy just waiting to erupt, an established structure of kindling awaiting a match. She wondered if that were the sort of thing it was acceptable to say. *I have a lot of the same books as you do, therefore we should be friends.* She suspected it wasn't, and yet wasn't this exactly why she was here? How did one establish a connection with someone when conversation seemed so stilted, so ill-suited for sharing important things? She wanted to run her fingers along these stacks of books, to establish even just a tactile connection with this woman whose mind ran along similar currents but whose breadth of experience, judging from the variety of these shelves, made Ava's own well of inspiration seem a meager stream in comparison.

Constance returned with a pile of cookies spread out on the blue-and-white figures of a plate of Delft china. Ava took one, glad for something to do with her mouth and hands.

"Take a couple, one is just torturing yourself. Indulgences are for the young, and you're so very young."

"Thank you." Ava clutched a stack of gooey circles and felt the chocolate stripes immediately start to melt across her palm. "Although, if you'll excuse me, you don't seem that old."

The high arch of Constance's brow lifted only slightly, but it was enough to cast her smile as an inquiry. "You're very polite. And I love people who still abide by a code of manners."

Ava wanted to tell her about all the Victorian etiquette books on her shelves at home, but shyness prevented her. "I haven't had a Girl Scout cookie in a long time," she said just to be saying something as she placed the first cookie in her mouth. Chocolate, caramel, coconut and vanilla cookie crumbled across her tongue, the combination almost forgotten but immediately recognizable.

Ava's eyes rested on the shelf nearest her line of vision where she noticed a group of familiar spines, their common interest. "Which translation is your favorite?" she asked, pointing, her annunciation slightly marred by caramel.

Constance was snapping into a Thin Mint with brittle efficacy. She turned around. "Of the Proust, you mean? Oh, I think it's hard not to love the first one you were exposed to. Although, it's difficult to say, I think Lydia should have kept going. Then it would be fair to judge. Do you like Proust?"

The many years of hiding this affection made her small nod feel like the confession of a long-secret shame.

"How wonderful." Constance's smile was just a bit devilish, and she asked, "Which volume is your favorite?"

Ava thought for a moment. *"The Captive."*

Again the dark, delicate line of Constance's eyebrow rose. "Really? That's an unusual choice. I feel like you can tell so much about a person from which volume they like best."

Ava found she was blushing and wasn't sure why.

"Poor girl, imagine having to put up with Marcel." Constance took another Thin Mint, holding it up for contemplation as she spoke. "The idea that women can satisfy each other perfectly well without them has always driven men to distraction. But a girl has to eat." She cracked the cookie with a sharp, pointed incisor.

Ava was starting to feel a little warm, and she pulled her blouse down from where it was creeping into her armpits. She had never really thought of Albertine this way, and she felt confused by this sudden opening of horizons like a curtain that had been pulled back too quickly, blinking in the unexpected infusion of light. "I thought she was just messing with him." Ava realized how insubstantial this sounded.

"You should be wary of putting too much faith in a narrator's point of view." Constance smiled. "It's not their fault, but they so often prove to be less than reliable. Especially if they're clever and charming and such pleasant company."

While they were talking, the back of one of Constance's shiny shoes had slid free from her crossed foot and now dangled from the tip of her toes, revealing the narrow bones and high arch. Constance moved her leg, the shoe wavered, and just as Ava thought it was about to fall, with a twist of her ankle she brought it to sit firmly on the back of her foot again. "So you talk like a writer—is this why you started your project?" she asked, looking at Ava with a curiosity that seemed to have sharpened.

Ava wasn't sure what to answer; everything felt filled with a flickering significance that welled up, flooding her with a confused elation, then subsided again beneath the flow of words. Finally, she had found someone to talk with about books in all of the ways she had always dreamed of. "Yes," she said. "Well, not really," she amended.

"Please, spare me the self-deprecation," Constance interrupted her. "I understand why you do it, but I just can't abide it." Despite the sharpness of her tone, this impatience felt strangely loving. "That's quite a club you seem to have put together." Constance recrossed her legs in the opposite direction, and Ava found she was staring at the other shoe waiting to see if this one would slip, as well. She wanted to stay in this apartment and talk to Constance forever.

"Well, I've been working as a librarian for the last few years."

"How orderly and quiet. I always had a fantasy of being a librarian. But maybe that's just because I used to like the way I looked in glasses."

"That might be why I took the job in the first place," Ava admitted. A strangely expectant silence hung between them at this acknowledgment of their physical selves. They both probably did look good in glasses, Ava thought and flushed at the idea. She wondered why she had assumed Constance would be so much older. Was she in her fifties? Maybe, if Ava had to guess. She wanted to ask and then suddenly felt very confused and embarrassed that she even wanted to know. What could it possibly matter? "Do you wear glasses?" Ava asked, and her voice made a funny wobble, out of place in such an innocent question. But the slight incline of Constance's posture shifted, as if the intimacy of the question seemed clear to her, and she watched Ava curiously. Ava realized she needed a plan. She had come in the excitement of finding a sympathetic acquaintance, but it now felt imperative that she have reason to come back, to yield to the strange magnetic force that circled Constance. She wanted to impress herself upon the material of Constance's mind and see the shape of the image she left behind, to find a reason to return to this apartment that smelled of old books and bergamot. "I read your book and thought it was amazing and was wondering if you might want to do a reading at our space," she said with sudden inspiration.

"It's a pretty glorious space to read in," Constance agreed.

Then remembering the precariousness of their position, Ava qualified quickly, "It would have to be in the next few weeks." She apologized.

"That's a little soon, but there's a chance I could do it. Why such a hurry?"

"We're having some complications at the Lazarus Club."

"Honestly, I don't know how you can stand that place. It's beautiful, but those people are deranged. That president asked me if it was my habit to wear trousers, generally. I almost told him it was my habit to bed anything in a skirt, *generally*, but then I didn't want his aneurysm on my conscience."

Ava was trying so hard not to appear embarrassed at this revelation, she found she couldn't decide where she was supposed to be looking.

"I'm sorry," Constance said, just a little archly. "Have I shocked you, my dear?"

"Of course not," Ava lied. "I've read *The Well of Loneliness*." She had, by accident as a teenager, thinking that Radcylffe Hall was a man's name. She had been mildly scandalized by the subject matter then and very impressed with what an intuitive, sympathetic author he turned out to be. She had actually read it twice.

Constance laughed. "I see."

Ava was feeling very funny now, as if the air in the room had become very thick and hard to breathe, but she didn't want Constance to notice anything, so she shifted again, accidentally bumping over a pile of books at her elbow. "I'm sorry," she said, picking them up, glad for a moment to be able to turn her back. "I love this book," she said, holding up a heavy volume. Again, this was the kind of thing she normally felt compelled to hide, and the thrill of confession struck her again, wild, liberating.

In order to read the title, Constance bent toward Ava, bringing with her the scent of gardenias. "Montaigne, I also always loved Woolf's essay on him."

Deciding this was getting ridiculous, Ava mentally committed to reading those books as soon as she got home.

She finished stacking the books and ate another two cookies. Still inclined to chat, Constance asked where Ava was from, and they had a spirited discussion of the virtues of raw oysters of which Constance was a fan. Eventually Ava knew she needed to go. She needed to leave before she did something to ruin this perfect afternoon. "I don't want to take up too much of your time," she said finally.

"It's been a pleasure. I look forward to seeing you again in the full glory of your salon. Just give a call about the details when you have them."

For one instant, the House of Mirth flickered around Ava, the glamorous, elevated endeavor she had intended. "Thank you," she whispered. "I will. Soon, I promise."

On her way out, Ava snuck a glance through an open door, a bedroom, another pair of high heels overturned on the floor. She wasn't sure why, but it made her happy that this impractical footwear was an established proclivity. For someone who moved as gracelessly as Constance and whose bones were so tiny, the gesture seemed both a rejection of frailty and the heightening of it to a near aggressive act. The shiny talons seemed so sexual, so assertive and yet the fear she might topple over at any minute bespoke a vulnerability that filled Ava with a confused empathy. As one who had agonized over the various messages that could be read in the trappings of appearance, Ava couldn't help but admire the contradictory, complicated, intriguing story bound up in these beautiful shoes.

Alone in the hallway, she stood for a minute in front of Constance's door and waited, she wasn't quite sure for what exactly, but the equilibrium of her world seemed to have rattled, and she needed a moment for it to settle.

Outside, the sun was still shining, and she stopped at a fruit stand on a corner and bought an orange. She dug her nails into the thick peel, ripping it free in large, satisfying chunks, and disposing of them conscientiously in a green wire garbage can. In the distance she saw the low, stone walls of Central Park.

The park was still bare, and high, spindly branches arched above paths lined with benches. A kid on a bike trailing pink streamers, a pair of runners in spandex, teenagers walking intertwined, their hands in each other's back pockets—Ava felt surrounded by what seemed like creatures from another world. As if a pair of blinders had been removed, the narrow walls that enclosed her previous life seemed to have shattered, and she looked with surprise at a universe that seemed new and glossy and full of interest. She sat on a bench, not far from an old lady napping into a twisted scarf, and finished her orange, happy to admire this vibrant pageant that seemed to unfurl in proportion to her pleasure in observing it. A toddler stumbled by on unsteady legs, a tiny drunk chasing an unflustered pigeon. A pair of Havanese carried the ends of their leashes in their mouths, proudly rendering their walker superfluous. People flew past on Rollerblades, bicycles, skateboards, all manner of wheeled contrivances, and the thought struck her—people exercised—and the strangeness and simplicity of it only underscored the attenuated parameters of the life she had been living. She wanted to talk to all of these people, to ride a bike, to engage somehow in the spectacle of life that was taking place. Orange pips burst in her mouth, and she wished she could express to someone the wonderful particularity of sitting on this bench, on this afternoon, the taste of citrus bright against her tongue, and the obscure sense of possibility that bubbled up through all of these impressions.

20

The next morning she woke up to a violent pounding on her door, and when she opened it, Stephanie handed her a brown paper bag. "I brought you some fucking chicken soup because there is no way you can possibly still be puking, and to be quite honest, I'm a little upset that you would pick a time like this to get sick when I am out there hustling like crazy to try and save our asses."

"Thanks," said Ava, thinking that she should still be mad, but knowing from experience the futility of waiting for apologies from Stephanie; she accepted the bag.

Stephanie looked her up and down. "I would have thought you would be skinnier."

Ava didn't answer, and put the soup down. "Do you want coffee?"

After a brisk nod, Stephanie sat down on the foot of Ava's bed, her fingers tented in deliberation. "So I found a lawyer who said he would meet with us."

"We don't have any—" Ava began.

"Pro bono. He's a friend of a friend," Stephanie interrupted her. "There's no way they can kick us out right now. We put way more than the seven thousand dollars they are asking for into that space in renovations. It's totally illegal. They're just trying to take advantage. Apparently they're desperate for money because the city keeps trying to sue them into fixing this building or something."

"I'm not sure it's illegal to trick people into doing your renovations for you. Stephanie, if you knew this was coming, why didn't you tell me?"

"I did. I left all the notices in that stack of books you were supposed to read." She had an icy glint in her eye. "Why? Have you not been reading any of the books I've been asking you to?"

Ava looked away, embarrassed, and she watched the coffee drip into the carafe, a patter of accelerating beats that matched her heart as a rush of anxiety about her future swept over her. "Oh god, oh god. What am I going to do? I live here. Stephanie, this is my home."

"Whatever, you can move in with me. The point is, we have to keep the club going. We've come so far. We can't lose this momentum. We need to stick together."

"I don't want to move in with you." Ava angrily reached for two cups. "The last time I lived with you, you just up and abandoned me. You know I never got our security deposit back or anything. I was basically about to be on the street when I got this job."

"I couldn't help it. I needed a break. I had just been broken up with and then that thing with the gallery happened, which totally wasn't my fault, but it was awkward."

"That gallery was a mess from the beginning."

"Well, it was going to be awesome, but I got stabbed in the back by some people I really trusted, and why are we even talking about this right now when we have to concentrate?" Stephanie's voice had risen almost to a shout.

"I'm just freaking out about the possibility of all of this

falling apart," Ava yelled back. "I'm in debt because of this. How can you not be worried?"

"Of course I'm fucking worried. This is my whole life, too. This is my last chance to make it in this city. If this goes bust, I just know I'll end up a low-level marketing exec with a summer place on the Jersey shore just like everyone expects from me, when I know I'm fucking Hamptons quality." She took a deep breath, joining Ava by the kitchen and ripping open a packet of Splenda with her teeth. White crystals fluttered over the counter, and Mycroft leapt up to dab at them with his tongue. "You're just feeling pessimistic because you've been sick. You'll see."

"Aren't the Hamptons just full of hedge fund traders and investment bankers? If all you want out of life is a place by the beach, then who cares? Why are we doing this?"

"No, the Hamptons are for the best of the best. The people that have risen and made it—the social and cultural elite." Then, getting annoyed by Ava's look of doubt, "High class," she finally blurted. "They're high class and no one's ever going to call me a trailer trash, low-rent, country bumpkin beauty queen ever again." She flushed a little and then, embarrassed at her outburst, added a little coldly, "You wouldn't understand because you grew up rich."

Anxious not to have Stephanie pursue this line of attack, which Ava had experienced in the past and knew just how mean it quickly became, she changed the subject. "I met a really cool writer the other day," she began.

"Later, we need to plan our strategy," Stephanie cut her off. Mycroft, unpleasantly surprised by the taste of Splenda on his tongue, shook his head and sneezed.

Ava didn't press it, but Stephanie's curtness didn't bother her as much as it usually did. She drank her coffee with a secret, private happiness that paced under all their agonized planning like a tiger in a cage.

★ ★ ★

Despite a terror that crept up on her in moments of repose, over the next few days, Ava's afternoon with Constance resonated like a stone cast into the surface of a lake,
and in between all the frantic conspiring with Stephanie,
ripples of Ava's personality began to reassert itself in small
ways she found unexpectedly cheering. She found she was
daydreaming again, long, elaborate sentences and paragraphs,
usually in conversation with Constance, as if her mind, recently aroused from slumber, was seized by an irrepressible
prolixity. Ava went out and bought a fern and a secondhand
tweed blazer that was only slightly too light for the damp
spring weather. It made her feel like Nancy Mitford, and
she liked that.

On the day of their meeting with the lawyer, trying to
look professional, Ava and Stephanie had both shown up in
navy suits and white shirts, an unintentional coordination
that made them look like airline stewardesses. They nervously explained themselves, handing over folders full of
press clippings and financial documents and letters of reference from some of their famous members.

Flipping through, Evan Brookmore, the lawyer, pulled out
their 501(c)(3) application. "Did you girls never file this?" he
asked somewhat incredulously.

Stephanie looked at Ava with a barely suppressed rage.
"That was your job," she hissed.

Ava looked at her feet. "I meant to," she said quietly.

"You didn't ever tell anyone you were a nonprofit, did
you?" he asked.

"No, I was very careful not to." Stephanie was practically
growling. "Which is lucky, since my partner is an idiot."

Evan Brookmore let out a low whistle as he closed the
folders. "Well, that's good, at least. The matter of the unpaid
rent is pretty straightforward. You say you signed a lease. I

wish you had brought it with you so I could see it, but there's not really any getting around that."

"But we put so much of our own money into fixing it up," Stephanie argued. "They can't kick us out now and then just get to use all that beautiful wallpaper and stuff that we paid for."

"Sure they can," he said, looking at them curiously. "Have you two never rented an apartment before?"

"But we were supposed to be a part of the Lazarus Club. We got them all this publicity, and we were doing all this to get new members for them," Ava said. "We were trying to help them."

"I get it and I agree, it's not very nice of them in spirit, but it's all perfectly legal. If I were you two, however, I would be much more worried about your close shave with the 501(c)(3). Advertising as a nonprofit and not being one is fraud. You could go to jail."

Ava gasped, but Stephanie recrossed her legs, annoyed. "You're not being very much help here."

"I'm sorry, girls. It sounds like a fun project. I love those *Master and Commander* books myself." He pushed the folders back toward them and asked Stephanie if she'd like to get dinner later.

Ava and Stephanie left his office and went straight to a bar where they did three shots of vodka to an admiring audience of one sleepy daytime drinker. Walking north in the blinding afternoon sun, Ava was trying unsuccessfully to light the cigarette the bartender had given her because she needed to do something, and this felt suitably destructive. Stephanie was keeping up a steady and voluble stream of curses at the Lazarus Club, the board, the members, the lawyer and everyone she felt wasn't walking fast enough on the sidewalk in front of them. "Come on." She stopped in front of a hot-pink storefront, pushing open a door.

"This place?" Ava asked, throwing away the cigarette she didn't want. The frozen yogurt shop was very, very bright, and an aggressive smell of fake sugar with a hint of bleach hit her full in the face from the open door. "We're going to eat ice cream? This feels a little clichéd, don't you think? Can't we just find another bar?"

"It's not ice cream, and it's going to make me feel better, so shut up." Stephanie pointed to a booth, and Ava sat down on the hard plastic.

"Here." Stephanie returned and set down two very large cups of frozen yogurt.

Something about seeing her friend stabbing this mound of frozen calories with a little pink spoon spoke more strongly to Ava of Stephanie's despair than mere words ever could have. The skipping buzz of Korean pop music playing behind them, the teenagers making out at the next table, everything conspired to drown Ava in an unbearable poignancy, and when she took a bite, the swell of artificial pomegranate melted around her tongue in disconsolate waves. "What are we going to do?" she asked.

Stephanie didn't answer, eating her yogurt with a frowning concentration. Ava waited, watching antic, animated music videos on a television mounted behind them. Finally, Stephanie threw her spoon down. "We just have to move, that's all. We pack up and start somewhere else."

"Go somewhere else? Where?"

"I don't know yet, but it's clearly our only option."

"But our whole club was based on that space."

"No, that space was nice, but we're the heart of the House of Mirth. If we go somewhere else, we just bring the magic with us."

"We could never afford someplace as nice as that."

"Look, we still have our members. The press loves us. We're still hot. I can't believe the Lazarus Club can't appreciate it." Stephanie bent her spoon in irritation and half of it flew off with a crack. "But other people will. I'll just set up some meetings with other private clubs. Someone is going to want us."

"I just don't see how we could manage," Ava said sadly.

"I'm sorry, Ava, but the clock is ticking on us. We don't have time to start over. There's nothing the world hates more than a middle-aged woman. We've got maybe seven years, and if we're not rich or famous by then, it's over. I might as well be in Boise smoking Virginia Slims at the back table of a Denny's waiting for cancer to eat me from the inside out."

"Stephanie," Ava said. "That's crazy."

But Stephanie was already tapping on her phone. "We can do this," she said, her old energy returning. "We have one last big party. We make it a fund-raiser. We can at least raise enough to hire movers and a month or two of storage. We've got this." Looking up and seeing Ava's expression, Stephanie continued a little more softly, "Trust me. Haven't I been taking care of you ever since that first day I saw you in the dining hall? You couldn't even figure out how to work the cereal bins."

"Those were very complicated," Ava objected. "They had those funny latches."

"Right." Stephanie reached over and gave her a loving pinch. "Don't lose hope now. This is just a setback. We're going to make it."

"I just can't see it." Ava played with the runny pink goo in her cup. Stephanie's enthusiasm was taking off again, but for once, Ava felt the funny stasis of watching it swoop past her from a place left far behind.

That night Ava woke up at two in the morning with a pounding headache and a terrible thirst. She tossed and turned for a little while, but the prospects for her future were too terrifying, and every time she tried to think her way through a possible outcome she got more and more anxious until, in desperation, she sat up and turned on the light. Where was she going to live? What was she going to do for money once she wasn't employed by the Lazarus Club anymore? At their best, the House of Mirth barely kept Stephanie afloat; it would never support the two of them. She was starting to drive herself crazy. *A Room of One's Own* was still lying next to her bed, so she picked it up and flipped through, searching for distraction.

Ten pages in, she was furious; why hadn't anyone made her read this before? This book was explaining the very essential dilemma of her life, her difficulty finding her voice as a writer in crisp, clear, delightful prose. She read eagerly, feverishly, a new sense of outrage blossoming within her, and when she finally paused, she looked up at all the other volumes crowding her shelves with a feeling of betrayal. All those books, all those wonderful, brilliant male writers that she loved so much, had tricked her, contorting her mind and impressions into an insubstantial echo of theirs and then leaving her to struggle with this deficiency out in the cold. This book had called her into a strange new shift in perspective, and as she saw herself from a great distance, all her old-fashioned ways and manners now seemed a little sad, a hollow imitation of a way of being in the world that had excluded her. A feeing of loneliness sprang up within in her, deeper and wider and more fearsome than anything she had ever felt.

She was startled when Mycroft yowled next to his bowl, paws pressed together in the bend of his tail, and got up to feed him, glad for the interruption. It wasn't until the first pebbles of the new, cheaper food she had to buy now hit the porcelain of his dish that he erupted in another quick, outraged yowl, little teeth flashing in protest. Ava almost dropped the box. "Jesus, Mycroft. I'm sorry. Okay?" In the refrigerator, she found a container of just-expired cottage cheese and set that next to his bowl.

Watching him push the empty plastic container around with his nose, this strange new enthusiasm returned, and she felt she needed to keep moving in order to dissipate its pleasantly uncomfortable urgency. There was a sense of things happening, shifting, and she wanted to be ready. Looking around, the clutter of her apartment and its fine layer of dust felt intolerable. What if she really was going to have to move soon? For a minute this thought didn't seem so terrible, and she began sorting through the elegantly arranged piles of things that covered every surface. After a while she caught herself humming a little.

Did she really need two separate lithographs of Napoleon's march on Moscow? Maybe it was time to get rid of the Edison wax cylinders that she had no way of playing. A single smashed creature, once part of a fur stole, whose glass eyes had fallen out, went into the trash as well as any vintage hats that didn't fit, of which there were a surprising number. She was considering a bunch of ukulele sheet music—what if she did learn to play someday?—but then she threw the whole stack of music down the shoot in the hallway and began sorting through a box of chipped tintypes of confederate soldiers.

The shearing off and reshuffling of her possessions calmed her and when she crawled back into bed as dawn was breaking, it was with a sense of accomplishment. She opened *Three Guineas*, curious to see what else this woman had to say, her words like the quiet, intimate whisper of Ava's secret unacknowledged self. She was startled and then transfixed to read a furious, feminist screed, a rejection of men and the

institutions they created. This was not for Ava. This was not
her style at all, and yet she turned another page:

*Therefore the guinea should be earmarked "Rags. Petrol.
Matches." And this note should be attached to it. "Take this
guinea and with it burn the college to the ground. Set fire to the
old hypocrisies. Let the light of the burning building scare the
nightingales and incarnadine the willows. And let the daughters
of educated men dance round the fire and heap armful upon
armful of dead leaves upon the flames. And let their moth-
ers lean from the upper windows and cry, 'Let it blaze! Let it
blaze! For we have done with this "education!"'*

Ava had to put the book down. "The daughters of educated men" was a strange construction—what about everyone
else?—but this call to destruction reverberated in her anger
and frustrations of the day, and she was lost for a moment in
wild imaginings: Stephanie and she, in orgiastic revel, their
bodies warmed by a raging conflagration. Then, feeling a
little silly, she turned over, pulling her covers around her
ears, and lay in the sheltering warmth of her bed for a very
long time without falling asleep.

She called Stephanie the next day, excited to tell her about
Virginia Woolf and all her new, thrilling ideas.

"Yeah, no shit. We all read that in college, Ava. And whatever, she's kind of a snooty bitch."

Hurt, Ava didn't pursue the conversation. "Okay, but
we've agreed, right? We can have Constance Berger read
for this last event?"

"Fine, Ava," Stephanie groaned. "Could you please just
stop going on about this woman like she's the greatest thing

you've ever met? I have a million other things to worry about."

"Have I been?" Ava asked, but Stephanie had already hung up.

21

Now that the knell had sounded, there was a certain relief to a doom that was settled rather than living in uncertainty. The House of Mirth and their future had splintered into an array of possible, implausible alternatives. Ava was done at the Lazarus Club, that was certain—fired as their librarian and consequently dismissed from her apartment, as well. She and Stephanie were going to try and keep having events at different locations to retain their members while they raised money and scouted a new space. Through all of the upheaval, satisfaction at having insisted at last on an event of her choosing, the reading for Constance, acted as a prophylactic, insulating Ava against the despondency of owing almost ten thousand dollars to the Lazarus Club and her credit card company combined. They were going all out on their last night because as Stephanie said, "Fuck them, what are they going to do, evict us?" Ava received two weeks of severance pay, which under the circumstances, she considered rather chivalrous.

It fell to Ava and George to pack up the remains of their enterprise. To secure as much of their stuff from possible impoundment by the Lazarus Club, they had been sneaking things out at night, ferrying the boxes in taxis to Stephanie's apartment. Stephanie had been missing, engaged on a mysterious project about which she kept sending them cryptic but encouraging text messages. Ava, floating in a constant, buzzing cloud of anxiety, was also slowly packing up her apartment, but since she hadn't decided where to go, she was sort of hoping that once Stephanie was gone, she might be able to linger, unnoticed in the quiet for an extra week or two before they threw her out. Being busy kept her from succumbing to the panic that welled up when she considered her future, and she concentrated on planning their event, a single-mindedness in the face of disaster that she had learned from watching Stephanie, and which she now acknowledged was pretty effective.

Balancing a stack of books in one hand, Ava leaned toward George and almost managed to pass them to him. Instead, they fell with a clatter on a pile of already packed boxes.

"Take care." He picked one up. "I don't know that we could replace *An Illustrated Guide to the Holy Land* or *Sex and Sex Worship*. Although I believe you should take *Hunting in Zambia*. I feel it belongs with you." He handed her the volume.

She held it to her chest in a wave of nostalgia. "Maybe I will. It's a Lazarus Club volume, though, not one of ours."

"You've earned it. I bet they wouldn't miss it."

"Not you, too. Stephanie's been joking that we deserve to steal everything that isn't nailed down. Let's keep some honor in all this." But she put the book aside. She climbed another shelf, noticing, now that they were almost empty, just how poor a job of staining and finishing they had done. "How did this get up here?" She tossed down a brassiere.

"This place has seen all varieties of high jinks." Packing tape roared out of the dispenser, and George pushed a closed box aside with his foot. "I won't say I'll be sorry to see the last of that freight elevator, though. The things I have managed to unload into this building." He started taping another box. "Speaking of, did we take the peacock?"

She nodded guiltily. "We've been very grateful for your resourcefulness, George."

"I know. I've been promoted. I'm now your director of members and operations."

"So you're sticking around?" She tried to jump down from the shelves as gently as she could, landing with a loud thump of Chuck Taylors on hardwood.

"I might as well. Careful. Wouldn't it be funny if, after all of this, the liability insurance we never bought went to your medical bills?"

Ava stayed in a crouch, drumming her fingers on the floor. Wearing sneakers and jeans with wide cuffs made her feel uniquely spry, a little like a five-year-old. "Still, you're young and free. Isn't there something else you would like to do that actually pays?"

George crossed his arms over his chest. "Since I was a kid I was always fascinated by all those great New York gadabouts, Styron and Wilson and Vidal and Kazin all crashing through each other's cocktail parties: a suit and tie, a fifth of scotch, and a head full of big ideas; it seemed to me the very pinnacle of living. Somehow in this moribund day and age you two managed to make that happen again. It was a gift, really. So yeah, I'll stick around." He shrugged. "I've got the rest of my life to be an orthodontist or a certified accountant."

He bent down for the next box, the hair sneaking out from under his cap curling like soft little feathers, and from the slipping of his waistband it looked like he had put his underwear on inside out, and Ava felt such a rush of sympathetic understanding that she found she had to wait a minute before she said anything. "You know, George. You might have been the best part of all this."

He ducked away from her with an expression of such desperate self-deprecation that, to spare him further embarrassment, she left to pack the last of their teacups from the bar.

Trying to imagine what it would look like to start this process all over again somewhere new filled her with dread, and to chase it away, she consoled herself again that in planning their last event, she would have finally made her mark on this mess of a project, impressing upon it, at last what she, and maybe George, wanted it to be.

The night of the event, Ava got dressed with an unusual amount of care. Her regular skirts and cardigans seemed boring and lackluster, but maybe it was just the unaccustomed disorder of her room that made it feel so odd to be putting on her usual clothes, as if she should physically reflect the change in her circumstances. Just for once she wanted to stand next to Stephanie and not suffer in the comparison. While packing, she had found the dress she and Stephanie had bought together so long ago, forgotten ever since, and now she decided to try it on. It felt different this time. She looked in the mirror, touching the soft underside of her arms with a caress that made her skin prickle. The dress skimmed her body, dark fabric revealing the outline of a figure she usually kept hidden, and she was surprised by a sudden desire to be seen. She looked good, after all, the pale skin of her chest and arms glowing, exposed. She looked like Natasha from the Rocky and Bullwinkle cartoons. She decided to wear it; although to ameliorate its effect just a little, she put on her glasses.

When she arrived at the library, George started a little. "You look—" he paused "—different."

"Get me a drink before I lose my nerve and put on a

sweater." A helpful volunteer ran into the bar and returned with a glass of wine, which he offered, standing too close.

Ava stepped a little farther away and looked around. Empty of all their things—the tufted couch, the extra books, the broken printer and the card table George used as a desk—the room expressed a melancholy grandeur. The shelves once again stood bare except for fluttering candles. Strangely, in this moment of dissolution, the space had regained the aura of limitless possibility, and the impression it made was curiously hopeful. "What we did here was really special, wasn't it, George?"

Before he could answer, Stephanie arrived with a large rectangle wrapped in brown paper and a flimsy easel under her arm. "Wait until I show you guys," she said, setting the easel down. "Not to brag, but I'm fucking amazing." She grinned and unwrapped the package. "I got Richard Denkins to donate a bunch of paintings. We're having a silent auction for our new place." She set the painting on the easel. "Isn't he a genius?"

It was an oil painting of a woman in red panties, legs spread, painted in such hyper-realistic detail that every tuft of pubic hair was discernable under the thin red satin. She sneered down at them over pendulous breasts. *"No,"* said Ava.

"Don't be ridiculous. These are so hot right now. They sell for like twenty grand. George, I left some more paintings down in the lobby. Go get them."

"It has an appeal," he said, glancing at the image as he left the room.

"Stephanie, I'm not going to ask Constance to read in front of a bunch of up-skirt pictures."

"Why not? Everyone knows she's a huge dyke. She'll probably love them."

"She's not like that," Ava said, defensive, before she could stop herself.

"Oh, spare me, Ava. She's just a midlist, midlife nobody that you are for some reason obsessed with. I'm just trying to add some dazzle to this event. I'm off to Richard's loft to pick up one more. Also you won't believe this, but I got Joe Reed to come, too. It's insane. Check your email. Tonight is going to be off the hook. Be back in like an hour." She waved triumphantly.

"Wait, this is Constance's event," Ava said, but Stephanie was already gone.

George came back with a large painting, a pair of glossy red lips tonguing a melting popsicle. "They have a certain je ne sais quoi," he said, propping it up.

"I don't want to talk about it." Ava shook her head. "Did you get an email from Stephanie today?"

"You mean you haven't seen it?" George ran for his laptop and held it open for her. "She sent this out a couple of hours ago. I thought I was accustomed to her abilities," he said philosophically. "But even now, she manages to awe."

Announcing the House of Mirth Grand Moving Benefit, featuring spoken word by Joe Reed, additional readings by Constance Berger. Silent Auction. Tickets $50 at the door. Cash only.

"Does she mean Joe Reed the rock star?"

George nodded. "I have no idea how she did it, but yeah. I guess he's reading some of his poetry."

"But this is not the event we planned. What is she doing?"

"I guess she's making good on her threat to fund our move."

Just then a young couple wearing Joe Reed and The Velvet Revolution T-shirts wandered in. "Excuse me, is this where we buy the Joe Reed tickets?"

More people started to trickle in, bunching up behind the

original couple, now claiming their spot with an aggressive immobility. "But my event. Constance. This was not supposed to be like this. How can she do this to me?"

George was looking toward the door. "We might want to get set up. I'm guessing this could get a little out of hand."

Struggling against a mounting panic, Ava grabbed the nearest volunteer and set him to tearing open packages of plastic wineglasses and stacking them on the bar. "Is Joe Reed really going to be here?" he asked, a wayward curl slipping down over one eye.

"No idea." People started arriving, and Ava began handing out wine.

"You guys are so cool," he said. She glanced at the young man, and his admiration seemed to bounce off her, leaving no mark. She was a brittle, reflective surface, a million years old. The noise had increased quickly. People soon lined up four deep, those at the bar fighting to hold their place. The event wasn't due to start for an hour. The thought of Constance Berger arriving to this chaos made Ava's heart sink. She needed to find her first and explain. She would wait for her outside.

"Do the best you can," she told the young man who paused every so often to rearrange his drooping curl with tentative, self-conscious fingers.

The next room was just as full. Looking for Stephanie, she struggled to the door where George, the patch pockets of his blazer bulging with money, stood cheerfully accepting twenty-dollar bills. He leaned close, and his breath smelled of marshmallow and juniper. "We are making so much money. I don't even know where to put it all." He bent down and took a large gulp of the drink at his feet. "Of the many difficulties I have learned to weather while working here, this is a new one."

A line of people stretched the length of the hallway and down the main stairs of the club. "Jesus!"

"Yeah," he agreed.

The Lazarus portraits looked especially put out as Ava followed the trail of impatient humanity. Two girls, their hair the same expensive shade of yellow, sat comparing manicures. A well-known writer asserted his prestige, asking loudly for Stephanie. A small white dog in a white leather bag let out an urgent yip every few minutes. Rodney caught up with her at the top of the stairs. He was carrying a large box.

"This is crazy." He cocked his head at the line. "Is it true? Is Joe Reed really playing at your place?"

"I don't know. He's supposed to read poetry or something. I had nothing to do with it. Has Aloysius seen this yet?"

"I don't think so. Last I saw him, he was bug-eyed and slurring—a sure sign he's been awake for too many days, so maybe he'll sleep through it all. I saw a few board members, and they looked pretty sore. But what else can they do, right? It's not like they're going to call the cops. At this point, I think bad publicity might be the only thing these guys hate worse than you."

"I think that's Stephanie's attitude, at least. What's in the box?"

"I figured you gals might not be prepared for these kinds of crowds." He dropped it against his hip and reached in to show her a bottle of Southern Ease whiskey. "They never drink this stuff downstairs. It's a little better than that bubble gum gin you ladies serve." Rodney raised the box over his head and weaseled through the crowd with a professional grace.

"Thanks."

Downstairs, Castor was writing in his notebook with a small gold pencil, ignoring the press in front of his desk. Ava snuck past into the balmy night. A few smokers had aban-

doned the queue, and Ava overheard much excited specula-
tion about Joe Reed. She wondered if Stephanie had in fact
succeeded in getting him to come or whether someone, likely
herself, would have to inform all these soon-to-be-drunks
that they should just go home. Maybe she should start telling
them that now. She anxiously drummed her fingers against
one of the brass poles of the awning. She had no idea what
she would say to Constance, or how to apologize. She was
straining to see into the shadowy back seats of passing taxis,
heart fluttering in her throat, when she was startled by a
voice at her elbow. "Hey, stranger," said Ben.

"What are you doing here?" she asked.

"I don't know. I wanted to say goodbye to my bar. I
worked pretty hard on that thing. Should I not have come?"
he asked testily.

"You did and you made something beautiful. I'm glad you
came. You deserve to be here."

"It was a cool thing you guys tried to do with this place.
I'm glad I got to be a part of it." He shrugged. "And I like
Joe Reed."

Ava felt the gentleness of this overture, and she remembered all the reasons she liked him. "Thanks. Look, I'm
sorry," she began.

Ben stopped her. "Not everyone is meant to date, and that's
fine, but if you wanted to chat about the Franco-Prussian
War or something sometime…"

"I would love to," Ava said. They smiled at each other
for a minute.

A taxi pulled up, and Constance Berger unfolded herself
from the back seat with the spindly precision of an egret
alighting. "Constance!" Ava waved an arm.

Constance's gaze climbed the Lazarus facade. "They really
should fix this up. It's criminal to let all that lovely stonework
just crumble like that." She glanced at Ava. "You look very

sophisticated." Ava hoped this was a compliment. "Is this your young man?" She extended a hand in Ben's direction.

"No," Ava said too quickly. "This is Ben Wheeler. He did some work for us."

Ben shook Constance's hand with a curious look toward Ava. "Nice to meet you."

"Quite a crowd." Constance discreetly turned her attention from the two young people.

"We had a last-minute addition to the evening," Ava apologized. "Joe Reed will also be reading. He has a lot of fans. We're having a sort of fund-raiser. I'm so sorry about all this. I was organizing a much quieter event and then things got a little out of hand." She held the door for Constance. Three old ladies in pearls were yelling their objections to everything at Castor, who was listening with a polite lack of interest.

"I remember Joe. We used to hang around the same clubs sometimes, but then everyone did. That was New York in the seventies."

"Really?" Ava tried to clear a path through the crowd. "I didn't think that was your type of thing, I mean. I'm sorry. I don't know what I mean."

"Well, we all have hidden depths," Constance said with a laugh.

Ben was watching them. Then he kind of laughed.

"What?" asked Ava.

"Nothing, don't worry about it. It actually makes me feel better about everything." He patted her on the back. "I'm getting a drink."

"I think I'll get one, too," Constance said with a sympathetic tilt of the head. She gave Ava an encouraging squeeze of the elbow, that sent an electric shock down her bare skin, and left for the bar.

Felicitously, Rodney appeared at her side. She nodded and held the back of his shirt for guidance as they pushed through

to the edge of the room where the crowd was a little thinner. Ava sat heavily on a radiator beneath an open window
while Rodney stood next to her, loosening his Lazarus bow
tie and scanning the crowd. "I'm pretty sure this is illegal,"
he said, handing her a bottle. "Fire codes."

Ava opened the bottle to the ripping sound of the plastic
cap and took a big swig. Alcohol and a thick coating of in-
determinate sweetness burned her tongue. She drank deeply,
trying not to gag at the powerful notes of grape soda and
dishwasher fluid. She indicated the room with the bottle.
"Why are you so nice to us, Rodney? This. Us. We're everything you hate."

He looked at the floor. "I don't know. It's just going to be
awfully dull around here without you two, you especially."

Just then Ava caught sight of a familiar shade of blond in
the crowd. "We're colorful. I'll give you that. Hold this."
She gave him the bottle and started toward the glint of yellow. Rodney took her place on the radiator with a sigh and
raised the bottle to his lips.

It wasn't Stephanie. Ava let herself be jostled by strangers
for a few minutes. She didn't find her business partner until
they had all gathered near the microphone, Stephanie waving
her over above the crowd. Joe Reed leaned his head back,
contemplating her through nearly closed eyes. "So you're
the other chick." Ava ignored him. "Hey, Connie, I haven't
seen you since the Cock closed down in '82."

Constance laughed. "Times change, don't they? And now
we're elder statesmen."

He nodded. "That's the truth of it. I hear you're working the uptown beat, selling your soul for a cushy, faculty
appointment."

Ava was indignant, but Constance answered with the indulgent tone reserved for naughty children. "I teach a few
classes."

"We're so lucky to have both of you to make our last night in the Lazarus Club so special," Stephanie interrupted. "It means so much to Ava and myself."

"Is this going to be okay?" Ava asked Constance.

"Oh, his sort is always very keen on integrity." Constance brushed off her concern. "That sort of thing stopped bothering me once I realized I like to pay my electric bills."

When Ava stood to introduce Constance, looking out into the crowd crammed into the large room that now felt so small, she once again had an ache for what this project might have been. Constance waited beside her, poised and enigmatic, keeping her place in the book she was about to read from with a finger that bore a huge jet ring. The audience sipped their drinks in wary anticipation. Even bereft of trimmings, this room had that ineffable feeling of enchantment that pervaded the Lazarus Club. These people would ask themselves, years from now, did we actually go see a reading in some derelict mansion where we drank alcohol that tasted like bubble gum and smoked illegal cigarettes with abandon? Or was it just a dream? That quality of unreality had felt so comforting to Ava, so welcoming, when so much of her life had been lived in that fluid space of daydreams and imagination. But now the sense of promises unfulfilled pressed in on her with the heat of so many bodies, and Ava wanted to apologize, for not knowing what she wanted, for having failed to enact it. She took a deep breath and then, despite having two full crumpled pages of introductory notes in her hand, Ava realized she had nothing to say. This was not her medium. This was not how she wanted to express herself. She had so many ideas and feelings, and she wanted to cover page after page after page with them, lovingly constructed and put together into sentences in the silence of her room. But here, beneath the expectant gaze of so many faces, all she wanted was to slip quietly onto the sidelines. She motioned to Stephanie, who accepted her place at the front of the crowd with some surprise and then a blinding smile of gratitude, which she then turned on the audience. "Let's give a round of applause for my beautiful, fantastic partner, Ava Gallanter," she said. "Now, what can we say about this magical journey we've all been on here at the House of Mirth? This journey that has only just begun as we leave our nest here at the Lazarus Club and prepare to spread our wings." Stephanie quickly warmed to her own eloquence, and it was quite a while before she let Constance finally take the stage, after many exhortations to everyone to be generous at the silent auction later that evening.

The next twenty minutes were as bad as Ava had been afraid they might be. No one listened, instead shuffling, fidgeting, spilling drinks, shouting impatiently for Joe Reed. Constance read on, unflustered and at ease, her figure a dark gash against the huge painting behind her—a woman in pink panties bent over a bicycle seat. Constance's reading glasses were black and round, and as she turned another page, she blinked, a sparrow amused by some secret joke. The magnificent amour of her self-possession hung around her casually, absently, without effort, and Ava wondered enviously at this imperturbability. Eventually, Constance finished and sat down to a resounding cheer, which was less appreciation than an enthusiastic farewell.

Mortified, Ava hid with a bottle of liquor, cross-legged on the floor next to the fireplace, surrounded by a thicket of calves and feet. Since they had unthinkingly packed their microphone, and since Joe Reed apparently talked like his jaw had been wired shut, his poetry was interrupted every few minutes by some yelling from the back to "speak louder." Reading from a small lined notebook, the shades of his large sunglasses flipped up, but with no lenses underneath, he grew more irritated at each outburst, and seemed to lower his voice out of spite. To curry favor, the audience at the front began yelling at the people at the back to "shut the fuck up." Through it all, Mr. Joe Reed mumbled on, refusing to pause for the disturbances. Now that everyone realized that they were not going to be able to hear, a dissatisfied murmur rose, causing even more people to demand that everyone shut up. Stephanie, standing at his elbow, listened rapturously, swaying just a little on her heels like a buoy in a strong current.

Eventually the reading ended, and everyone began moving about with purpose. A tall woman with high cheekbones and sad eyes looked at Ava curiously. A handbag bumped against her head. Ava joined the throng, milling aimlessly. After a moment she realized she was standing next to the coat closet, empty because she had just cleaned it out, and she slipped inside. She couldn't face Constance after that embarrassment of a reading, and the dark, enclosed space felt forgiving. She sat on the smooth bare floorboards and, feeling the need for a desperate courage to get through the rest of the evening, drank with intent.

When she emerged, the first thing she saw was Stephanie, nearly naked. She had shed her dress during the evening, and now clad in underwear and a rugby scarf, a rakishly tilted mortarboard on her head, she was swigging champagne, a pinup sprung from the fervid dreams of some university provost. "Amazing, isn't it?" she called to Ava. "Someone just gave it to me." She laughed and swung the tassel to the other side of her hat. "We're graduating to bigger things."

Her lack of self-consciousness almost transfigured her into something, if not quite innocent, somehow resplendent, but Ava grabbed her narrow wrist, and dragged her through an appreciative audience into the bathroom. "Why aren't you wearing any clothes?" Ava asked once they were inside.

Stephanie pressed her back against the closed door with an elated expression. "I think we've outdone ourselves tonight."

She kicked off her shoes, sighing with the relief of feeling her feet flat on the floor. "I think this party is going to make it a cinch to find a donor with a new space. The world loves a rock star." Then, she added seriously, "He wants to use me on his new album. Can you imagine? Me and Joe Reed."

"You can't sing."

"That's not the point." She held Ava's hand for a moment, her drunken smile transfigured by joy. Then, she took a lipstick out of her bra and turned to the mirror. "Whatever. At least I'll be able to use him for more fund-raising." The lid of the lipstick case snapped open, abrupt in the tiled room. "I'm always looking out for us. Want some?"

Ava shook her head. "Tonight was a disaster. You ruined everything."

"No, I saved everything," Stephanie said sternly. "It was you who wanted to ruin everything by planning our last event around some boring old lady." She looked at Ava in the mirror. "This was supposed to be about us. It's our event. Our project and all of the sudden you're acting like all you care about is this woman just because she wrote some books and wants to talk about Proust or something."

"It's not my fault no one ever wants to talk about Proust with me." Ava stopped. Stephanie was avoiding her eyes, and a slow realization began to dawn on her. "You're jealous. You sabotaged this whole thing on purpose. You ruined my event for Constance because you're mad that someone likes me better than you."

"I would never," Stephanie protested, but with less conviction than usual.

"After all the loyalty I've given you, following you around like some subaltern." Stephanie glanced up, but Ava didn't feel like stopping to explain. "All these years of it always being about you, and finally I found one person, just one, who thinks I'm cool, too, and you can't handle it."

"Oh my god, Ava, you act like you're in love with her. Ever since you met her, 'Constance writes books, Constance is so smart.' I mean, seriously, can you even hear yourself?"

"That's just not true," Ava objected. "And I've spent all my time since I met her running around with you trying to save this hopeless business. For you." Ava found herself spurred by the injustice of it all. "Practically everything I do is for you. And has been forever. Since I've known you." The years unfurled in Ava's mind, so many passing moments in the company of Stephanie, prey to the whims and schemes of her imperious friend. Staying up nights to help her write papers in college, following her to New York after gradua-tion, being dragged to parties and events she hated, cover-ing their rent when she needed to, deferring to Stephanie's wild impracticalities, a series of endless choices made against Ava's better judgment. Viewed in concert, this proof of her relentless flow of devotion seemed almost absurd. "No won-der my mom hates you and thinks I'm crazy. At this point she probably thinks I'm in love with you."

Ava happened to look over, and stopped short at Stepha-nie's distinctly unsurprised expression. "Wait a second." She spoke slowly, considering. "Do you think I'm in love with you?" Stephanie didn't respond, waiting. "Oh my god." Ava closed the lid and sat down heavily on the toilet, trying to think through this new information. "You've been taking advantage of me all these years because you think I'm in love with you?"

Someone opened the door, and they both yelled, "Occu-pied!" The door was quickly shut with apologies.

"You're kind of weird sometimes, and you were always really bad with guys," Stephanie started halfheartedly and then stopped in the face of Ava's stricken expression. "I don't know, I just figured. I don't know what I thought."

They were both silent as Ava tried to process what Stephanie seemed to be implying: a friendship that had taken up most of her adult life could have a totally different narrative than the one she knew. Her past, her very memories seemed to dissolve, acquiring a nebulous film of uncertainty. Had she really been so unaware of what had actually been passing between the two of them? Had all those years been a lie? Viewed in this light, a love and faithfulness that Ava had given so freely now appeared ridiculous in the light of Stephanie's cold self-interest. And it was this loss, the sudden theft of the integrity of her own experience that Ava felt most keenly. Over the course of their friendship, Stephanie had betrayed her in all kinds of little ways, a casual profligacy that Ava barely paid attention to, but this was different. This dissimulation shattered a friendship she had built her life around. This felt unforgivable.

Stephanie had set her mouth in a frown, but it was starting to wobble, and she chewed on her lip. "What?" she finally exploded. "What's so wrong if I did think that? Why don't I deserve to have one person, just one person in this whole dirty stinking world that actually cares about me? That actually thinks I'm more than just some dumb blonde tramp? You were the only one, Ava. The only one in my whole life." She looked at her feet, her hair slid down and covered her face, and she didn't push it back. "I needed you."

Behind Stephanie's head, Ava noticed another place where they had messed up the wallpaper. A white crack almost two inches wide ran down the wall, spreading and then narrowing, a slick of plaster cutting across a field of red that brought Ava back to the present. "You never wanted a literary salon. You've been taking advantage of me, and now we owe thousands of dollars because you don't care who you drag down with you."

"We don't," Stephanie said.

"Excuse me?"

"We don't owe thousands of dollars. I went back and had dinner with that lawyer and brought a copy of the lease with me. We signed as an LLC. That means we can dissolve the company, and we aren't liable for its debts."

Ava was just about done with Stephanie's revelations. "What are you talking about?"

"I was going to surprise you." Stephanie sadly played with her lipstick. "At the end of the night. I made George get champagne for us and everything."

"What about my credit card?"

"Oh, you still have to pay that. It's in your name. But we can make that back in two seconds once we reopen."

"So I'm still in debt, but you aren't?"

"Yeah, but we will pay it off. Once we get our own town house, and start attracting the real money, that debt is going to be nothing."

"I'm done." Ava stood, and walked quickly out of the bathroom. She was half listening for Stephanie to call her back, and when she didn't, Ava was a little surprised at the relief she felt.

The exasperated person waiting outside spoke irritably. "Could you have taken any longer?" He walked into the bathroom and saw Stephanie motionless in the center of the room. "Goddamn it."

The crowd was sparser and drunker. Guests sat on the hardwood floor, laughing and ashing the cigarettes that they shouldn't have been smoking into plastic cups. An effete young man lay, one leg crossed over the other, pointing at the painting just above him. "It's the curve of the pudenda that makes it such a devastating indictment." He tried to sip from a cup without raising his head, and alcohol splashed over his upturned collar, while another young man nodded in grave agreement.

Ava stepped over them; she was done. She was free of them

and their ilk. She was done with Stephanie and the years of affection she had wasted. A heady mix of freedom and sadness, terror and relief poured over her—was this what divorce felt like? Was she really free of this union that she had contorted herself into so many unlikely shapes to accommodate? Could it just be renounced like that, so easily, and would she continue to bear its shape like a tree root that has grown into and around a crack in a sidewalk? Who was she without her best friend?

In the bar, she saw Constance wedged between the broad backs of young men facing other conversations and Ava squeezed in next to her, nodding to the intern to pour her a drink. One of the men frowned before moving away to give her room. "He was having the most amazing conversation," Constance said, folding a cocktail napkin into a small triangle. "Did you know there is a Bulgarian bar somewhere on the Lower East Side where people dress like forest animals and dance all night? This city never ceases to amaze."

"I didn't." Ava picked a napkin up from the bar and started fiddling with it, too. "But I never hear about those kinds of things." The lights around the bar had grown halos, an extra aura of sparkle that was making Ava squint a little.

"We seem to be in the middle of something not that far off right now." Constance looked around. "It's so much more satisfying that this is all happening in the Lazarus Club. I always thought of it as such a pearls and dentures kind of place."

"I think they would agree with you. We are currently less than welcome around here—not that I really blame them." She accepted the drink and took a large sip. "I want to apologize for tonight. I'm so sorry. I wanted it to be different." Again, Ava was struck by the nebulousness of her expectations when her disappointment felt so acute. Strange that she could be so sure she didn't have what she wanted, and yet so unclear as to what exactly that might have been. Maybe that was why Stephanie was always so frustrated with her. "My salon is all assholes."

"Aren't they always?"

"But they always seemed so amazing in all those novels."

Constance sighed. "I know. I love them, too. But they're not really for us."

Distracted by the inclusion, Ava lost her train of thought. "Us? What is for us?"

"A million things that have yet to be written. But I don't want to sound too radical. I like tea lights and velvet curtains and stodgy old men, too." She waved an arm at the room, indicating the club around them. "But I would take Edith Wharton over Henry James any day." She spoke with a conspiratorial tone that warmed Ava like a furnace. "As I assume you would too, judging by the name of this thing."

On the bar next to her, a tea light guttered its last and sank into a pool of wax. The heady collision of newfound freedom and unconsidered horizons rushed toward her, tremendous, exciting. What if Stephanie was right? Without thinking, Ava surged forward and kissed Constance once, lightly on her lips. As if she had shattered all the previous days and hours of her life, tiny shards of the unthinkable erupted at her wild and wayward daring. Without the hard, large pressure of a masculine jaw, Ava felt like she was falling forward, a descent into softness that yielded at her touch and smelled of gardenia and smoke. Constance neither resisted nor pursued the kiss further, but her lower lip parted just enough for Ava to feel the smooth, wet crest of it, a possible invitation, and Ava pulled back, terrified, but ringing with a tremulous exhilaration. "I'm sorry."

"That's one way to make up for a mess of a reading." Constance smiled.

"I'm so sorry." Ava needed to escape, to run from the audacity she had just committed, and pressed backward until the crowd behind her yielded enough to let her slip away. "Excuse me. I'm so sorry."

Constance watched her kindly. "No need to apologize, my pretty thing. We've all got to start somewhere."

The library stank of the end of a party. The noise had died to a slurred rumble over which laughter, high and shrill, burst forward and then crept slowly away. Candles flickered out amid the smell of hot wax and smoke. An empty wine bottle rolled in circles around the floor, kicked by unsteady feet. Across the room, Stephanie was tearfully explaining something to an older man, who listened, a hand consolingly brushing the elastic of her underwear.

George stood near the door, resting an elbow on an empty shelf, humming "It's a Long Way to Tipperary." Seeing her, he set down his drink and held out his blazer. "Observe these pockets. For the first time ever, I am so flush, I couldn't even think where to store this lucre."

Ava reached into one of the patch pockets on his hip and withdrew a wad of crumpled bills. "I'm going to take this." Then, suddenly sentimental, she hugged him. Her arms wrapped around his narrow frame to the elbows. He was as slim as a lizard, all sinew and bones. "You're the best, George," she said into his damp shirtfront.

"Goodbye, Piccadilly. Farewell, Leicester Square," he sang.

The trip back to her apartment was difficult. The ground tilted under her feet, the gentle rocking of a ship at sea, and she found the act of directing herself in a straight line to require more concentration than usual. In the endless hallway to the elevator, she had to stop a few times, leaning against the wall until the wallpaper, a terrible pattern of black arabesques on a yellow background, stopped spinning. She wouldn't be sad to see the last of it. If she kept a low profile, it would undoubtedly be a few days before anyone remembered to kick her out of her apartment. Maybe this handful was enough for a month's storage. She desperately needed a job, but New York was big, full of restaurants and temp agencies. The elevator bell dinged at her floor, and she stumbled a little as she left, knocking over one of her neighbor's cats. She shrugged as the shattered remains went careening loudly down the garbage chute. One couldn't take everything to heart.

She looked around at the piles of boxes in her apartment—no job, no home, no Lazarus Club—the uncertainty of it all, normally so terrifying, felt like a gift, like she had escaped a fate, the true peril of which she hadn't even realized. She wasn't tired. The nervous energy that had been bubbling quietly inside her since her moment with Constance rose up again, insistent. She wanted to dance or sing, to set the whole world on fire. This prompted the echo of a thought still rattling around her brain—rags, petrol, matches—and she crossed to her old black phone, not yet packed up, and dialed. When information picked up she asked if there was a hotline for the inspections department of the NYC Landmarks and Historic Buildings Commission. She wrote it down and hung up with a smile. To hell with the Lazarus Club, she thought. *Let it blaze for we are done with this education.* And she gave Mycroft a kiss on his small pink nose.

EPILOGUE

The YWCA residence for girls of slender means was a large, square building from the turn of the century, solidly functional, although not without its charms, among which were pretty little porcelain sinks in each room and certain quaint, old-fashioned rules—no married ladies, no overnight guests, no male visitors above the second floor. But most important, it was cheap. So cheap that by working a temp job and eating all her meals in the residence cafeteria, Ava was able to slowly, with great satisfaction, winnow a bit of her credit card debt each month.

It was strange living in a world so totally absent of men. Ben, with whom she had resumed a slightly strained friendship, had helped her carry over her boxes. "Looks about right," he said with a grin, reading the awning. But it had since been weeks. Even Mycroft was gone, boarding with Constance for the moment. Ava found it remarkable the way the young women living here seemed to expand to take up all the extra space. Dancers prowled the hallways, taut and nervous, their thin, hard legs shifting around like cranes about to take off; and actresses hurried to auditions, a contradictory picture in bright, dramatic makeup and casual yoga pants. Older residents carried an air of mystery—

why were they still here, in cardigans and orthopedic shoes? Ava delighted in them all. Someone on her hall practiced scales every night, her voice ascending and falling in a weird primeval cry that soothed Ava to sleep in her narrow bed. They were all broke, or they wouldn't be there, but ambition seemed to float through the dingy hallways like a pheromone, filling the air with the sharp tang of desire.

Ava glanced through an old *New York Post* while standing in the residential lounge, trying not to watch her ramen turn with agonizing slowness in the rickety communal microwave. She had worked late and missed dinner again. She was updating the files of a huge investment company, a task that agreeably seemed to expand to suit the hours she needed, and she spent entire days alone and content in the quiet climate-controlled archives surrounded by stacks of yellowing paper.

But walking home that night through the warm spring evening, the trees exhaling a scent rich with sap and dirt, for the first time in a long while, Ava felt a sort of restless longing for things she couldn't quite describe. She wanted to get drunk, to eat something delicious, to shake off the rigorous asceticism of her recent life, to giggle something stupid to a receptive ear. Normally she found comfort in the austere virtue of her solitude, but just tonight the gentle breeze called an ambiguous but seductive invitation to her, and she felt melancholy. Even the prospect of her nightly three pages— she had thrown out her old novel and was happily writing a scandalous autobiography of Irene Adler that the Baker Street Irregulars were going to hate—even that hadn't been enough to console her today.

The microwave whirred interminably, and Ava turned another page. She had been regularly reading the gossip columns as they gleefully reported each descending step in the Lazarus Club's upheaval. They had received a surprising amount of bad press for kicking Ava and Stephanie out.

"The Lazarus Club Eats Its Young" was Ava's favorite headline, and their departure started a trail of dominoes falling as years of malfeasance came to light, most of which was tangled up with Aloysius. The board tried to kick him out, a bunch of lawsuits followed, accusations of hoarding and misuse of funds, some scandal involving a bunch of dead finches. Eventually they all settled out of court, and Aloysius was outed from his apartments and temporarily banished from the establishment. Following all this had become one of Ava's few indulgences. She chuckled in anticipation and turned to Page Six.

She almost dropped the paper. There, immediately recognizable, even with her head slightly turned from the camera, was a picture of Stephanie getting out of a car, maybe a limousine, Ava couldn't tell. A male hand was extended toward her, and from the angle of the shot, it almost looked as if she were crouching away from it, although maybe she was just hiding from the blast of flashbulbs. Her short skirt had ridden up even higher, and a small strip of bare thigh was visible. The caption only listed her name and whatever party she was going to. Ava held the paper closer, trying to coax from the blurry newsprint any further information, some small clue as to what her friend was doing now, whom she spent her time with, whether she was happy, but closer inspection only revealed the thick pixels of the photograph, a refusal to betray deeper secrets. With a slight ache, Ava recognized the specific strap of her bra.

She had tried calling once. In her new happiness, the expansive air of possibility in which she now lived, Ava found she was becoming nostalgic. Stephanie couldn't help who she was. And Ava had noticed a funny thing: as she wrote her book, she found she was giving Irene Adler more and more of Stephanie's characteristics, and as she crafted this portrait of her friend on the page, the sting of betrayal had started to fade a little and she was left with a complicated admiration for her friend's strange, dynamic personality. She missed her. Stephanie had answered in what sounded like a crowded restaurant. "Who?" she asked, though she had clearly heard the name. "Oh, sorry, Ava, I can't talk now, I'm very busy." Ava managed to give her phone number and address just in case. Then a few days later she had received five pages of hand-scrawled vitriol, hysterical self-defense and character assassination, which Ava folded and put away in a drawer. She decided to give up on getting back in touch with Stephanie for a while.

Ava walked back to her room, slurping noodles, still intent on the picture when she almost bumped into her neighbor, a tall brunette she often exchanged shy smiles with while they fumbled with their respective keys.

"Oh, don't eat that stuff," said the neighbor with a laugh. "I do it all the time too, but it's too depressing. Instant ramen is, like, the taste of sadness. I have a toaster. I could make you a slice of toast." She paused and blushed, looking at her sneakers. "If you wanted."

Her faded blue T-shirt had the name of a band Ava had never heard of and freckles burst across her nose when she smiled and Ava tried to bite free from the noodles dangling from her chin. "I love toast," she said and then thought it sounded silly.

"Okay, I'll come over in a little while. Do you like lemon curd?"

Ava could only nod.

The neighbor smiled and disappeared back into her room.

Safely behind her own door, Ava set aside her noodles and paced, trying hard not to listen for sounds from the next room, because it seemed too eager and a little creepy. From the mailboxes she knew her neighbor's name was Kate, and this sounded like such a wonderfully prim name. After a while, she sat down at her typewriter, hoping that a distraction might make the time pass; it felt like the last five minutes had taken forever. At one point she even got up to check, but when she picked it up, her old alarm clock ticked quietly, humming against her ear, and Ava sat back down, scrolled in a blank page, and started a new chapter.

★ ★ ★ ★ ★

ACKNOWLEDGMENTS

Thanks to my brilliant agent, Dana Murphy, and my incredible editor, Liz Stein, for making this happen and especially for all your help and support in that final stretch of unexpected difficulties. I'm so grateful to have such a pair of amazing women on my team. My thanks also to everyone at Park Row Books who worked on this for me.

Thanks to my writing group, teachers, and early readers: Madeline Stevens, Karen Havelin, Joe Ponce, Yardenne Greenspan, Emily Barton, Rebecca Godfrey, Heather Aimee O' Neil, Zachariah Pickard, and especially Lauren Leblanc for all the advice, support and encouragement. I could have never done this without all of you.

Thanks to André Aciman for twenty years of unwarranted faith in me. It's a debt I may never repay, but I'm working on it.

Thanks to my mom and dad and the circle of friends to whom I owe my education, Jon Newlin, Henri Schindler, Ersy Schwartz.

Thanks to David Brooks for sharing your name and your inspiration with me.

Thanks to my friends, my support: Kris Alexanderson, Alison Fensterstock, Robert Starnes, Janet Peters, Callie Field.

Thank you to Brooke Geahan, a friend, a genius, a force of nature, one of a kind.

A very special thanks to David Shamoon and Ian Davey Volner, as well as old friends and new friends who helped make something magical.

And finally thanks to my husband, Matt, for making me a better person, a better writer, for offering your calm waters up in service to my hurricane, and for tolerating all the nonsense it took to get here.

And to Oliver and Violet, my loves, thank you for sharing your gestation and infancies with this book.

ABOUT THE AUTHOR

Iris Martin Cohen grew up in the French Quarter of New Orleans. She holds an MFA from Columbia University and studied Creative Nonfiction at the Graduate Center, CUNY. She currently lives in Brooklyn. *The Little Clan* is her first novel.